SINAI DECEIT

AN ARCHAEOLOGICAL THRILLER

DARWIN LACROIX ADVENTURE SERIES
BOOK 5

DAVE BARTELL

ISBN: 978-1-957269-00-9

To Tenny Wright, who taught me how to put my soul into my writing

The Monastery of Saint Catherine is the oldest continuously active monastery on Earth.

"Few places on earth have played so decisive a part in the history of mighty nations as this largely barren, sparsely populated peninsula. There would have been no Egyptian empire in western Asia, no spread of Islam in north Africa, no Alexandria, no Arab conquest, had Sinai not provided a critical thoroughfare." Jill Kamil, author of The Monastery of Saint Catherine in Sinai

"Moses... remove your sandals from your feet, for the place on which you stand is holy ground."

PROLOGUE

Nile Delta, Egypt
24 August 1799

Henri Lacroix stepped off the sloop in Rasheed under a blood orange sky and strode toward the frigate *Muiron*—the fastest remaining vessel in the decimated French fleet. His mission accomplished, he rushed to stow his precious cargo and escape the marauding British. The sun, tinged by the dust over the vast Saharan desert, cast a pall over the eerily quiet quayside as Henri searched for an officer. All work had stopped and the dock hands prostrated in Maghrib, the evening prayer.

Henri caught a young lieutenant's eye and motioned him to a stack of five crates. "Load these immediately. We sail within the hour," he said.

"As you wish, sir," replied the junior officer.

Henri placed silver coins into the man's palm and glanced at the workers. Then he eyed the lieutenant to emphasize his point. "Don't be stingy with the bonus. The cargo's precious."

He moved on to chat with another officer. In less than five minutes, the Egyptians finished their prayers and began moving Henri's crates.

When the cargo net closed about them, Henri ran aboard and stood by the hatch as the crates were lowered into the hold.

On deck, lanterns held back the twilight as the frigate's crew scurried about readying for departure. Henri looked south towards Cairo as a strong northerly breeze rippled the frigate's sails and cooled the deck planking, still warm from the day's sun. He caught a whiff of exotic spices and freshly baked aish baladi, which caused his stomach to growl as he envisioned sweeping the flatbread through fava bean paste. A firm hand grasped his shoulder, bursting the comfort food moment.

"Did you succeed?"

Henri stiffened at a voice he knew well and turned to face Napoleon Bonaparte. The thirty-year-old general scrutinized Henri from behind deep-set gray-blue eyes. With his Egyptian campaign in tatters, he needed Henri's expertise to elude the British. Napoleon's shoulder-length hair lashed about in the swirling wind as he waited.

"Yes," Henri replied. "Smith's fleet will turn northeast at eight o'clock. We sail along the Alexandrian coast until we see the signal. Tell your men to light it no earlier than 4:00 a.m., or we'll have the English upon us."

Napoleon barked an order, and a junior aide sprinted down the gangplank where he shouted at the cavalry who galloped away.

"Did he buy it?" asked Napoleon, turning back to Henri.

"Who, Smith? I doubt it. He's a spy," Henri snorted. "I assured him you're a royalist. But he's still trying to get out from under Nelson's shadow and could very well move to capture us."

"Yes. I suppose we'd make a career-defining catch," said Napoleon, staring upriver into the gathering darkness before he turned back to Henri. "Join me in the stateroom for dinner. You'll need your strength to navigate the coastline."

Henri said he would and returned his attention to the hold. As the crew finished tying down the crates, he reflected on his frenetic movements. Six days ago, Napoleon's aide had burst into Henri's Cairo studio, informing him they were leaving Egypt. Henri had protested that he could not leave his work. But as four soldiers entered, the aide had retorted it was not a request. With a mere two hours to pack, Henri had grabbed only the most critical samples, equipment, and notebooks before the four-day journey up the Nile.

Yesterday, Napoleon had sent him on a diplomatic errand to speak with Sydney Smith, the Royal Navy's captain tasked with maintaining the British blockade. The two had become acquainted while being held in the Temple prison in Paris: Smith on arson charges for burning French ships and Henri over a prize capture gone wrong. They had bonded as each possessed a renegade spirit that bristled under the yoke of more powerful leaders.

Henri had negotiated with Smith to allow Napoleon's escape from Egypt and keep his own priceless cargo from falling into British hands or, worse, sinking into the depths. After a tense tête-à-tête and a gift of exquisite gold artifacts from the French expedition in upper Egypt, Smith had finally agreed to look the other way.

Henri's thoughts returned to the present as sailors shouted and the *Muiron's* sails snapped. Dockhands cast off the mooring lines, and the bow swung into the current. They were leaving Egypt on the very day Salim, the alchemist, had finally promised to take Henri to the source.

Damn you, Napoleon. Henri stomped the deck as the quayside retreated.

Two hours later, during the main course in the *Muiron's* stateroom, a middle-aged diplomat in civilian dress asked Henri, "You're both from Corsica? Did you and Napoleon know each other?"

"Our families fought together for Corsican independence," said Henri.

Napoleon overheard and looked over. "Yes, Henri and I terrorized the streets of Ajaccio while the grown-ups plotted and schemed. Do you remember the time we stole the wine merchant's cart?"

"As I recall, it was you. It only became *we* after you were caught. Perhaps if *we'd* not drunk so much of the cargo."

Napoleon roared with laughter. Henri, the diplomat, and the ship's senior officers joined in. When the moment had passed, the captain shifted the conversation, asking Henri, "Are you sure this will work?"

Napoleon answered for him. "Henri's the best privateer I've ever met. He's worked the Barbary Coast since he was thirteen."

"Understood, but do you know this section of the north African coast?"

"Well enough," said Henri. "It will be a tense night—"

A rap on the door interrupted and drew their attention, and a junior officer opened it. "We've left the river mouth," he said.

"Light's out!" commanded the captain. "All unneeded hands below decks, now!"

Henri followed the captain to the foredeck, where they surveyed the dark coastline. He repeated earlier instructions to maintain course into deeper water to avoid shallows caused by the river Nile's silt deposits.

The captain ordered the Union Jack raised. It would be difficult to see at night, but would give them an element of protection if spotted by a British vessel. In less than a quarter of an hour, the first officer ordered a turn to port, when the Alexandria lighthouse came into view.

Nearly seven hours later, the *Muiron* glided past the sleeping city of Alexandria so close they could hear the surf. Henri's heart pounded as he traversed the port side decking, studying the water and listening to the depth soundings called out. To avoid dangers dead ahead, keen listeners had perched on the bowsprit.

Onshore, a few lamps burned at this hour, but still glowed enough to silhouette the frigate to any ship farther out to sea. To alter their profile to that of a smaller vessel, the captain had ordered the furling of all sails aft of the foremast. At the same time, high in the rigging, sailors stared out into the Mediterranean Sea for British ships.

An hour later, the city's lights faded as the *Muiron* rolled along the calm black sea, and a crescent moon rose, orange in the Saharan haze. Its faint glow was just enough to highlight their sails.

"Signal to port!" yelled a man from aloft.

Henri spun toward the sea of sand beyond the breakers and, minutes later from his lower vantage point, saw the fiery glow of the signal. The view through his telescope confirmed the fire on the high walls of the Taposiris Magna, an ancient Ptolemaic structure west of Alexandria. *At last,* he sighed and his shoulders relaxed as he crossed to the starboard railing and scanned the sea. He saw nothing, but his heart resumed pounding while waiting for the order to turn. They'd have few defensive options if caught this close to the coast.

Finally, they drew parallel with the bonfire, and the captain gave the order to turn. The vessel heeled and picked up speed as men, working like spiders in a web of rigging, unfurled the sails. The bow wave kicked up and Henri instructed the watchers on the bowsprit to stay alert for treacherous shoals. He maintained vigil throughout the waning night, until, as dawn tinged the eastern sky, the captain sent a junior officer to relieve him.

Once lying in his bunk, he thought of the crates in the hold below and his lost opportunity with the alchemist in Cairo. *I was so close to the discovery,* he lamented, but at least he had the crystals. As sleep eluded him, he began plotting his next steps.

Corsica, France
8 October 1799

The British fleet dogged the *Muiron* for over a month until it made port in Ajaccio on the first of October. Napoleon ordered a quick resupply, only to be trapped in the harbor by the contrary Corsican winds. He paced the decks, itching to get back to the mainland. He'd received a message about more French defeats at the hand of the second European coalition and his brother assured him the time was ripe to seize power. France had had enough of government by committee following the Reign of Terror and needed a true leader.

At last, a week later, the winds subsided, and Napoleon issued the command to sail on the morning tide. Henri's wife, Aglaé, organized a send-off dinner for Napoleon, his officers, and the elites of Corsica's capital city at the Lacroix mansion on Rue des Oranges. The home radiated elegance and the sumptuous meal reminded the men, who had been warring for two years, of the pleasures of French society.

Long into the night, after the guests and officers had departed, Henri dismissed the servants so he and Napoleon could speak privately.

When the two were alone, Napoleon said, "Come with me, Henri. Lucien assures me the Republic needs my leadership. I need trusted men. The Directory's corruption has bankrupted the nation."

"I think not," said Henri, beckoning his friend into the library. "I'm sure your brother has enough good men. This past week has shown me that my place is here. The shipping company needs a firm hand." He poured cognacs, and they sat silently for a time.

Napoleon finally asked, "What did you do in Cairo during my campaign in the desert? You never said."

Henri gazed into the amber liquid and swirled it around the snifter. His thoughts drifted back to a day two years ago when he'd gone to Cairo to inquire about an object found in a tomb. In a small dark shop, a neatly robed man worked over a small flame, heating an iron pot. When Henri held out a crystal found in a tomb near Saqqara, the man's eyes went wide. Henri tried to ask a question through broken Arabic, but the man waved him off, turning to a pot.

He increased the flame under it and removed several jars from a shelf. He added precise amounts from the jars into the pot, sending a heady aroma into the closed space. "Put it there," said the man, pantomiming the action so Henri understood. Then, the man gently stirred the now boiling mixture around the crystal and pinched a powder from a pouch around his neck.

He waved Henri closer, then tossed in the powder. A cloud billowed from the pot. Henri reeled as a vapor enveloped them. The shop swirled in a kaleidoscope of color as the robed man grew in stature. Henri felt weightless and steadied himself against the table. Suddenly, his mind emptied. The mental restlessness he'd experienced before accompanying Napoleon to Egypt was replaced by a growing sense of connection—he'd found the purpose he so desperately sought.

The air cleared, and the room settled again; everything had sharp clarity. The man removed the crystal with a pair of tongs and held it up for Henri. It glowed brightly from yellow spots beneath its glassy surface and he placed it on the table, its heat scorching the wooden surface.

"Give me a coin," said the alchemist.

Henri placed a five francs silver piece in the man's outstretched palm. The alchemist grasped its edges with the forefinger and thumb of his other hand. Slowly, he moved it until just above the crystal, then let go. The coin wobbled, suspended in mid-air.

Henri crouched down, no stranger to conjuror's tricks. But, as if to dispel Henri's doubt, the old man lightly stroked the coin's edge. It spun slowly. Henri tore a page from his notebook and slid the paper between the coin and crystal, expecting it to fall. Nothing happened. Whatever force levitated the silver could pass through other material.

"Mon Dieu!" He touched the coin, stopping its spin. Then he spun it again. The back of his neck tingled, and the feeling spread through his limbs. He stood and looked at the alchemist. "What is it?"

"Takwin," said the man.

For the next two years, while Napoleon fought the Ottomans, Henri worked with the robed man, delving into the mysteries of the strange crystal. He learned it was a diamond after showing it to a mineralogist in the French expedition. In time, Henri's Arabic improved, but he could never grasp the meaning of takwin. His frustration grew as the old alchemist spoke in riddles, saying, "the crystals came up from the ground." He kept promising to show Henri its source, but always had an excuse not to. The day after he finally agreed to take Henri to the crystals, Napoleon's messenger had showed up.

"Henri? Where did you go?" asked Napoleon. "Each time I ask about Cairo you withdraw. What happened my friend?"

"I met someone," said Henri, sipping more cognac.

"You sly dog. I heard the women in Cairo have a devilish charm." Napoleon swayed in his chair, mimicking a dancer.

Henri had not intended to insinuate it was a woman, but it deflected his friend from probing further. They toasted to "the woman" and a short while later Napoleon declared he must go.

As Henri watched his childhood friend depart, he fingered the diamond he always carried in his vest pocket. Tomorrow, he would move the equipment he'd secreted away from Cairo to his other house up the mountain behind Ajaccio.

Henri turned beneath the portico, mounted the mansion's steps, and stopped in the foyer. He withdrew the diamond and held it up to the bright candelabra. The tiny black flecks inside the diamond drew him in. His investigations in Cairo had proved the diamond could move metal objects many times larger. *I'll figure you out.* He rubbed it with his thumb. *Even if it takes the rest of my days.*

He returned the diamond to his vest pocket and walked upstairs to bed.

1

Bocagno, Corsica, France
Present Day

Eyrún Stephansdottir made tea in the kitchen of her house on the mountain above Ajaccio. While it steeped, she looked out the window at her husband, Darwin Lacroix, clearing the detritus from an overnight thunderstorm. She never tired of the view out the wall of glass doors onto the flagstone patio. Many nights they sat at its firepit that overlooked a vast gorge and stargazed in the warmth of a crackling pinewood fire.

Eyrún binned the tea bag and carried her cup down the short steps to the living room to her own project—organizing the hodgepodge. Books and notes had piled up since their return from Pantelleria, Italy where they'd shut down an antiquities looting ring.

She gathered books, stacking them on the fireplace coffee table. She reached for another book on its lower shelf, a small, leather-bound volume that bore no title. Curious, she opened it and, seeing the handwriting, remembered it was the diary written by Darwin's third great-grandmother. The cursive script flowed across the unlined pages; its blue ink thicker where the vintage pen nib had doubled back.

While lovely on the page, she could not read the Corsican calligraphy. Still, she sat on the floor, leaning against the sofa, and turned to the cover page. Using her mobile, she translated the text as:

A Lacroix family history and,
Resolution of the great vendetta
Letizia Lacroix nee Paoli
1921

The great vendetta? Darwin never mentioned this. She turned the page, and a note with a computer file name fell onto her lap. Knowing where Darwin kept family research, Eyrún retrieved her tablet and navigated to the file's cloud location. She began reading. Most of the early pages listed family members' births and deaths and who was related to whom.

Eyrún skimmed ahead until reaching pages on Pasquale Lacroix's life, someone she knew from Darwin's family stories. She'd been told Pasquale loved to boast, especially about a box of Roman scrolls he'd found in 1867 buried in Herculaneum. But his wife, Letizia, recorded a different view of the man Darwin revered.

Pasquale loved to boast. He was a superb storyteller, but we all knew his tendency to exaggerate. Much of his gasconading, he appropriated from his grand-père Henri Lacroix, who, with the backing of the French crown, suppressed the last vestiges of Barbary pirates. Some of this history is documented. The rest I have gathered orally and recorded here.

That's interesting. Eyrún remembered snippets of the Lacroix family history told by Darwin's grandfather, Emelio. He lived in the family mansion in Ajaccio and loved pointing out family heirlooms that harkened back to when the family had entertained Napoleon Bonaparte and other society members of the French Republic. She was pretty sure Emelio had mentioned Henri once or twice.

Not eager to get back to cleaning, she went downstairs to the library and located the black leather-bound volumes of the Lacroix

Shipping Company records. Beginning in 1617, the books lined two rows of shelves. She pulled out one covering 1850 to 1875, Pasquale's younger years, but they were unreadable except for the numbers, which she figured related to cargo. She imagined her own relatives in Iceland during this same period, eking out a living in a harsh climate. Her family had kept spotty records, and she had never understood Darwin's cavalier attitude toward his family history.

The old records rekindled another urge to explore something she'd seen in this room, but had always put off to another day. *Why not now?* On a whim, she went to the spot on an upper shelf and ran her fingers along it, feeling for a concealed latch. Two years ago, she'd seen Darwin open a secret wall to hide the box of Herculaneum scrolls from intruders. She'd not been inside the hidden room since.

Eyrún was about to give up when she found and unfastened the latch. The shelf rotated toward her into the library. Cool musty air poured from the opening. Eyrún flicked on her phone's light and stepped inside the five-meter-wide space that went about fifteen meters deep. Pine furniture, layered in dust, made up a crude living area, with four beds lining one wall and a table and food-preparation area opposite. A door concealed a pit toilet. She wrinkled her nose despite it emitting no odor.

A massive armoire dominated the rear wall. She moved to it and tugged one door open. Plates, cups, and bowls were stacked with linen, unused for decades. As she lifted a blue and white porcelain bowl, the shelf support gave way. The heavy ceramic tipped the board and took down the lower shelves. The armoire's top broke away as its contents cascaded down.

She dove backwards as the decrepit pine collapsed before her eyes—a dust cloud billowing. A coughing fit drove her out of the room. *Oh, no!* She sighed heavily at the destruction wrought by her curiosity. Then she got a larger light from the library and went back inside to survey the damage.

As she stepped over the carnage strewn about the floor, she could see the whole upper part of the cabinet had fallen away, and its backing boards were angled precariously. They could reassemble the armoire, but the dishes were a total loss. She grasped one backing board and pulled it away.

What? She removed another board. *Something's behind this.* Two minutes later, she had pulled ten boards free, exposing a wooden door set into the wall. Her heart raced. Over the next half-hour, she cleared the broken mess enough to access the hidden door. After pulling its iron ring several times, she put a foot against the wall and, grasping it with both hands, yanked multiple times until a body-width space opened.

She paused to catch her breath. *God, I hope this isn't some forgotten Lacroix crypt.* The hair on her arms stood up as even colder air spilled from the blackness.

Steeling her resolve, Eyrún shone the light behind the door. Its beam revealed a rough-hewn tunnel. The frigid air carried a moldy odor of decay. She paused, closed her eyes, and sniffed. *No human decay.* Darwin had taught her to distinguish smells during their digs in Egypt and beneath French cathedrals.

But there's something else. she thought while squeezing through the body-width opening. Her top snagged on a splinter and, working it free, she slid behind the thick oak door. She brushed a cobweb off one shoulder and peered deeper inside.

A bright light hit her face, and she immediately put a hand to her eyes. Something metallic and red loomed before her. She thrust a hand up in defense as she leaped backwards, thudding against the heavy door. Nothing moved.

She moved the beam toward the object and snorted at what had scared her. A menacing suit of armor stood in the corridor not three meters away. Two round mirrors mounted on its shoulders had reflected her light, and a vibrant red cross on the knight's tunic had combined to startle her. *Well, it worked,* she mused, dusting herself off as she studied the tunnel's entry and armor in her path.

An oil lamp mounted on the right side wall would have lit the corridor in ages past. Two swords and a lance hung on a wooden rack below the lamp and, looking down the tunnel, she noticed other lamps farther in. The knight's arms held a cocked crossbow pointed at the doorway. *That's scary.* She shone the light around the armor's feet, looking for a stand, but saw nothing. *Guess I just go around it.* She took a step.

The knight lunged, firing the crossbow. The bolt flew at her face. She dove, screaming. The fletching scraped her neck as it slammed into the door. A dust cloud engulfed her as the armor shuddered to a stop an arm's length away.

Violent coughing doubled her over, stars filling her vision as she felt her neck. It stung. A half minute later, the spasm passed, and she picked up the light and brought her fingertips into its beam. *Blood!* She felt again, probing the burning wound, but confirmed it was not deep. Then she turned to the door behind her. The iron tipped half-meter bolt stuck fast in the thick oak.

Oh God! I could have been killed. Her vision tunneled as she sucked in deep breaths, trying to overcome the shock. *Dammit, who…* but the wooziness continued to expand. A voice shouted her name. "Eyrún!"

She spun to see a light behind the knight, farther down the narrow stone corridor. *Someone's in here.*

"Hey," she yelled, shoving past the armor. Oblong, brass-framed mirrors lining the left wall cast the light's stark white beam onto paintings on the right wall. She banged against one portrait and careened into the opposite side before steadying herself.

"Eyrún!"

I'm coming. She pushed off the wall and, a dozen steps later, she found another door. This one was covered in mirrors that gathered and expanded the rich colors in the paintings behind her. *Beautiful,* she thought. Her breaths quickened as she stepped toward the door, then froze. A woman, older than her, with long chestnut hair and wearing a simple white gown, appeared in the mirror. Her hand lowered to the doorknob.

"Come," said the woman, her voice both soft and commanding. The door swung inward to a crypt.

The other voice echoed again, "Eyrún." Like a muffled whisper, it came from all around her as she entered a dank chamber of less than two meters square. A small chapel stood against its rear wall and tombs were embedded in its side walls. The voice seemed to emanate from the wall on the right.

Eyrún turned and stared at the portrait of a young woman hanging over one tomb. *I've seen you before. But where?*

She set the light on the floor and grasped the tombstone, but could not grip its edge. Studying it for a moment, she pounded a fist on one side until the stone moved inward, causing the other side to pop out. She grabbed that edge and worked it back and forth until the stone came free. She laid it on the floor and shone the light inside the grave.

She leaned back, gagging as the fetid decay nearly overwhelmed her. It reminded her of a crypt she and Darwin had forced open in Sainte Lazare to recover a Knights Templar object. She came forward again, lured by the light glinting off a small box between the corpse's finger bones.

"Eyrún," came a distant, muffled voice. "Get out."

What? Her head swam. But the voice was unmistakable. *It wants me to find this box. To get it out.* Her heart pounded as she gently removed the box and carried to the altar. Placing it atop the flat stone, she moved the light closer.

It's a music box. She opened its gold lid and one by one, miniature cloisonné figures moved to the accompaniment of a delicate music. The bewitching melody morphed into the voice of a young girl, and Eyrún found herself drawn into a dream she could not escape. A vision of an older, pre-Christian world. The antediluvian world of the Old Ones, as ancient as the Earth itself. A place on the edge of oblivion where the boundaries between the living and the dead, matter and spirit, earth and sky, were porous, permeable and fluid.

It's magical.

The crypt filled with translucent light. She felt herself fading into the dream.

"Eyrún."

The voice called her name one last time before she lost consciousness.

2

W*here'd she go?* Darwin Lacroix had finished his post-storm cleanup when he noticed a corner of Eyrún's garden box had fallen apart. She'd talked about replanting and he wanted to know when so he could schedule repairs.

"Eyrún?" he called out. He saw a stack of books on the fireplace table and surmised she must have carried some downstairs to the library. Wiping his dirty palms on his jeans, he scooped up the books and headed to find her.

A cold breeze greeted him on the lower level and he checked the bedrooms whose outside sliding glass doors opened onto the stone patio. But the bedroom's inside doors were all closed. *Odd. Nothing's open.* He continued straight toward the library. A few strides closer, he saw the rear shelf rack turned at an angle. His lips drew into a wry smile. Now her whereabouts made sense. Eyrún must have opened the secret safe room again and decided to explore.

Built in 1733, the Lacroix family mountain house had been constructed as a redoubt against pirates that regularly trolled Corsica's coastline. Over the centuries, the room had been converted to storage and modified again as a safe room during World War II. He'd not been inside for two years and, as far as he remembered, that was the only time Eyrún had seen it.

As he neared the library's door, he looked at the small brown leather volume atop the stack he carried: Letizia's diary. He'd attempted reading it a few times, but had always lost interest. This was partly because her handwritten Corsican was mind-numbingly difficult to read, and because he cared more for the ancient past, not the boring stories of his family's shipping business. Except for Letizia's husband, Pasquale, the Lacroixes were merchant sailors—duller than dirt.

But he'd hired someone to translate the diary into English, figuring Eyrún would enjoy Letizia's yarns. Darwin's grandfather, Emelio, born two years after Letizia's death, loved to tell tales of Pasquale and his marauding across the Mediterranean. Emelio had the gift of storytelling. In his youth, Darwin had loved hearing about treasure hunting, privateering, and vendettas that passed through generations of Corsican families. But as he matured, Darwin learned to believe half of what he saw and nothing of what he heard from Emelio's stories. Still, he hoped there was a glimmer of truth in the legends.

"Eyrún? Are you in there?" he called. His stomach clenched as she screamed. Heart pounding, he ran to the library and through the open bookshelf into the safe room. *What the hell?* "Eyrún!"

A dim light shone through a doorway he'd never seen. He dropped the books on the nearest bed and struggled over a mess of broken porcelain and pine boards. "Eyrún? Where are you?"

A noxious smell of mold hit him as he approached the door. He gagged and coughed, turning to look for a cloth. Grabbing some linen from the floor, he pressed it to his face and switched on his mobile light.

He squeezed through the opening, shuddering at the frigid air rushing out. "What the ..." his voice trailed off at the sight of a full suit of armor. He swatted at something that brushed the back of his head and turned. "*Merde!*" He touched the bolt driven into the freshly splintered door and followed it back to the crossbow. Blood smeared the knight's arm.

Putain! He shone his meager light around the armored figure to see Eyrún's form waver in the distance. "Eyrún! Get out of there."

She disappeared. Without thinking, Darwin dropped the cloth from his face and grabbed a sword hanging on the wall. He pushed around the knight while drawing the weapon from its ornate scabbard. Its blade sparkled in the light and, grasping the hilt in a ready position, he glanced at the row of portraits along the wall. "What the hell is this place?"

Something brushed against his leg. He swung the sword down, missing whatever it was, and crumpled to the floor, metal clanging on stone. He struggled to his feet, groping for the weapon. Swinging the light from side to side, he ran to the spot where he had last seen Eyrún. The mirrors on the left wall aided the illumination as he stopped at an open door.

Inside, Eyrún stood at a shrine, her back to him. She swayed as if in a trance. "It's beautiful," she said, just before collapsing.

3

Ajaccio, Corsica

Eyrún pushed open the heavy wooden doors of the village church and was confronted by a row of vicious-looking knights perched on life-size marble statues of stallions. They had frozen in mid-gallop and blocked her path. In the center, taller than others, was the knight who had confronted her in the tunnel. His stare bore into her. "What do you seek?" he asked, leveling a pike at her chest.

"The music box."

The knight raised the weapon, and the mounts parted as she walked between them toward a door with a portrait of the same young woman she had seen in the crypt. The door swung away, revealing the church library. She approached a book of illuminated pages, turning slowly on their own. Vivid drawings depicting the supernatural and the macabre stopped on a picture of the antique music box when she got close.

To the side, a woman she had not seen said, "Be wary. Its contents may be lethal."

"Why?" asked Eyrún as the library turned pale and a yellow light warmed her side.

"We won't know which kind exactly until the tests come back, but like I said, it's possibly lethal," said a form near her feet.

"She's awake! Eyrún?" A hand grasped her arm.

People came into focus. A woman in a white coat moved quickly toward her, blocking the warm light. The hand on her arm gently squeezed. "Eyrún? Love? Can you hear me?"

"Darwin?" she croaked.

"It's okay," said the woman's voice. "You're in a hospital."

Rapid beeping and an alarm sounded. "Breathe easy." A click and the alarm stopped. "Easy now. You're fine," said the woman. The noises settled, and Eyrún tried to sit up, but hands pressed her down. "Not just yet. You're too weak."

"Why am I in a hospital? I was in the library. The room. Oh, my God—" Her hand swept to her neck, touching gauze bandaging.

"You found a tunnel behind the safe room," said Darwin. "I followed and saw you collapse. Then brought you here."

"This morning?" asked Eyrún, looking at the setting sun outside her window.

"No, Love. It was two days ago."

Before Eyrún regained consciousness, the doctors feared she'd been exposed to a black mold or powder from *Amanita phalloides,* one of the most poisonous mushrooms. Darwin had spent two frenetic days worrying about its extreme toxicity. He remembered a workshop on excavation techniques that warned about dangers in old graves. Charles VI, the Holy Roman Emperor in 1740, had been assassinated using *A. phalloides*. Therefore, all crypts had to be examined with the utmost caution. But, fortunately, Eyrún's blood tests had showed no liver distress.

In the hour after she awoke, Eyrún regained full awareness and her appetite returned. Darwin ordered delivery from a favorite local restaurant. While waiting for dinner, she described what had happened in the tunnel: the animated armor, the voices and colors, and the vision in the mirror.

The toxicologist confirmed Eyrún had been overcome by an entheogenic substance. "Basically, they are like magic mushrooms," he said, "and, fortunately, not life-threatening."

"Would it help to have samples from the area where Eyrún was infected?" asked Darwin.

"Yes, greatly. We could narrow down what affected her."

"What about the danger to me?"

"Wear gloves, goggles and an N95 mask, and you'll be fine," said the doctor. "If it's psilocybin, you could end up tripping. Your wife got hit with a massive dose."

Bocagno

The doctors then advised they keep Eyrún one more night to ensure anything hazardous was out of her system. After strolling the corridors with her, Darwin drove to the Agrippa Center for Archaeology (ACA), the foundation they'd established in Corsica three years ago. He went to its chemistry lab to get a hazmat kit and an organic vapor respirator. He figured the fitted mask and thick filters were overkill, but he was taking no chances.

Once home at the mountain house, Darwin stepped into the bunny suit and fitted the mask over its white hood. Then he adjusted the goggles and pulled on nitrile gloves, snapping the stretchy material over the hazmat cuffs. He lit a match, shook it out, then waved the smoke around the respirator. *Good. No smell.* He headed downstairs. A glance in a mirror reminded him of an American cop show he had seen while getting his PhD at the University of California at Berkeley.

He opened the hidden bookshelf door, sniffed, and smelled nothing but the synthetic mask. Stepping over the broken dishes, he moved around the still-open oak door. He shuddered at seeing the bolt stuck in the oak and shook off what could have been. *She's fine. Let it go,* he thought, and opened the test kits.

It took five minutes to swab the bolt, the door, and the surrounding surfaces. He sealed the bags and, looking down the tunnel past the armor, decided to test the crypt. Eyrún had described hallucinating before reaching the tomb, but he wanted to be thorough, and, besides, he was curious. *Why did my ancestors build this place?*

After taking samples in the crypt, he stopped in its doorway to the main tunnel and looked deeper inside. The tunnel curved about fifteen meters distant. He walked toward the curve and, moving the light along the right wall, saw another oak door. The voice of caution warned against exploring on his own, but another, more urgent, drove him to pursue answers to what had happened to Eyrún.

The door's smooth oak panels fitted tightly, held fast by two iron bands, hinged into the wall. He pressed the latch on the unlocked handle and pulled. He stayed behind its protective bulk while shining the light through the opening. He saw a wooden cabinet with glass paneled doors overflowing with containers of various sizes and shapes. He looked above and around the door for any booby traps, and seeing none, opened it wide.

A large granite table occupied the room's center. A brass balance scale sat on its left edge and three hourglasses were grouped in its center next to a mortar and pestle. A wood-fired stove covered by an expansive hood that vented into the ceiling filled the far wall. *What the hell?* Finding a chemistry lab here was beyond his wildest guess.

Darwin gingerly peeled back the edge of his mask. An astringent, mildly sulfurous odor permeated his nostrils, a reminder of university. He pulled the mask away, sniffed sharply, and closed his eyes while processing the smells. There was no mold. A distinct soot smell hung in the background like he'd experienced when he helped his grandfather examine an old fireplace flue. He studied the stove and pushed the bellows handle that hissed, pushing up an ash cloud.

Stepping away to an adjacent wall, he surveyed the flasks arranged on the shelves. He recognized yellow sulfur, salt, and one full of mercury. He lifted it, swirling the vibrant silvery liquid, and set it down. Many of the labels made no sense, and he turned to the table, where, behind the hourglasses, lay a book, its brown leather cover embossed with *Henri Lacroix*.

Darwin's heart thrummed as his fingers traced the lettering. *What is this place?* He knew Henri, of course. He was a childhood friend of

Napoleon Bonaparte, who had later increased the Lacroix Shipping Company's fortunes with fat contracts hauling around Napoleon's army. But Darwin knew little else about him.

His fingers ran along the cover's edge before flipping it over and reading the title page.

Enquête sur les propriétés chimiques du Takwin découvert lors de recueil des observations et des recherches qui ont été faites en Égypte pendant l'expédition de l'armée française 1798 - 1801
Henri Lacroix

His eyebrows raised as he smiled, realizing his five-times great-grandfather had participated in the famous French exploration of Egypt. The civilian scholars and scientists who had traveled with Napoleon's armies had produced a massive body of work, known as *La Description de l'Egypte*—the foundation of Egyptology.

Oh, to be part of that team. Darwin drifted into a fantasy of opening long lost tombs in the Age of Enlightenment. His skin tingled, and he got lost in the daydream for a long moment before refocusing on the journal.

He turned its pages, pausing to read passages about the investigations on the chemical properties of takwin. *What's takwin?* He looked over the table and glanced in the mortar. *That?* He reached inside its bowl and withdrew a thumb-sized diamond, crude and impure, riddled with black flakes. Wiping it with a finger to ensure it was an internal flaw, he held it to the light. Distinct black specks, one to two millimeters in size, were frozen in the crystalline matrix.

After pondering the room for a while, he realized he needed to return the mold samples to the toxicologist and these mysteries would have to wait. He pocketed the diamond and grabbed the journal before closing the lab door. Less than a quarter of an hour later, he was headed back to the hospital, his head spinning with questions.

4

Ajaccio

Eyrún awoke to dim light cast through the partially opened hospital room door. Laughter came from the corridor, followed by a voice saying they should get back to work. A glance at the clock showed it was just after ten. Darwin had left an hour ago, and she estimated with a ninety-minute round trip to the mountain house and an hour to take samples, he might be back around midnight.

When sleep would not return, she eyed the binder with Letizia's translated diary that Darwin had brought from the house on his last trip, along with pajamas and other things. She manipulated the bed's controls to sit up and turn on the reading light, then grabbed the binder from the side table and read from a page she'd dog-eared.

Pasquale and I fought again last night. Today, he left on the Hermes on the usual route to Tripoli and Sicily. We parted amicably, but I could feel the tension. He says he's searching for something, but will not say what. I fear it's the Spanish woman. I've seen her hovering about too many times recently.

Eyrún read on. Letizia wrote when the muse caught her. Sometimes more than once a day and other times not for days. She tried to think of how long Pasquale would be at sea and, reaching for her mobile, googled speed in the age of sail power. A quick calculation estimated a journey from Corsica to North Africa, Italy, and back could take two to three months. Returning to the diary, she read about Letizia's lunch with her mother-in-law six weeks after writing her worries about Pasquale's affair.

Anne broached the subject of my happiness and asked if a pregnancy had caused my moodiness. I said no, and when she probed, I mentioned my fears of an affair. She enquired about Pasquale's behavior and her reply set me back, emphasizing that I tell no one what she was about to say.

A soft knock at the door announced a nurse who came in on her rounds. When Eyrún assured her everything was fine, the young man left, and she returned to the diary.

Anne said that at the end of his days, Pasquale's grandfather Henri spoke of a great treasure hidden away. Pasquale, nine at the time, become obsessed with finding it. Pasquale's father, Gaston, had insisted the treasure was the ravings of a lunatic. Anne told me Pasquale's fantasy will pass and to give him a lovely family, sons to carry on the Lacroix Shipping Company. But it sounded to me like Gaston carried some resentment about his father, Henri.

Eyrún flipped to a page where Letizia had drawn a family tree and studied it a few moments before turning back. Letizia's mind must have settled after the conversation with her mother-in-law, because her writing shifted to mundane descriptions of everyday life.

Eyrún skimmed ahead again until reaching an entry made after Pasquale's return from Italy in the early summer of 1867.

He goes on and on about the box he found near Mount Vesuvius. He writes letters ceaselessly to scholars in Paris about the scrolls found inside it. His father and the Company directors have told him to focus on running the shipping business, but I see him reluctantly drag himself to the offices each day.

But, he is tender with me. This morning before leaving, he stopped to ask how I felt and placed a hand on my belly. I told him it was too early to feel anything. He kissed me, saying I was his greatest treasure. His smile warmed my heart and I swear I felt the baby for the first time. I must go. Anne is coming to help design the baby's room.

The following entries spanned significant time gaps as babies came along. First daughters, Isabelle and Charlotte, then, eight years later, sons Henri, Charles, and lastly Dominique in 1892. Her infrequent entries mentioned christenings and her daughter's weddings, then stopped in the middle of the First World War until an entry on 13 April 1921.

I had lunch with Caroline today. She told me the sale of the Lacroix Shipping Company had completed and she was moving to Paris with my grandson, Antione. I begged her to stay, but I cannot blame her. The dark cloud of grief still hangs over us. She asked me to go with them, but I cannot. I would find no joy in Paris.

After lunch, we visited the family plot so she could say farewell. Little Antoine looks so much like his father did at his age. She's right to take him away from this place. The war took our joy, our future, our men.

As we parted, Caroline gave me an envelope and made me promise not to read it until she had left for Paris. When I made to open it, she grabbed my wrist, insisting I wait. Tears flowed, and she lowered her face as she begged me to wait. I promised, but it is all I can do not to give in.

Eyrún turned the page to learn what was in the letter when Darwin knocked on the door. She closed the binder as he walked in.

"You're up, Love. How're you feeling?"

"Fine. I can't wait to go home tomorrow."

He looked at the closed diary in her lap. "Anything interesting?"

"Just your family history," she said, fingering the binder's edge, itching to find out what was in the letter. But she distracted herself. "Did you get the samples?"

"Yes, and you'll never guess what else I found."

The following day a light rain fell as Darwin drove them around Ajaccio harbor. The ferry from Nice had arrived and disgorged a dozen cab-over semi-trailers and a handful of cars, mainly Corsicans, who had visited the mainland. Stopping as one long truck swung onto Cours Napoleon, Darwin shrugged his shoulders and rubbed a kink in his neck. He had slept on a roll-away bed in Eyrún's room and, between its lumpy mattress and the hospital noises, he felt like he'd been run over by the truck in front of them.

The toxicologist had confirmed the swabs from the bolt and the armor contained a ground psilocybin mushroom and sent samples to a specialist lab in Marseilles. With no other symptoms, they had discharged Eyrún just after breakfast. Darwin suggested they could stop at Emelio's for a proper breakfast, but Eyrún had said, "I just want to get home."

Five minutes later, they rounded the traffic circle next to the airport and headed up the T20 towards the mountain house. As the road rose from the alluvial plain that had supported humans since Neolithic times, Eyrún asked, "Have you read Letizia's diary?"

"Some. I stopped partway," said Darwin, easing them into the first turns on the winding climb up Monte d'Oro's southwest slope.

"I thought Henri's talk of treasure would interest you."

"Sure, but Ajaccio's full of tales about lost treasures. Remember the coins I found on the big Sanguinaires island?"

She nodded. Years before they'd met, Darwin had discovered a cache of gold coins dating to the sixteenth century.

He confessed, "I found it boring. I couldn't get past Letizia's writing about the family, buying the latest dresses from Paris, and who went to which parties." He patted a hand to his open mouth, feigning a yawn, but added, "I asked Emelio if he knew anything about Henri and a treasure."

"What did he say?"

"That Henri succumbed to dementia and began wandering Ajaccio, talking crazy about pirates and treasure. He became an embarrassment to the family, and they tried to institutionalize him. Emelio said there was nothing else in the diary about Henri. Mostly, we talked about Pasquale and the Box," he said, referring to the Roman scrolls that had brought estrangement between Darwin's father and grandfather.

"Did he say how Pasquale died?"

"Yes, but that's well known in the family." Darwin recounted the story as it was told to him. How tragedy struck the Lacroix family in World War I, as it had, disproportionately, so many Corsican families. Pasquale and Letizia's youngest son, Dominique, Caroline's husband, undertook a mission of mercy to bring the remains of Corsican boys from the killing fields of northern France home to be buried on native soil. Sadly, their ship went down, losing all souls about ten kilometers from the Sanguinaires Islands on the outskirts of Ajaccio harbor.

"Emelio said the tragedy broke the wives, Letizia and Caroline. Letizia's other two sons died earlier in the war, along with her sons-in-law."

Eyrún put a hand to her mouth and looked out the side window. She was silent a long moment before asking, "Letizia wrote Caroline moved to Paris with Antoine. How did Emelio get back to Ajaccio?"

"After Letizia's death, the house on Rue des Oranges lay empty until Antoine fled Paris in early 1940. His wife Elizabeth was Jewish and he, rightly, feared the worst." He paused to focus on a series of tight turns below the town of Bocagnano.

Eyrún remembered the letter Letizia had mentioned and grasped the pages from the back seat. She read while swaying with the car's motion, then inhaled sharply.

"What?"

"Pull over. You have to read this."

He rounded a traffic circle that split the road toward town and up the mountain and pulled into the small market at the junction. Eyrún spread the open binder across the center console.

I now know why Caroline wanted to leave this place. If the letter is true, it tarnishes the memory of her husband as the faithful man he claimed to be. An American woman wrote saying she had a child by Dominique. She claims they met while he was in hospital in Nice. I burned the letter. No one must know. This family has suffered enough.

"*Merde…*" said Darwin.

"Does this mean you have relatives in America?"

5

Baltimore, Maryland, United States

Mike Carson stood in the attic of his grandmother's home in Baltimore, staring at the stuff of a lifetime: toys, out of style lampshades, and stacked boxes, all layered in dust. Five days ago, she'd died from a stroke, less than two weeks since he'd last visited. She'd appeared healthy and mentally alert, but her doctor said a sudden stroke was not uncommon at her age.

The void returned, and he sighed. *If only I...* He looked up, squeezing his eyes against the tears. *Stop it. You can't go back now.*

His grandmother had raised him following his mother's death from a drug overdose a month before his first birthday. The divorced older woman had to work to support herself and his uncle and aunt—twins who'd also inherited their father's addictive behavior. Mike had struggled for attention and left home at his first opportunity, having had minimal contact with his family for almost two decades.

But, in the last three years, his relationship with his grandmother had improved and, when they'd had lunch together on his previous visit, she had forgiven him. They'd planned lunch again this week, but instead he got a call from the hospital. *It's like she knew her time was coming.* He sighed. Another disappointment in a life that had more than its fair share.

Yesterday, he'd obtained a copy of the will and an attached letter from his grandmother. She'd left the house to him, but the letter described documents in the attic that would lead to a "greater, rightful" inheritance. She did not say what it was other than she knew he was bright and curious and had a knack for figuring things out.

He pocketed the letter again after reviewing its instructions. *The location's right.* He counted the ceiling joists again. But none of the boxes in this spot contained anything valuable—just clothes and photographs—and had not been moved for a decade. He was about to give up when he stepped on a board that levered up on one end and, when he removed his foot, it banged down, kicking up a dust cloud.

Mike sneezed and pinched his nose. *Could it be?* He kneeled when his head cleared and lifted the board to reveal a large box imprinted with a picture of 1970s-style boots. The box contained folders full of documents. One labeled birth certificate immediately caught his eye. Downstairs, his dysfunctional relatives argued over the house's contents—all old and worthless. He tuned them out.

Opening the manila folder, he read the handwritten note atop the birth certificate. *What?* His heart palpitated. His great-grandmother was the product of an affair in 1917 between an American army nurse and a wealthy French naval officer. *Grandma's been trying to prove that her mother was owed an inheritance?*

The attic door banged open, causing Mike to jump.

"Goddamn Terri's talking shit about me. On a binge. Bitch is slurring," said his uncle Jeff, ranting about his twin sister. But the crackhead was barely coherent himself. Mike shoved the documents back into the box and leaped to his feet as Jeff growled, "It's mine. I'm the one who deserves it."

"It's just a collection of crappy poems," said Mike.

Jeff's eyes widened. He lunged. Mike stepped back, tripping over a ceiling joist, and banging his head on a rafter as he fell. Stars whirled as he tried to sit, but his uncle was on him.

"It's mine." Jeff thrust hands around Mike's neck.

"Get off me," Mike sputtered. He hesitated at the surprise attack before his defense training kicked in. He drove both fists upward into the man's jaw. Teeth banged in a sharp crack. Jeff howled and rolled off.

Mike jumped to his feet, sucking in air while staggering a few steps away from the drug-crazed man who had grabbed a baseball bat from a pile of toys. Jeff lunged, swinging wildly. Mike arched, pulling in his gut as the bat swept through the hollow space, just missing him. He used Jeff's momentum to kick out his legs, sending him down hard onto the plywood. He dropped a knee into Jeff's gut and one-punched him into oblivion.

"Asshole," said Mike, checking the man's pulse—rapid from the drugs coursing his body. *Probably won't remember a thing.* He stood and, gathering the box, swept the attic for anything else he might want. He knew his mother's siblings would take anything they thought would bring a dollar and their next fix. *God, I hate this family.*

He picked up the bat before going downstairs, just in case his aunt Terri's latest boyfriend had shown up. He had not. Mike walked out the front door, ignoring Terri's questions about the box tucked under one arm, and dropped the bat on the porch before heading down the street. Two blocks later, he glanced back to confirm no one was following and ducked into a convenience store where he bought an energy drink. What Mike really wanted was a beer, but he knew that was never happening again. Twenty-five minutes later, his ride share dropped him off at a hotel across town.

Once in his room, Mike opened the box and laid the folders and documents on the bed. He'd done this many times in prison when other inmates had asked for his help. They were all inside because of their lies and deception. But sometimes an innocent person was caught in a riptide of evidence they could not refute—facts assembled to support only a guilty point of view. Sometimes, Mike could reassemble them to show a person's innocence.

Unfortunately, in his own case, he was guilty. His conviction, a decade ago, had come after a series of poor decisions while in Iraq.

He'd joined the US Army on his eighteenth birthday, two months after September 11, 2001. Like many at the time, he'd wanted to get back at those who'd attacked his country. But deeper down, Mike was drawn to a sense of purpose and belonging. The Army's predictability suited him. His grandmother had cared for him, but given him little guidance as her own life had been shattered by an addict husband and three children who'd all succumbed to alcohol and drugs.

Mike's spotty grades showed he had the intelligence to master subjects. Still, without support at home, he'd drifted aimlessly through school. A couple of teachers had tried to help him, but he was soon passed on to another year—caught in a system geared to produce average.

Between tours of duty, he took college courses. When he showed an aptitude for leadership, he was recommended and accepted into Officer Candidate School, where he discovered an interest in law. He had joined the military police on his fourth tour in Iraq when he made a career-ending mistake.

His downfall began with the addictive behavior that had ruined his family. Hard drinking among colleagues in a combat zone led to his introduction to corrupt police who saw a chance to profit in the war's chaos. For Mike, it started small, taking protection payments from local shop owners, but it slowly escalated into trading Army supplies for looted antiquities.

He got caught in a sting operation that put him in military prison for seven years. Unknown to him, the antiquities hidden in Army shipments back to European bases also contained heroin. In prison, he cleaned up, realizing how alcohol had clouded his judgment. He completed a college degree and studied law, helping other inmates present their cases and advocating for his own release. Despite his reforms, no one would employ him as a lawyer upon his release.

Instead, Mike had found a job with a freight forwarding company, rising to shift supervisor after two years. He volunteered as a paralegal on his days off, hoping to find a way to a less dirty job. His grandmother had helped him rebuild, and he had been applying for a job in a small law office in western Maryland when he got the call that she'd died.

6

Ajaccio

Three days later, Eyrún and Darwin visited Emelio at Maison Lacroix on Rue des Oranges in Ajaccio's old quarter. Home to the Lacroixes since the late 1600s, it was here that Henri entertained Napoleon after escaping Egypt. Over appetizers, Emelio had insisted on using the champagne flutes given to Henri by Napoleon.

Later, they dined on one of Emelio's favorite meals paired with a Bordeaux Darwin had brought up from the cellar. The last bottle of 1994 Clos du Marquis from Saint Julien did not disappoint. Darwin enjoyed the less pretentious wines from this tiny appellation sandwiched between more famous producers.

"Good pick, Darwin. *Santé*," said Emelio, holding up his glass.

Eyrún and Darwin responded in kind. Then, Emelio and Darwin tipped their glasses toward the portrait of Pasquale Lacroix that dominated the wall at the table's end. The two had invented this nod to their forebear after solving the mystery contained in a box of Romans scrolls Pasquale had found in Pompeii. Their progenitor peered down at them through bright green eyes, one shaded by lush gray hair hanging across his forehead.

During their meal, Darwin and Eyrún told Emelio about the crypt and alchemy laboratory. The old man peppered them with questions and shifted to his seat's edge. He possessed bottomless curiosity and drank up new information, like a man reaching an oasis. He asked, "We never knew Henri had a daughter. Are you sure?"

"Yes," said Eyrún. "She died at seven."

"Aw. That's tragic. I wonder why they kept it a secret." Emelio pushed back from the table, looked up at Pasquale, and draped an arm on the captain's chair, much like the man in the portrait. He sighed and swept back his hair before turning to them. "What did your father tell you about the family?"

"Not much."

"Hmm." Emelio glanced at the portrait a moment and turned back to them, his green eyes clouding with sorrow. "Both Pasquale and my grandfather were killed in the closing years of the Great War. My grandfather's two brothers had died earlier in the war. Letizia was devastated and my grandmother, Caroline, that's Dominique's wife, couldn't bear to live with all the grief in Corsica. So many families lost their men."

He took a breath, as if reliving the experience, then continued. "In 1919, Caroline sold the Lacroix Shipping Company and moved my father, Antoine, to Paris."

"Darwin told me you moved back to Ajaccio in 1940," said Eyrún.

"Yes. Dad was teaching at the Sorbonne when he married your great-grand-mère, Elizabeth, and had me in 1936."

Darwin perked up. He'd wanted to hear this part of the family history, but Emelio always brushed it aside. Now he waded in. "How could Caroline sell the company? I thought it passed down through the male heirs."

"It did. But Caroline served as Antoine's trustee in 1919. Letizia and the surviving board members agreed with her decision. There was no one to run the company," he said and, looking toward Eyrún, added, "The loss of her husband and sons consumed Letizia. Antoine was the sole heir, so Caroline acted on his behalf to sell and establish a trust with proceeds that continues to this day. It provides for the properties and funds our educations."

"Did you ever live in the mountain house?" asked Eyrún.

Emelio sighed again. This time, his whole body sagged as if a great mass settled on his shoulders. He studied his folded hands for an uncomfortable period. Darwin leaned forward, anticipating a long-sought answer. Emelio finally raised his head and through wet, red eyes said, "Yes. We fled Paris because my mother was Jewish. But even Corsica became unsafe. There were informers who would turn people in for favors from the Nazis." His voice broke. He paused to settle ragged breathing, before going on.

"Mother and I lived in the safe room under the mountain house. Father visited us when he could and entertained me with stories. It wasn't until the Allies landed on Corsica that we returned to Ajaccio. After the war, we learned that Mother's entire family, all who had stayed in Paris, were gone." Emelio's shoulders rocked. The old grief poured out.

Eyrún rushed from her seat, and dropping to her knees, grasped his hands.

Darwin moved beside Emelio's chair and wrapped his arms around his beloved grandfather. He swallowed hard against a pain welling up in his chest. *"Desolé, Grand-père. Je suis sincèrement désolé."*

A tear dropped on his arm as he imagined his grandfather's unwanted memories. The secret room had been a hideout, a place to play for Darwin and his sister. But it had been a dungeon for Emelio.

7

Baltimore

Mike poured a second cup of coffee from the hotel room set up and went back to his grandmother's documents arranged on the bed. He opened the top folder and read the note and birth certificate again. His great-grandmother Judith Davis was born on September 21, 1917, to Clarice Davis in Baltimore, Maryland. The document listed the father as Dominique Lacroix of Corsica, France.

Why didn't she mention this? A moment later, he answered himself. *Probably because she couldn't prove it.* But a memory surfaced. During his third year in high school, she had, out of the blue, visited France, saying she had always wanted to go. His aunt and uncle had been furious that she was wasting their inheritance. His grandmother left him in their care, but he had mostly stayed with friends. Oddly, she'd returned less happy than he figured from the journey of a lifetime, explaining she was just tired.

As he opened a folder full of receipts, he realized her fatigue was likely true. She had made eleven trips between Paris and Ajaccio, Corsica. A quick estimate of time aboard trains and ferries showed she had spent nearly two weeks of her month-long trip dragging around luggage.

Besides the receipts, seven folders of legal documents, many in French, lay in one pile. Another contained folders with correspondence between her local attorney and the inheritance experts in New York. He rubbed his brow at the daunting paper trail and sipped his coffee. Fortunately, she'd kept detailed notes, and he dug back in.

Sally Carson, his grandmother, had found her grandmother's birth certificate in the 1970s. Mike remembered once hearing about his great-great-grandmother Clarice—fiercely independent, active in the Suffrage movement, and a Red Cross volunteer in World War I. The details of her life scrolled across the pages before him.

While working as a Red Cross nurse, Clarice Davis had had a fling with a charming French naval officer who was under her care. He resumed duty in 1917 and she returned home to the United States to discover her pregnancy. She journaled that their daughter Judith was the product of a "deliriously intoxicating weekend in Paris with a man whose far-away emerald eyes and deft touch aroused passions I've not experienced since."

Clarice had looked up Dominique Lacroix after the war to let him know about their daughter and was devastated to learn he was killed. Clarice focused on raising her daughter, Judith, while pursuing a successful career as a surgical nurse for the Veterans' Administration, including distinguished service in World War II. She never married and died in 1979.

Judith Brown, nee Davis, the daughter of Clarice and Dominique, and Mike's great-grandmother, had lived an upper-middle class life, marrying a prosperous surgeon, George Brown, in 1940 and raising three children—Mike's grandmother, Sally, was the oldest child. Mike knew he had two great-aunts, but they had moved west and the families had fallen out of contact as his branch succumbed to addiction and poverty. He'd met one of them during an Army trip to Oakland, California, but it had been like oil and water. While they shared DNA, it was clear they had nothing else in common.

Mike read on: Sally Carson nee Brown had become interested in genealogy after taking a community college night class in 1977. Her studying led to interviewing her grandmother Clarice in the year before she died when Sally learned about Clarice's affair with Dominique Lacroix.

A wave of sadness moved through Mike on seeing his family's rich history. He would have loved to talk with his grandmother about it. He sighed, shaking off another missed opportunity. *It's passed. Let it go.*

His grandmother's notes then took on a more serious tone—one of building a case to claim an inheritance from her great-grandfather's family. Sally had compiled a history of the Lacroix Shipping Company. Caroline Lacroix had sold it in 1919 after her husband Dominique had died in 1917 and the fortune went to their only son, Antoine.

Below the typed notes, his grandmother had drawn a family-tree showing Dominique Lacroix's only children as Antoine and Judith, Mike's great-grandmother. As he dug deeper, the implications astonished him. Sally Carson had tried to claim Judith's rightful inheritance as an heir to the Lacroix Shipping Company fortune.

He set down the folder and googled the Lacroix Shipping Company. He followed a link to the Wikipedia history of the extinct company headquartered in Corsica. Founded in 1617, it had grown massively in the early years of the French Republic, especially during Napoleon Bonaparte's rule. The long and detailed entry ended with the company's sale in 1919 to an Italian corporation that had gone bankrupt in the aftermath of World War II.

Mike felt he had a potential case as he had once helped a fellow inmate recover an inheritance from a great-grandparent. But he could see tremendous obstacles—mainly that it involved a distant generation and another country's estate laws.

Well, start with the basics, he thought and began writing questions:

Is there any money left?
Who are Antoine's heirs?

He studied the family tree in his grandmother's notes. Antoine Lacroix had one son, Emelio, born in 1936. *He could still be alive.* On a hunch, Mike went back to the Wikipedia page and clicked its history. Most changes had been made by a user named *Agrippa.* He followed the link to find Emelio Lacroix's profile page, that listed an extensive series of contributions to archaeological research pages.

Mike scanned the dates. Emelio's last update had been done three weeks ago. *He's alive.*

Another half-hour of searching led Mike to determine the Lacroix family still had money, plenty of it. *My great-grandma's entitled to a share of Lacroix Shipping. That means I deserve a part of the fortune.*

He leaned against the desk and tossed his mobile on the bed. For the first time in years, he truly felt that something was about to change for the better.

8

Bocagno

The next day, Eyrún and Darwin took Emelio to the mountain house to explore the tunnel. He'd visited them many times during their remodel and since, but had always stayed on the upper floor or outside. During the drive up, Darwin had thought about the house's condition when they had first adopted it as their home. It had appeared unoccupied for at least a decade. Darwin's family had used it during happy summer holidays, but he guessed Emelio had stopped going after his wife's death thirteen years ago.

After a toilet break and a glass of water that Darwin figured were mostly delay tactics, Emelio finally said he was ready to look at the tunnel. Darwin led the way and Eyrún held Emelio's hand as they entered the library's secret door. The old man paused just inside the safe room while Eyrún described how she'd opened the armoire on the back wall and the shelves had collapsed to reveal the hidden door.

"Don't worry about the dishes," said Emelio, looking around. "I never wanted to see them again. Let's see what you found."

A path had been cleared, and most of the dismantled armoire

stacked on one bed. The massive oak door had been pulled open a full meter where it stuck fast because of a shift in the floor.

"Imagine that," said Emelio, stopping at the door and looking back at the room. "Father told me adventure stories in this room for three years and, all along, a big adventure lay just behind the armoire."

Darwin smiled at seeing his grandfather's bright eyes dart around the space—curiosity was winning out over sad memories.

Emelio moved around the door. "*Mon Dieu.*" He put a gloved hand on the crossbow bolt deep in the oak. "Eyrún, I am so sorry, my dear. You could have been killed."

"It's not your fault, Emelio."

They pushed past the armor that had been moved aside, the booby-trap mechanism disabled. Emelio took in the medieval props before walking deeper into the tunnel. "You have some wacky relatives, Darwin," he joked and, passing the mirrors, added, "I imagine this would be eerie in a drugged state."

"It was like a nightmare. Terrifying and beautiful at the same time. I couldn't stop myself from going farther," said Eyrún.

A few steps later, they entered the crypt, and Eyrún described her movements as best she could remember. The gravestone remained open and emanated rot into the chilled air. Emelio shone a light inside. Light brown hair covered a skull. Its arm and finger bones that had held the music box lay askew. He stepped back and read the tomb's inscription:

STÉPHANIE LACROIX
1817-1826

"This is strange," said Emelio, running a finger over the engraving. He turned to the crypt on the opposite wall. "Henri and his daughter died within three years of each other. There's more mystery here, but show me the laboratory."

They walked to the lab door farther down the tunnel's opposite side. But as Darwin opened the door, Emelio stopped them with a question. "Where do you suppose that goes?"

They stared down the dark passage that bent sharply left about ten meters past the lab. "Only one way to find out," said Eyrún, leading the way.

Once around the bend, the path began a steep descent, and Darwin held Emelio's arm. Darwin noticed his grandfather, while still hale at eighty-six, did not have the strength and balance of even a few years earlier when they had maneuvered a hillside together in Scotland.

In a couple of minutes, they caught Eyrún, who had traveled at a faster gait and now stood before a pile of granite rubble. "This didn't collapse on its own," she said. "Someone purposely sealed it."

"What could be down there? Do you think it leads to a way out?" asked Emelio.

"Possibly," said Eyrún, picking through the pile. "But it's just as likely to block people from getting in."

"Makes sense," said Darwin. "I'll guess we're headed in the direction of the gorge behind the house. I'd say…" he searched the overhead rock as if looking for the house before adding, "it's on the right side. There's a wooded ravine we explored as kids. There's lots of places a tunnel could come out and remain hidden."

"Well, before we go poking around the canyon," said Emelio, turning around, "let's go back to the lab. I think we need to understand what our long-dead ancestor was up to."

The up-slope journey taxed Emelio, and Eyrún used the slow return to check out the tunneling work and bedrock. She commented there was nothing remarkable about the tunnel. Miners had been cutting their way underground and working granite for millennia.

Inside the lab, Emelio wandered about, his fingers grazing everything. Occasionally, he picked up an object to examine before placing it down. While studying the glassware, Emelio said the laboratory reminded him of an exhibit in the *Musée des Arts et Métiers* in Paris, before asking, "And you say his journal covers all his experiments?"

"*Oui*," said Darwin. "I haven't read far, but he mostly worked with these diamonds." He picked one from the mortar on the main table and held it close to his light. "Henri called them takwin."

"I've heard of it," said Emelio, taking another diamond and rolling it between his fingers. "It's alchemy, right?"

"Yes. Well, not exactly. Takwin's more conceptual from what I read."

Emelio's eyebrows scrunched. "How so?"

"It's hard to describe." Darwin opened a note on his mobile and read. "An ancient alchemist, Jābir ibn Hayyān, wrote about it in his ninth century *Book of Stones*. He even pointed out that the topic was supposed to be confusing to all except those whom God deemed worthy."

"There's a way to diffuse your critics," said Emelio, squinting as he stared into the largest diamond before continuing. "I know alchemical principles imply all things come from elemental particles. Epicurus called the smallest particle an atom, and that was over two thousand years ago. Now we know about protons, gluons, and whatnot. I can't keep up anymore." Emelio waved a hand. "The other day I read a story that said everything is energy when broken down to its most fundamental."

"Then alchemy wouldn't have been so far off," said Darwin.

They replaced the diamonds in the mortar and moved toward Eyrún, who was studying the hood above the stove.

"This has to vent someplace," she said. "I think it's somewhere near the pines in our drive. I looked yesterday, but the brush is too thick."

Darwin thought about it and mentally traced his steps back through the tunnel into the secret room and up through the house. He had been in enough underground places to gauge relative position. "That seems right. The trees may have been planted to conceal a chimney and, now, two hundred years later, are huge."

"Hey, you two. Look at this," said Emelio, who had wandered across the lab and opened a cabinet full of leather-bound notebooks. "It's all of Henri's journals going back to Cairo in seventeen ninety-nine."

They joined him and each took a volume and page through. Darwin had drawings of different equipment set-ups. He put it down and reached for a much smaller black book. "*Merde!*"

"What?" They turned to him.

"It's Henri's personal memoir."

9

Vatican City

A week after Eyrún's incident under the mountain house, Darwin returned to his office in the Vatican Apostolic Archive. He stood over his fourteenth-century mahogany desk, its surface barely visible under books on alchemy and esoterica. He'd come back specifically to research what his ancestor Henri had been up to and Darwin's official role as the pope's Director of Special Archaeological Investigations gave him unfettered access to the Vatican's vast resources.

So far, he had learned that alchemy applied to a vast body of work spanning millennia. At its core, it was existential and philosophical. Its practitioners concerned themselves with life's most burning questions: where did we come from? And what are the elements that make up our universe? If they could answer these questions, then they applied what they learned to transmute particles.

The archaeologist in him was pulled deep into these mysteries that had been lost in time. He'd long been absorbed by the gap in understanding human development. The idea of concealed inner wisdom resonated within him, that, perhaps being locked in this earthly plane, likewise closed our view of the universal. He'd also pondered the radical shift when humans began expressing themselves and leaving behind their legacy.

He'd seen exquisite 35,000-year-old cave paintings that depicted coordinated hunting and sophisticated human and animal relations. They must have had language, but he was flummoxed at how slowly human communication had evolved in the ensuing eons. He couldn't conceive how their brains, as large as his own, thought and reasoned.

He refocused on his notes that traced the development of alchemy. All of it tracked backward to a few sources: one, a fabled Emerald Tablet. The Greeks attributed its cryptic to a god-like figure, Hermes Trismegistus—a fusion of the Egyptian god Thoth and the Greek Hermes. But the origins became more diluted the farther back one went until, before written language, this mystical knowledge faded in the mists of time.

His thoughts spiraled as his brain overflowed. He was about to get a cup of coffee when his watch buzzed, alerting him to a meeting.

10

Ajaccio

Eyrún sat at her desk reviewing the previous month's financial statement for the Agrippa Center for Archaeolgy when her friend Katla Einarsdóttir called. Eyrún and Katla had become close during graduate studies in geology at the University of Iceland. Eyrún had been waiting since Katla messaged her earlier that morning that Eyrún's overnight package had arrived in Reykjavík.

"Halló, Katla."

"Halló, Eyrún. Tell me the weather there is gorgeous because it's so damn cold here."

"It's sunny and warm," said Eyrún, knowing it was relatively true compared to Reykjavík. Morning showers in Ajaccio had given way to broken sunshine, and now a cool breeze blew in from the western Mediterranean Sea. "You know the offer to visit is open any time."

"I know. I know. Asa told me she and Petûr had a wonderful time on your boat, but my parents are too old to watch Tinna. We're hoping for some holiday time alone."

"Bring her," said Eyrún. "Darwin and I will watch her a few days. He's talked about kids."

"Are the two of you—"

"No. Not anytime soon and it'll do him good to get a firsthand reminder how much work they are."

They talked a while longer before Katla said, "Tell me about this diamond you found. I've never seen anything like it."

Eyrún stood and closed her office door while giving an abbreviated version of its discovery before asking, "What did you find?"

"At first, I thought it was just a green diamond, but I knew you wouldn't have sent it just for that. I ran a test to determine if it had been artificially created, that is irradiated. The beam knocks an atom out of place in the carbon lattice and it refracts light, but the Raman spectroscopy lines showed a fluorescence consistent with naturally occurring radiation. Which means it's more valuable. You said it was found in Cairo?"

"Originally, yes," said Eyrún.

"That's odd. Most green diamonds are colored with GR1. Sorry, that's the natural radiation exposure, separate from the H3 Nitrogen related defects, and most of the GR1s come from alluvial deposits in Zimbabwe or the Central African Republic. There are other places in the Americas and India, but maybe only India had trade with Egypt in the seventeen hundreds."

Eyrún scribbled notes and nudged the conversation along. "So, these are naturally green diamonds from—"

"No. Actually, your diamonds are even more rare. They're what's known as chameleons. Like the name implies, they change color. When heated, they turn a pale yellow, almost white, then back to green as they cool. The same happens when they're left in darkness and then exposed to light. And under a short-wave UV light, they phosphoresce a slime green color."

"How?"

"We don't know. The color shift mechanism remains unclear, but it makes them highly sought after," said Katla.

"What about the flecks? Did you see the three inside the big diamond?"

"Yes. Could be any kind of impurity that adds to their rare quality. But there's something else."

Eyrún straightened in her chair. This was what she had been waiting for.

Katla continued, "One day, after sunset, when the automatic timers switched off the lab's lights, I was about to wave my arms to turn them back on when I noticed the larger diamond glowing on its own. It had not been heated or exposed to UV light, everything's LED here, yet its color fluctuated in greenish hues, almost pulsing. On a whim, I put it in a radiation detection chamber."

"Uh huh," said Eyrún. She had used one at her old company Stjörnu Energy in Iceland to monitor the materials ejected from the steam vents used in power generation. Most of the stuff was benign, but they needed to carefully regulate the amount of Radon gas near areas with human and animal populations.

"I got a strong radiation signature."

"Oh, my God, Katla. I had no idea. What did you—"

"I'm okay. I wasn't around them for long, and it was below our exposure threshold. The diamond gives off seventeen point one micro-Sieverts per hour. I looked up a comparison, and it's roughly the amount of parts of Pripyat, that's the abandoned city near the Chernobyl reactor. People visit all the time. It's an extreme tourism thing. Sorry, that's not important. I just meant it's not super dangerous, but you don't want to keep one in your pocket for any length of time. Anyway, I've put the diamonds in a shielded box to send back to you. Where are your samples?"

"In a thick safe in the lab, but I'll move them today."

Eyrún scribbled on a Post-It note and stuck it to her laptop's screen. Katla probed further about the diamond's source, but Eyrún kept her answers vague, saying it was from a crypt Darwin had come across, then she turned the conversation back to Katla's visit to Corsica who ended the call with a promise to discuss it with her husband.

11

Vatican City

Darwin walked a short distance down the hall and knocked on an opened door frame. Yesterday, when he'd asked the head librarian about alchemy and Egypt, he'd been told, "You need to talk with the Purple Lady."

Angela Tucci peered over a stack of books and papers. Her shoulder length white hair, with a whisper of purple tint, was parted in the middle and styled with a subtle inward curl that met a string of smoky-gray pearls around her neck. At the interruption, she looked up, her eyebrows arching above violet framed reading glasses.

"Buongiorno, Signora Tucci," he said.

"Buongiorno. Come in, Mr. Lacroix. I've heard a lot about you." She stood, smoothed her eggplant colored skirt, and, rising to nearly his height, moved from behind the desk to shake his hand. Her flawless skin concealed the age of this scholar who had served under five popes, and her periwinkle eyes cemented her nickname in Darwin's mind.

He returned her firm grip as she added, "Please. It's Angela. Let's sit," she said, waving to a table and chairs. "Espresso?"

She had the capsule in the machine almost before Darwin answered. He surveyed the office and, as she placed the cups on the table, he asked about the wall of photographs behind them. In addition to popes, she had posed with multiple world leaders and one black Labrador Retriever. "That's Ari, short for Aristotle. He keeps me young. You just missed him. My assistant took him out for a walk."

They talked about his family on Corsica before the conversation zeroed in on Darwin's reason for the meeting.

Angela asked, "You mentioned alchemy in your email. What would you like to know?"

Darwin opened by explaining the laboratory and journals. "As best I can tell, Henri became obsessed with alchemy during his time in Cairo with Napoleon. He wrote about tutoring with an alchemist, an old man who both created a sense of wonder and frustrated him with his mystical rantings."

"Yes," she said, drawing out the word in agreement with his observation before adding, "Alchemy's full of contradictions and the occult. How can I be of help?"

"To find out why he thought this diamond's related to alchemy," said Darwin, taking it from his pocket and placing it on her palm. "His first journal mentions the old alchemist in Cairo sought something called a takwin, and this diamond was key."

Angela held it to the light and, retrieving a jeweler's loop from her desk, stared into it.

"There are flecks inside," he said. "All the diamonds we found in his lab, about twenty, contain them."

"It's a beautiful green, but diamonds aren't my thing." She handed it back, asking, "Where the alchemist find them?"

"Henri never found out. Napoleon withdrew from Egypt, taking my great-grandfather with him. Henri wrote he returned four years later, but the alchemist had died and his lab was remade into a bicycle shop."

He tossed back his espresso, then asked, "What is it? The takwin. I've read about it, but it makes little sense."

Angela put two fingers to her lips and drew in a breath as she closed her eyes. After a long moment, she breathed out. "Takwin is not a thing. It aims to create artificial life—akin to the power of genesis or even resurrection. But it also refers to purification or spiritual regeneration. It's a highly esoteric branch of alchemy first documented by Arabs in the ninth century."

"That was Jabir ibn Hayyan? Right?" asked Darwin.

"We suspect the writings attributed to him are compilations of older works, but let's take a step back." She paused, as if considering how to continue. "Alchemy, as I'm sure you've read, has at least two etymologies: one from the Greek term *khēmeía,* meaning to work with metals and, another from the Egyptian *kēme,* meaning black earth. The Arabs added *al,* to make it *al-khēmeía* or *al-kēme,* depending on which root you want to follow."

"This found its way to Europe when crusaders happened upon the Arab texts. In turn, these writings influenced the development of thirteenth century esoteric philosophy—the Kabbalah—which posits all creation emanates from a supreme being and the soul exists from eternity. In the fifteenth and sixteenth century, thinkers like John Dee and Edward Kelley—"

"Who discovered the Enochian language," Darwin chimed in again.

"Yes," she said through a forced smile. "the angelic dictations they scried, but let's move on. I'm giving you a highly compressed version of the history for context. Essentially, these philosopher chemists studied divine nature in order to unlock hidden wisdom. They further strove to avoid heresy by applying their ideas to Christianity. But, of course, we know few escaped the Inquisition."

"Heretics were burned. Books as well, but fortunately, a significant number of survived—concealed—as you've found, in the deepest recesses of our library."

Darwin thought of the stacks on his desk and his struggle to figure out Henri's work. The most promising link had to do with the medieval European alchemist's pursuit of *prima materia* or first matter —which could give rise to any other element. He asked Angela about it.

"Have you read Newton?" she asked.

"I skimmed the *Principia*."

"We commonly know Newton as the mathematician physicist, but his genuine passion was alchemy. He straddled the worlds of magic and chemistry. He spent years working on the Philosopher's Stone."

"What?" Darwin sat up.

"It's true. Among other things, he was a Rosicrucian, the spiritual movement that embodied the Kabbalah. Later in life, he wrote the *Principia*, but all along, Newton believed that a single invisible force moved everything in the universe. Some believe he invented calculus to find this emanation. Did you know he also calculated the apocalypse would occur no earlier than the year twenty-sixty?"

Darwin massaged his brow, trying to wrap his head around Angela's discourse. He knew alchemists' claims of turning lead into gold and creating the elixir of life were false. But their precise measurement and meticulous documentation enabled later practitioners to improve upon techniques, paving the way to modern chemistry.

He felt lost in a fog and threw out the first thing that came to mind. "Didn't alchemy also emerge separately in China and India?"

She smiled warmly, as if sympathizing with an inductee's struggle over a labyrinthian topic.

"Yes, but let's leave that for now. Tell me about this Egyptian alchemist your great-grandfather found. While *kēme* refers to the black or fertile land surrounding the Nile, it also relates to the Egyptian black arts. Some pseudo-archaeologists push wild ideas about the funerary texts in the *Book of Coming Forth by Day* or, as we know it from a poor Prussian translation, *The Book of the Dead.*"

"They—" Her eyes locked on the diamond. A ray of sunlight had pierced her office window, changing its color to yellow.

"It does that," said Darwin, following her stare. He picked up the diamond and held it in his closed palms for a long minute, then removed a hand to show the diamond had returned to its original green color.

She jumped from her chair and pulled a book from the pile on her desk. "Look at this," she said, carefully turning pages before stopping on a drawing of a fractured stele. Its upper left corner was missing, but the lower half of an Egyptian god sat on a throne facing three objects: a green stone, a yellow stone, and, between them, a bush with radiating flames.

"*Mon Dieu!*" said Darwin.

"My thoughts exactly."

12

Ajaccio

Eyrún went straight to the lab and removed the diamonds from the safe. Seeing no obvious place to store them, she put them inside the radiation test chamber. The ACA archaeologists used it to measure faint radioactivity given off by the samples. The decay rate of known elements helped date artifacts.

She switched on the machine and, within seconds, the cumulative bunch of diamonds registered 114 micro-Sieverts—eight times higher than the readings Katla got. Her heart pounded. *Okay. It's significant but not life threatening. But what about cancers?*

She rushed to a computer workstation and googled radiation exposure. A quarter hour later, after scanning multiple sources from various nuclear regulatory agencies and filling a notepad with figures and references, she felt reasonably comfortable with the calculations.

She consulted the exposure charts again. "Shit!" she yelled in the empty lab. For exposure to over 100 micro-Sieverts daily, for a year, the chart read:

Fatal cancer in 5% of people exposed, many years later.

She, especially, hated the vagueness of "many years later" and looked around for a safe storage container. Finding none, she sealed the radiation chamber with a strip of blue builder's tape and wrote:

DANGER! DO NOT OPEN.

That'll have to do for now. She stepped back. *Oh my God! Darwin's got one in his pocket.*

13

Vatican City

Back at his desk, Darwin placed a print of the photo he'd taken in Angela's office beside two early alchemical texts. The office dimmed as a thunderstorm gathered, and he switched on a lamp as he settled into reading.

His search now expanded to include ancient Egyptian deities based on the potential link between the diamonds and the stele. He pulled up notes he'd taken earlier on Hermes Trismegistus, a mythical figure who came to prominence during the Ptolemaic Kingdom after Alexander the Great had cast a Greek influence over Egypt. Also referred to as Hermes the Thrice Greatest, this odd, syncretic melding of the Egyptian god Thoth with the Greek god Hermes had intertwined with alchemy.

Darwin looked closely at the stele photo and compared it to a seated likeness of Thoth. The fracture cut off the figure at chest height, but a mark on the stele fit where Thoth's ibis beak would have extended. The yellow and green gems hovered at head height. If these were the diamonds in question, Thoth was the right Egyptian god.

He'd given humans the gift of writing in the form of hieroglyphs.

Hermes, the other "half" of Hermes Trismegistus, escorted souls into the afterlife. Some people in Christianity's first centuries believed that only ancient beings like Hermes Trismegistus could communicate with this fundamental spirit. Thus, alchemy became a means to unravel human's earthly bindings and open a portal to divine experience.

Darwin finished tapping notes on his iPad from the books spread across his desk, then gazed out his office door. The recondite topic reminded him of a university course in metaphysics. A quick glance back at his watch showed he'd been researching for two straight hours after meeting Angela, and he stood and breathed deeply while rubbing his stiff backside.

After stretching a couple of minutes, his eyes fell on the diamond and he picked it up, rolling it between his fingers as he surveyed the open books. He picked up the photo with the other hand and looked back and forth between the diamond to the glowing stones in the photo. *What's the connection?*

He set down the photo and reread a paragraph Angela had highlighted about Hermeticism—the notion of primeval, divine wisdom. "Hmm." He looked out the window at the passing storm. The idea that single theology wove through all religions had a certain resonance. He considered the Egyptian connection. *Maybe—*

His phone rang, and he jerked, dropping the diamond.

"Hi Love," he answered Eyrún's call.

"Where's the diamond? Get away from it."

"What?"

"It's radioactive Darwin. Where is it?"

He backed off from the desk, studying his fingers as if expecting to see a burn. "It's on the desk. How bad is it?"

"Bad if you're exposed for a long time. Find a shielded container. The museum laboratories must have something. I put the samples here inside the radiation chamber for now."

"Okay. On my way," he said, filling her in on his discoveries while walking to the basement lab.

Eyrún recounted her conversation with Katla, including her invitation to visit Corsica.

"That's great," he said, pausing atop the stairwell to the lower levels. "Listen, I'll lose the signal when I go below, so I'll call you back later."

"Okay. But do you think Henri had any idea about radiation? I mean, he was exposed for years. When did he die?"

"Er ... 1850s, I think. But that was long after he found the diamonds, right?"

"Yes, but I don't want us taking any chances."

He agreed and said goodbye before trotting downstairs, the elegant Italian marble of the upper floors giving way to plebeian concrete as he descended.

14

Morgantown, West Virginia, United States

Mike relaxed his eyes by looking out the window of his rented mobile home in West Virginia. Hours of studying documents the last two days had brought mental and physical fatigue. This morning, he'd reorganized the stacks to prepare for writing out his action plan.

Across the ramshackle trailer park, children yelled in a playground and the squeak from the rusted swings could be heard inside Mike's unit some thirty meters away. It didn't surprise him, as the trailer's thin aluminum skin and scant insulation barely served as a windbreak from the elements. He shuddered, imagining life here in the depths of winter or an unbearable July. *Thank God I'll be gone.* If all went as planned, he would spend most of the summer in France.

The place served his need for cheap rent and anonymity from his relatives, who had come with hands out during the sale of his grandmother's house. She'd left it solely to him, explicitly cutting her addict-children out of the will. But they hired lawyers to press for a share, and as soon as the money from the sale hit Mike's bank account, he spread the cash across a series of regional banks. If they somehow found him, he didn't want all his assets frozen.

Screaming erupted from his neighbor's trailer and two kids shot out its side door, heading to the playground. *Wife must be home.* He stood and stretched. It was just after nine. The woman next door worked the graveyard shift at a pork processing plant. The husband or boyfriend had usually left by now for the dayshift in the same plant. *Probably hungover, and didn't get up.*

Mike stared at the playground. His gut clenched, remembering the same desire to get out of the house and run away. Escape. Pretend the horribleness would be gone upon returning home. He wanted to tell them that not all life was like this, but his head just sagged, shaking slowly from side-to-side. *You can't help them.*

Mike returned his attention to notes on genealogy. He had calculated a six percent DNA match with Dominique Lacroix, at best. His grandmother would be a greater percentage, but depending on how prolific the generations, there could be hundreds of people who could claim a similar inheritance.

But hundreds are not making a claim. I am.

He looked at the kids again, mentally pushing back from their hopeless situation. Even if he tried to help, the parents would take the money to buy booze or drugs. He'd experienced it once when a generous employer had helped his grandmother and his uncle stole the money. The state did nothing. It put his uncle right back in the house when his grandmother refused to press charges.

His cheeks flushed hot at the memory of friends who had supportive families. *And money.* He flashed on his own wasted chance in the Army and launched into a familiar self-deprecating maelstrom.

It's your own fault. You piece of shit. You had a great thing going and fucked it up. Just like your—stop it! He reflexively yanked open a kitchen cabinet. The same move he'd made in the Army to grab for the bottle. Make the world feel better.

But in place of a bottle, he found a note he'd written to himself for just this situation:

The answer's not here asshole

He banged the cabinet shut and looked outside as the neighbor slammed his trailer door. The man spewed invective that was silenced only by the roar of his dilapidated pickup truck. The oily exhaust clouded the view of the playground.

A moment later, Mike centered himself by making a glass of iced tea. *This place is temporary. Stay focused on getting out. Keep working on the plan.* He repeated the mantra while stirring the ice and carried the glass back to the table.

By early afternoon, he'd outlined a plan. Caroline Lacroix, Dominique's wife, had sold the Lacroix Shipping Company in 1919. When her son Antoine died in 1967, the fortune went to his only son, Emelio. Mike's grandmother, Sally, had determined during her 1997 trip that the record of the sale would be in the *Chambre Arbitrale Maritime de Paris,* a court of arbitration. Mike learned little from its website, and besides, he sought a hundred-year-old record that was not likely to be digitized.

He needed to go to Paris, but without the ability to read French or even competently explain his search, he would be stuck. He looked up bilingual law firms, but those would cost hundreds of dollars per hour. Traveling and hotels would burn cash at a fast clip and he would need a large reserve to pursue the claims once filed.

He picked up an article from the document pile. Emelio Lacroix and his grandson Darwin stood before an institute they'd established in Corsica, the Agrippa Center for Archaeology. He tossed it back on the pile.

These people have money, he seethed at the thought of his great-grandmother, left to raise a child alone, cast off by this wealthy family. *I need an open and shut case or the bastards will tie me up in court until my money runs out.*

He stared again at the photo of Darwin, smiling, one arm around his grandfather and the other around a beautiful woman. *He benefitted from his family's shipping empire, while I was raised by impoverished idiots.*

How different my life would be if I… His mind drifted a few moments thinking of a big house, holidays full of joy and not fighting, before snapping back to reality.

That should be me. That will be me.

15

Ajaccio

Eyrún warmed her hands on a ceramic mug as she stood on the catwalk overlooking the dig site, five meters below. As Managing Director of the Agrippa Center for Archaeology, she'd been supervising a building expansion when human remains were dug up in the car park. They had quickly determined a settlement from the Neolithic period lay beneath their feet and reimagined the expansion as a living museum and teaching facility. Lower down, another catwalk crossed the pit where visitors got an up-close view of modern excavation and could talk with the archaeologists working on the site, many of whom were interns. A middle-aged man with a thick graying beard stood with a group of students beginning a three-month internship.

"Good morning, Barry," she called down.

"Oh, hi, Eyrún." Barry Hodgson had joined the ACA as director of archaeology after leaving a professorship in northeast England. He had been Darwin's favorite professor and advisor during his post-graduate studies.

"Carry on," said Eyrún, and watched him turn back to the group.

Barry's reputation as a field archaeologist had made his digs highly sought after. He loved to teach, but hated academia's constant pressure to publish and fight for budgets. His role at the ACA freed him from both, and the weather in Corsica had made the move a straightforward choice. Barry's wife, Zoe, a professor of languages, thrived on teaching remotely and loved how her garden prospered in the Mediterranean climate.

A young woman, hair covered in a tangerine hijab, waved, and Eyrún returned the gesture. Illi, from a village, the Siwa Oasis, in the western Egyptian desert, had joined this internship group before entering university in Cairo. Illi's family had played a vital role during Darwin's investigation of a disused tomb in the Siwa Oasis intended for Alexander the Great. Eyrún had funded the local school and promised to help foster Illi's strong intellectual ambition. Young women in the oasis were just beginning to seek education and fulfillment beyond their traditional roles.

Eyrún sipped her tea and smiled, feeling a glow from more that the liquid's warmth. *It's working*. Just that morning, she had received a letter from the president of an East African country praising the ACA's work in helping them mitigate antiquities looting.

She turned to the second-story doorway and walked to the physical sciences laboratory she had personally outfitted. Besides the equipment needed for forensic archaeology, she had installed a spectrometer and tools required for her expertise and passion: geology. Her PhD in volcanology had focused on geothermal power to convert flue gases into petrol. The royalties from the technology licenses had contributed to the wealth she and Darwin had used to found the ACA. While she loved the hard sciences, she had come to realize the importance of understanding human development and assisting impoverished countries in preserving their abundant cultural history.

She set the cup on the worktable, switched on a bright task light and examined the music box from the crypt. The gold box was six centimeters square and half as tall, with paws at each corner that raised its base slightly. Its sides had been fashioned like a packing crate —etched with fine lines that mimicked wood grain. Atop the box on either side of a tightly fitted turntable, a golden puppy chased a red and blue cloisonné ball. She flipped it over, but as she had observed before, its bottom was sealed with no means of opening. An engraved message was written in a fine script:

Joyeux anniversaire Stephanie

There was no age or year, but Eyrún guessed a delicate gift like this would have been given no earlier than four years. She sighed, knowing from the dates on the tomb in the tunnel, the girl had died at seven. A twinge in her gut surfaced a painful memory.

Eyrún's father, also a volcanologist, had perished in an explosion under a glacier when she was eighteen. Almost two decades later, the ache lay dormant, like an old injury, until triggered by a certain movement. She thought about how different things might have been, but then, sighing heavily, released the pain to its familiar niche.

She looked out the lab's rear windows at the mountains above Ajaccio and pictured all the goodness in her life: her sister, a medical doctor, and her happily remarried mother, both living in her native Iceland. Eyrún had achieved her own successes and found a partner in her husband, Darwin Lacroix. Together, they were building a future in the ACA for themselves and for others.

The pain faded, and a warmth and sense of connection replaced it. She took a cleansing breath, then refocused on the music box.

This must have been made in the early 1820s. She jotted down it down. Darwin was still working out a timeline of Henri's work. Setting the box on the table, she pushed a minute switch on one corner. A mechanism inside whirred faintly as a tune played and the dog and ball rotated on their gold disc.

It took her a moment to pick out the melody as the internal scroll plucked the comb, but the unmistakable notes of Frère Jacques fell into place. She smiled at how this would comfort a small child, then her brows knit as she focused on the conundrum that had brought her to the lab—*how does this run?*

She rotated the object in her fingers. The tune played consistently, not slowing or pausing. She flicked the switch to stop the music and put on magnifying glasses. The box instantly enlarged, her fingers blurry pink and huge at the edges of the visual field. While beautiful at normal resolution, the gold surface showed pits and scratches from wear. A minute of careful study showed no screws or other means of getting inside. The only openings were a gap where the switch slid back and forth and the ring between the turntable and box.

She gently grasped the dog and ball and wiggled, but the disc held fast. She used a plastic pry tool from a computer repair kit to lever the turntable. Again, no movement. "Huh," she said, before setting it down and removing the glasses. Her mouth scrunched as she considered the next move which came to her as she looked across the lab. One of their staff, Lina, who had recently joined from Lithuania, was an expert in ancient jewelry. Eyrún carried the music box to her workstation and was about to write a note when, on a whim, she took it to a radiation detector. The diamonds had been removed and safely stored in a lead-lined container.

She placed the music box inside and closed the door. To her astonishment, the box gave off faint radiation consistent with the diamonds. Her heart thrummed as a world of possibility danced.

A diamond powers the box. But how? An idea sprang, but in the same instant, she suppressed it as wild imagination. *But what if it is? It would be a revolution.* She pictured the possibilities, but again checked her excitement. The scientist in her needed proof. *I need to see what's inside!* shouted her inner entrepreneur. She ran off to find Lina.

16

Vatican City

The next morning, Darwin opened Henri's first journal, begun in Cairo in 1799. A shielded box containing the diamond and marked with radiation warnings lay on the desk. The previous night, after finding the box in the basement, he had read up on radiation and learned his exposure had been minimal. He also learned that Henri would not have known about the dangers, as radiation properties were not documented for another century when Röentgen, Becquere, and Curie ran their famous experiments. Even then, the actual dangers did not hit home until workers who painted radium on watch dials began dying.

He sipped his go-to morning triple shot cappuccino as he untangled Henri's two-hundred-year-old scrawl. It was clear Henri had been taken in with tales of Egyptian dark magic and the incantations the alchemist Salih used as he tried to achieve takwin. Salih claimed he could read the ancient language, but Henri was not convinced.

Salih uses some narratives to support his ideas, but I have sketches from the tombs that he cannot read. Pierre, the expedition's linguist, calls the symbols hieroglyphs from the Greek "sacred engraved letters." I feel a world will open to us when we discover the key to this language.

Darwin chuckled at knowing the same French expedition had also found the Rosetta Stone and decades would pass before its deciphering. History was full of men like Salih, who claimed power by guarding their esoteric knowledge. *Not unlike keeping the Christian gospels in Latin,* he thought, *but there's more going on here.*

He read on as Henri described fantastical visions when Salih would claim to interpret the hieroglyphs by "waving the diamond" over the text.

I began to observe Salih's ritual more closely. Each time, before consulting the texts with the diamond, he poured a fine brown powder on one palm, rubbed it against the other, then clapped his hands vigorously to disperse the powder. He kept the powder in a jar and would not tell me its source. He called it holy.

One day, I arrived and stood outside his curtain to watch him put a dried plant into a mortar and grind before pouring it into the jar. Later that day, I took some of the plant from the place he kept it. It is a mushroom. Later I put a small piece in my colleague's coffee. In less than twenty minutes he began spouting ludicrous notions and babbling about the "wonderful colors" in the servants' clothing. I knew then, Salih used this mushroom drug for his illusions.

"*Bien sûr!*" Darwin smacked the desk. While he knew the world to be full of the unexplainable, more often than not, a physical manifestation was unveiled upon careful examination. Like a magician's sleight of hand, Salih had used a psilocybin to distract his audience. Like Eyrún drugged in the tunnel, Salih's clients would be convinced some magic had occurred.

Merde! He tensed, thinking of Eyrún in the tunnel. *Henri had used the same tricks.* He pushed down the emotion. *There's something else behind these diamonds, otherwise Henri wouldn't have obsessed over them. Something to do with the radiation?*

Darwin closed the journal as his assistant alerted him to a weekly meeting of department directors, but spent most of the meeting daydreaming about Henri's journals. At one point, he confirmed his late afternoon flight back to Ajaccio and messaged his assistant to prepare a special document to transport the shielded box containing the diamond.

He'd carried the diamond in his shoulder bag on the flight over. *How the hell did security miss that?*

17

Ajaccio

Eyrún had interrupted Lina enjoying the ACA's rooftop lounge and asked her to help with the music box. A half-hour later, the disassembled box now lay in the lead container with the diamonds. Lina's experienced hands knew where to pull with the right amount of force. Eyrún had videoed the process and taken high resolution photos. She now studied those. Gold wires had suspended the diamond inside the box. When the switch on the box's side was opened, the plates spun, turning both the musical armature and turntable.

She played the video forward and backwards and studied the photos, but could not figure out how the mechanism worked. She donned a radiation suit and placed the lined box inside the shielded workstation. Without the turntable, she could see inside the box and watched the plates spin when the switch opened. She got a flexible pinhole camera and held it just inside the box. The switch pulled back a pin that held the internal plates from spinning. *Magnetic?* She wondered and got a magnetic field meter from a lab drawer.

It gave a strong reading. *But what does the diamond have to do with it?*

She set the music box aside and placed a loose diamond from the lead-lined box on a wooden tray. Then she took apart a magnetic latch from one of the lab's cabinets and, using tongs, she placed the magnet over the diamond. It resisted. *Interesting*. She opened the tongs, and the magnet floated five millimeters above the diamond. *Could it be?*

Eyrún sat back, staring in disbelief at the scientific equivalent of the Holy Grail—a room temperature superconductor. *At least it behaves like a superconductor.* Her spirit soared at the prospect, but she needed confirmation. And she knew from research that verification would require a high-energy physics laboratory.

She messaged a friend who would grok the situation in a heartbeat: Zac Johnson.

18

Morgantown

The solution hit Mike while running along a former railroad line through the Appalachian countryside. Sun warmed the air after a passing thundershower had damped down the pollens. The undertone of decay in the shadows competed with floral fragrances in the sunlight clearings. Life burst forth everywhere: a doe and her fawns looked up from a meadow, comfortable with the human traffic crisscrossing their forest.

A gunshot, likely illegal hunting, startled them and, for Mike, brought back memories of patrolling in Iraq. In such a moment, his team would have grouped into a protective formation. As the forest noises resumed, he pictured their faces and one in particular, a member of the Algerian special forces who had joined the coalition. *Ramy speaks French.* As Mike turned back toward the trailer park, he pictured his friend's wide smile and confident manner.

Ramy Touré came from a well-to-do family, had multiple university degrees and, during compulsory military service, had found he liked to fight. After working his way into a special forces unit, he was sent to Iraq as part of Algerian support for joint action against the insurgents.

Mike had been raised to think everyone in the Middle East was a terrorist, so he'd been surprised at developing a friendship with Ramy, even though their backgrounds could not have been more different.

It had been Ramy who introduced Mike to taking bribes and smuggling, which had gone well for three years, but when the shit had hit the fan after the heroin bust, Mike had landed in prison. Ramy got deported back to Algeria, where the government said it would deal with him.

Deal with him, my ass. Mike ground his teeth. The last he'd heard, Ramy lived in Paris. During the return run, Mike kept thinking about other potential solutions. He'd sworn to never contact his old accomplices, but no other options came to mind. He needed a native French speaker and reader and could also use a cheap place to stay.

Son-of-a-bitch. He pushed the idea from his mind the last mile as he tried to enjoy the peaceful spring day. He knew there would be little time for reflection once he set the plan in motion.

Mike stared at the long email draft. He'd been rewriting it during the last three hours, debating how much to say. Ultimately, it came down to trust. *Do I trust the bastard? No.* Ramy had saved his own hide while deserting Mike. But he also knew trust was not a blank check. It had different accounts. He had trusted Ramy with his life while on patrol, as the man had a sixth sense for danger. But, beyond combat, he trusted him with little else besides Ramy's own well-being.

Dammit! Mike's finger hovered over the send button, the email edited down to just the essentials. He needed help with research and legal translation and could pay if Ramy were looking for a side hustle. If Mike remembered correctly, Ramy's degrees were in history and global business. If Ramy discovered too much, Mike would have to cut him a share of any money he inherited.

His internal debate over reconnecting to his bitter past tied him in knots until, realizing he had no better options, he smashed the mouse, zipping the email into the ether. He walked away from the laptop, poured another glass of iced tea, and then looked for cheap flights to Paris.

In less than twenty minutes, Mike's mobile rang with the caller ID showing a French country code.

"Hello?" he answered in a flat voice, suspicious of a robocall.

"Mike! Buddy! How are you?" A thumping music faded and street noises increased.

"Ramy? How'd you get my number?"

"Of course it's me. I pinged a few people on WhatsApp. Got your number from Skunk."

Mike's nose wrinkled at the mention of their colleague Russ Jones, whose recalcitrant hygiene had earned him the dubious nickname. He'd heard Skunk went back to Europe after serving time. "*Where* are you?" he asked.

"At a club near the opera. Stepped outside to call. It's great to hear from you. What's this about needing research help?"

"I'm a lawyer now and got a client who wants to pursue an inheritance from French relatives."

"Sounds like you need a genealogist."

"No. They've got DNA and know the family tree. What they need is evidence of the money trail."

"Why me?"

Mike could hear Ramy talk to someone, saying he would be back inside in a minute.

"My client doesn't have a lot of money and I'm not fluent in French. I don't know what your financial situation is and—"

"You thought I might like to make a little on the side," said Ramy.

"Exactly."

"I might be. Listen, I'm with these two girls from Calais. It's their last night in Paris. Call me tomorrow about this time. Hopefully, I'll be awake," he said, laughing.

They ended the call and Mike remembered Ramy's other passion: women. In their countless nights out, Ramy had never gone home alone. Sadly, his lust had also been their downfall when a police-paid informer had infiltrated their group. Mike pondered this potential problem, then set it aside, reasoning he only needed Ramy's translation skills. *Nothing illegal in that,* he thought, and refocused on booking a flight.

19

Bocagno

That night, Eyrún stopped in the village just downhill from the mountain house. The carpark at *I Mazzeri* market overflowed, and she had to squeeze into a spot on the road's shoulder. The once dilapidated building had been remodeled into a cafe and specialty foods market by two chefs from Paris who had come to the island for its less hectic lifestyle. Soon after their arrival, Sylvie and Anne had also revived traditional Corsican cuisine.

Few people were in the market and only two cafe tables were occupied, which perplexed Eyrún. She was about to ask about it when laugher erupted from the rear kitchen area. When Eyrún looked through the doorway, Anne answered Eyrún's unspoken question. "The cooking class."

"That's right. I meant to sign up. How's it going?"

"It's been wildly popular, especially with the tourists."

They talked about the upcoming schedule and, after Eyrún had chosen a cold stone-cooked trout and a ratatouille to take-away, she wandered over to the basket of fresh rustic breads. She enjoyed cooking, but when Darwin was away, it was easier to pick up small dishes from the market. While Anne wrapped her selections, Eyrún looked in on the class.

Ten people, mainly couples, surrounded a long butcher-block table prepping food. From their lively, loud conversations, she guessed the wine had been flowing. A woman who appeared in her seventies had stopped at one couple's station and corrected their cutting technique. A moment later, she looked up and caught Eyrún's eye and held the stare. The old woman's eyes narrowed as she peered over Eyrún's shoulder.

Eyrún's neck tingled, and she looked over her shoulder where the woman had focused. Nothing. She turned back. The woman was gone, but she jumped as a hand gripped her forearm. The woman, a head shorter than Eyrún, had moved around the table in those brief moments. They locked eyes again, but up close, Eyrún could see the woman's left eye wandered, giving her the feeling that it was searching.

"Beware the cancer in your family."

"What?" asked Eyrún, her body tensed, heart pounding.

But the woman turned and went to another couple struggling with their preparations. Eyrún was about to call after her when she jumped at another touch.

"Sorry, Eyrún. I didn't mean to startle you," said Anne, holding out a bag with Eyrún's order.

"Thanks."

"Are you okay? You look pale," said Anne.

"Er ... yes. I mean no," she said, glancing at the class, then back to Anne. "Who's that woman? The teacher."

"That's Giséle. The wife of the sausage maker. Did she say something?"

Eyrún was about to answer when Giséle looked up, as if she could hear them. Eyrún gently guided Anne across the store, out of the kitchen's view.

"She said to beware of cancer in my family."

Anne gasped. One hand covered her mouth, then her fingers played with a kitchen cloth on her apron. "I'm sorry, Eyrún. Some locals say she's a seer, a *mazzeri,* but other villagers say she's crazy. We named our restaurant *I Mazzeri* as a bit of fun and a connection to the local legends. I can talk to her. Giséle's a brilliant cook and the guests love her stories."

"No. That's okay," said Eyrún. "It was weird. That's all."

"Okay, but you let me know if it happens again."

Once home, Eyrún poured a glass of white wine from Calvi in northern Corsica. As the ratatouille and trout warmed, she dragged a piece of bread through olive oil and gulped down half the wine. The house held the chill from the overcast spring day and she switched on the gas fireplace.

She gathered the plate and sat on the hearth, absorbing the flame's heat, but shivered at the memory of Giséle's proclamation. She would have thought it crazy were it not for unearthing a cache of radioactive diamonds in her own home.

An hour later, her watch chimed, alerting her to call Zac. She knew he rose early and timed her call to catch him before his day got busy.

20

Oakland, California

Zac Johnson finished his last set of single arm pull-ups following a parkour run in his native Oakland, California. Now in his mid-thirties, he kept up the dawn routine he'd adopted as a US Army Ranger following graduation from the West Point Military Academy. The fluid movement through the urban space preserved his ability to move spontaneously. The skill had served him well during tours of duty in Afghanistan, and a few places not officially acknowledged.

After fulfilling his service obligation, he'd completed a Master's degree in plate tectonics at the Colorado School of Mines, followed by a PhD in earthquake early warning detection. He applied this knowledge at the US Geological Survey where he'd met Darwin Lacroix at an archaeological site on California's San Andreas fault.

Zac's team had been placing sensors when they discovered human remains and called in a team from the University of California at Berkeley. Darwin, who had recently completed his PhD, got the call and the project led to their friendship.

Two years later, Zac had joined Darwin on an exploration of a lava tube in Iceland, where they discovered a massive diamond chamber.

Zac had used his windfall to found a company that had launched dozens of micro-satellites to form a global earthquake prediction network. But the other investors had cared more about financial return than the value of saving lives. When they pushed too hard to monetize, Zac sold his shares and went back to primary research.

His workout done, he walked into his favorite local coffee bar and, while waiting, switched his phone off silent. He smiled at seeing a message from Eyrún and his eyes ballooned on reading it. He took his drink outside to call her.

"Zac! Hi!"

"Hey, Eyrún. Just got your message."

"You won't believe what I found." She launched into a rapid account of what had happened under her house and the later discovery of the diamonds and music box.

Zac sat on a sun-drenched concrete planter and put the phone on speaker, so he could scroll through photos she'd sent. He grinned at the description of Henri's alchemy lab. They'd also met in Iceland and shared a passion for geeking out on technologies. He listened to her investigation of the diamond's odd properties, knitting his brows when she got to the radioactivity part.

"Which element?" he asked.

"I don't know, but one gives off over a hundred micro-sieverts and passes through everything except metal, so it's definitely gamma. My mass and optical spectrometers can't register the flecks inside the diamond, just the carbon matrix itself. But whatever it is, it's acting like a superconductor, right?"

Zac shifted into the shade and zoomed in to watch the video she'd sent. Tongs held a magnet over the diamond and then shifted out of frame. The magnet wiggled as if alive, animated by an unseen energy. His heart raced, and his fingers moved instinctively, grasping and pulling at the video to get a better look. "It is, but ..." he trailed off, thinking about the only superconductors he'd seen—in environmental conditions of massive pressure or super-cold temperatures.

It's beautiful. He played the video again, becoming absorbed in possibilities, but he pushed the ideas aside. "How many of these do you have?"

"Twenty-three. Darwin's got one with him in the Vatican, where he's been researching the alchemy angle." She recounted what he had told her about Thoth and the hieroglyphics.

"You two get into the craziest shit."

"Not me. My life was normal until I met him."

Zac laughed so loudly that a nearby group of women stared.

"I thought of your project when I saw the superconducting behavior," she said.

Zac was currently at Lawrence Berkeley National Laboratories developing micro-sensors in the Molecular Foundry, a facility specializing in nanoscale research. He'd returned to California after a year in France and a relationship that hadn't worked out to pick up on his earthquake detection passion.

He watched the video again. "Wow, Eyrún, if this is a room temperature superconductor, it's a breakthrough. You said Darwin's forebear found these at an alchemist's shop in Cairo. Any idea where he got them?"

"No. That's what Darwin's trying to find out."

"Something's in that fleck. Can you send one of these to me?"

"I was hoping to help figure it out in person."

"That's a better idea. I'll start a visiting scientist application with the lab. How soon can you get here?"

21

Roissy, France

Mike disembarked from a Norwegian airline's Boeing 787 at the Orly airport near Paris. He had found a cheap, one-way business class seat on the carrier offering bargain travel to Europe. The upgraded seat also came with a pass to the shorter line at passport control, but the only one booth was staffed.

A few minutes later, a second agent entered another booth. *About time,* he thought, but after the current traveler, the first agent shut her window. Mike groaned at the ceiling. *French efficiency*. He settled back in the booth, realizing he'd better get used to it as he was about to go digging into records stored not long after the French Revolution.

Two hours later, he arrived at 17 Rue Etienne Marey, the address Ramy had given him. A placard on a fence surrounding a weed-infested lot promised a new building. *What kind of sick joke is he playing?* Mike let an expletive trail off as a woman pushing a pram walked by and his head sagged from a desire to be sleeping at what was 3:00 a.m. body clock time.

He tapped Ramy's number and blocked his wheeled case with one foot as it drifted on the sloped sidewalk. A mobile sounded out immediately behind him and he spun to see Ramy walking up.

"Mike! Buddy, it's good to see you." Ramy embraced him and explained he lived a few buildings down the block. "I don't want my address publicly known."

Mike decided not to ask why and followed Ramy through a five street intersection onto Rue de la Dhuis. A hundred meters farther, Ramy said, "It's here," and keyed them into a six story building covered in scaffolding. Its bottom apartment windows were barred. "The whole building's under renovation. The neighborhood's transforming and the owner kicked out all the families so he could triple the rent."

"Nice guy," said Mike as they mounted the stairs.

"Yeah, he's a piece of work. All the families are immigrants with dubious status, so there's not much they could do."

"Why do you live here?"

"Security," said Ramy. They reached the top floor. "These are mostly finished. New tenants move in soon. I get to live here until the building's done."

"Then what?"

"We'll see. You can stay in this one." Ramy opened a door and Mike followed him inside. The rough planked floor was covered in grit and paint splatters. Boxes of hardware flooring were stacked against one wall. "It's rough, but the plumbing works. There's a roll up mat in the bedroom and a spare towel in the toilet. No eating's allowed, so you'll have to get your meals out. But the price is perfect."

They agreed to meet up in two hours after Mike showered and took a quick nap.

Just before three that afternoon, they emerged from the metro at *Place du Trocadéro*. Mike squinted, one hand shading his eyes, while looking at the Eiffel Tour across the Seine River. Its dark spire shrank behind the Musée de la Marine as they crossed the street.

Inside, Mike paid their admission fees, and they went to an information booth where he greeted the middle-aged docent.

"*Bonjour*," she replied.

"*Parlez vous anglais?*"

"A little."

Mike asked how to find the research library, and the woman unfolded an exhibits map and drew a line on it directing him to the right place. He thanked her and joined Ramy who stood admiring the photos and displays surrounding the Jules Verne trophy, named in honor of the author's renowned story of an eighty-day round-the-world journey, that was given to sailors who broke the global circumnavigation record. The current holder had circled the planet in just under forty-one days.

"Impressive, until you consider the space station has gone around the Earth three times since we woke up," said Ramy.

Their footfalls on the wood floor echoed in the gallery as they strolled past paintings of seascapes and long dead captains. They turned into a short hallway where a placard listed various offices and pushed a button on the library door. After being buzzed in, Mike explained the reason for his appointment. The librarian introduced them to the digitized catalogue and how to request volumes.

Mike was pleased to find much of the search index in English, but knew the volumes would be French. Ramy busied himself with his mobile while Mike waded through records, jotting down the books he wanted to pull. Twenty minutes later, he handed an initial list to the librarian and continued searching the digital catalog while the volumes were retrieved.

"What should I look for?" asked Ramy, opening to the page number Mike had scribbled.

"Documents of sale for the Lacroix Shipping Company. In particular, names and amounts paid. Was it one person or many?"

"Why is that important?"

"My client is descended from one branch. If they split the money, I need to know the amount we're after."

Fortunately, it did not take long to find the data in question. The purchaser, Mythos Shipping, had paid 73,000,000 French Francs to the estate of Dominique Lacroix, who was the sole shareholder of Lacroix Shipping. Ramy tapped away on his mobile, then whistled. "That's six-hundred thirty million euros today."

Mike raised his eyebrows on hearing the amount, but he reined in his enthusiasm. "It depends on how much is left. It's been a hundred years. What's this note here?" He fingered a section beginning with *sauf* that he knew meant "except."

Ramy read it aloud: "The Lacroix Shipping Company assets do not include prizes won by Henri Lacroix under the letter of marque issued 21 May 1798."

"What the hell does that mean?"

Mike carried the leather-bound book to the librarian, who read it and said, "a *lettre du marque* from the French government authorizes the bearer to engage in privateering on behalf of the government."

"Pirating?" asked Mike.

"No. No, it's different. During a war, a privateer could legally capture a vessel belonging to the enemy, even a non-combatant. The captured ship is called a prize. It sounds strange today, but in the age of sail, an elaborate global system existed to rule on seized vessels."

Mike's eyebrows scrunched as he tried to get his head around the concept. It sounded like piracy to him. "Is there a way to find this, uh, *lettre du marque* issued to Henri?"

"Perhaps," said the librarian, who turned to a monitor and clacked away on a keyboard.

An hour later, Mike's fingers ached from scrawling notes on his pad and on pages copied from various record books.

The letter of marque had led him to a case in the *Conseil des Prises,* the French maritime prize court, in which Henri asserted title to all cargo on an American ship. He'd seized the *Demeter* and its Aztec gold cargo off the coast of Nevis on 13 June 1798. The French court in the Caribbean had ruled in Henri's favor, but the Americans claimed no state of war existed between France and the United States and the seizure, therefore, amounted to piracy.

Mike asked Ramy to reread the French court decision, but they found no clear amounts awarded. A last line in the French document referred to "The Demeter" case in the Boston Prize court.

"Back to America?" asked Ramy.

22

Above the Tyrrhenian Sea

Darwin arrived at the airport in Rome for the short flight home to Ajaccio. His Vatican credentials avoided deeper scrutiny of the diamond in the sealed envelope, and as the plane pushed back, he opened Henri's memoir and began reading. Up to now, he'd focused on alchemy and figured it was time to get the measure of his five-times great-grandfather.

He'd previously skimmed the early sections and found them mostly accounts of Henri's life growing up in Ajaccio. Now, he concentrated on the jumpy scrawl of an older hand as Henri wrote of learning the Lacroix shipping trade. The dry account tugged at his eyelids until he came across:

My life seemed destined for the ordinary until The Fates landed me in prison with Sydney Smith.

What? Darwin wriggled upright in his seat. He switched on the reading light and dug in. Henri wrote he had been caught smuggling arms for the Corsican nationalists in 1795 and brought to Paris for trial.

While being held in the notorious Temple prison, he'd met a Royal Navy officer, Sydney Smith, who was being tried for burning the French fleet in Toulon.

Sydney is a man of adventure. One who risked his life taking action behind enemy lines. But also he also speaks of the fickleness of politics. He complains bitterly of being passed over for admiralty by less capable men. He told me, if I want my fortune, I must seek it myself. Be willing to take colossal risks, and to choose sides wisely.

When I asked him which side, he answered with two questions.

Can Corsica withstand France? And, when the fighting ends, which side would be the most profitable for me?

As the plane throttled back for descent into Ajaccio, Darwin read Henri gained release from prison through the influence of his childhood friend Napoleon, who was quickly rising to power. The two had been born into well-to-do Corsican families the same year, 1769, and had fought for Corsican independence, until Napoleon had joined the greater power.

Napoleon is, as ever, self-assured. He told me he will run the country one day. He confided in plans to attack Britain, but he needs more capability at sea. I found myself agreeing to help in exchange for a quick dismissal of all charges against me.

Darwin gripped the memoir tight as he went through the landing preparations. Henri was made a junior officer in the French navy and posted to one of the fastest frigates on orders to disrupt British shipping. Two years later, as the French-British conflict escalated, Henri was given a special assignment. The Americans were helping the British in their war against France. As the French admiralty had deemed Henri a competent commander, they made him captain of a decommissioned frigate and issued him a *lettre du marque*.

At first, Henri wrote:

I thought it was a demotion. The crew of the Mercure were rejects from the navy, but the first-mate soon indoctrinated me into this lucrative world. The crew, while undisciplined, was highly motivated.

Henri wrote of the American ships the *Mercure* captured over the next two years and how he had used his share of the prizes to commission three new ships for the Lacroix Shipping Company. Soon afterwards, he wrote:

Our personal accounts swelled but nothing compared to our greatest prize—the Demeter—an indistinct three-master but, carrying a massive gold horde bound for Boston.

As the wheels bumped onto the runway, Darwin read about the *Mercure* engaging the *Demeter* in the Narrows between Nevis and Saint Kitts. Once the *Demeter* had surrendered, the *Mercure* escorted it to the French half of Hispaniola. Riveted to his seat as the plane emptied, Darwin scoured the prize court trial details. The *Demeter*'s cargo was unremarkable: cloth, dried-beans and twelve horses, until the *Mercure*'s chief carpenter noticed new construction in the hold—a false wall that concealed over a thousand gold bars.

Henri ordered the wall resealed and promised the carpenter a larger share if he kept quiet. But it was Henri's next action that took Darwin's breath away.

Before leaving Cape Francois, I followed Sydney Smith's advice to act for myself. Knowing the gold would flow into the coffers of the corrupt Revolutionary government and leave me but a tiny share. I bribed a port authority to swap a shipment of lead from Brasilia for the crated gold. Later that night, I purchased a schooner from a bankrupt trader and, before dawn, set sail for Corsica.

Darwin's heart thrummed at this firsthand account of mercenary action in the age of sail. He'd heard tales of the Lacroix men outmaneuvering Barbary pirates in the Mediterranean Sea. But here was a tale of his forebear sailing for France as a—*Merde!* His romantic vision froze.

Henri was a privateer! He expanded the company with stolen American gold! Darwin flipped back to the section where Henri had written he'd commissioned three new ships. But that was before the *Demeter*.

He sat, eyes closed, shaking his head. He'd always been told Lacroix Shipping had fought off pirates, not engaged in piracy itself. The logical side of his brain tried to rationalize the new knowledge. *It's more than two hundred years in the past. It is what it is now. I can't change the past. And it's got nothing to do with me.*

But Darwin's moral compass always sought true north. He and Eyrún had founded the ACA to prevent looting. Henri had used an ill-gotten windfall to amass a larger fleet. Darwin had been told of the company's exponential growth in the Napoleonic years through the Great War. But now, he wondered, what would the family fortunes have been without the privateering bounty?

"Is everything all right, sir?" asked a flight attendant.

Darwin smiled and assured her it was. He shut the memoir, stood, and pulled his case from the overhead bin.

While trudging up the jet bridge, he tried to shake off the feeling that everything he'd been told about the Lacroix family's fortune was a lie.

23

Paris

Mike spent that night in an internet cafe researching online US court records on prize cases. Unfortunately, from his Paris location, many resources were blocked. Shortly before 2:00 a.m., he came across a website for a maritime law consultant who had also authored books and articles on commercial shipping. He claimed to be a maritime history buff on the age of sail.

What the hell, he thought and called Wilson Cartwright III, whom he imagined as a wizened guy whose windblown hair flailed beneath a captain's hat.

"Wilson Cartwright," said a throaty voice.

"Hi Wilson. My name is Mike Carter. I'm a lawyer researching a case for a client involving a spoliation case. Do you have a few minutes to answer some questions?"

"Now there's something I don't get every day. Sure I have some time. I was about to take my sloop out, but got a squall warning. In my younger days, I might have chanced it, but I think it's best to wait it out," said Wilson. He paused as a radio squawked in the background, then added. "Tell me about what you got and we'll see if I can help."

Mike described being in Paris chasing a potential inheritance for a client, and finding the notation about the letter of marque on the sales contract. "I'm trying to research this prize case involving the *Demeter* from here, but the US privacy laws are stopping me. I don't want to fly back home, just to get access. Also, I'm no expert on this business of privateering."

"Well, it's a fascinating slice of history. I can tell you that much. Like a game of cat and mouse on the high seas."

"Sounds like piracy to me."

"Oh, it was," said Wilson. "The European powers fought each other all over the globe. While the navies supported troops on colonial lands, their governments allowed private contractors, privateers, to arrest the flow of goods to their enemies. The letter of marque you found is an authorization to seize cargo. They created prize courts to adjudicate based on the law of war. But here's the important part, crews kept the seized goods as compensation. Successful privateers made three or more times a sailor's annual wage."

Mike heard the rigging on Wilson's boat clang from the incoming weather. "Do you know how to look up the *Demeter* case? And what do you charge?"

"Oh, I'm retired now and mostly do this kind of research for fun. Let's see what I find. If it looks helpful, then perhaps a fee based on any settlement you get," said Wilson.

Mike agreed and said he would send details as a thunderclap on Wilson's end brought the call to a quick close. Mike tapped out an email summarizing what he knew so far and sent it to Wilson before calling it a night.

24

Ajaccio

Thoughts had log-jammed in Eyrún's brain all day, but the cancer worried her the most. She'd kept her concerns at bay by staying busy: booking a flight to San Francisco, finding a cancer screening clinic, and working the dig with Barry and the interns.

Just after four, she picked up Darwin from the airport, wanting to talk about what the old woman Giséle had said. Instead, Darwin ranted about his family's pirate legacy. Her frustration poured into her driving as they wound their way up the T20 toward home. She zipped around slower traffic, working her way up to a slow-moving lorry. *Gotta get him before the up slope.*

Eyrún's modified Porsche Macan soothed her need for speed. She'd been an ice rally driver in her twenties and had joined an amateur category team on the Dakar Rally. She'd looked up the next year's route as a distraction earlier and had been itching to get behind the wheel.

"Whoa." Darwin gripped the passenger hand-hold as they rocketed around the truck before the curves tightened. "That was close."

"We're fine."

"Er ... anyway, I can't believe Emelio never told me about the family's pirate history."

"Is the envelope safe?" she asked.

"Yes. I told you at the airport. It's lined with a lead film. We tested it in Rome." Eyrún downshifted into a curve and, while she powered out of it, Darwin asked, "No comment about Henri?"

"Don't take this the wrong way, but why does it matter? It was over two-hundred years ago. A different time. Different ethics."

"But—"

"We've got a bigger problem." He turned to her, but she was concentrating on a series of curves and spoke toward the windscreen. "We've got a pile of radioactive diamonds under our house, and yesterday an old woman at *I Mazzeri* told me to beware of cancer in the family. Anne said she's a seer and everyone in the village knows about her predictions. This morning, I mentioned it to Hervé. He's a Corsican native. He crossed himself, then ran to the break room."

"C'mon, Love. You're getting sucked into Corsican superstition."

"Really!" She glanced at him, eyes ablaze. "How else would she know we've been exposed to radiation?"

"She doesn't. How do you know she doesn't tell every other stranger the same thing? It's not like cancer's rare. The *mazzeri* tradition goes hand-in-glove with family vendettas. Tourists love this stuff. The stories are part of our backward island charm, downright Shakespearean."

They rolled through the traffic circle at Bocagno, and Eyrún studied *I Mazzeri* market. She thought about confronting the old lady, but the near empty carpark meant there were no classes today. *Forget it. It's just a coincidence.*

"What did Zac say about the diamonds?" asked Darwin.

"He agrees they could have superconducting properties."

"Which means?"

"In simple terms, it means these diamonds could produce a never ending electric current. Stéphanie's music box could, in theory, run non-stop for thousands of years."

"That's crazy. How—"

"I'm going to California the day after tomorrow. Zac's getting us time on the Advanced Light Source at the Lawrence Berkeley lab."

"You really think the diamonds are that dangerous?"

Eyrún turned off the road onto their gravel drive. The Macan's wide tires amplified the soft crunching sound that meant home. She switched off the engine and the mountain silence enveloped them. She sat for a moment.

Darwin made to open his door.

"Wait," she said, putting a hand on his arm. He turned to her, and she continued, "Yes, I think the diamonds are dangerous. We don't know what we're dealing with. That's why I need to go to Berkeley."

"Okay."

They exited the car and Eyrún said, "I still think we should get scanned. All of us. You, me, and Emelio. I made appointments at a clinic in Nice."

Once inside the house, Eyrún asked the digital assistant on her phone to create a reminder to call her sister. Siggy was a nuclear medicine doctor in Reykjavík.

25

Paris

Mike awoke the next morning to a hammer drill whose incessant vibration drove up his blood pressure. He showered, dressed, and went to a cafe on the corner where he took an outside table. He ordered coffee and relaxed in the sun's warmth radiating off a building in the narrow street. A faint breeze carried a barnyard undertone that perplexed him until he traced it to the fromagerie next door.

Some minutes later, Mike's mood brightened as the cafe creme worked its magic. He tore off a piece of croissant, its flakes disintegrating as he slathered it with raspberry jam. Tension from the rude awakening receded in the sunshine of a summer's day in Paris.

Halfway through the croissant, his laptop chimed, and he wiped his buttery fingers on the napkin. Wilson had replied. He pushed the croissant aside and leaned into the screen.

```
Hi Mike,
Assuming there's any money left, you've got
an interesting one. The Demeter's owners
```

brought a spoliation case against the French government in 1801, claiming that under *jus belli* or the law of war that no such declaration of war existed between the US and France and seizing the *Demeter* was illegal. Historians back up that claim by calling the undeclared naval skirmish the Quasi-War.

The owners claim the *Demeter* carried gold bound for the US Treasury under a government contract. The French argued the *Demeter's* seizure was just and further claimed it was partial repayment of the loans it had made during our Revolutionary War.

I dug into the history and the US Congress had indeed suspended loan repayment, which led to France seizing American ships and this state of quasi-war.

The case went cold after Napoleon Bonaparte came to power and normalized relations with the US, but the French refused to settle the Demeter spoliation claim, saying it had received no gold.

The case file mentions Henri Lacroix as captain of the Mercure, the vessel that seized the Demeter, and that he took the Demeter to the prize court in Cape Francois. BTW, that court had a reputation as notoriously corrupt.

Do you suppose Henri made some kind of deal and took the gold himself?

```
Good luck. I've attached a pdf of the case.
Let me know how this turns out.
Wilson
```

Mike reread the email and googled "Quasi-War" where he learned about the short conflict that existed during the period Henri got the letter of marque and his seizure of the *Demeter*. He then read the case file Wilson had sent. The plaintiff argued that to capture a neutral vessel on the high seas, a state of war must exist *de facto,* and the neutral party must have knowledge or notice of intention from the belligerent. As no declared war existed, the plaintiff asserted the *Demeter*'s seizure by a French privateer was illegal.

The document described the details, such as the *Mercure* firing on the *Demeter* five leagues west-southeast of Nevis before boarding and escorting it to Cape Francois. Its manifest listed passengers and precious metals valued at $19,000,000.

Mike ran a quick calculation based on inflation since 1799 and found the *Demeter*'s gold would be worth nearly a half-billion dollars today. He leaned back in his chair and considered different scenarios. *Henri grabs a half-billion in gold and heads back to France. Or maybe not.*

He considered the French government's assertion that it never received the gold. *Henri didn't want the government to get it, so he takes the gold to some out-of-the-way place. Corsica? It's not exactly out of the way. But Henri's family owned a Mediterranean shipping company. He would know a lot of out-of-the-way places to hide a treasure.*

He started a list of actions, beginning with finding what they could about the *Mercure* and other ships owned by Lacroix Shipping. Maybe knowing their ports of call would yield a clue about where Henri had dropped a load of stolen gold.

26

Berkeley, California

Three days after her call with Zac, Eyrún watched the Golden Gate bridge out the window of the morning flight from Paris to San Francisco. The California coastline tucked under the jet's massive wing as it traveled southward down the widening peninsula before arcing over Silicon Valley and back toward the airport. As they descended, the San Francisco bay's gray-green water seemed to rise, and, just about when it felt like they would land on its placid surface, a spit of runway flashed beneath them and the plane touched down.

Barely twenty minutes later, she emerged wearily from the international terminal. The brisk San Francisco wind and the blazing afternoon sunshine instantly jump-started her.

"Eyrún!" Zac called out.

She crossed the curbside lane, and he bear-hugged her. They kissed cheeks, and he grabbed her case as the automated trunk of his car swung open. "You didn't tell me about this," she said, running a hand over the matte graphite finish of his Tesla. The car seemed to absorb light, like a stealth fighter jet, except for its glass roof and bright red brake calipers.

Zac beamed as he tapped the recessed door handle on Eyrún's side before crossing around the front to his side. They buckled in and Zac told the car, "Navigate home."

"You got full self-driving?"

"Of course, but I like the hands-on experience." He gripped the steering wheel that looked more like one you'd see in a Formula One race car. As they rolled silently into traffic, he asked, "How's Darwin?"

"He's good, but obsessing over alchemy."

"That's Darwin. Plunges headlong into stuff."

"Phht," Eyrún expelled. "Drives me crazy. At least he's got his Vatican gig to—" The G-force crushed her backward as the Tesla shot from forty to a hundred in two seconds. "Oh, my God! How fast can it go?"

"I don't know," said Zac. "Specs show over two hundred, but I'm not trying it." Their speed then dropped to a crawl as they hit the downtown San Francisco traffic. Zac let the car take over in the tedious start and stop the flow onto the Bay Bridge to Oakland as Eyrún described what they'd found under the mountain house.

Zac asked questions about the alchemy lab, but she had little to add, as Darwin had not yet translated the journals. When they had passed Treasure Island halfway across the bay, he said, "We'll go back to my place so you can shower and unwind. Then, let's go up to the lab to get you signed in. The place is full on, so we have to work around other experiments, but I got time booked in the Geothermal Rock Lab starting tomorrow morning at five figuring you'll be up early."

"Sounds good," she said.

At quarter to five the next morning, Eyrún pulled her scarf close against the damp chill, the opposite of yesterday's warm afternoon, when they had visited the lab security office to get her checked in. As they walked up to the rock lab, the predawn mist drifted through cones of light cast by the lampposts along the concrete path. Near the doorway, puddles had gathered from the fog drip off the surrounding trees. They each badged in, and energy saving lighting switched on as they snaked their way through the hallways leading into the Geothermal Rock Lab. Few people were in the building at this hour, save for scientists who'd been monitoring all-night experiments.

"Tea?" asked Zac as they passed a kitchen.

"Love some." She checked emails on her phone while the tea steeped. The bergamot aroma mixed with a waxy smell from the gleaming floor tiles and something else, like ozone or flint; she wasn't sure, but it was familiar. The geology labs at her alma mater, the University of Iceland, smelled the same.

She felt at home upon entering the main lab. While she was now on another continent, she knew all the instrumentation that crammed into the counters and shelves. Wheeled carts, some topped with butcher's block, occupied the open areas surrounding the permanent benches. She had access to this gear at the ACA or at universities in France or Italy, but she hadn't come for this lab. It was just a precursor to the main event.

Zac put the diamond into the shielded hood and manipulated it through the leaded glass. They duplicated Eyrún's levitation experiment and measured the strength of its magnetic field.

"I've never seen anything like it," he said after a stack of weights tumbled. "It supports over thirty times its own mass."

"Zac, we're ready for you now," said a woman wearing a beanie and a zipped up puffer jacket beneath a white lab coat.

"Thanks, Adrienne," he said.

Eyrún used tongs to put the diamond in its shielded container and carried it to the next door lab. Adrienne's outfit made sense as the CT lab made the foggy morning seem warm. Banks of instruments lined each side of a black conveyor belt–like bed of the scanner. Eyrún placed the diamond on a plastic tray and, when the operator's voice over the in-room speaker confirmed the correct position, she joined them in the control room. The dull hammering penetrated the wall as a monitor showed the tray pass through the scanner's large magnet ring.

"It's crystalline," said Adrienne as she manipulated the scan on another display. "Where did you find this?"

"Africa," said Eyrún, truthfully, but used the continent to keep the answer vague.

"Here we go." Adrienne brought up the first pass of the CT. "It looks like a cubic structure. What did the x-ray crystallography show?"

"About the same. We got the squared sides, in the same staggered pattern." Eyrún's finger ran along one side of the monitor. "But the diamond's tight matrix makes it difficult to figure out the chemical makeup of the flecks."

"You need time on the ALS," said Adrienne.

"We've got a slot at dark thirty tonight," said Zac, referring to the Advanced Light Source facility perched atop a hill at the lab's highest point.

After a hearty breakfast at an organic place full of students and faculty from the University of California, Zac drove them forty minutes north toward the wine country where he'd promised to pass the time until their turn on the ALS late that night.

"Where're the grapes?" asked Eyrún as they rolled along a two-lane highway surrounded by brown grass hills.

"No wine tasting today," replied Zac as he turned and entered the gates of the Sonoma Raceway. He continued through the empty car park and to the trackside garages, stopping near one emblazoned with a famous racing school's logo.

Eyrún's heart rate kicked up as she walked toward the garage.

"Nope. Not that. This way."

She followed Zac, wondering what he was up to. She'd always wanted to try one of the powerful NASCAR machines, but it was silent despite a group with laptops and radios under a trackside umbrella. Suddenly, three cars flew by on the main straight with no more sound than the rushing wind.

"Over here," called Zac. She caught up as he explained, "My startup used SpaceX to launch all our microsats and one of their execs said if I ever wanted to have some real fun down here on Earth ..." He trailed off as he sent a text.

A moment later, a woman exited the side door of an unmarked

racing stall. "Zac?" When he nodded, she said, "I'm Jillian. I got a DM from the big boss that a VIP was coming today."

Zac introduced Eyrún and Jillian asked them to sign a non-disclosure agreement on her tablet. "I hear you raced Dakar," she said to Eyrún.

"Amateur division," said Eyrún.

"Don't let her modesty fool you. Her team finished fourth, and she came in second at the Iceland ice rallies last winter," said Zac.

"Well, you're in for some fun today," said Jillian, tapping on her phone. The paddock door scrolled upward to reveal a candy-apple red roadster with broad racing slicks. "Welcome to our test kitchen."

A half-hour later, following several orientation laps with a professional test-driver, Eyrún buckled up the racing harness and adjusted her helmet's microphone before giving the thumbs up to the crew.

She rolled out of the pit area and, seeing the green safety light onto the track, mashed the accelerator. The otherworldly torque from the car's four electric motors propelled her to 120 miles per hour in seconds. She braked hard into turn one. The EV hugged the track like a sled on rails.

"Whoo!" she yelled two minutes later, going over 200 on the main straight. *I need one of these,* she thought, as she passed the trackside crew and began her second lap.

27

Ajaccio

The warm Mediterranean air enveloped Mike as he exited the Ajaccio airport and walked to the taxi stand. Fortunately, the connecting flight through Nice had been on time and, if all went well, he'd be on the return flight in just under three hours. He breathed in the humid sea air and gulped water from his bottle.

Two days earlier, he had sketched out a potential suit against the Lacroix family and realized he'd have a stronger case with DNA evidence to back up the genealogy. On a whim, he'd emailed Emelio, posing as a PhD candidate researching the Quasi-War between the US and France. He'd found records mentioning the Lacroix Shipping Company and Napoleon Bonaparte.

Emelio had replied that, to his knowledge, Lacroix Shipping had no dealings outside the Mediterranean, but if Mike was traveling to Corsica, he'd be happy to meet.

The taxi rounded the airport as Mike looked back and forth between the harborside view and the alluvial plain that stretched up toward the mountains. A series of commercial buildings came into view, followed by a massive two-story glass structure that fronted the

Agrippa Center for Archaeology. A mound with three crude granite sculptures occupied the center of its carpark.

"That's the institute founded by our famous native son, Darwin Lacroix. Well, not like Napoleon, but he's long dead," said the driver.

That's a good sign. Mike smiled, head swiveling to study the building as they passed. "What made him famous?"

"He found a Templar's treasure a few years ago. Good on him to invest it in his hometown." The driver continued pointing out the sights along the harbor road into the old city, but the commentary fell on deaf ears. Mike was thinking about the lawsuits. If the Lacroix fortune served as seed money for Darwin's fortune, then the chances of a settlement looked brighter. *I could live on two to five million.*

Mike knocked on Emelio's door and greeted the old man. "*Bonjour,* Mr. Lacroix. I'm Mike Carson." They shook hands.

"A pleasure to meet you, Mike. Come in," said Emelio. "Coffee?"

"Yes. Thanks. I'd love some."

Emelio led him into a front room and told him to make himself comfortable while he got their coffees. Mike set his shoulder bag on a chair and took in the room. Tall ceilings, twelve feet high in Mike's estimation, gave the room an expansive feeling. Heavy drapes framed a window that overlooked a well-tended garden with a fountain and two marble statues. Male and female figures sensuously motioned to each other from either side of the water feature.

He turned his attention back inside. Ceiling height bookshelves lined two of the walls with an old-fashioned ladder on rails to reach the highest volumes. The elegant furnishings bore the ornate signature of centuries past, their surfaces inlaid with intricate wood and gold patterns. Overall, the room smelled of beeswax, old books, and leather.

The parquet floor creaked underfoot as he crossed to the nearest shelf and tilted his head sideways to read their titles. He ran a finger lightly across the leather spines and slid one out. He expected French, but found Latin and replaced it, moving along the shelf, stopping at four volumes: Napoleon I through IV. Mike pulled out the first and opened to the title page to a faded ink dedication signed:

Napoleon

Mike closed it at the sound of rattling cups. "That was a gift to one of my forebears," said Emelio. "He and Napoleon grew up here in Ajaccio."

They talked about the history of Ajaccio and Corsica while drifting toward the reason for Mike's visit.

"As I said in my email, I'm writing a history of the Quasi-War. This period seemed unusual given our two countries' cooperation and common enemy: England."

"I've not studied it much myself. You said Henri was involved. How so?"

Mike explained the *Demeter*'s seizure and the subsequent case by the US to recover stolen gold. "The court records show that Henri Lacroix of Corsica captained the *Mercure*, the ship that captured the *Demeter*. Do you have any records, perhaps a memoir, that might explain Henri's involvement?"

Emelio shrugged. "Not that I know of. Henri only ran the shipping company. We had our share of struggles with the Barbary pirates, but I've seen nothing to suggest he privateered."

The denial seemed too glib for Mike. *Especially how he said 'our share of struggles.' He knows more than he's saying.* Mike continued, "I can understand. It's an old American case. I'm visiting the *Chambre Arbitrale Maritime* in Paris tomorrow to study the records first hand. Is there a maritime museum in Corsica?"

"None, other than a small fishing museum," said Emelio, blinking rapidly.

The facial tic deepened Mike's suspicion. "I know the company was sold after the war, but did you keep any company records I could study?"

"No. I'm afraid it all went with the sale, years before I was born."

Emelio stood. "Forgive me, but I need to use the toilet. An old man's bladder."

Perfect. Mike sprang from his seat and went to Emelio's chair when he had departed. He found it in seconds: a long white hair. He bagged it for later DNA sampling, then went to a spot on one bookshelf he'd been studying. As Emelio returned, he moved along the shelf as if examining more books.

Mike drew the conversation to a close, then excused himself, saying he wanted to visit the Napoleon museum before catching his return flight to Paris.

Later, as he stared out the window of the plane, he thought about the house. *He's got money.*

Paris

The next morning, Ramy took Mike to the lawyer he'd met during the tenant evictions. The young man, Hamid Gandlarz, was sharp and hungry, but his degree from a lesser school had excluded him from the corporate law firms in La Defense or the high-end firms along Boulevard Haussmann. However, he fit Mike's meager budget, which required an avocat who could extend the US lawsuits into French civil law.

Mike had filed a paternity suit in US court before he left Maryland, claiming his great-grandmother, Judith Brown nee Davis, was due a share of the Lacroix Shipping Company sale. To further the harassment, Mike submitted a second suit to go after assets that Henri Lacroix used to fund the shipping company.

That case, filed on behalf of all heirs of the *Demeter,* alleged that Henri Lacroix committed an act of piracy when he captured a shipment of gold bound for the United States. In addition, the French government became complicit when its Kangaroo court in Cape Francois ruled in favor of the *Mercure.* Using the data dug up by Wilson Cartwright on the *Demeter,* Mike used the 1801 spoliation case claim of

$19,000,000 as a basis to calculate the present value: a staggering $443,090,472.

Hamid read a summary of Mike's filings in the US before saying, "You realize it's long past the prescriptive period, what you Americans call the statute of limitations."

"Yes, I'm aware of Article 333 in your Civil Code, but I have evidence that my great-great-grandmother wrote at least three letters between 1917 and 1919 to the Lacroix family and included a photo in one. My great-grandmother, Dominique Lacroix's daughter, wrote again in 1933 and hired a private investigator who learned Dominique was killed in the war, but his family still lived in Corsica," said Mike, feeling hot under the collar.

He took a breath, then held up a folio. "In 1997, My grandmother presented evidence directly to Emelio Lacroix, but he blew her off. I have letters dismissing her outright, denying paternity, so, in my eyes, it's a case of miscarried justice. We fulfilled the requirement to establish paternity within the required period. The Lacroix family unjustly denied my great-grandmother's inheritance. And I want to shame them into doing what they should have done for my family years ago."

Hamid shrugged. "Okay, it's your money. I'll file the cases on your behalf. Give me two days to prepare them."

28

Berkeley

Very late that night, a waxing gibbous moon cast its silvery light on the ALS building's cupola, its profile much like the Dome of the Rock. And like Jerusalem's holy structures, seekers visited from all over the world hoping to find answers.

While Darwin was pursuing the metaphysical, alchemy and the occult, to discern the diamond's invisible influence, Eyrún was about to do the same with high-energy physics. *But each new answer precipitates new questions, especially at the sub-atomic level.*

"What's so funny?" asked Zac. When she told him, he continued, "Yeah, I think about that, too. We've reached the point where the smallest particles give way to pure energy. Then what?"

He badged into the main door and security staff validated their IDs. The lowered lights at 2:30 a.m. gave the appearance of a facility asleep, except for a low hum from the experiments running on the ALS downstairs.

The hairs on the back of Eyrún's neck stood up. She'd studied results from facilities like this, but had never been inside one. The synchrotron below their feet drove electrons at near light speed around a storage ring, where magnets then forced some electrons into a slalom-like path. Alternating polarity then separated beam lines toward each experiment.

She looked up at the dome's underside: a mass of girders and corrugated steel. A crane mounted a story above them, poised to move gear to the lower level. They strolled along a pathway around the structure that was lined with pallets of equipment cordoned off by orange traffic cones. Eyrún lifted a tarp to peek under on the pallet when footsteps drummed on metal stairs. She dropped the flap and turned as Adrienne emerged from below.

"Nice to see you again," she said, explaining she'd been curious about the flecks in the diamond.

"Likewise," said Eyrún. "What time did you get here?"

"Hours ago. I've been working on another project with Dr. Bopardikar and invited myself to stick around. C'mon, we're setting it up for you."

Zac nodded for Eyrún to go first and, as they descended, asked, "You know how this works, right?"

"In principle," she called back.

Zac answered in a loud voice over the drone of the high-energy array. "The electrons in the ALS emit electromagnetic radiation from visible through ultraviolet and x-rays. Then they're shot into hutches with instrumentation. That's where we'll put the diamond."

They reached a door labeled Hutch 23 and Adrienne swiped her badge. Inside, she introduced them to a man with thick dark hair and an Albert Einstein mustache who was all business after their brief greeting. "We have little time," he said, adding, "you must know someone high up in the lab to get a slot in the schedule so fast."

Zac grinned, but left out that he'd become good friends with the head of the US Department of Energy.

Dr. Bopardikar removed the diamond from its shielded envelope and placed it in a receptacle at the end of a long, rectangular conduit channel. The two-meter channel entered the room at the opposite wall.

Zac explained, "The beam line comes down this path," he said, running a finger from the wall to where Dr. Bopardikar checked the instruments arrayed atop a thick granite-topped table. Eyrún, Zac, and

Adrienne stood against the wall in the tight space as he moved quickly, making adjustments.

"We do the rest outside." Dr. Bopardikar motioned them outside the hutch.

An hour later, they went back to Zac's temporary space in another of the Lawrence Berkeley Lab buildings to study the results. The sky had just begun to lighten as they went inside, and Eyrún marveled at how fast the procedure had gone. The beam had been diverted for less than a microsecond, its energy deflected by the diamond's atomic matrix and splattered onto sensors that recorded everything. Most of their time in the ALS had been spent confirming the data quality.

"It's a perovskite, like you thought. A calcium silicate variant, unless I'm reading the data wrong," said Zac.

"Looks right, but," she pointed to a pattern modeled on the ultra-high resolution display, "this shouldn't exist on the Earth's surface. Unless—"

They jumped as her phone rang.

"It's Darwin," she said, answering it. "Hi ... What? Oh, my God. When?"

29

Ajaccio

Earlier that day, Emelio Lacroix stood in the family plot overlooking Ajaccio harbor, moaning to his former wife. "You warned me, Marguerite, and I never listened."

The late morning sun cast his hunched-over shadow across the tombstone and he moved a hand to protect his neck against the building heat. The downslope breeze mitigated the warmth and bore the earthy fragrance of maquis, a Mediterranean perennial that blanketed Corsica. Its lavender, sage, and faint sandalwood aromas usually soothed him, but yesterday he'd been served two lawsuits.

One, a paternity suit, alleged the Lacroix family owed an inheritance of €2,000,000 to Judith Brown from the estate of Dominique Lacroix, Emelio's grandfather. He was not surprised, just perplexed at the timing, as he thought it was long forgotten. He'd known about Dominique's potential heir since the late nineties, when a woman had visited him in Corsica, claiming she was Dominique's granddaughter.

At the time, Sally Carson had given him a copy of a 1918 letter from his great-grandmother, Letizia Paoli. She'd written in reply to Sally's grandmother, Clarice Davis. Letizia stated Dominique had died in the

Great War and claimed he had always been faithful to his wife. Sally had also shown Emelio a photo of Dominique and Clarice in Paris, taken in 1917, three months before Dominique's ship went down.

Emelio had been consumed with work and didn't have time for Sally's distraction nor the inclination to share the Lacroix money. He hid behind lawyers who caused Sally to chase records in Paris and Corsica before she ran out of money and retreated to America.

Marguerite had scolded his selfish possession of an inheritance that he'd done nothing to earn. The incident had added to the strain in their marriage, tense from the time and money he'd thrown at proving a far-out theory about ancient Rome. In addition, their only son had become estranged because of Emelio's obsession.

Now, with his past come back to haunt him, Emelio stood over the love of his life. *What have I done?* He swallowed against a tightening in his throat and looked around. A lone woman at another grave faced the opposite direction. He turned back and lamented. *I should have helped her, Marguerite.*

She'd forgiven him thirteen years ago as a cancer took her life. Darwin had also got his father, Olivier, to reconcile with Emelio. But the shameful chapter of denial weighed heavily on his aging soul. *I should offer something to Dominique's heirs.*

But the second lawsuit truly frightened him. It claimed that Henri Lacroix, his three-times great-grandfather, had wrongfully used a *lettre du marque* to seize gold from an American ship. Its owners had been held financially accountable for the cargo bound for the US Treasury and the suit alleged that Henri's "act of piracy" had led to the bankruptcy of the ship's owners. A consortium of survivors sought a payment of €600,000,000 from the Lacroix Shipping Company Trust.

While the lawsuit sounded preposterous, he knew fighting against it would bankrupt him. The trust had little left in it, as he'd exhausted it by chasing his Roman ideas. He'd not told Olivier or Darwin, and feared the day when he'd have to confess to wasting the family fortune.

How can I tell them I'm a failure? He owned three properties that garnered modest rents, but aside from his government pension, he had nothing.

A sharp pain cleaved his chest. Heart attack. He massaged his breastbone as the spasm subsided. He convinced himself his family didn't need the money. Olivier and his wife were tenured professors at the height of their careers. And Darwin and Eyrún had remodeled the mountain house with their own money. But it was still owned by the trust and the house on Rue des Oranges desperately needed repairs. The lawsuits would sweep them away.

He knew Darwin and Eyrún had accrued significant wealth, but his pride prevented him from asking them to pay for his failures. The pain struck again.

Mon Dieu. His vision tunneled. A hand clutched his chest. "Oh Marguerite," he gasped, collapsing atop her grave.

30

Oakland

After the pre-dawn call with Darwin, Eyrún booked a seat on the Air France afternoon flight from San Francisco to Paris, then went back to Zac's place to get some sleep. She awoke before noon, took a shower, and went to lunch with Zac.

"Give Darwin a hug for me," he said, when dropping her off at the airport. He promised to finish the experiments and send the data.

"I will, Zac. Thanks." She trudged through the terminal, keeping to herself. Thankfully, the flight was on time and her seat provided privacy to quietly process the day's events.

Eyrún's heart held a special place for Emelio. From the moment they'd first met in Scotland, he'd been the loving grandfather she had never known. And in the years since she and Darwin had moved to Corsica, she and Emelio had lunched together regularly. Eyrún cherished those times. Emelio never judged, and his advice, more often than not, came as questions that guided her toward a solution.

She kept in touch via inflight Wi-Fi throughout the seemingly endless day, but sitting alone over Hudson Bay produced a rudderless sensation. Eyrún craved structure. The thought of Emelio being gone closed like a vise in her chest.

Ajaccio

Eyrún landed in Corsica and got a taxi. A half hour later, she traversed the blue line along the white corridor that led to the ICU, her insides quivering as she pushed back worst-case scenarios that had begun twenty-four hours earlier when Darwin called her in Berkeley.

After her initial shocked reaction, he'd answered her questions. "We don't know what happened. He was visiting my grandmother's grave when a woman heard him cry out. She turned to see him fall and hit his head on the granite covering the plot. The doctors ruled out a heart attack, but they don't know what caused him to collapse."

"Is there any—" She'd cut the question short, fearing the answer. Emelio's sharp, inquisitive mind had kept him going.

"No. They also did an MRI and found no deeper trauma. There's swelling in his brain, so they're keeping him in an induced coma for two or three days as a precaution."

Eyrún arrived at the ICU's door and the staff buzzed her through, directing her to Emelio's room, where she found Darwin dozing in a chair. She paused a moment to take in the scene; a faint beep from another room was the only sound breaking the preternatural quiet. Emelio slept peacefully, elevated by two pillows, and looked like he could've been on his sofa, except for the oxygen tube under his nose and electrodes on his head for the electroencephalogram.

Darwin's dark brown hair was swept every which way from his habit of running a hand through it when stressed. His five-day beard meant he'd also neglected his usual grooming routine. Her throat tightened as her eyes flooded. In addition to her love for Emelio, she knew he meant the world to Darwin.

Setting down her bag on an empty chair, she gently put a hand on Darwin's. "Hi Love." His eyes fluttered open, and he rose, wrapped his arms around her, and began sobbing. She reflexively joined in his pent up release.

A few minutes later, Darwin blew his nose as they sat facing each other and he updated her on what the doctor had said an hour ago. "He's stable. The brain swelling's gone down. His EEG shows normal activity, but they won't know for sure how he is until he's awake."

She studied Emelio's face, then looked at Darwin. They shared the same green eyes, but dark circles hung beneath Darwin's and his body sagged with fatigue. "You're beat, Love. Go back to the house and get some rest. I'll come along later when the visiting hours end."

He gathered his mobile and put a hand on Emelio's shoulder while whispering in his ear. Then he kissed Eyrún and slipped out of the room.

Eyrún scooted the chair closer to the bed and put her feet up on the other chair. "I'm here, Emelio," she said, stroking his arm. "We're all here, Grand-père. Come back to us when you're ready." She leaned against the elevated mattress and the weight of fatigue soon pulled her into sleep.

She woke an hour later when a nurse came in to check on Emelio and informed her that visiting hours were ending. Eyrún messaged Darwin for someone to pick her up and said good night to Emelio. She paused at the door, watching the various colored lines march across the monitors. *Please come back to us, Grand-père*. Then she walked out into the soft evening air. Summer's heat had not yet arrived, but spring's chill had retreated up the mountains. The fragrant woody maquis combined with the harbor's tang, creating a heady combination of earth and sea.

She closed her eyes and took in a cleansing breath. Three exhales later, her fatigue abated somewhat and her ears pricked up at the familiar growl of her Macan. It stopped at the entrance and the passenger door swung open.

"Siggy!" Eyrún's heart leaped as her sister stepped out. "Oh, my God, Siggy."

They hugged each other, Eyrún's head tucking against her taller sister's shoulder. While Eyrún was over average height, Siggy beat her by half a head. Both had long dark brown hair and matching glacier blue eyes, features stressed by very pale skin, and they often joked that Siggy's extra height must be from a secret Dutch relative.

"I had to come," said Siggy, pulling away and wiping a tear from Eyrún's cheek. "Darwin had just picked me up from the airport when you called."

They piled in the car and Siggy peppered her about Emelio's condition, but Eyrún could only offer what the medical staff had told her.

"The normal brain waves and reduced swelling are a good sign. He'll be fine. I'm sure of it," said Siggy.

Eyrún's stomach rumbled as she realized her last proper meal had been breakfast before landing in Paris. "I'm starved."

"Great timing. The whole family's here and we've cooked a feast. Better get your energy up because you're gonna need it," said Darwin.

Eyrún turned to Siggy. "You're about to meet your doppelgänger. Darwin's niece, Chloe, is a force to behold."

31

Eyrún and Siggy were still chatting up a storm when they arrived at the Maison Lacroix on Rue des Oranges. The light blazed beneath the portico in the deepening twilight as Darwin switched off the engine. Seconds later, a blonde-haired girl burst out of the front door, squealing, "*Tante* Eyrún!" only to freeze as Siggy got out first. The girl's mouth hung open at her changed aunt and, when Eyrún emerged from the Macan's other door, knitted her brows. "Two *Tante* Eyrúns?"

The adults laughed as Eyrún explained and made introductions. "This is my sister, Siggy."

"You're tall," said Chloe, looking between the sisters, then grabbed Siggy's hand. "Come see my fort in the library." Her younger brother, Nathan, ran after them.

"Eyrún, my dear." Darwin's dad Olivier hugged her, followed by his wife, Carmen.

She got more hugs from Darwin's sister Marie and her husband, Julien, who said, "Dinner's just ready. You must be hungry."

Eyrún answered, "Famished," as the aromas of a rich roast and yeasty bread permeated the house. She moved to the dining room, where dinner had been set on the antique sideboard. A cast-iron casserole pot brimmed with a veal leg confit and plenty of carrots—rustic Corsican comfort food and just the medicine she needed. Darwin poured glasses of Myrtus, a red wine from Sartène, and she tucked in.

During dinner, the Lacroixes regaled Siggy with stories about the family, and Chloe proclaimed she wanted to be a pirate. At one point, Siggy looked between Darwin and a large portrait of his three-times great-grandfather, Pasquale, hanging over the table's end. Pasquale's long hair swooped down, shading the left of his vibrant green eyes and nose that bent ever so slightly to the right. He keenly resembled Darwin.

The conversation soon drifted to Emelio's condition, and they debated his health and the burden of caring for such a big house. "He's been fine," Darwin said, but acknowledged Emelio was slowing down. "We see him two or three times a week, and he's got help with cleaning and the garden."

Eyrún asked Siggy for her opinion of what happened to Emelio. "Well, I haven't examined him or seen the scans, but from what you told me, the head injury's the main issue. He appears to have suffered no other trauma, like a heart attack or stroke, that would have caused a fall. It's possible he tripped. Balance declines with age."

The questions fell away as each person seemed to consider Emelio's fate. Darwin praised his mom, Marie, and Julien for a sumptuous dinner and gathered the dishes with Olivier. Chloe and Nathan insisted that "both tante Eyrúns" read them a bedtime story.

After the kids were asleep, Eyrún fought off fatigue to sit with her sister. "Thanks for coming," she said, warming her hands on an herbal tea.

"I know how much Emelio means to you, and I needed to get away."

"How's it going?"

"Better. Marcus joined *Médecins Sans Frontières* and went to Mauritius for a year."

"I'm sorry."

"We'd been falling apart for some time, even before I learned of his affairs."

Eyrún wrapped an arm around her sister. *Good riddance.* She'd never liked the arrogant surgeon, who she thought had proposed to Siggy far too quickly. "You're welcome here as long as you want to stay. Come home with us. You know the trails. It's a great place to forget."

"Thanks," said Siggy, leaning her head onto Eyrún's.

They said good night, and Eyrún went down the hall to her bedroom.

Darwin was cleaning his teeth before bed and said, "Zac messaged that he's coming tomorrow."

"He doesn't have to," she said.

"He's bringing the diamond. Said he needs to talk in person."

"Okay." She finished washing her face and slid into bed. Despite the fatigue, her brain raced with the possibilities of room-temperature superconduction. *If Zac's flying in, there's a lot more to this.*

32

Late the next afternoon, Eyrún again sat with Emelio in the ICU. Darwin had gone to pick up Zac from the airport while the children had lured Siggy and the rest of the family to a park. Eyrún had spent most of the day at the ACA before arriving with Darwin at the hospital that strictly enforced its two-visitor policy. The fatigue from jetting to California once again pulled her into a catnap. Some minutes later, her eyes popped open when a nurse came in to take Emelio's vital signs.

"You're awake," the nurse said to Emelio. "Can you talk?"

"Yes—" Emelio coughed.

The nurse held a cup of water for him and carefully monitored his swallowing.

"That's better." Emelio cleared his throat. "Where? How? Eyrún!" He smiled upon seeing her. "I thought you were in California."

"Easy. One thing at a time," said the nurse. "You came to us after knocking your head." He studied Emelio's pupils while asking basic questions, such as his name, date of birth, and where he lived.

When they had finished, Eyrún answered Emilio's question. "I was in California, Grand-père, but came back when you hit your head. You gave us quite a scare. How do you feel?"

They chatted while the nurse took his vitals and told the attending ICU doctor that Emelio was awake and alert. The doctor came in two minutes later, and Eyrún said, "I'll let everyone know you're up."

She messaged the family group as Emelio remembered what had happened. "I was visiting my wife's grave when I felt a pain in my chest. My head felt light, and everything went dark. Then, I woke up here."

The doctor explained the scans they'd made and the precautionary coma they'd kept him in for two days to let his brain heal from the internal swelling. Emelio said he felt fine except for a headache. The physician tapped instructions on his tablet to move Emelio out of the ICU when a bed opened up in another ward.

"How's Darwin?" asked Emelio after the medical staff had retreated.

"He's great. Anxious about you, as we all are. He's at the airport getting Zac."

Emelio's eyebrows shot up.

"You scared us, Grand-père. The whole family's here." She explained that Olivier was due to come to the hospital in an hour as the ICU allowed only two visitors in at a time.

"Eyrún, I need to tell you something before Olivier and Darwin get here."

She angled her chair to face him and took his outstretched hand. "Are you sure? The medical team wants you to rest."

"Yes. I'm sure. I must get it off my chest."

Eyrún waited a long moment for Emelio to gather his thoughts. She tried recalling family secrets and wondered if it was due to the feud between father and son. Darwin had told her about an incident when his dad, Olivier, was seventeen and, in a moment of anger at Emelio, had sold Roman scrolls from the family's prized collection.

"I've lied about our past. The Lacroix's, I mean," Emelio began. "We're not the kind, benevolent family we appear to be. I let Olivier and Darwin believe the adventurous tales of Pasquale because it's nicer than the truth, which is that the Lacroix Shipping Company was built with blood money."

Emelio reached for the water. She helped him drink, then sat back after dabbing his wet chin with a tissue.

"When you found the tunnel under the house, I knew secrets about Henri would surface. Henri's grandson Pasquale was a rascal, and he found the box of Roman scrolls in Herculaneum, but his pirating stories came from Henri. You have to promise you'll keep this between us." He locked onto her eyes and squeezed her hand. "At least for now."

"I promise," she said. "Darwin and I don't keep secrets from each other, but I'll wait for you to tell him."

His grip relaxed. "Thank you. I'll tell them. I just need more time to work it out." He paused and sipped more water before going on. "My grandmother, Caroline, told me about this. She was Pasquale's daughter-in-law. Bear with me, there are many people in the family tree, but this concerns Henri's journals you found in the tunnel."

She nodded.

"Henri's not an innocent explorer, researching alchemy for fun. He was a close friend and confidant of Napoleon, and over the years, the Bonaparte and Lacroix families fought for Corsican independence. But as France took over, Napoleon went to the French mainland to the military academy, and Henri became a corsair."

Eyrún's eyebrows raised.

"It's true. Only later did he become the controlling partner of Lacroix Shipping. Then he used his friendship with Napoleon to win contracts during the Napoleonic wars. The company's profits soared, and by the time of the Great War, we had enormous wealth and grew even richer in the new war. But it caught up with us. Pasquale was in his sixties when two sons were killed in 1916. When his other son, Dominique—my grandfather—was injured, Pasquale captained one of the Lacroix's vessels to bring Dominique and other Corsican boys home. But their ship was torpedoed and sank on the return journey, losing all souls. Dominique's wife Caroline and her mother-in-law Letizia were overcome with grief."

Eyrún put a hand to her mouth, and Emelio took a deep breath before continuing. "I know this is a lot of names for you, Eyrún, but you'll need the context for the story."

"I've got it so far," she said, biting her lower lip and trying to imagine what was coming.

"In 1919, Caroline, acting as trustee for their son Antoine, sold Lacroix Shipping. She wanted nothing more to do with a business that had brought so much misery. And to compound her tragedy, a letter addressed to Dominique arrived, announcing his daughter's birth. It was from an American nurse with whom he'd had an affair in Marseilles, where he'd been convalescing.

"The Lacroix family denied Dominique's paternity twice. Once from the American nurse's original inquiry and," his expression darkened as he looked down at the sheets, "again in 1997 when Dominique's granddaughter came to Corsica."

Eyrún calculated dates and guessed Emelio would have been in his late fifties or early sixties at the time. "Did you see her?"

"Yes."

She waited.

"Just once, but I hid behind our lawyers. They countered all her documentation and sent her on a wild goose chase after old records. After a month, she went away, and I never heard from her again."

Eyrún sensed there was more, and gently coaxed him along. "But something else must've happened. You're not telling me this because of the tunnel. How does it relate to Henri?"

"A relative of Dominique's American daughter is suing me, claiming denial of inheritance."

"Is it true?" she asked.

"Yes. And it gets worse. And here's where Henri comes into the picture. The same law firm has also sued the Lacroix trust for an act of piracy committed by Henri against an American ship. They're asking for a staggering amount of money, and my lawyer says it could cost us dearly to fight the allegations."

As the weight of Emelio's confession settled, Eyrún thought, *Why now? It makes no sense. The paternity claim's a hundred years old. The piracy trial is over two hundred.* Her face reddened as the puzzlement turned to anger. "This is bullshit, Emelio. Ignore it."

But the tired man looked away toward the floor, and Eyrún sensed his guilt at having lied to the woman who had visited decades ago. *He wants to make amends.* She softened her approach. "It's okay, Emelio. What if you pay off the relative? Settle for a modest amount."

"I can't," he said, voice breaking, his eyes red and wet. "There's no money. I've lost it all."

33

Paris

The next day in their lawyer's run-down office, Ramy waved the letter he'd just translated aloud for Mike. "It's bullshit. They're lying."

Mike suppressed his urge to swear while considering the next step. "Chill, Ramy. It's part of the negotiation. I didn't expect they'd pay on the first letter. They could have ignored it, but they responded. That means there's something to chase." He steepled his fingers in thought. He hadn't expected the *Demeter* case to elicit anything but the go-pound-sand letter from Emelio's lawyer:

> Henri Lacroix was an upstanding citizen whose actions were authorized by the French republic. As such, he cannot be held personally liable, especially for spurious claims, while acting under the French flag.

He'd filed the *Demeter* class-action suit as a red herring to increase the stakes in the paternity suit. He'd use the piracy story on social media if needed to force a larger settlement on the other claim.

> My client acknowledges an ancestry allegation made by Sally Carson, granddaughter of Clarice Davis, but, to our knowledge, she dropped it in 1997. In addition, the prescriptive period has long passed, and my client has no obligation to respond to this uncorroborated claim.

The letter said the proceeds from the Lacroix Shipping Company sale had long been exhausted, and their client, Emelio Lacroix, now lived on a French government pension.

"What do you want me to do?" asked the lawyer through Ramy's translation.

"We send them this DNA report and go after the grandson."

"I have an idea," Ramy offered.

"I'm all ears," said Mike.

34

Ajaccio

Late that afternoon, Eyrún sat with Darwin on the swim deck of her twenty-one-meter powerboat. The two dangled their feet in the cool Mediterranean Sea as they enjoyed the last of a second bottle of rosé. Zac was up on the flybridge teaching Siggy to pilot the boat around Ajaccio harbor, and the rest of the family was visiting Emelio, now in a regular hospital room. The sun seared their skin, and Eyrún felt they were on a giant rotisserie as the craft moved in broad circles.

"What's up, Love? You're brooding. Emelio's fine," said Darwin, rubbing a foot underwater against her calf.

"I can't say."

"Is it about the letter?"

"He told you?" She nearly knocked over a wineglass.

"No. He left it in the desk drawer. I went looking for the advanced directive. You know … in case. But he's okay now."

Eyrún emptied her glass and gazed at the Sanguinaire islands on the harbor's edge. "He asked me not to tell you or your dad."

"I don't know what the big deal is. Some ambulance-chasing American lawyer thinks they can get money. So, let's just pay them off."

She studied his face. *He doesn't know about the trust.* Then, turning back to the clear water, she slowly kicked her legs, its coolness flowing between her toes. She'd been thinking about how they could use their money to help Emelio, but also shield themselves and the Agrippa Center for Archaeology from liability. Any settlement could be an admission of piracy, however long ago, and the stolen gold in question belonged to the US government. *Why does this keep happening to us?* She thought back to a recent entanglement involving antiquities thieves who went after the ACA.

She nearly gave in to her urge to spill Emelio's financial situation when Zac called down. "We're getting hungry. How about oysters at that quayside place?"

When Darwin agreed, she exhaled in relief. The powerboat's massive engines rumbled as they climbed off the swim deck.

Ramy watched the yacht speed up and arc toward the marina. He had spent the early part of the day searching the mountain house and then Emelio's home until a half hour ago when he'd heard the children and their parents return.

The letter from the older man's lawyers stated there was no money, but Ramy had seen firsthand the mountain of wealth inside the houses. He had been about to explore the basement when a sensor he'd set up alerted him to a car entering the drive. He had slipped out the back door and gone to the harbor, following devices he'd attached to Eyrún's car and powerboat.

He would have to search the basement while the family slept. It was not optimal, but as there were no bedrooms on the ground floor, it would make it easier. He messaged Mike what he'd discovered, then returned to his hotel room to rest before the long night.

A little before eleven that night, the four adults settled into soft leather chairs in the library. Marie and Julien had said good-night earlier and gone up with the kids. Olivier and Carmen followed shortly after, saying they'd got up with the sun.

Zac leaned back in his chair and propped his feet on an ottoman. "Do you think this paternity suit has any legs?"

"It appears so from Emelio's story. The timing lines up, and Dominique was in Marseilles. And they claim there's a DNA sample," said Eyrún.

"But we don't know the percentage and, even if we did, Dominique's, what, four generations back from you, Darwin? Even you'd only test about five percent related to him," said Siggy.

"Pay them off." Zac waved a hand.

"What about the piracy lawsuit?" asked Siggy. They'd talked about it over dinner when Darwin had brought the letters to the table. Olivier had confessed to knowing nothing about Henri beyond the family story of being friends with Napoleon. She upped the speculation with, "Maybe the gold's hidden in that tunnel under your house?"

"Dunno," said Darwin. "A month ago, we'd have laughed at you, but after what happened to Eyrún and then finding the alchemy lab ..."

Eyrún added, "We'd need a full-scale mining operation to get through the blockage." She yawned, causing the others to follow.

"Cut that out," said Zac, straightening up.

Siggy also sat up and said, "I want to hear about the diamonds."

Zac looked at Eyrún as if asking permission. She said,"Go ahead. We're family here; besides, Darwin's the only one who might struggle to follow."

"Hey!" Darwin objected.

"We'll dumb it down for you," said Zac.

Darwin made an obscene gesture.

"Siggy, you're in nuclear medicine. How much do you know about superconducting?" asked Zac.

"My undergrad and master's degrees are in high-energy particle physics," she said.

"From Oxford," Eyrún cut in. "She worked at CERN before deciding on medical school."

"Well, okay then. I guess I'm in the dummy group with you." Zac glanced at Darwin, who mouthed, "Touché."

Zac explained the tests he and Eyrún had run at the ALS in Berkeley. "The spectrographic data shows the specks in the diamond are a calcium perovskite. The pure carbon matrix exerts enough force to mimic the intense pressure in the mantle and hold the perovskite intact, but there's more. Besides the traces of thorium you found, Eyrún, one diamond, has uranium. After that, I needed to get the samples and data out of the lab as people got curious."

"Slow down," said Siggy. "Radiation?"

Eyrún explained the measurements she and her colleague Katla made.

Siggy continued, "Okay. So not deadly, but you wouldn't carry them around in your pocket unless you wanted to sterilize yourself. Darwin, is this what Henri was studying?"

"Yes," he replied, "but he couldn't have known about the radioactivity. That was about a hundred years too early."

"I gotta hand it to Henri," said Zac. "He was onto something. He just didn't have the knowledge or tech to understand it fully. Anyway, before leaving Berkeley, I modeled the data and got this crazy picture." He passed around his phone with a photo of a blue donut-shaped ring surrounding a black center. "Look at that toroidal energy field. These diamonds are like miniature suns, or fusion reactors. They could power satellites in deep space forever. Or with proper shielding medical devices inside bodies."

"Or a tokamak," said Siggy, passing the phone to Darwin.

"A what?" asked Eyrún.

"Tokamak. Short for *toroidal'naya kamera s magnitnymi katushkami.*"

"Easy for you to say," said Zac.

"I studied Russian. Anyway, it's one of their experimental devices to confine a thermonuclear explosion," said Siggy. "How many of these did you find?"

Darwin answered, "Twenty-three, but Henri's journal describes a massive cache."

"Where?" Siggy shifted to her seat's edge.

Eyrún's and Darwin's eyes widened, and Zac's heartbeat picked up at her sudden intensity.

"Dunno? Why?" asked Darwin.

"There are governments who *will* kill to find it."

Ramy sat ramrod straight, overhearing the conversation from the microphones he'd planted earlier. He never believed the lawsuits would amount to much but had gone along with it because Mike was paying. *But a nuclear device? Wow!* He didn't understand the science, but he knew of a source that was always looking for a unique weapon and would pay handsomely to get it.

35

Hours later, Zac awoke to a hand shaking his shoulder and calling his name. Moonlight poured through the window and backlit a tall figure, whose long hair swept forward as it leaned over. He recognized the perfume. "Siggy?"

"Shhh. Yes. Get up. There's someone in the house," she whispered and turned away. He threw off the sheet and yanked on his jeans, and as they moved toward the upstairs hallway, she added, "I went downstairs to refill my water and saw a hooded figure go into the basement."

"Maybe it's—"

"No. They're using a tiny light. Your room was closest and, well, I thought with your training..."

"Okay. Get behind me." Zac looked about for a weapon and, seeing none, continued into the hall toward the stairs. "Stay close to the wall." He motioned, knowing from experience that the less traveled sections of the hardwood were more solid and less noisy. He stopped halfway downstairs to listen.

A squeak, like a door hinge, came from the kitchen where the basement door was. He continued down and picked up a candlestick from an alcove at the base of the stairs. Footsteps now headed to the library. Zac waved Siggy back. She stayed for a moment, then followed.

A faint light played on the wall, highlighting its sage green in the darkness, then disappeared into the library. Zac moved toward it and cautiously peered in. The hooded figure scanned the bookshelves and, then, the desktop. When it moved toward the table between the leather chairs, Zac stepped through the doorway, candlestick raised in his left hand. As best he could tell, the figure was not armed: one hand held a small light while the other probed the objects on the table.

Zac rushed in, yelling, "Hey!"

The figure turned, hurling a water glass. Zac blocked it, but the move allowed the figure to get around him.

Siggy tripped the figure, sending them rolling. It jumped as its hood slipped off, revealing a man with dark hair and a short beard—waving a blade.

"Knife," yelled Zac.

The hooded man lunged. Siggy parried the knife with a book and rounded with a kick to his midsection. The man thudded into the opposite bookshelf, spun upright, and sprinted for the door.

Zac jumped over a chair to cut him off, but collided with Siggy doing the same. That split-second allowed the man to get past them down the hall. They rushed to stop him, closing the gap near the foyer, when Darwin crashed into them. The hooded man flung open the door as Zac, Siggy, and Darwin tumbled together in a heap.

A quarter-hour later, Zac was still holding an ice pack to his temple where he'd whacked the wall after colliding with Darwin.

"I could have caught him if you hadn't taken us out," said Siggy, rubbing her ankle.

"*Desolé*," Darwin shrugged, holding an elbow.

As they nursed their wounds, Eyrún looked over at the scene in the library. Everything was as she remembered it before going to bed, except for the broken water glass.

"Nice moves against the knife, Siggy. Where'd you learn to fight?" asked Zac.

"Judo lessons."

"She was on the Icelandic Olympic team," said Eyrún.

Zac raised his eyebrows at Siggy. She shrugged.

"Nothing seems missing from the basement," said Olivier as he and Carmen returned from the kitchen. The entire family had gathered on the ground floor after the incident, but Marie and Julien had taken the children back to their room.

"We should call the gendarmes," said Carmen.

Olivier agreed and moved toward the landline in the hallway.

Eyrún picked up the envelope, counting rapidly.

"Shit! Stop Olivier! Don't call the police." When they all looked at her, she finished, "One of the diamonds is gone."

Mid-morning the next day, Ramy reported to Mike.

"You went back in?" asked Mike, his voice booming through the phone's tiny speaker.

"I needed to see the basement."

"You could've waited until today when they were out."

"I took *one* diamond," said Ramy, muting Mike's rant while he ordered a coffee in a quayside cafe.

"C'mon, Ramy. We need to focus on lawsuits. Sell the diamond, but stay out of the house. If they link the break-in to us, the lawsuits are done."

He unmuted. "Fine. I'll skip the basement."

"When are you back in Paris?" Mike asked.

"A couple of days," said Ramy. "The weather's nice, and there's this Italian woman." He disconnected while muttering, "Asshole." He carried two coffees back to the boutique hotel, sipping his as he walked.

That's rich. Telling me to focus. Like the lawsuits aren't some bullshit paper game. He felt for the diamond in his shirt pocket. Good, he'd learned not to leave valuables about. Most of his one-night stands were harmless, but some had wandering fingers. Turning up the hotel's street, he reviewed what he'd heard last night before breaking in.

The black specks are some kind of rock, a perov—no, that's not right. Doesn't matter. It's the radioactive part. One's got uranium and produces, he paused, trying to recall the word, but couldn't do better than remember it was Russian and began with a T. *But the taller woman knows.*

Ramy flashed back to the fight, heart skipping at the thrill. He'd always felt most alive in combat. He pictured her improvised weapon as she deflected the knife and smiled at how her night dress lifted when she kicked. *Love to get her in the sack.* He let the fantasy play for a long moment before refocusing on the diamond.

These are worth something to the right people, like Ali! The face of a former special forces colleague popped into memory. *Yes, he'll know. He was always talking to the Chinese or the Iranians. Hell, even the Saudis would pay to bury a competing energy source—screw Mike.*

36

The following morning, Eyrún suggested she, Darwin, Zac, and Siggy got to brunch after the others had gone to see Emelio. She also wanted to discuss the break-in, as they'd been too tired the night before to explore beyond a cursory basement search. While waiting to fall back asleep, she'd puzzled over the theft. *Why only one? If they thought it was a diamond, then why not take them all?*

As Zac mopped up the hollandaise sauce with a piece of crusty bread, she voiced her concern out loud. "I don't understand the break-in. I mean, the house is full of antiques. He could have taken a lot more, even all the diamonds. Why not?"

"Or the timing," said Siggy. "Why break into a house full of people?"

"I've been thinking the same thing," Zac added, eyeballing a sausage on her plate.

"It's like he was looking for it," said Siggy, pushing her plate toward him.

Darwin jumped into the conversation. "We haven't mentioned the diamonds to anyone, unless he overheard us at the restaurant the other night?"

"We didn't talk about it then," said Eyrún. "The only place we discussed the diamonds was in the library last night."

"Oh shit," said Zac, through a full mouth.

Back at the house, twenty-five minutes later, Zac had them sit in the leather chairs and talk about the boat trip while he searched the sitting area. Last night, Eyrún had promised to take them on a day trip to the Sanguinaire islands and show Chloe a pirate's cave. She rattled off a list of food to bring as Zac moved about on hands and knees. At one point, he circled his finger for them to keep talking.

"What makes you think there's a pirate's cave on the island?" Siggy asked Darwin.

He started on the history of Ajaccio harbor and its use by pirates over the centuries when Zac stood and pointed beneath a lampshade. Darwin paused awkwardly, so Eyrún jumped in. "Let's get ready. They'll be back in fifteen minutes."

Zac waved them from the room as he said, "Hey Darwin, how about we bring a few more bottles of the rosé?"

"Yes. That was fabulous," said Siggy.

Eyrún asked Siggy to help her in the kitchen as they left the library, and Zac stopped them by the cellar door. "There's definitely a microphone."

"Didn't you take it out?" asked Eyrún.

"No. We don't want whoever's listening to know we think it was anything but a random smash and grab."

"But they know what the diamonds could be used for and took one to get proof," said Eyrún. "Siggy, how dangerous do you really think these things are?"

"I'm no expert, but that toroidal field concerns me. The flecks are tiny, but in the realm of nuclear physics, the energy could easily power a destructive device: one small enough to miss detection on a plane or a packed venue."

Zac's stomach dropped. He'd seen too much wanton waste of life during his tours of duty.

Darwin motioned to Zac to follow him outside to the garden and when far enough from the house, said, "Something's not right here. Think about it. When did we first talk about the diamonds?"

"Last night," Zac and Siggy said at the same time. Eyrún agreed.

"That means the microphone was already in place, meaning someone's been listening. We only learned the diamonds' inner details when you were in Berkeley, right?" asked Darwin. They nodded, and he continued, "That's, what, three days? Who knew about this in Berkeley?"

Zac and Eyrún talked through who they worked with. "The doctor guy in the hutch," said Eyrún.

"He was annoyed we bumped something on his calendar. Definitely had his knickers on too tight," said Zac. "It could also be Adrienne who got into the ALS with us. I thought she was too enthusiastic."

"You're right," said Eyrún. "I didn't like her nosing about. Could she have stolen the files?"

"Maybe. But tracking us here that fast sounds CIA or military," said Zac.

"The guy we fought was a pro," said Siggy.

"Could Adrienne be working for the military?" asked Eyrún.

"Hang on," Darwin said. "We're leaping to conclusions. Let's work the problem."

They were silent a long moment before Darwin spoke again. "Suppose it's military. Siggy, you said governments would kill for this. But they won't want a handful of diamonds. They'll want them all. Who could tell us about the technology you mentioned? This tokamak?"

"Err, maybe a former colleague from CERN. She studied Russian weapons technology for NATO."

"Would she talk to you about it? I mean, it could be classified stuff," said Zac.

"I don't know," said Siggy.

"But she could answer basic questions about the data you found, like how dangerous it might be?" said Eyrún.

"She would, but said not over the phone."

"Then, let's go to Geneva," said Zac.

Eyrún went into planning mode. "We need to figure out the danger, find the source, and get back the stolen diamond if we can."

"Then let's set a trap," said Darwin, waving them farther away from the microphone to explain his idea.

37

Geneva, Switzerland

That Sunday, Zac adjusted his ball cap against the afternoon sun and watched the riot of vessels on Lake Geneva. Amidst dozens of sailboats, the ferry from Genève to Lausanne cruised the lake's windswept surface. Whitecaps marched with the southwest wind as a group of windsurfers rounded a marker.

"She's in first," said Siggy, eyes stuck to a pair of binoculars.

"Cool," said Zac as he soaked in the legendary European summer playground.

They had taken a flight from Ajaccio to Nice, then a high-speed train to Geneva, before a forty-minute car ride had brought them to a breathtaking lakeside estate. Once inside the security gate and, while rolling past a twenty-room house, Siggy had explained her friend Vanessa "just rented the boathouse."

But the three-bedroom upper floor of the boathouse was larger than Zac's penthouse in Oakland. Its lower floor had taken his breath away: half workshop and half garage—a boater's dream. One roll-up door opened directly into the lake where a gleaming mahogany cruiser had been lifted on davits to protect its hull. The other door allowed sailboats to be wheeled out and down a ramp. A dock ran between the doors to a broad sitting area where Zac now stretched his long legs.

Besides her day job at CERN, Vanessa windsurfed on the Swiss Olympic team, and was training for the summer games in France. Siggy had said she currently ranked third globally and hoped for a podium finish the following summer. "Go, go, go!" Siggy bounced on her toes, urging her friend toward the finish.

Zac smiled at her intensity. He remembered meeting her in Paris at a Lacroix family celebration when the President of France had awarded Emelio the *Légion d'honneur*. Each had been with a partner at the time: Siggy with a fiancé, and Zac with a woman whom he loved.

He flashed on the bittersweet moment when he'd decided to move to France for their relationship. He still harbored potent feelings, but her cave biology passion kept her away more often than not. They'd parted friends and, except for an intense fling that had ended badly, Zac now avoided dating.

Siggy burst his memory bubble. "Yes!" she yelled, thrusting a fist toward the lake as Vanessa crossed the finish in first. Zac had to take her word for it, as all the sails bore the red and white Swiss colors.

The other classes finished over the following minutes, and their crews slackened the sails. Vanessa stopped briefly at the mahogany cruiser that had gone out to watch the regatta. Its stern bore a blue-green flag with a pharmaceutical company logo. The CEO owned the estate.

Vanessa sailed to the dock with the other competitors, jumped off the board into the water, and walked it up the boat ramp. Once in knee-deep water, she hefted the sailboard onto dry land. Her shoulder-length black hair streamed water down her broad shoulders as she carried it onto the lawn. Once her rig had been secured, she led them to a cabana, where a staffer took their lunch order. Other guests sat at tables along the lakeshore. Zac looked around while stirring his mojito. "Is it like this every day?"

"No. It's for the regatta. The drug company sponsors teams in each class and invites key employees and friends," said Vanessa.

Their lunches arrived, and Zac's stomach leaped at the aroma of grilled entrecôte topped with grilled spring onions and chimichurri.

He'd gone for robust, having suffered a meager breakfast. The first bite did not disappoint—the tangy sauce spiked the rich, salty meat.

"God, I can't wait until my training's over," said Vanessa. She'd downed a special post-race shake and now ate a plain white fish with lemon juice, recording the macros on her phone in between bites. "Three hundred and seventy-one days, then I can eat like you." She shoveled in another bite.

After lunch, she sighed, staring like a hungry puppy at Zac's caramel gelato. He offered a spoonful. "No!" Her hand went up like warding off a curse. "When I get on the podium in France, it's the first thing I'll eat. Well, after the champagne, of course."

"Why not gold?" Siggy asked.

"Silver maybe, but May from Thailand has been unbeatable."

"But, as you said, it's a year away," said Zac. "And you only need to beat her when it matters."

A fire kindled in Vanessa's jade-green eyes. "You're right. When it matters."

That afternoon Zac embraced a new hobby as Vanessa showed him how to sail an iQFoil. Once he'd got the balance right and kept the underwater fin level, he stopped porpoising. He'd enjoyed previous experiences windsurfing, but this was flying.

38

Vatican City

Darwin was back in his Vatican City office on Monday morning, researching locations for the diamond cache. Emelio had gone home where Darwin's parents would care for him until their return to London later in the week. By then, the doctor had assured them Emelio's life would be back to normal. Darwin's sister and family had departed with Zac and Siggy, who'd continued to Switzerland. And Eyrún refocused on a critical project at the ACA.

While Emelio's collapse had shaken Darwin, Vatican City continued catering to its global empire. His assistant caught him up on developments during his absence. Darwin thanked him and asked not to be disturbed for two hours. Now, surveying the sea of books and papers on his desk, he began looking for the diamond's origins.

Once formed deep in the earth's mantle, diamond-rich rock was forced upward in volcanic columns called kimberlite pipes. These deposits were found worldwide, and mining operations dug vertically to extract the gems. But Darwin wasn't aware of any kimberlite in northern Africa, which led him to think of a southern trade route.

Maybe from Botswana or South Africa?

He, Eyrún, Zac, and Siggy had divided the research by expertise: geology, particle physics, and archaeology, or, in this case, anthropology. Alchemy fell into this discipline of humans seeking understanding. Archaeology studied objects and past civilizations. This current conundrum involved a mash-up of disciplines. And knowing how the diamonds were used could lead to their origin.

Darwin ran a finger along a map following Arab trade routes through the Middle East, India, and southern Europe. Traders stopped at ports throughout the Indian Ocean. *Maybe from Somalia through the Red Sea? But if Henri's notes are correct, these diamonds had arrived in ancient times. And wait—*

He pulled up the photo of the broken stele from the purple lady's book. He guessed it was old, from the late 1800s, as the original black-and-white photo plates had been hand-tinted before printing. The caption further described the colors as yellow and faded green. An oblique fracture cut through the lower seated figure, but a sharp triangle point remained in the upper half. The author had concluded that the seated deity was Thoth and had hand-drawn the upper section of the god's profile, fitting its ibis beak to the point.

Darwin concurred with the author's logic, as the ancient Egyptians credited Thoth with inventing science and magic. *If these colored stones represented the diamonds, then this stele could reveal their location.*

Minutes later, he stood in Angela Tucci's office studying the stele's photo in the book, but looking at the actual page was no more revealing than the picture on his phone. "Where did you find this?" he asked Angela.

"A book fair in Berlin in the early seventies. The seller said it had come from a collector's estate. You can see the publishing date, 1879, and the publisher is long defunct."

"What's this in the corner?" Darwin pointed to a small white marker in the photograph he had not captured in his close-up snap.

"Looks like a catalog marker," she said. "Like the stele was in a display case."

Darwin borrowed a magnifying lens. "It's in English, but the resolution's too poor to make it out." But he could make out a series of numbers separated by dots, followed by four lines of text, probably a description. "This looks like an old catalog reference I've seen in the British Museum."

"Could be. What have you learned about the diamond?"

"The flecks are a rare perovskite."

"Which means?"

Darwin explained that a compound like the perovskite in the diamond had been theorized but never seen as it couldn't exist on the earth's surface.

She squinted. "Sounds like there's more to it than that."

"Could be. We're not sure yet," he answered vaguely and thanked her again.

39

Geneva

Zac, Siggy, and Vanessa sat on the boathouse deck above the dock. Zac's forearm muscles thrummed as they recovered from the constant tension from holding the sail. The air had cooled as the sun angled behind them, but was still long before setting. In an hour, they would go to the big house where the CEO had invited them to dinner.

Vanessa turned to Siggy. "Tell me about what you found and the urgency of your visit."

As a security measure, Zac had requested they leave their phones inside next to a speaker playing loud music. He described the diamonds and the testing he'd done on the ALS. Siggy said the toroidal field reminded her of the Russian's tokamak work. Zac then handed her printed photos of the blue donut-shaped field and a chart showing its strengths.

Vanessa's brows furrowed as she studied the photos and chart. "What about radiation?"

"The thorium diamonds give off twelve to twenty-one micro-sieverts, but the one with uranium is three times that," he said, and handed her a diamond from a shielded envelope. "This one's thorium. An hour's exposure should be like a chest x-ray."

"Astounding. We spend all our time trying to synthesize this on billion euro machines, and here it is lying on the ground." She held the diamond up to the bright sky and studied the flecks. "Not much to see."

Vanessa put it down as Siggy asked, "I thought of your expertise when Zac showed me the photos. What can you tell us?"

"A tokamak controls a magnetic field to confine the plasma in a torus shape. That's the donut in Zac's photo. The Soviets conceptualized the idea in the 1950s and, fast-forward through the Cold War, we're building a massive joint tokamak fusion reactor right now in southern France."

"ITER?" asked Siggy.

"Yeah, the International Thermonuclear Experimental Reactor. It aims to duplicate the sun's energy here on Earth. We're all cooperating, now. Well, mostly anyway."

"Why do you say mostly?" asked Siggy.

Zac jumped in. "Poke at nuclear science, and the military's not far away."

"What is it with warmongers?" Siggy growled at him.

"Don't look at me, Siggy. But I can tell you first-hand that there are people intent on destruction. It's nothing new. Some Neolithic dude sharpens a stick to feed the tribe, and another uses it to steal from the neighbors."

"Doesn't make it right." Siggy crossed her arms and looked across the lake.

"No, it doesn't," said Vanessa. "But there's legitimate science going on with tokamaks. You know that from your days at Oxford, Siggy. Fusion technology gets us to the dream of cheap, clean power generation for a device-hungry world, but just like dynamite, it's a double-edged sword."

Two jet skis passed close to shore, their water-muffled exhaust reverberating through the surrounding trees. Vanessa studied the diamond in the conversational lull.

Zac watched Siggy wrap her arms around pulled-up knees and stare at the jet skis. He puzzled over the reason for her vehement reaction. *Something must've happened. Her father maybe?* He remembered Eyrún talking about his death and guessed Siggy would've been fifteen. He studied her profile, her forehead creased, eyes empty and distant.

Pain. He'd seen it before in his troops. A dull vacancy brought on post-trauma. *Shit, Syria.* He'd overheard her telling Eyrún about volunteering in *Médecins Sans Frontières* and describing people's desperation.

"Siggy?" Zac asked and continued when she made no response, "I have to ask Vanessa about the Russians. It's why we came. Do you want us to go inside?"

"No. Sorry. Go ahead."

He nodded, then asked her friend. "Does it have weapons' potential?"

"It's difficult to tell because toroidal fields require massive energy to produce. We know from a report—can't say how I got it—that the Russians were working on devices that could produce a localized Q field. There are plenty of Russian scientists at CERN and working on ITER."

Zac nudged the conversation in a direction he felt Vanessa was uncomfortable going in. "What about trust? Any concerns about the GRU?"

Her eyes flicked away momentarily, confirming his suspicion. She tried covering herself. "Not really. That's all past."

Not really, Zac thought. He loved Europe and Europeans, but too many thought the long peace since the world wars was permanent. But he knew from colleagues in defense intelligence that the Russian security machine had only gone underground. The KGB's former leader sat in the president's chair, plotting a return to the Soviet glory days.

Zac took in the summer playground before him and let Vanessa's comment rest. He needed answers, not a debate, so he replied, "We all hope so. What's your opinion about weaponizing a tokamak?"

"A few of us at CERN have studied it. It's different from nuclear bomb technology. The current arsenal uses high-powered explosives to trigger a runaway fusion event on enriched material. The tokamak does the opposite. It creates a magnetic field that contains a fusion reaction." She rolled the diamond between her fingers again. "I'll wager that the pressure of the diamond lattice that keeps the perovskite from breaking down also acts like a tokamak."

"You mean it contains the fusion reaction that's causing the superconductive field?" asked Siggy.

"Yes. I'd love to study this thing."

Zac burst her bubble. "But what if it were fractured, not with a hammer, but by explosives? Could it go nuclear?"

"I need to study the data, but in theory, if an explosive force were applied, yes, it could start a fusion reaction," she said, setting the diamond down as if it were toxic waste.

"How bad?" Siggy sat up.

"Depends on the mass. We can measure it with further scans. But judging by sight, I'd say it's milligrams. It wouldn't be anything like Hiroshima, but definitely a large city block."

Two hours later, as dessert was served in the big house, Siggy turned to Zac, "I just got this alert."

He looked at a warning on her phone about a device that had been tracking her since leaving Corsica. "It must be in my purse or case," she said. She had brought only her phone with her to dinner.

When the evening at the main house ended, they thanked their host and returned to the boathouse, where Siggy emptied her purse onto the counter. Zac switched on the bright vent hood lights. A white circular disk lay atop the purple silk lining in the bag's bottom.

"Dammit," said Siggy, placing it atop the dark granite counter.

"Don't those find lost keys?" asked Vanessa.

"Yes, but there's a downside to any tech. Stalkers, ex-boyfriends, and such use them to follow victims," said Zac.

"Not anymore!" Siggy pulled a meat tenderizing mallet from the kitchen tools by the stovetop.

"Wait!" Zac grasped her arm.

Siggy's brows nearly fused as her eyes blazed.

"There's another way to play this game. Someone is following us. I'm guessing it's the guy in Ajaccio who broke in. So, let's give him something to follow."

40

London

Darwin flew to London the next morning, where he visited the British Museum's Egyptology research department. He asked around about the photo, pointing out the blurry catalog marker. "It looks like one of yours."

His queries got him to the senior expert on Egyptian steles, Giles Hampton, who said, "I know that one. Haven't looked at it for years." The older man looked like a museum piece himself in a three-piece suit, a gold chain looping from his vest.

Darwin followed him into a subbasement, moving slowly as the antiquarian navigated with a cane reminiscent of the Victorian age. Giles's pant legs bunched at his ankles, and Darwin pictured him standing tall in a top hat at the Royal Ascot when the suit, most certainly bespoke, had first come from the tailor.

They eventually reached an expansive room with rows of cabinets full of wide, flat drawers. Giles navigated along the rows, stopping to read the description of each. *Patience,* Darwin coached himself at the glacial pace as Giles asked over one hunched shoulder, "I read your paper theorizing how Julius Caesar used lava tunnels under

Londinium to rout out Boudica's uprising. Did you ever prove that out?"

"I published a follow on—"

"Ah, here we are," Giles interrupted, seeming to forget his question, and turned down a row, his left fingers following the drawer numbers. He pulled out a drawer, then another, before shifting to the next cabinet. "It's this one," he said, stepping aside. The wide, shallow drawer contained multiple small fragments, but the stele, set in a wooden frame, took up most of the space. Its surface appeared as fresh as the day it had been carved—the paint retaining vivid shades of ochre and blue on the seated figure and orange for the flaming bush.

Darwin held a hand over the frame's glass to cut the overhead light's glare and leaned in to study the colored stones: one a vibrant yellow and the other green. The tablet-sized stele had been fractured cleanly, cutting through the seated figure's midsection. In addition to the triangle point the book's author guessed was Thoth's beak, an outstretched hand remained. Darwin had not given it much thought when looking at the photo, but now, seeing it live, he could see a pit in the palm's well. Something had fallen out, or he thought, *was more likely taken out*.

"What do you know about this one?"

"Came to us that way, frame and all," said Giles.

"May I?" When Giles nodded approval, Darwin lifted the frame, tilted it to study the stele's edges, and then looked at the frame's backing. A note had been glued and varnished to it.

Found by Captain James Allison-Clark during the North Africa campaign, 1942

"Found?" Darwin asked rhetorically. He'd seen far too many objects with similar provenance. Someone stole it from Saint Catherine's Monastery, and, later, Captain Allison-Clark had bought it, or, perhaps, a guide had planted it, promising rare objects in a tomb. Whichever the case, Allison-Clark's estate bequeathed the looted stele to the British Museum, which used his story as legitimate provenance. Darwin's stomach churned with the memory of a recent fraud involving Tuscan vases at the ACA. He stared at the stele's broken edge; it was too clean to have been done in antiquity.

"Do we know where in Egypt James *found* it?"

"Possibly. The stele's picture appeared in an article about its donation in the 1960s. Shortly afterward we got a letter from a priest at the Saint Catherine's Monastery in Sinai requesting its return, stating it had been stolen. He claimed to have the missing piece, but would not show it to us."

"But the British Museum declined the request, despite knowing the stele's spurious provenance," said Darwin, his voice dripping with sarcasm.

"I wouldn't know. That's above my pay grade."

Darwin's blood boiled at the bureaucratic dodge of responsibility. He took photos of the stele, especially its broken edge, and thanked Giles before heading back to Heathrow for his return flight to Rome.

Geneva

The following day, Vanessa drove Siggy and Zac to the Swiss post office, where they put the tracker in an envelope addressed to a fictitious officer at the US military base in Spangdahlem, Germany. "That will throw them off," Zac said.

Back at the boathouse, Zac called Eyrún at the ACA from a landline to update her on what they had learned and the tracker in Siggy's bag. "Be vigilant. Someone's tracking us."

"Got it," she said, "Darwin's in Vatican City. How many people do you think they've got following us?"

"We still don't know who, let alone how many. Tell Darwin what we found out. We'll stay here another two days while the tracker draws attention toward Germany."

"Agreed," said Eyrún.

Vatican City

Darwin met his friend Richard N'Dembele for lunch at their favorite restaurant, two blocks from St. Peter's Basilica. The owner had reserved their usual table, where they settled in surrounded by the fragrance of the herbs growing under the front window. Richard gathered his cassock as his colossal frame made the chair look like it came from the kid's table.

"Tell me, how is Eyrún?" his voice rumbled. "What does she see in you?" He laughed, and Darwin blushed at their old joke.

They'd met in Clermont-Ferrand, France, where Richard was assistant to a bishop, now a cardinal. Aside from his duties for Cardinal Santos, Richard served as the go-between for the pope and Darwin. Twice Darwin had made profound discoveries from obscure Vatican records besides uncovering a forgery operation inside the Vatican museums.

"She's great, as always, and asked about you."

Richard clasped his hands and smiled broadly. "I love that woman. You know, had I not taken vows, you'd have had tough competition."

Darwin grinned while shaking his head. A warmth spread at the joy of being with his friend, different from Zac, more like a beloved older brother. Then, after a server took their order, Darwin explained what they'd found under the mountain house up to the diamond theft.

"That is troubling." Richard took the diamond Darwin had removed from a protective pouch. Eyrún had determined the radiation from this diamond was lower—no more than a dental x-ray. The big man had studied geology and worked in a South African diamond mine before entering the priesthood. "I've never seen anything like it. And there's thorium inside the specks?"

Darwin nodded, and Richard examined it further while listening to the technical details of what Eyrún and Zac had discovered. He raised his eyebrows at the alchemy, especially the connections to the Egyptian gods.

"Fascinating. You'll have to tell me more one day," said Richard. He'd come to Christianity later in life and, while faithful, had, from time to time, discussed mystical practices with Darwin. He handed back the diamond when their main courses arrived.

Darwin, who went through food like a wolf, slowed, realizing he'd finish before Richard was halfway through his meal. Eyrún had been after him to slow down and be more social. He forced himself to pause between bites and asked, "I need to see the other part of the stele in Saint Catherine's monastery, but they turned me down. Do you think His Holiness could persuade the abbot to grant me access?"

"Sure," said Richard, pulling his phone from beneath his cassock, "I'll text him now." Darwin's eyes widened. "No, His Holiness and I don't have that kind of relationship." He laughed at pulling Darwin's leg again.

"But you are in his contacts," said Darwin, who was getting better at responding to Richard's pranks.

"True. And Cardinal Santos is scheduled to see his holiness tomorrow. Perhaps I can slip your question into the agenda."

41

Holy Monastery of the God-Trodden Mount Sinai

As sunset neared two days later, Darwin arrived at Saint Catherine's Monastery. The sun's primary heat radiated from the ground and buildings as the temperature cooled. The mountain air held little moisture and, at over 1,500 meters, spared the residents from the Sinai desert's punishing heat. Long shadows crept over the mountains like an incoming tide.

Darwin, relieved to move about freely after a grueling day of travel, rubbed his low back while waiting for the driver to unload the luggage. His day had begun with a flight from Rome to Istanbul and followed by a connecting flight to Sharm El-Sheikh on the Gulf of Aqaba and a three-hour minivan ride over the St. Katherine-Nuwiebaa Road. His other option had been a flight to Cairo and a six-hour bus trip, but either choice had meant a butt-numbing journey.

His eyes roamed the twenty-meter-high protective wall with granite blocks cut from the surrounding mountains. Portals opened at regular intervals where defenders could fire upon attackers. Most curious was a wooden shack, which was like a guardhouse, mounted two-thirds up the wall. In times of trouble, he'd read that the monks sealed the gate under the wall, making the only point of entry a basket lowered from above.

Just left of the gate, the wall bulged outward with the tower of Saint George, home to the manuscripts a millennium ago, until the monks relocated them to a formal library. Darwin had seen pictures of the recent renovation of the oldest library in the western world and craved the opportunity to peruse its stacks.

A tingling spread to his fingers as he recalled entering a disused tomb in the Siwa Oasis in the western Sahara desert. Its preternatural silence and magnificent frescoes amplified the privilege of being the first human to witness it since the fourth century.

"Sir?" the driver's voice grabbed Darwin's attention away from the memory of hieroglyph-covered walls. He turned to find that the other visitors had gone ahead.

"Thanks." He tipped the driver, collected his case, and walked to the guest house among buildings in the monastery's outer compound. Low walls divided single-storied structures shaded by trees that were carefully tended in this water-scarce area.

"*Monsieur Lacroix?*" asked a monk.

"Yes."

The monk gave Darwin a tour of the grounds while escorting him to a room. "Dinner will be at seven in the dining room near the garden," he said. "Is there anything you need?"

Darwin thanked him, said no, and entered his room, pleased to find it more like a modest hotel than the monastic cells he'd pictured from medieval times. After plugging in his phone, he washed off the desert's grit. A muezzin's call drifted through an open window, drawing the local Muslim faithful to Maghrib, the sunset prayer, a reminder that, like Jerusalem, all three Abrahamic faiths converged here.

Wanting to explore the famed monastery before dinner, he left the room and headed for its side gate. The dark tunnel under the thick wall emerged from what looked like a cramped village, its buildings an eclectic combination of styles and age. Its flagstone streets were immaculate.

He saw no one and crossed to the basilica. Behind its stout door, the desert fortress gave way to gaudy opulence. Gold, bronze, and silver—centuries of gifts—adorned the walls and hung from the ceiling. Darwin arched his neck to follow the chains suspending dozens of candelabra. Anchored high in the ceiling, they were inlaid with a gold pattern and held aloft by the original sixth-century beams.

His survey drew him to the altar, where he paused in the apse, its half-domed ceiling filled with a sublime mosaic. Brilliant gold tiles gathered candlelight, illuminating the blues and whites used in the Christ figure and his disciples. Darwin stood transfixed at this monumental work of art, leaning backward to take in the scene. The church was silent as a tomb, except for a palpable whooshing in his ears, created by his head's extreme angle.

He looked down, stretching his neck muscles, and ran a shoe lightly over the intricate black and white marble inlaid floor. He continued along the south aisle and entered the chapel of Saint John the Baptist in the southeastern corner.

He spent a long moment before continuing to his objective, the Chapel of the Burning Bush behind the apse. Many visitors considered this the innermost shrine. He'd been steeped in the Catholic tradition, French on his father's side and Puerto Rican on his mother's, and the story of God speaking to Moses through a fiery bush had captivated him since childhood.

Darwin stepped out of his shoes as a soft, waxy aroma from the muted candlelight greeted him. He paused before a four-pillared altar directly over the bush's location. Elaborately patterned tiles adorned the walls. While moved to be in the presence of living antiquity, he'd always imagined it would be a natural rocky alcove.

He sat on the floor and meditated a short while before leaving the basilica to look for the dining room.

42

Paris

"I knew it." Ramy put down his phone. Over the last four days, he'd watched the tracker in Siggy's purse go to Geneva. It had stayed a day before moving to its current location: the NATO air base at Spandgahlem, Germany. But shortly after arriving, it had stopped working.

He smiled. *Forget this bullshit lawsuit. They confirmed its nuclear properties at CERN and took it to the US military. That verifies it's weapons-grade. If the US wants it, then others will too.*

He compared the screenshot he'd taken when the tag arrived to the live Google map. While he could zoom in on the base, getting decent resolution on a US Air Force refueling tanker, the buildings were nondescript. Not that he expected them to be labeled. *No matter. I can use it to up the ante. What I need are the bidders.*

Ramy messaged a former special forces friend in Algeria:

> found something your friends in the east might want

Ajaccio

That night, Eyrún received a call from Astrid, her avocat at the Paris law firm.

"I've got a lot to send you on the lawsuits and the background check. I'll email it, but let me give you a summary," Astrid said.

"I'm ready." Eyrún popped in her earbuds and started taking notes.

"Both lawsuits come from a small-time lawyer named Mike Carson from Baltimore, Maryland, and were filed in the district courts. He's using a Paris attorney, Hamid Gandlarz, to file the motions here. He's clever. I'll give him that. The spoliation suit is wildly creative as the US never rescinded its privateering law.

"On the paternity suit, we have confirmed that Mike is a direct descendent of Clarice Davis. But DNA testing to establish paternity is not allowed under French law—"

"It isn't?" asked Eyrún.

"No. Not by a private party. DNA testing in a paternity case can only be ordered by the court. It's structured this way to preserve peace within families. It's complicated," said Astrid.

"Does Mike Carson have a real claim?" said Eyrún.

"Well, yes, and no. Yes, in that his documents and a DNA test confirm a relationship. But at least sixteen other descendants of Clarice Davis could claim a share of any inheritance. And there's another law in our favor. Last year, the French Civil Code added Article 913 that complicates any inheritance claim from outside France."

"What should we do?"

"We think Mike Carson hopes to collect the entire class action monies himself. I'd advise you to fight it. Or, if Emelio wishes to settle his conscience, offer a modest settlement to the closest living descendants of Clarice Davis, and each subsequent generation can fight for its share. It's all documented in the email."

"Okay. I'll read it. What about the spoliation claim—the *Demeter* case?" asked Eyrún.

"As I said, it's creative. We think it's a red herring to get you to settle the paternity suit. Our interns researched records in the Museé de la Marine and the *Conseil des Prises*, our maritime prize court. They found the *Demeter* carried gold it had seized from Spain, so, in effect, the *Demeter* was privateering for the US Treasury. True, the Quasi-War with the US had never been declared, but privateering was a quirky phase in maritime history. Every nation did it. Henri stole gold from people who stole it from Spain, who looted it from the Aztecs. It's safe to say we could tie this up in the courts. We recommend working with your PR firm to acknowledge the history and deflect the article."

"Thanks, Astrid. I appreciate the fast work, and I'll think about a settlement." Eyrún ended the call and checked her email. The files included a photo of Mike Carson after passing the bar. He stood against a light background, brown eyes set in a round face topped with short sandy hair.

He doesn't look anything like Darwin. Somehow, she'd pictured a man with a vague resemblance. Still, the man in the photo looked nothing like the Lacroix family members she'd seen. She printed the documents for each lawsuit and tucked them in a folder that she stuck in her laptop case before returning to the day's work.

43

Saint Catherine's Monastery

The young monk who had greeted Darwin when he'd arrived at the monastery now led him to a table. Two older monks stood as they approached.

"Your Grace, this is Darwin Lacroix," said the young monk to the archbishop.

"Pleased to meet you, Archbishop," said Darwin.

"And you as well, Monsieur Lacroix. Welcome to our monastery."

The young monk continued, "This is Father Theophilus, the head librarian."

"It's an honor to host a distinguished Vatican guest," said Theophilus, a man whose stiff formality reminded Darwin of his peer at the Vatican. The man's emphasis on protocol and orderliness fit, as he bore the fiduciary weight of the western world's earliest library.

"The honor is mine," said Darwin as they all shook hands. "Thank you for seeing me on short notice."

He sat in the offered place across from the archbishop, with Theophilus to his right and the young monk to the left. The archbishop asked the young monk to lead the blessing. In the process of questioning, the archbishop had raised one dark eyebrow. Darwin's mind flashed a picture of the man as Sean Connery's double. *Trim the beard and lose the hat.* He bowed his head to suppress a laugh and, fortunately, had regained composure when the long blessing finished.

As their dinner was served, a chicken dish with an earthy tagine fragrance, the librarian asked about Darwin's work at the Vatican. "What is the pope's Director of Special Archaeological Investigations?"

Darwin swallowed his first bite and looked ardently at his full fork before answering. "The Vatican Apostolic Archive restricts access to documents the Roman church found suspicious or censored. For example, a diary written by Hypatia of Alexandria was purposefully hidden within the archive. A millennium ago, one Vatican librarian thought it pointed the way to gnostic scripts. Thankfully, instead of destroying it outright, he buried it, so to speak."

"Like someone with a broader sense of curiosity thought the diary might be worth interpreting at another time," said the librarian. He squinted through thick glasses that he kept pushing up a razor-thin nose. "And how did you, an outsider, come by this role?"

The man's demeanor, while polite and casual, bristled with suspicion. Darwin adjusted his approach. "His Holiness values my perspective and intuition as an outsider. But I'm not the sole expert. I supervise a team of tenured Vatican archivists and preservation experts. I've also got a steganographer to evaluate encrypted texts. We examine the historical context and 'declassify' them, so to speak, returning them to circulation. Anything questionable, we route to the pope for his decision," said Darwin.

He locked eyes with Theophilus, steeling himself for the next question, but the archbishop steered the conversation towards the Agrippa Center for Archaeology. Darwin described its work as preserving ancient cultural heritage. The librarian shifted his inquiry to the ACA's role in repatriating looted antiquities. Darwin answered them patiently, guessing this must be a test of his intentions.

Eventually, the conversation drifted toward life in the monastery while they finished dinner. When tea was served, the archbishop asked, "Now that we know you better, tell us about this object you seek and why my brother in Rome suggested I listen to your urgent request."

"We found diamonds with superconducting properties that make them desirable for scientific research," said Darwin.

The statement raised the eyebrows of the three holy men, and Theophilus asked, "Why—"

"They're also dangerously radioactive." Darwin cut him off.

"How do you know these are near our monastery?" asked the younger monk.

Darwin summarized Henri's alchemy notes, which led to finding the picture in the German book of the stele in London. "I went to the British Museum to see it and learned three things. One, the stele's fracture did not happen in antiquity. And, two," he said, laying a picture of the stele on the table, "we think these yellow and green stones represent the same diamonds we found that react to bright light."

The monks passed around the photo.

"What's the third thing you learned?" asked Theophilus.

"That its provenance shows someone stole it from you, and its other half is here," said Darwin, looking at the archbishop who held the photo.

"Is this the burning bush?" said the archbishop, tapping the picture.

"Could be," said Darwin and reached across to point out the fracture, "but if we knew which Egyptian god this is, we might make more sense of it and get a precise location." He looked from face to face and saw the archbishop nod to the librarian, who produced a flat box and laid it on the table.

"We think this is the missing part." Theophilus removed the lid, folded the cloth, and handed Darwin the upper piece of the stele.

"Hathor!" said Darwin, looking at the top half of the seated figure, whose long black hair draped across one shoulder. Atop her head rested a U-shaped crown whose black horns supported an orange disk. A yellow cobra looped the disk, its head facing toward the gems and bush. Blue flowers floated above Hathor's crown.

"Do you know what it means?" asked the archbishop.

"I think so. Hathor's either the mother or the consort of Horus and

Ra, the sky and sun gods. She represents maternal care and sexuality," he blushed, "er, joy, music, and dance. See, the headdress of cow horns wrapped around the sun disk blends the maternal and the celestial. But in our case, the Egyptians also connected Hathor with semi-precious stones."

"Then this might be the stone missing in your picture." The librarian laid a thumb-tip-sized piece of turquoise on the table.

Darwin picked it up and held it next to the photo. The scale was off, but its shape matched the stele in the picture. "Wait," he paused, mentally reviewing his research before continuing, "the Egyptians mined turquoise in Sinai, and the enslaved people doing the work worshipped Hathor as their protector. The mine must be close by."

Theophilus covered his hand with the cloth in the box and palmed the stele. "We think so," he said, allowing Darwin to see its backside.

A demotic script ran over the top of a map, cut off by the fracture lines. But before Darwin could get a closer look, the librarian placed it back in the box and moved it off the table.

Darwin's jaw dropped and, after a moment, he said, "Wait! That means the other part of the map ..." He let the statement hang while visualizing Giles closing the drawer a few days ago.

"Yes. The rest of the map is on the *donated* piece in the British Museum. Return it to us, and you may photograph the complete map," said Theophilus.

"You mean steal it?"

"Not exactly, Darwin," said the archbishop. "You've described your talent for repatriating looted antiquities. The British have never taken our requests seriously before. We're hoping you can be more convincing."

44

Paris

"Dammit!" Mike dropped the letter from a prestigious Paris law firm on the counter of his flat. *The old man must have involved his grandson.* This would much more difficult than he had imagined. Mike had figured on the local attorney in Corsica lacking the skill to fight and encouraging the family to settle. But a high-end firm in Paris could bury Mike in work.

This was a worst-case scenario: an expensive, years-long fight. He looked again at the settlement offered: €50,000 for each first-generation child of Clarice Davis to be divided among each child's descendants.

It's an insult. They must know Clarice was an only child.

Even if he kept it all to himself, he'd already incurred nearly $20,000 in expenses. He walked to the balcony and stood at its railing. *Bastards.* He stared blankly at the building across the street. After controlling his emotions, his mood lifted slightly. *It's just another round in the fight. They beat grandma once. Now it's my turn.* His hands squeezed the thick round railing as he plotted. He'd opened with a ridiculous sum. They had counter-punched low.

But they did come back with an offer, which means we struck a chord.

Although he hadn't expected to get anything close to what he'd asked for, he considered $1,000,000 his walk-away amount. *It's doable,* he reaffirmed to himself.

Now it was his turn to fight dirty. *A little bad press about the ACA's money will increase the numbers.* He fired off an email to a journalist.

Seconds later, his phone chimed, reminding him of a meeting with Ramy, who'd said something about another plan. He tucked the papers away in his case, pocketed the phone, and walked to the cafe.

Ajaccio

Darwin, Eyrún, Zac, and Siggy sat on the flybridge of Eyrún's powerboat, Hypatia. They'd dropped anchor on the lee side of the big Sanguinaire island outside Ajaccio harbor.

While the others talked about Darwin's visit to the monastery, Eyrún brooded about Emelio's predicament. Earlier in the day, the Paris firm had sent their recommended responses to the lawsuits. At first, Emelio had been uncomfortable with the idea of settling. But she'd told him not to worry about the money. She would take care of it and help him explain the empty trust to Olivier and Darwin.

She left out telling him she had hired an investigator through the Paris firm. The microphone and break-in at Emelio's house might have been coincidental, but the tracker in Siggy's bag was not. She hated not being able to tell the others about Emelio's lawsuits. *Damn his foolish pride,* she fumed, trying to cover her emotion behind her wineglass.

"What's up, love?" asked Darwin.

"Something I forgot to tell Hérve," she said, reaching for her mobile and messaging her assistant on an unimportant issue. She set down the phone as the first stars appeared on the eastern horizon above Corsica. Behind her, the western sky's orange rim faded.

Siggy blurted out. "You can't be serious. Steal an artifact from the British Museum?"

"I am," said Darwin. "We need it. Besides, it's looted antiquity—"

"What!" Eyrún almost shouted.

Siggy recounted the conversation for her sister.

"Just take a photo of its back," said Eyrún.

"Won't work," he said. "We went over that. The monks want the whole piece reunited—in Saint Catherine's."

They argued about the ethics a while longer before Darwin reminded them, "Look. I get it. This isn't just about the stele, but how else will we find the diamonds' source?" He stood and went to the flybridge's railing and stared at the lighthouse atop the island.

Eyrún went to him and stroked his back. "How will you do it? Break in, I mean?"

Darwin explained his idea, and Zac shook his head. "Needs some work, bro."

As sunset neared, they went below to the galley to cook dinner. Zac switched on a reggaeton playlist, and they spent the evening refining Darwin's plan until they thought it was good enough.

Paris

Mike sipped an iced tea at the corner cafe. An afternoon rainstorm had broken a heat wave but left a cloying mugginess. He'd been working on his response to the lawyers when Ramy arrived.

"Hey buddy, what's up?" Ramy asked, bumping fists with Mike and taking the adjacent seat facing the sidewalk.

"Just chilling."

Ramy ordered a drink, then said, "When I left Corsica, I saw the friend, Zac, and Darwin's sister-in-law at the airport."

"Did they—"

"No. They didn't see me." The server arrived with Ramy's cocktail, and they waited for her to move away. "But I dropped an air tag, you know, one of those Apple devices—"

"I know what they are. What the hell are you doing? I told you if they connect me to your break-ins, the lawsuits are screwed. Hell, Ramy. I thought you were smarter than that."

"I am," said Ramy, placing a diamond on the table between their drinks.

Mike snatched the dirty crystal. It looked more like the quartz he'd found as a kid, but he could make out the specks inside that Ramy had described. He held it under his phone's light, as Ramy suggested. After a minute, he closed his hands over the diamond and peeked at it.

"See, it glows," said Ramy. "They talked about its radioactivity and acting as a superconductor."

"How radioactive?" Mike handed it back.

"You probably got a chest x-ray worth just now. That's why it's best to keep it in here," he said, closing it in a metal box. "One x-ray isn't bad, but continuous exposure would take a toll."

"Shit." Mike rubbed his palms against his jeans, then realized the stupidity of the motion. Radiation wouldn't rub off. He gulped his tea, then asked, "What do we do with it?

"Sell it." When Mike's face screwed up, Ramy added, "It's got to be weapons-grade. They took it to a German NATO base after they visited a Russian nuclear bomb expert in CERN."

"Jesus, Ramy. Keep it down," Mike hissed. He glanced at the building and nearby lampposts for cameras. Paris wasn't as bad as London's surveillance, but the French anti-terrorist teams remained on high alert, especially after the 2015 attacks in this arrondissement.

"This area's clean, Mike. That's why we're at this cafe." Ramy pocketed the box. "But you're right, walk with me." He left a twenty euro note under one glass, and they headed down the street. A block later, he said, "I got in contact with Ali."

Mike flinched.

"Relax, I used Proton."

Mike's stomach sagged. Memories of the heroin bust made him want to turn and run, but at least Ramy had the good sense to use a point-to-point encrypted email service.

Ramy continued, "Ali replied that the Iranians or North Koreans might be interested. The Chinese bureaucracy's too big to get through. Pakistan maybe, but they might not have the tech."

A few strides later, Mike played along. "What next?"

"That's more like the old Mike." Ramy punched his arm, and when Mike shrugged, he continued, "Ali said to give him a week."

Ajaccio

The following day, Eyrún lay wide awake before sunrise, the details of the lawsuits buzzing in her brain. She slipped out of bed and quietly padded up to the main deck. The kettle was already hot, and a light bergamot fragrance hung in the galley. Wet footprints on the deck led up to the flybridge, and she guessed Zac must've made good on his commitment to a morning swim. She popped a new bag in a cup, poured over hot water, and mounted the steps.

"Morning," said Zac, towel around his shoulders. His curly wet hair sparkled in the sun, spilling over Corsica's granite spine.

"I couldn't sleep any longer," she confessed before being asked.

"Hmm." Zac sipped his tea.

Eyrún smiled. *He deserves to meet someone nice.* Zac had confessed in Berkeley that he'd stopped dating to clear his head. She'd thought about girlfriends she could introduce, but all were in committed relationships. She sighed.

Zac had been looking out to sea and missed her sad moment. He turned back. They both spoke simultaneously, "Something's been bothering—"

They stopped. "You first," he said.

"Erm." She stared into her cup. "I need you to promise you won't say a word of this to Darwin. I can't keep it to myself any longer."

"Why not tell Siggy?"

"I can't. She doesn't have the context. Not like you."

"Okay."

Eyrún told him about the lawsuits, Emelio's financial situation, and how she had hired the Paris law firm.

When she finished, Zac smirked and wagged his head. "Gotta love Emelio, but he can be stubborn. And I thought the Lacroix boys got over their feud?"

"They have. This is a case of Emelio's pride."

"How can I help?" he asked.

"You already have. I needed to get it off my chest. What did you want to tell me?" asked Eyrún.

"About the turquoise mines Darwin's looking for. The diamonds don't fit the scenario. I mean, not unless somebody dumped them in the mine."

"Yeah, I thought about that, but was so wrapped up in the lawsuits. Could they have been traded from elsewhere in Africa?"

"Possibly," said Zac, "All the kimberlite in this part of the world's sub-Saharan. What about a meteorite?"

Eyrún listened while he laid out a theory of an extraterrestrial impact that brought perovskite-laden diamonds to Earth.

"But wouldn't the impact destroy the diamonds?" she countered.

"True," he conceded, "but the entire peninsula's been subject to plate tectonics between Africa and Asia. Suppose part of the mantle extruded into one of the rifts? Then a meteorite blows away the surrounding rock, and the wadis erode it for the next million years, exposing a deposit."

"I suppose that might make more sense than traders packing a bunch of diamonds," she said.

"Exactly. I'll put a query out to the OSINT. Tell them we've found microspherules and nanodiamonds in the soil of an ancient settlement and seek satellite data on an impact." The Open Source Intelligence community used publicly available satellite feeds to ferret clandestine activity, from smuggling to illegal military movement. "I'll offer a bitcoin bounty for data. That should get us a fast result."

"Sure—" Eyrún stood at a loud splash off the swim deck.

Siggy had dived in. Her long pale form glided beneath the azure water before surfacing and stroking away from the boat.

"Hey, you two. There you are," said Darwin, walking up from the galley, coffee in hand.

"Your secret's here," said Zac to Eyrún while tapping his heart. "I'll let you know what I find with the sats."

45

Algiers, Algeria

Ramy's flight landed that afternoon at Houari Boumediene Airport. He'd expected nothing from the lawsuits and, figuring they needed another option, took matters into his own hands. Besides, in his view, Mike had always been reluctant to join in risky ventures.

After passing through border control, he hired a taxi that dropped him off eight kilometers away along the Bay of Algiers. He watched the taxi drive away on Rue Verte Rive before entering a restaurant. He wove his way past the tables and the kitchen before exiting in a rear alley. Pausing long enough for a cigarette and checking whether anyone had followed him, he walked three blocks up the passage to a car park. Ramy tapped the dark-tinted passenger window of a white BMW M5. The door unlocked, and he got in.

"Were you followed?" asked Ali, a bull-necked man whose meaty hands strangled the steering wheel.

"No."

Ali rocketed out of the car park, made a series of rapid turns, and entered the N1, where he paid little attention to the speed limit. Ten kilometers later, he braked hard onto an exit ramp, then kept to the posted limit as the road arced toward the Hilton Algiers. He drove around the large hotel and picked a spot in the car park.

Knowing Ali as a man of few words, Ramy had said nothing during the drive, and, besides, most of what they had in common was a past Ramy cared not to dwell on. Yesterday, when he'd laid out the barest of explanations, Ali said he knew a North Korean who had been sniffing around. Now, with the engine idling to keep the air-conditioning on, Ali turned and, holding out a hand, said, "Show me the diamond."

Ramy dropped it in the colossal palm and waited.

"What do you know of it?" Ali held the diamond up, the waning daylight pouring through the windscreen.

Ramy explained the fleck inside the gritty, unpolished crystal as best he could.

"Sounds like guessing."

"No. They took it to nuclear research facilities in California and CERN. Then went directly to the American base in Spangdahlem, Germany. That tells me it's dangerous."

"Hmph. We need more for this guy. He says the American sanctions have hurt them and their glorious leader's looking for ways to make a statement."

"Then we show him this," said Ramy, unfolding a paper. As Ali studied it, Ramy described the blue donut shape. "It's called a tokamak. I'm no physicist, but I heard them describe it as a magnetic field containing high-energy plasma. Break the field, and boom."

"How big?"

"Enough to take out the hotel." He thumbed at the building behind them and held up a USB stick. "All their conversations and data are on this."

"Let's go." Ali stuffed the diamond and USB stick in his pocket, ignoring Ramy's comment about not keeping it close to his family jewels.

"Wait." Ramy grabbed Ali's forearm, not allowing his brusque colleague to control his deal. "What do you know about this guy?" Ali crunched his brows, and Ramy felt the ropey muscles tense. "C'mon

Ali, the more I know, the better we can play this guy. You know that," he said, releasing his grip.

"He's been westernized. Went to the university in Beirut. Speaks fluent Arabic. Officially, he brokers contracts for raw materials."

"And unofficially?" Ramy probed.

"He's like any other agent for the hermit kingdom, looking for access to military technology."

Paris

Mike hit the streets for a run the day after accusing Ramy of sidetracking his inheritance opportunity. They had argued, and Ramy had called Mike naïve to think he could take on a powerful Paris law firm. The legal motions requesting more data on the *Demeter* and Henri Lacroix's direct linkage as captain supported Ramy's comment.

Initially, Mike had calculated he could afford to play this game for two years if he stayed rent free at Ramy's flat, but the builders would be done before the holidays. Ramy was looking for another squat, but if Mike had to pay rent, the Paris firm would easily outspend him.

After sprinting the last hundred meters of his run, Mike stopped and bent over, panting, hands on knees. *Maybe selling the diamonds would work. How many did Ramy say the Lacroixes have?* He didn't remember, but if they got a few hundred thousand for them, that would tide him over. *It could work,* he thought, walking under the shade from the trees lining the street when he remembered the journalist.

He turned into a tabac shop. *"Bonjour."* Mike exchanged greetings with the proprietor and scanned the news rack. The Global Investigative Journalism Network reporter had told him the story should be out today. At first, she'd not been interested, but after researching, she'd come back wanting to write a report on modern piracy and thought Mike's lawsuit would get readers to connect Somali piracy with France's shady past.

He found the smaller journal she'd mentioned in the rack next to the major papers. Its headline jumped out:

Aztec gold in Corsica

He grabbed the edition and dropped a two euro coin in the wooden tray. The shop owner nodded as Mike headed outside while reading. Following the opening paragraphs about piracy in the Horn of Africa, the article picked up what Mike had planted:

> France engaged in its own state sponsored piracy against the fledging United States. In a newly filed spoliation lawsuit in Paris, the heirs of the *Demeter*, an American merchant vessel, make a convincing claim that a Frenchman, Henri Lacroix, illegally seized the *Demeter* in 1801. But, before the US could respond to the judgement by the corrupt French prize court, Henri had taken the *Demeter's* cargo.
>
> The gold is long gone, but the lawsuit exposes records buried deep in the Conseil des Prises archives and, its modern trail shows the gold may have been used to build the Lacroix family's shipping empire. And, they went on to profit from the French state with lucrative contracts during the world wars. While the company is now defunct, its assets remained with the family and are rumored to have funded the high-profile Agrippa Center for Archaeology in Ajaccio, Corsica. Another example of the privileged class building its fortunes on the back of the taxpayers.

Nice, he grinned. *That'll shake up the fancy Parisian avocats.*

46

Algiers

Ramy awoke, head thick from an evening entertaining Agent Park, but the pleasant ache in his groin compensated for the excess alcohol. A quarter-hour later, while toweling dry, he glanced in the mirror and sighed—the long nights had become harder to shake off. He rubbed the dark circles under his eyes, splashed cold water on them, and, when dried off, noticed the empty bed. *Good*. She'd taken the hint after he'd rolled off her that morning, saying he had to get ready for a breakfast meeting.

He dropped the towel, stepped into the room, and threw open the drapes. *Home*. He squinted at the bright daylight coming off the Bay of Algiers. *No*. He turned away, rejecting the nostalgic moment. His family and military had disowned him, and he felt nothing for the place now. Yesterday, he'd half expected to be detained or, at least, questioned at passport control, but they'd waved him on like any other citizen. He rubbed the veins in his throbbing temples.

He surveyed the room. As expected, the woman had rifled through his bag. Last night, Ali had shown the diamond and USB stick to Park, then handed both to Ramy, who put them in his room's safe. Ramy laughed. The nightclub's reputation as a haven for thieving escorts remained intact, but he suspected Park had hired her. His interest in the diamond had seemed too casual at the time.

Ramy removed the tiny camera he'd clipped to the drapes and reviewed the video on his phone. The woman had tried to open the safe using a black light to detect the fingerprints on its keypad. *Not exactly a rookie move. Why buy something when you can steal it? Sneaky bastard Park.*

His phone chirped.

Ali: downstairs in 10

Ramy: got it

Forty minutes later, they sat in a crowded cafe within walking distance of the North Korean embassy. Ramy cleared his brain fog with a strong coffee before Park arrived with a woman fashionably dressed in a dark blue pantsuit and heels.

"Good morning, gentlemen," he said, "I trust you had pleasant evenings." His mouth spread in a toothless grin.

Ali grunted.

"Most definitely," said Ramy, smiling and studying Park's face. Last night when their business was done, Park had introduced them to two women and left the club shortly afterward, saying he had a very early morning call.

Park introduced his colleague, Kim, who was all business. "Let me see it," she said.

While stylish in appearance, Ramy had no illusions about her role —an agent of the People's Republic of North Korea. He placed a small envelope in her outstretched palm. She tapped the diamond into her other palm and studied it between her manicured fingertips.

Ali and Park went for a smoke as Ramy studied Kim. He knew most of their global espionage was now done in cyberspace by fast-tracking their brightest kids into hacker school. But the weapons trade required old-fashioned face-to-face dealings.

Ramy remained placid as Kim took out a small device, switched it on, and set the diamond on top. She snapped a photo.

"What's that?" he asked.

"It's radioactive," she said, ignoring his question.

"Yes, that's why we thought you might be interested."

"What else does it do?"

Ramy knew Park must have briefed her, including handing over the print-out of the blue toroid, but he placed his phone on the table and played the recording from the Lacroix's library. He'd gotten used to each level of superior officers asking the same questions as if they did not believe their underlings.

"Who are these people?" she asked.

"That information comes along with the diamonds," he said, dropping the diamond back in the envelope while adding, "that is, if you're interested."

"We might be. How many do you have?"

Now we're getting somewhere. He studied her face. Pretty, but her severe expression and brusque manner set him off.

She must have read his mind and smiled warmly, exposing perfect teeth. "My apologies. Park has brought too many things of dubious value to my attention. I rarely see such a unique item. If it is capable of what the people in your recording say, then I am very interested. Where did you say you found them?"

"I didn't." Ramy liked her new congeniality and flashed on what she might be like in the sack, but he'd honed his skills in war-torn Afghanistan. Misjudge someone's intentions, and you died.

She laughed. "You're good, Mr. Ramy. Let me lay it out for you. If this diamond has the superconducting and nuclear properties you claim, and if you can get a lot more of them, my people would be willing to pay. But," she held out her palm again, "we need to validate the merchandise."

"Fair enough. How long will it take?"

"You're in luck, as I have to courier another item tonight personally."

He handed the diamond back to her as Ali and Park returned. "We'll be in touch," she said, standing and saying something in Korean to Park as they departed.

47

London

"Follow my lead like we planned," Darwin said to Siggy. He carried a volume on the tombs at Saqqara, which he'd requested two hours earlier, and took it back to the research desk and thanked the librarian. Now at half-four, they left the round reading room in the center of the British Museum as thunderstorms darkened the atrium. They passed the exhibits, and Darwin badged into the staff entrance just before the men's WC. They kept their heads down to minimize what the security teams saw.

Earlier in the day, a car service had dropped them off at the museum after a flight to Heathrow from Ajaccio. Barry Hodgson, Darwin's former professor and now Director of Archaeology at the ACA, had lent them his still active research pass.

Inside the offices, most employees were wrapping up their day. Darwin's plan counted on the workday's end, covering their movements.

To blend in, Siggy opened a manila folder with photos of artifacts and questioned Darwin about one vase. They looked like two researchers going about their business to anyone in the area. Darwin held a door open for Siggy, and, once in the corridor, he pressed the down button on a nearby lift.

They reached the sub-basements and found the cabinet row in less than three minutes. He opened the drawer, turned over the framed stele, and used a small screwdriver to remove its backing. Once out, he turned to hand it to Siggy.

"Take a photo first," she reminded him.

"Right." He laid the stele face down on the cork in the drawer's bottom, but paused as the map sucked him in. He traced a finger along a route northward from Saint Catherine's monastery.

"Darwin! We don't have time. Take the picture."

He snapped a half-dozen times with his phone, pocketed it, and swapped the stele with a fake Siggy had brought in her purse. Fixing the frame as best he could, he replaced it in the drawer and closed it. They turned to go when Darwin grabbed Siggy's arm, pulling her down into a squat behind the cabinets.

A man's voice boomed from across the room. "Hello! Is anyone about?"

"Shit!" Siggy hissed.

"I said hello. This is museum security. Stand where I can see you."

"What do we do?" Siggy asked, as her pale complexion seemed to grow even lighter.

"Plan B." Darwin pulled a small windup toy from his pack and aimed it between the cabinet legs toward the voice. The toy buzzed as it shot under the cabinets and drew the guard down a far row.

Siggy and Darwin went on hands and knees in the opposite direction. Nearing the wall, they heard the guard call for backup. They moved along the last row and reached a door marked "Emergency Exit - Alarm Will Sound." Darwin pulled the next part of their getaway kit from his pack: a wire with clips on each end.

"Here," said Siggy, pointing to sensors: small rectangular blocks mounted on the door and its frame. She took the wire and clipped one end to the door half of the sensor and the other to the doorframe half. Darwin risked looking across the room and saw three more museum guards enter.

Siggy pushed the door handle and opened it carefully. The wire kept the alarm circuit closed, and they went through. "Good," she said on the other side, and gently closed the door. But as it latched, a piercing alarm went off. "Shit. Shit. Shit. The wire must have popped off."

"Nothing for it, then. C'mon." Darwin led her down a short corridor to a stairwell. A dank, moldy odor assaulted them.

Siggy pinched her nose while looking at the slimy streak on the wall that flowed onto the downward steps.

"We go up," said Darwin. "This exits near the museum's front entrance."

But partway up the stairs, a door opened two floors above and someone yelled, "They'll have to come up here."

Siggy's hand went to her mouth. "What now?" she rasped through her fingers.

"Plan C."

"You never told me about a plan C."

"Didn't think we'd need it," he said and turned. "We go down."

"Ew." She grasped the handrail for balance against the slippery steps and followed Darwin down three floors. The tight stairwell doubled back on itself six times. The lights did not activate at this level, and the dim light from above barely prevented total darkness. They stopped at a metal door that appeared not to have been opened in decades, but its newer-looking padlock suggested otherwise.

"Now what?" The footsteps from above came lower. She reached for her phone.

"No lights," he said. "Hold this." She took his pack, and he rummaged out two large spanners. "Hope this works. Saw it on the Internet."

"Tell me you didn't." But Darwin had already worked the spanners in place. The mouth of each fit the bolt's shaft on either side of the lock mechanism. The spanner's round heads met with their handles at near ninety degrees.

The voices above them quieted as they entered the emergency exit from the subbasement with the cabinets.

"They'll be back soon. Look away," said Darwin, pressing the spanners together. He strained, then crunched his arms and core together. The bolt split like a firecracker. The spanners clanged together, and one hit the floor. Darwin danced, wringing one hand while biting back a yell.

"Let me see it," said Siggy.

"No time. It's just bruised." He collected the spanners and pushed open the door. Once on its other side, he handed her a light from the pack and said, "Now I need a light."

She held it while he wedged a spanner in the door's bottom gap, using the other to hammer it.

"That'll hold awhile." He pulled another light from his pack and shone it down a long corridor.

"Where are we?"

"Someplace I've read about. Hopefully, it goes where I think."

"Oh great. My sister told me about your thinks."

"They work out. Mostly. C'mon. Our only other choice is with them." He nodded towards the door.

"That's career limiting. Let's go." She fell in behind as he jogged. In a hundred meters, the corridor turned right, then, in another fifty, angled right, dead ending at another metal door.

"Please work," he muttered, grasping the handle. Siggy held her breath, but the door opened easily, and they stepped inside an enormous white-walled tunnel.

"What is this place? It … it looks like a Tube tunnel."

"It is. More or less. Keep going. I'll explain as we go."

Siggy marveled at the riveted metal panels holding back the London clay as Darwin explained they were in the BT Kingsway Exchange. "British Telecom moved its switches down here during the Cold War. Before that, Londoners used the place as a bomb shelter in the war."

They moved through a vast space with old electronic equipment, and she nearly crashed into Darwin when he stopped suddenly. "Here we are." His light focused on a sign for High Holborn Street.

"No good," said Siggy, her light running over four weld marks between the metal door and its frame.

"*Putain!* It's been sealed since I was here last."

"We're stuck?"

"Not yet, but we need to know if they followed." He put a finger to his lips. A moment later, the tunnel rumbled. Siggy's nails dug into his forearm. "Darwin?" her voice went up an octave.

"It's a train—the Central Line. Don't worry. It's passed through here eighty times a day for the last hundred years. We're safe." All went quiet, and Darwin tried to ignore Siggy's excited breathing as he strained to listen farther down the tube. Seconds later, a metal scraping sound echoed from the direction they'd come.

"Damn, they got through. Follow me. I wish I had your sister's speed."

"Me too," Siggy huffed from behind. "I kickbox, not run."

The tunnel felt endless, though Darwin knew its entire length was a thousand meters. *God, I hope that door opens from the inside.* He remembered the unique key used to open it from the outside.

"How much farther?"

"We're close." He looked over his shoulder to see lights coming toward them, still a long way off. *If the lift isn't down, we're screwed.* But luck favored them, and the industrial lift sat at their level. Darwin hauled the rope that opened its wide door and jumped inside, Siggy right behind him. He punched 0 for street level.

Nothing.

"No power. Dammit." Siggy kicked the panel, cracking the up button.

"There's gotta be another way." Darwin jumped out, scanning the area with the light. "Workers would need an emergency escape." He moved around the lift's far side. "Here." He yanked open a door. "Go!"

Siggy went in. He pulled the door closed and followed her up the tight, winding shaft. He lost count at eighty steps, his thighs burning.

"How far down were we?" she yelled.

"Dunno," he gasped. But seconds later, they reached the landing and piled out of the shaft. Both sucked in huge breaths before Darwin looked up at the door to the street.

"Please, please, please." His legs moved like lead as he studied the internal latch and blew out upon seeing a simple mechanism. He pushed open the door and stepped outside 39 Furnival Street, never happier to walk into drenching rain.

48

Paris

That afternoon, Mike met Ramy on Pont des Arts to appear as competition to the North Koreans. The footbridge between the Louvre and the Left Bank was a meeting place for lovers, who attached padlocks to the railing and threw the keys into the Seine River as a sign of their commitment. But when a structural engineer calculated the danger posed by the extra tons of fixed weight, the city cut away thousands of the locks.

Mike had called Ramy's phone mid-span over the Seine River, and they found each other, after which Mike looked at a diamond Ramy showed him. They talked for a few minutes until Ramy saw Kim approaching from the Left Bank.

"There she is. Go now. Don't look," said Ramy.

Mike pocketed a fake diamond, and they shook hands. He turned towards the Musée du Louvre, where their plan called for him to keep up the illusion by hiring a taxi to the American embassy in case the North Koreans followed him.

"*Bonjour*," said Kim.

"*Bonjour*. Nice day in Paris," said Ramy. "I've always liked this view." He turned to face the point that split the river's flow around Île de la Cité. A couple sat on one bank opposite a large family picnic on the other, but someone with a long-range camera lens who stepped into the shadowy canopy of a willow tree drew his focus.

Kim covered the moment. "Who just left you? A friend?"

Ramy rested his hands on the railing, trying to pick out the photographer. "Another interested party." He couldn't be sure if the guy had taken pictures of Mike, but decided if he had, he'd ID Mike as former American military. He turned to Kim and, seeing her frown, added, "Nothing's settled yet."

"I thought I was exclusive." Kim pouted and pressed in close, like a lover. Her hand slipped around his waist. "I want it, Ramy," she whispered.

Ramy's heart jumped, and he pushed into the embrace but got poked in the ribs. He glanced down at a gun in her riverside hand—its fat silencer angled upward—at his heart. He reflexively sucked in his gut. All sounds went dead in his hyper focus. His logical brain tried to control the situation, but his lizard brain pushed one foot backward to run.

She shoved the barrel harder. "You thought I wanted something else?"

"Don't you?" Ramy went on instinct and peered into her brown eyes while letting a hand cup her ass. *She won't kill me. Not if she wants the diamonds.*

"Flics! Kiss me."

Ramy did so, finding her lips much softer than her frigid demeanor. The gun's pressure withdrew, and her perfume—oud—enveloped him. Its dark incense and musk added a strangely erotic element. She pulled away when the gendarmes passed. Ramy thought he detected pleasure in her expression—fleeting, but her hard veneer had softened.

He smiled and took control before she could. "What did your people find out about the diamond?" He leaned against the railing and lit a cigarette.

"We're running more tests, but it shows promise. We're prepared to pay, but only if you call off the Americans."

So, they know. He'd have to be careful. "I might be. How much are you talking?"

"There's an envelope in my jacket. Kiss me again and take it," she said.

This time, Kim lingered as Ramy transferred the fat envelope to his pocket, giving the man with the telephoto lens plenty of time to capture the transaction.

49

Bocagno

The stele lay on the mountain house's kitchen counter where they'd left it the night before. Darwin had woken up thinking about it and, after brewing himself a triple-shot cappuccino, slid onto a stool to study it. As the drink warmed him, the silence in the house reminded him of the British museum's sub-basement. He looked out the mountain house's expansive windows, where a light haze hung in the canyon. The sun rising over Mount Oro behind him cast its coral hue onto the far ridge.

Two days earlier, he'd been asleep when their Eurostar from Saint Pancras station in London had reached Paris. Two uniformed conductors had roused them at the Gar du Nord station. He'd leapt up, thinking they were police, and spent the next hour in the station looking over his shoulder before taking an overnight TGV to Nice. He hadn't relaxed until Eyrún picked them up, following their flight to Ajaccio.

Per the original plan, Barry had told the London police that his badge had been lost. But Darwin, still edgy from their cross-Europe run, half expected the authorities to connect the missing badge with his visit to London.

The front door banged open. Darwin jumped, sloshing hot coffee as two figures shot into the room.

A hand slapped the entry table. "I won!" yelled Siggy.

"*Putain!*" Darwin sucked the hot drink off his hands and ran them under cold water.

"Whew," said Zac, "it's hotting up out there."

He moved toward the kitchen, followed by Siggy, where they both got glasses of water. Zac chugged half of his, refilled it, and perched on a stool across from Darwin, who was wiping coffee off the floor.

Siggy looked at the stele on the counter. "Figure anything else out?"

Before he could answer, Zac said, "I still can't believe you two stole it from the British Museum. You've done some crazy shit, Darwin, but this beats all."

Darwin wadded up the towel and tossed it next to the sink. "Yeah, it might be hard to regain my reading-room privileges."

"Ya think?" said Zac.

Darwin then answered Siggy's question. "It doesn't tell me enough. I need to see it with the other piece. After we scan it today, I'll take it back to Saint Catherine's."

"Good morning," said Eyrún, coming upstairs from her office where she'd been answering emails. "You two better shower. I need to be there in forty minutes."

"Got it," said Zac and headed downstairs.

"Can I use your shower?" asked Siggy.

Eyrún said, "Sure," as she prepared her breakfast. A moment later, when Siggy had gone, her phone chimed with a message from her assistant.

Hervé: Trouble

She followed the Tweet he'd included and banged her tea mug on the granite counter. "Dammit!"

Darwin looked up from his remade cappuccino, brow raised in question. She forwarded him the text.

"*Merde,*" he hissed, "these people don't stop." And after a minute of reading, she added, "Isn't this the same journalist who tried to frame you for antiquities fraud?"

"It is. That bitch! I thought we had a gag order on her."

"Wait. Don't respond," said Darwin, seeing Eyrún tap on her phone.

"I'm not. I'm calling Astrid."

"*Oui, allô,*" Astrid answered.

"*Allô, bonjour Astrid. C'est Eyrún.*"

"*Bonjour, Eyrún. Ça va?*"

Eyrún switched to English. "I'm not having a good day. I've got Darwin with me. You're on speaker." He and Astrid exchanged greetings before Eyrún continued. "I sent you a link to another article by Nathalie Ruelle. This time she's published a story about piracy. I'm sure it's a plant for the *Demeter* lawsuit."

They heard a keyboard clacking as Astrid said, "It's coming up now."

Eyrún explained and added, "I thought she couldn't publish any more sensationalist lies."

"She can't. Not without consequences, but this article reads as factual."

"What about the tweets? My assistant has already got two calls."

"I'll get our team on it. Don't do anything. Darwin, you either," said Astrid, and promised to update them before the day's end.

"We won't," said Darwin. The call ended, and he added, "I still don't understand why Emelio doesn't pay these guys off. We've got a bigger problem with these diamonds."

"He—" Eyrún stopped and sipped her tea.

"He what? I asked Emelio the same thing the other day, and he said you were handling it."

Eyrún's insides churned. She hated keeping secrets from Darwin, but she'd promised Emelio. She'd talked to Astrid about using her money to settle the lawsuit, but the firm had advised waiting until it completed researching the Lacroix Shipping sale. So far, they'd learned that the Lacroixes had kept a seat on the board of directors. The fact that the acquiring company had shuttered didn't remove the liability.

Darwin pressed on, "I heard you and Zac talking about Emelio, but you changed the subject when you saw me."

Eyrún looked at her phone, searching for words to explain that might also not break Emelio's trust.

He put a hand on hers. "What is it, Love? Let me help you."

"I promised Emelio."

"Yes, you did, but he's my grandfather and a proud old man. Look, I love him and will do anything for him, but his vanity's always been a pain in the ass. My dad and I know he spent much of the trust chasing the Roman lava tube idea, but he won't let us help him, even as trustees. So please, you can tell me. What is it?"

She flushed. "Emelio didn't spend *much* of the trust. He spent all of it."

Darwin stared out the window as Eyrún drove them down the winding T20 to the ACA. Her revelation about the exhausted accounts had explained so much of Emelio's behavior over the last decade. He had avoided updating the trust documents after Darwin had secured his fortune. And two years ago, Darwin and Eyrún had offered to buy the mountain house at the market rate, but Emelio had said the trust forbade selling the properties. They settled on renting it for one euro per year and then spent €500,000 on remodeling.

It makes perfect sense, he thought, watching the pines give way to maquis. The house needed massive repairs. Emelio had explained its dereliction by saying he no longer wanted to go there after his wife died. But the remodeling revealed the eighteenth-century house had suffered decades of severe neglect even before that. Now he knew why. Emelio had no money to fix it.

He fumed at Emelio's obstinance, one hand squeezing the passenger door grip, his forearm muscles pulsing. *He could have asked me.* Now, the trust was empty, and the properties were exposed. *I could lose my family's legacy.*

Darwin ground his teeth. He understood all too well his grand-père's obsession with the lava tube hunt. He'd been consumed by it himself. *But would I have thrown away my family's fortune chasing that?* He thought not as they swept through the last wide turn off the mountain and onto the alluvial plain.

Siggy thumped his seat back. "Didn't you hear us, Darwin?"

"Huh? Sorry, I was thinking." He tuned into the conversation going on between the others.

"See. He does that," said Eyrún.

Zac joined in the gibing. "C'mon, Darwin's just better at mindfulness than the rest of us mortals."

Darwin flipped him off.

"Zac suggested a connection between the timing of your visit to Berkeley and the microphone being planted in the library," said Siggy. "What if someone in Berkeley tipped off the military?"

"It's possible," said Zac. "But suppose the microphones were there before. I mean, whoever's behind the lawsuits just happened to hear us talk about diamonds. Too bad Emelio didn't have a security camera on the house. We'd at least know what the guy looked like when he ran out."

"Oh, my God. I forgot. Astrid sent me a picture of the lawyer. Darwin, look at my phone," Eyrún said.

Darwin grabbed her phone from the cupholder and swiped into the photos app after tapping in her code. He held up a mug shot he didn't recognize.

"That's him," said Eyrún.

He handed the phone to Zac in the back seat.

"That's definitely not the guy who broke in," said Siggy.

50

Ajaccio

Eyrún pulled into the ACA car park, and the four got out to finish their conversation behind the SUV. Eyrún showed Siggy the photo again, emphasizing that the library had been dark during the fight.

"Not that dark," said Siggy. "This guy's got blond hair, and the guy I fought also had a thinner face."

Zac chimed in. "This has got to be connected to Carson. He's ex-military with a conviction for drug smuggling in Iraq. Bastard. His bullshit fueled the insurgents and put my team at risk, cleaning up the damage."

"Are you saying Mike hired someone to break in?" asked Eyrún.

"I'd bet on it. He pays a guy to plant microphones to get Emelio's reaction to the lawsuits. Instead, he overhears us talking about diamonds. Then he sends the guy back later to steal one," said Zac.

"But why not take all of them?" asked Eyrún.

Zac threw up his arms. "Probably hoped we wouldn't notice. They took one to shop it around, then tracked Siggy to CERN, which fueled their suspicions."

Darwin saw too much emotion and coincidence in the accusations. He had no other suspects in mind, but knew they needed more evidence to ground their assumptions. He pictured the library, the break-in, and the subsequent stalking of his sister-in-law. *Mike doesn't have enough to solve this either,* he reasoned. *What if they're still listening, hoping to catch something?*

"Wait," Darwin cut in. "The microphone's still in the library. Let's draw them out." He paused a beat, then continued, "Tonight after dinner, we go see Emelio. Then back at the house, we have a scripted conversation," he emphasized with air quotes. "Then we watch what they do."

"Good thinking. I like it," said Zac.

Siggy nodded in agreement.

"Then it's a plan," said Eyrún, checking her watch. "Let's review it over dinner. I've got a meeting in three minutes."

That night, after having their conversation for the microphone, Darwin left through the basement in Emelio's house. He thought their exchange had gone well and they should get a reaction from their two main points. Their first about fighting the lawsuits wouldn't be a surprise. But their made-up second point should—that the police had a video of the thief. Tomorrow, Eyrún, Siggy, and Zac would go about their normal business, while Darwin slipped away to Saint Catherine's Monastery to get a head start on finding the source of the diamonds.

During the eighteenth-century construction of the home in Ajaccio harbor and the mountain house, the Lacroixes built a safe room in each. Over the years, various generations had used the redoubts during incursions by pirates and, more recently, WWII combatants.

Darwin passed the safe room's living area and exited into an escape tunnel that split in two. He followed the left passage toward the basement in the house behind Maison Lacroix. He emerged from the cellar doors outside a home owned by Emelio's neighbor and lifelong friend, Mateo. Darwin rounded the house to a detached garage, where Mateo was cleaning the windscreen of a lemon yellow Citroën CV2—its engine running to warm up. Darwin, who'd learned to drive in this car, grinned at the throaty growl of its modified motor and a memory of his last ride in it. Eyrún had driven the Citroën, racing another car in a getaway.

"Hi Mateo," said Darwin.

"Darwin!" Mateo dropped the cloth on a workbench, and they embraced. The tall, lean man wore a black leather jacket, and a cap pulled low over his long white hair. "Giving someone else the slip, eh?" he asked after their greeting.

"You could say that," said Darwin, squeezing into the cramped back seat. Mateo tossed a blanket over him and then drove at a snail's pace. Mercifully, it was only four kilometers to the private air terminal, where Darwin thanked Mateo and waited in the hangar.

Minutes later, his phone chimed with a message from Richard Ndembele in Vatican City:

All set for tomorrow

Richard had arranged for Darwin to join a Vatican diplomatic visit to Israel, where he would slip away from the group at Tel Aviv's Ben Gurion Airport and board a tour bus to Saint Catherine's. The escape felt like overkill, but he wanted to return to Sinai without tipping off Mike Carson.

Zac had put out feelers to his former military-intelligence colleagues to get more background on Mike. At the same time, Eyrún had asked her lawyer, Astrid, to discover the identity of Mike's collaborators in the events that had led to his court conviction.

Darwin responded with thanks to Richard as a small jet drifted down the alluvial plain and landed on the main runway, disappearing behind the main terminal. A minute later, the plane taxied into view. Its white metallic paint glowed translucent as a pearl in the mix of yellow and white airport lights. At twelve meters, the Embraer Phenom 100EV was the smallest jet he'd ever seen. Its sharp nose and short body reminded him of a stubby pencil, albeit one with two engines and a carbon-fiber whale tail.

Nice. Goose flesh rose on his arms. He hadn't been looking forward to the lengthy bus ride tomorrow, but this would be a great start. The jet throttled to a whisper, and the stairs folded open as the pilot popped her head out. She waved him aboard, as he'd been told this would be a fast pickup.

"Welcome, Mr. Lacroix. It's just you to Rome," said the pilot as she stepped into the sleek jet and set his pack on a seat. Then she added, "Would you care to sit up front?"

"Absolutely!" He followed her into the cockpit and buckled into the soft fleece seat.

She dialed in the route and conversed with ground control as the engines spun up. Darwin surveyed the cockpit, taking in the three flat panel displays—his mirrored the pilot's to his left and currently showed the airport map and a digital instrumentation cluster. The center panel showed their route. While the pilot entered the flight coordinates, he imagined holding the video game-style yoke, but he kept his hands on his knees and instead scanned the airport through wraparound windows.

Seven minutes later, after waiting for a commercial flight, the Phenom shot out over Ajaccio harbor. Once at altitude over the Tyrrhenian Sea and the lights of the Italian coastline on the far horizon, the pilot asked, "Would you like to fly it?"

The plane handled like a dream, responding to the barest touch. Twenty-one minutes later, Darwin reluctantly let go of the yoke as the pilot took back control for the approach to Rome. His only regret was the shortness of the flight.

51

Paris

The following day, Ramy sat at the corner café, drinking coffee and scanning a newspaper. Cars hissed by on the wet pavement as he read the forecast for rain throughout the day. He laid down the paper and thought about the moment with Kim on the bridge. He'd tried fantasizing about her last night with a woman he'd brought home from a club, but it wasn't the same. It lacked real danger.

He was imagining finding the diamond cache and Kim offering herself as a reward for a job well done, when a passing scooter drove through a puddle and showered his shoes and pant legs with muddy water. Ramy swore and wiped them off with a napkin, then sat up and checked his phone. It had overlooked an alert—a new recording from the microphones he'd planted in the Ajaccio house.

He popped in noise-canceling earbuds and began listening to the same four voices as in the original recording. He closed his eyes to distinguish them better. One man spoke with a deeper voice, and he decided it was not the grandson. The women had the same lilt, and he found it impossible to tell them apart. He used a fifteen-second skip-ahead function until the lawsuits entered the conversation. Three minutes later, he paused the recording and messaged Mike:

Ramy: Where are you? You gotta hear this.

Mike: I'll be down after finishing an email

Ramy ordered two coffees and, when Mike arrived, gave him one earbud and played the relevant section together.

One woman said, "I got the research back from the lawyers today. It's nice work."

"And?" asked the other female voice.

The first woman continued, "A small-time American lawyer, Mike Carson, filed the suits and used a Paris firm to file with the French court. Our lawyer called the piracy case 'very creative' but hopeless to win."

"She said the paternity suit has potential. However, that many generations back would make the DNA evidence weak, even with birth certificates. Astrid recommends fighting both cases, as she suspects Carson has little money."

The porcelain cups clanged as Mike brought a fist down on the table. The man they figured as the grandson spoke next.

"I feel bad that my family screwed over an heir. What if we met with Mike to work something out?"

"What? For a damn ambulance-chasing lawyer?" said the deeper male voice, adding, "Did they say anything about the break-in? The coincidence still bothers me. I think it was this Carson dude."

"They sent a photo of the guy," said the first woman. The recording picked up a rustling sound before she added, "Here."

Mike's eyes widened.

"That's not him," said the second woman.

"Definitely not." The deep voice concurred. "The man we fought had a thinner face and dark hair. It was night, but I'm sure it's not this guy."

"What about the video we got from the neighbor's cameras? Have the police gotten anything yet?" asked the grandson.

"Soon. Astrid sent a copy to a security firm with state-of-the-art digital enhancement tools. They forwarded the enhanced video to Europol."

"How long until we have an ID?"

"End of the week. Astrid said Europol's backed up, but if there's any link between Mike Carson and the guy in the video, she said it's game over for his lawsuits."

Mike knocked over the chair as he stood, yanked out the earbud, and threw it at Ramy before stomping off.

Mike fumed as he walked fast, looking down at his feet. He had no destination in mind. *Just move.* He needed time to think to make sense of another of his life's opportunities gone bad. Ramy had followed him for a few blocks, insisting there was no way they could ID him from a video, but Mike ignored him.

Eventually, Ramy left him alone, and Mike turned into Père Lachaise cemetery. Its quietude fit his dark mood. At one point, he waited out a downpour under the eaves of a long-dead family's mausoleum, where he stared through the deluge at another tomb. Three minutes later, the rain passed, and he started up again, keeping to the street's center as the heavy drops splattered from the leaves in the wind that chased the storm.

He exited the cemetery, rounded Place de la Bastille and turned on another, more minor street alongside Canal Saint-Martin, its docks jammed with houseboats. Few people were about on the quiet weekday. He climbed a pedestrian bridge over the canal about halfway along its length. He stopped mid-span and stared at a woman feeding pigeons while his life's failure reel played: his miserable childhood; joining the army as a way of escape; and finding an aptitude for policing and law, only to make stupid decisions that landed him in prison.

Mike thought he'd turned things around by passing the bar, but found no one would hire an ex-con. This lawsuit was supposed to have set him up in his own practice, but now it too was fading. *Why can't I catch a break?*

A moment later, Mike realized he'd gotten a break when his grandmother left him the house and the documents, but he'd ruined it by reaching into his past for help. His head shook slowly. *God damn Ramy. I should never have trusted the son of a bitch.*

Two hours later, he found an envelope shoved under the door of his squat. "Shit!" He kicked it before picking it up, expecting a note telling him to vacate, but found a wad of euros and a message from Ramy.

Sorry, buddy. I didn't mean to screw up your deal. Here's €5,000 to offset your expenses.

Also, listen to the file I emailed to your secure account. You walked away before the best part. They said the American Department of Energy offered $50,000 a diamond. Looks like we can get the NKs to up their bid.

Mike counted the cash. It didn't cover all his expenses, but it was a good start. He didn't like the idea of dealing with the North Koreans, but it sounded like getting a large settlement from the Lacroix family could be more expensive than it would be worth.

52

Saint Catherine's Monastery

Darwin arose at Saint Catherine's monastery to a sun-filled valley and ran along the trail to Mount Sinai. Its day climbers had long departed, which left him mostly alone. He'd arrived late yesterday afternoon on a luxury tour that had taken some discomfort out of the six-hour journey. Four hours in, they'd reached the Sea of Aqaba. Its vast blue lulled him into daydreaming until a short stop at the Egypt border control. Once cleared, the coach zig-zagged in and out of sight of the water before climbing into the Sinai mountains. The extreme contrast between the ocean and the desert highlighted the precarious conditions of life in this part of the world.

After stretching, he showered, got breakfast, then sat in the olive garden to wait for the monks to complete their morning rituals. Small birds darted in and out of the protective canopy. A quarter-hour later, he headed to the library. Inside the fourteen-hundred-year-old hallways, candle wax and ancient wood smells permeated the dry air. Fine dust triggered a nasal itch, and he rubbed his nose to avert a sneeze. The high-desert climate created a favorable environment for preserving ancient manuscripts.

The librarian, Theophilus, whom he'd met at dinner, arrived a minute later. His sandals scuffed softly on the stone floor, and keys jangled on a ring affixed to his black habit. They greeted each other, and once inside the library, Darwin sat at a reading station under a light while the monk retrieved the other pieces of the stele.

"I trust all went well at the British Museum," he said, setting down a wooden box, tilting its cover, and placing the smaller pieces of the broken stele on a cloth.

"If you mean I'm not in prison, then yes." Darwin said, smirking, remembering how the guy had pushed his buttons the last time they'd met. He then placed the larger piece he'd taken from the British Museum on the table and watched as Theophilus fitted the two pieces together that formed the upper half of the stele and joined them to the lower.

Hathor's head slid perfectly onto her body and formed the final rectangular shape, slightly larger than the monk's palm. Four lines of script covered the two upper sections, but before Darwin could study them, Theophilus folded a cloth over the pieces and used it to turn them over. Darwin wriggled forward in his seat, half expecting him to put the whole thing back in the box. But he unfolded the cloth and leaned back.

The map was crude, almost childlike in its simplicity. An outline of the monastery walls marked with a simple cross sat at the rectangle's top, and halfway down, a sizable upside-down V had been marked with another cross. "We think that's Jebel Musa, Mount Moses," said the librarian. A few smaller upside-down Vs marked other mountains, and a north-south range dotted the stele's bottom left.

Darwin's stomach sank as he realized the completed map told him little more than he knew before. "You had me break into the British Museum for this?"

"You did that on your own, Monsieur Lacroix."

"That's bull—" he cut off the expletive in deference to the location. He took a long, slow breath and massaged one temple to soothe a throbbing vein. He also realized the monk's statement was technically true.

"We're sorry to disappoint you, but you presented too great an opportunity. It was the archbishop's idea," said Theophilus.

Darwin looked up, shooting icy daggers at the librarian.

"The pope said you are uniquely gifted at finding things. No?"

Darwin squinted. It was true—he'd been nicknamed The Great Finder for his preternatural ability to discover what others had overlooked—but what was this guy getting at? Theophilus remained poker-faced, and when it felt like he'd wait for eternity, Darwin responded, "I've heard people say it."

"Then we would greatly appreciate your help in solving a mystery." He flipped the stele back on its front side. "What do you see?"

Before concentrating on the script, Darwin studied Hathor, the colored gems, and the burning bush. "It's demotic, right?"

Theophilus nodded.

Darwin switched on his phone's light, leaned close to the letters, and then ran a finger along the stele's edge. Unlike the stele's other borders, it was sharp. "It's been broken. There must be another piece."

The librarian's beard expanded beneath a wide grin. He reached into the box and laid another identical rectangle next to the Hathor piece.

Darwin's eyes widened like saucers. "*Merde!*" He drew out the expression, forgetting his earlier trepidation.

Horus, the falcon-headed consort to Hathor, sat facing his partner on the opposing half. He wore a *pschent*, the double crown for the rule of upper and lower Egypt. Its inner white crown, shaped like a bowling pin, rested inside the scalp-tight cylindrical red crown. The god held out a bowl as if offering it to Hathor.

A half-dozen or so objects stood upright in the bowl, shapes that Darwin could only think to describe as penises. His face screwed up as he looked at the librarian.

"Yes," he said, "you can see why we've kept this hidden."

"This doesn't fit with the diamonds and the burning bush shape unless this represents some grotesque ritual," said Darwin, comparing the two gods on the stele again.

He noticed that the fracture line united three lines of characters flowing across the stele. He knew demotic—a cursive-like form of hieroglyphics—was used in the centuries before Christ. But in the Ptolemaic period, the Greeks had replaced it with Coptic. While he couldn't read the script, he knew the stele dated before the common era.

"Have you translated it?" he asked.

"No. I'm not a demotist," said Theophilus.

Darwin immediately thought of the purple lady. She'd mentioned being an expert in reading demotic. He snapped a picture of the complete stele and considered the odd puzzle before him.

"Maybe this represents an obscure esoteric cult? Alexandria's flow of people and ideas resulted in a collision of beliefs. But a mutilating sacrifice? That doesn't fit with anything Egyptian, Greek, or Roman I've seen."

Theophilus said, "Now you see why the archbishop wants you to look into it. And the piece you returned to us answers another question." He turned all the pieces over again and continued, "You see, we didn't know the monastery's relative orientation before. Now we see Jebel Musa directly south and," he pointed to the convergence of the mountains, "this place might have significance."

His finger paused over a single mark, cut with a deeper groove and somewhat apart from the others. "The Egyptians mined this area two millennia before Christ. Maybe this mountain has something to do with your diamonds?"

Darwin stared at the map. He'd have to compare this to Google maps to make any sense of it. *Hopefully, the demotic isn't just an incantation.* He looked at Theophilus. "Looks like I've still got my work cut out. How long can I use the library?"

"The abbot said as long as you like."

53

Ajaccio

Eyrún sat with Zac and Siggy as they scrolled through high-res satellite images. Zac had offered a bitcoin bounty to anyone in the OSINT, the Open Source Intelligence Network, who found evidence of meteorite impact in the Sinai Peninsula. The loose confederation used publicly available sources to uncover deception and misdeeds by corporations and governments.

Earlier, Zac got a ping from *obiwan43* with evidence of a crater rim near Khetiu Mafkat. By late morning, they'd arranged a compilation of images that showed a faint arc passing through the mountains.

Circling 200 kilometers above the Earth, the satellites created a unique viewpoint. This enabled a talented observer to composite the images captured in different spectra and to tease out what lay hidden from human view.

In this case, *obiwan43* had placed a purple arrow indicating the meteor's likely impact point in a mountainside. The images revealed the barest indication of a crater. Weathering over many millennia had formed deep wadis that washed away any evidence visible at ground level.

Eyrún pored over separate images that showed a circular difference in soil type. "They're talented and thorough," she said. "We need to sample the soil within the crater ring for microspherules. How close is it to the mine?"

"The problem is there are multiple mines," said Zac. "I'm looking at ground photos of entrances scattered across fifty kilometers."

Siggy spoke up. "Look at this." She zoomed in on another image taken from a satellite on a polar orbit whose primary purpose was to monitor the radiation from the Chernobyl reactor. Fortunately for them, its path from Antarctica northward went over the Red Sea on its way to Ukraine. "There's a faint radiation increase as the satellite passes over the impact zone here." Her finger hovered over the dark image with light yellowing.

They superimposed images, aligning them with GPS data, and found the yellow radiation signature beneath the purple arrow.

"Well, last time I saw X marks the spot was an Indiana Jones movie," said Zac.

"*The Last Crusade*. I loved that one where the smart German spy seduces both father and son," said Siggy.

"And they found the grail in Petra—the same part of the world as Sinai."

Zac and Siggy riffed on trivia before Eyrún said, "Enough! We'll have movie night later."

Siggy made a face at her older sister, and Zac laughed at the sibling skirmish.

Eyrún got them back on task. "Let's focus. If we think this is the likely location, how do we narrow down which mine?"

While Eyrún left to attend a meeting with a visiting dignitary, Zac and Siggy spent the next two hours comparing recent images of the mines near the impact spot with older images in NASA's Earth observatory image database.

"We've got forty-three tracks," Zac said, rubbing his eyes to relieve a mild headache.

The scarred landscape's grays and tans made it difficult to distinguish the features. In addition, the 3D images taken from varying directions caused the brain to mix up concave and convex. As a kid, Zac had always wondered why the moon had bubbles and craters until a teacher explained the visual mind fake.

Siggy moved the images into a computer folder while Zac set up a query using the powerful artificial intelligence application in the ACA's digital lab. The chief scientist, Lupita Kimani, was on holiday visiting her family in Kenya, but Zac was adept at working with her algorithms. He pointed the AI to the photos in the folder, tapped enter, and pushed back in his chair. When all looked in order, he stood. "Let's go outside. My eyes need a break."

"How long will it take?" Siggy asked as they walked onto the rooftop oasis.

"Not long. Couple of hours max."

They leaned on the teak counter at the roof's edge and looked over the harbor. The late afternoon sun cast long shadows across the water, and the onshore breeze broke its surface into a million sparkles. Tiny sailboats schooled like minnows near the large yachts anchored in the deeper water.

All was quiet except for the flap of the shade sails over the elaborate entertainment space used for exhibits and fundraisers or moments like this when employees needed a break. Siggy looked up as a jet's rumble drew her attention, and she followed its path toward the European continent. Her profile captivated Zac.

Look at those lashes, he thought, watching her dark hair feather in the light wind, one glacier blue iris just visible from his angle. And her gently sloped nose had a short kick out, like a ski jump.

Siggy drank from her water glass, and the swallowing motion drew Zac's eyes down to her shoulder, exposed from her sleeveless summer top. The memory of a former lover blossomed. She, like Siggy, was tall and dark-haired. But the hurt crushed the thought—she'd used him to deceive Darwin and Eyrún. The relationship had ended badly, and Zac still kicked himself for being so gullible, so blinded by the spectacular sex.

Siggy bumped his arm while putting her cup down. Zac reflexively pulled it in.

"Sorry," she said, smiling broadly.

He flushed. "No problem. Just tense," he said, glossing over the moment.

As if feeling the same, Siggy's gaze flitted down, then returned to the harbor. "Which dock has Eyrún's boat?"

Zac leaned into her as he pointed quayside. "That long one," he said.

She looked down the line of his arm. "I see it," she said, her cheek resting on his shoulder.

His pulse skipped a beat, and he let his arm drift down, but not before lingering on her scent: a mixture of hair products and a floral perfume. It was not the exotic muskiness of his former lover, but lighter, like a summer morning. He stole another whiff of her fragrance, trying to place it before mentally pushing away. *It's too soon.* He backed away from the counter. *Besides, she's Eyrún's sister.*

"Let's go see what the AI's turned up," he said, turning to the rooftop door.

Inside the dim computer lab, Zac was all business as he pored over the results. Eyrún had joined them a few minutes ago and looked over Zac's shoulder at the monitor.

"The AI graded the trails based on changes between the photos. Accounting for differences in time of day and the seasonal changes of the light angle, it found seven trails that have been traveled regularly, But …" He tapped on the keyboard and manipulated another image as he trailed off.

"But what?" asked Eyrún.

The screen zoomed out, and Zac answered. "The seven trails are all in the radiation zone, but spread across this terrain."

A triangular peak filled much of the screen, its sides wickedly steep. A wadi had carved the mountain, leaving treacherous cliffs. The seven trails led into different locations within the cliffs and mountain, each terminating high above the wadi's floor.

"The only way in is here." Zac zoomed out four clicks and indicated the serpentine canyon that fanned out near a dirt road. "That's about a five-kilometer hike, and that dirt track's a long way from anywhere."

"What's that?" Siggy pointed to a white rectangle.

Zac centered and zoomed in until the satellite image pixelated; then he backed off one mouse click.

"That's a minivan," said Eyrún. "And here," her finger moved along the wadi, "those look like people."

"Somebody's going there," said Siggy.

54

Saint Catherine's Monastery

Darwin had to admit Theophilus was a showman. *He could've just laid all the pieces on the table and let me have a go.* He smiled at the man's guile. A few minutes later, he stood, stretched, and glanced at the librarian across the room, reading glasses perched on his nose, tapping away at a computer. The oldest library in the world had digitized key content, and its global audience wanted access to more.

Darwin looked again at the stele and paused. *Wait. This picture of a plant with flames might not be related. We only assume so because the pieces were brought to a monastery with a history of a burning bush.* It was not the first time he'd succumbed to unconscious bias. He turned to Theophilus. "Do you have any idea where this stele was found?"

The man peered over his readers. "A cave, but that's all the librarian at the time documented. He didn't even record a date. I only discovered it by locating his name in the list of librarians. He served from 1623 to 1637."

"How did he get them?"

"A Bedouin from a clan living near the monastery found them. Unfortunately, the librarian was not curious and just filed them away. A remodel in the late eighteen hundreds brought them to light again. That's probably when someone took the photo you saw in the Berlin book."

Theophilus refocused on his emails, and Darwin returned to the stele. He accepted the plausibility of its local provenance. The Egyptians had run significant mining operations in Sinai and built at least one temple dedicated to Hathor.

Before his first visit, he'd read the monastery's history. Some of the local Bedouins, the Jebeliya, had descended from Roman soldiers who had come in the seventh century when Emperor Justinian commanded the monastery's construction. Over the centuries, the Jebeliya and the monks had developed a symbiotic relationship.

He ran a finger over the flaming plant on the Hathor stele as he considered the librarian's request—investigate whether the ancient Egyptians had found a similar burning bush. Again, bias suggested a connection. *But is it the logical leap*?

He looked in the direction of the basilica. It had been built around the bush's traditional location. *But that was over 2,000 years after Moses saw the bush.* He knew Christianity overlapped with the tail end of Egypt's Ptolemaic period as the Roman Empire took over. And by the time Justinian commanded the monastery's construction, Rome was in decline, and Egyptian mining in Sinai had long played out. *Way too much speculation and hopeful coincidence.*

He shifted to the Horus stele with its bowl of phallic objects. He'd heard of bizarre practices in ancient Egypt where the people had built elaborate and enigmatic monuments for four millennia. *But penises? Perhaps an abstruse ritual? I suppose anything's possible.* Darwin sat back, tapping a finger to his lips. *Who would know?* The face of Cardigan Ford popped into his head.

He'd met Professor Ford during his doctoral program at the University of California. He'd been named Cardigan because his upstate New York hippie mom liked the sweaters, and was a gifted storyteller whose lectures frequently had students rolling with laughter. But in Darwin's opinion, Cardigan was a first-rate thinker who wove a tapestry of eclectic ideas into his lectures and he sat in whenever possible. He now recalled one class billed as Egyptian exotic-erotic.

He googled "erotic papyrus" on his phone and followed a link to the Turin erotic papyrus. Found in Deir el-Medina, near the Valley of the Kings, the 3,000-year-old images depicted sex acts. Darwin remembered Cardigan describing the differing opinions about its purpose, but with no similar examples ever found, most historians attributed no meaning to it beyond erotica.

He considered this possibility for the phalluses on the Horus stele, but shook his head. *It doesn't fit. Horus offering a bowl of severed penises is way too twisted.* His eyes drifted from the bowl to Horus's crown. *Wait! The White Crown.* It had a similar phallic shape to the objects in the bowl. He remembered another of Professor Ford's lectures had suggested the Egyptians had experimented with hallucinogens.

What's that paper? He googled "Egyptian crowns esoteric" and sifted through the results. *There.* He clicked a link to the *Journal of Ethnopharmacology* and read its abstract. The author theorized the Egyptian White Crown symbolized entheogenic mushrooms. The paper argued that Egyptian high priests used psilocybin in their rituals. That little had been documented because a passage from the *Book of the Dead* explicitly stated: "Let no stranger anywhere have knowledge of it."

He looked at the stele again. *No, not phalluses. They're mushrooms. Now it makes sense.* The flowers above Hathor's crown were blue lotuses that signified a dream state, a rebirth, or enlightenment. Horus was offering a means to achieve an altered state of consciousness.

Darwin felt the pang that accompanied an impending discovery. He recalled Henri's journal, and how he wrote that the alchemist used ground mushrooms to fake a mystical experience. *The diamond's magnetic superconductivity is a magical prop.* He pictured Henri's lab under the mountain house and the bizarre trap he'd set up with the knight. *The psilocybins that overwhelmed Eyrún came from the same cave as the diamonds.*

He shivered.

Straight from the Book of the Dead.

55

Bacagno, Corsica

That night Eyrún, Siggy, and Zac had dinner at *I Mazzeri* in Bacagno. The bistro teemed with tourists, but the owner-chefs, Sylvie and Anne, always kept a table or two for locals. The warm evening air mixed with the cooler currents flowing off Mount Oro, shrouding them in a rich blend of maquis and roses from the patio's lattice. They had ordered appetizers and were well into their first glasses of a local white wine whose oily minerality flowed off the tongue, leaving the crispness of the ancient Roman grape on the palate.

"Mmmm," Eyrún sighed. The soothing hum in her chest deflated the day's tension. This was what she loved about Corsica, her adopted island home. It was French in administration but independent at its core—blending Genoese, Italian, French, and bits of North Africa—a waypoint in the Mediterranean. Isolated yet accessible. A peaceful place full of savage beauty. *Not unlike Iceland.*

She came out of her moment to Zac drumming fingers on the table in time with a gypsy jazz group whose tunes reverberated off the restaurant's back wall.

"Oh yeah," he said, "it's not every day you hear Django Reinhardt." He clapped loudly as the song ended. As the guitar player began a softer bluesy number, he turned to Eyrún. "Did Darwin answer?"

"Oh crap, I forgot. A call came in before we left."

"No worries."

Eyrún tapped out a message to Darwin about the mining location they'd found and sent it. She snorted at a random text offering lotto numbers as Siggy excused herself for the toilet. Eyrún dropped the phone in her purse and looked up to catch Zac lingering on Siggy's retreating figure. She'd been about to comment when appetizers arrived and, having not eaten since breakfast, dug in. A few minutes later, Siggy returned, and Zac excused himself. He dropped some euros in the tip jar as he passed the band.

When he'd disappeared inside, Siggy asked, "How long is Zac visiting?"

"I don't know. He comes and goes, even though he talks of settling down." Eyrún studied her sister's face. "Why?"

"No reason." Siggy swished back her remaining wine.

But Eyrún knew a covering move when she saw it. As the older, more reflective of the two, Eyrún had worked to alleviate Siggy's burdens when their father died. At times, Eyrún lived vicariously through Siggy's easy-going life and her brows knitted as a resentment resurfaced. The jealous protector pounced. "You said you needed space from Marcus before getting involved."

"I do, but you have to admit, Zac's gorgeous."

Eyrún had noticed. But she'd fallen for Darwin and now considered Zac like a brother. "I—"

Zac appeared behind her as the players launched into Minor Swing, Django's famous *pompe* driving the beat.

"C'mon." Zac grabbed Siggy's hand, and they joined other couples dancing in a tight space in front of the band.

Eyrún swayed as the sultry fiddle traded riffs with the guitar, and Zac spun her sister. She let go of trying to influence Siggy, deciding Zac could handle himself. A minute later, her soul reveled in the perfect evening. *Well, almost. It would be even nicer if Darwin were here.*

56

Saint Catherine's Monastery

Darwin walked among the olive trees enclosed within the monastery's protective walls. The vast peaks surrounding Saint Catherine cast the valley in darkness. At the end of one row of trees, he glanced up at the western sky. The massive black shape of Ras Safsara was framed by an indigo hue as the brightest stars winked on for the night. An owl's hoot startled him, and he tracked the sound to eaves that hung over the garden's wall. Another creature, a ground squirrel, he thought, rustled nearby as a different kind of night bird called from across the garden.

He'd spent the day following potential trails, but a link between the Egyptian esoterica and the diamonds had remained elusive. Early in the day, he'd avoided asking Theophilus for help as he sensed the man would laugh him off. But with multiple threads and no clear connections, Darwin decided to risk it. Unfortunately, the librarian had to attend afternoon prayers, which meant Darwin's time in the library had ended for the day.

He rounded another row of trees nearer the monastery guest rooms when Eyrún's ringtone sounded on his phone. His heart jumped. She'd broken the communication silence. He grabbed it out of his back pocket and, squinting against its harsh glare, read:

Eyrún: Found it. See usual location

A little cryptic, he thought, but she'd also sent a photo of Zac and Siggy dancing with a caption:

Wish you were here

He recognized the patio at *I Mazzeri* and sighed. While entranced by research and, most of the time, comfortable in the solace of his internal universe, a twinge in the back of his throat reminded him that everything he truly cared about was in Corsica. He replied:

It's beautiful here, but missing you

He returned the phone to his pocket and headed to his room, where he could use his laptop to view what Eyrún had put in a cloud storage folder. They used this dropbox to share files without having to send links that could be intercepted.

Paris

Later that night, Ramy sat in a nightclub with a woman who said she was from Toronto. His phone, face-down next to his drink, buzzed. He flipped it over.

Kim: He's in Sinai - Saint Catherine's monastery

Ramy: what's there

Kim: Don't know yet, following his trail

Ramy: how did you find him

When no reply came back, he put it down and watched his date snap selfies using the brightly lit bar as the backdrop. The phone vibrated again.

> Kim: meet tomorrow, bridge, 0930, i'll know more then

Ramy figured Kim had compromised Darwin's phone. *Probably mine as well,* he thought, stuffing it in his jacket. A quick look at his watch brought a frown to his face. Kim's meeting time meant it would have to be an early night.

The Toronto woman adjusted her ample breasts for another selfie. She caught him looking and smiled. *Or maybe not,* he decided, and whispered something suggestive in her ear.

She moved a hand to his inner thigh and squeezed, pulling him along as she slid out of the booth.

Ajaccio

"I hate these," said Eyrún while checking for a message from Darwin.

"What?" asked Siggy.

"I got another junk text offering winning lotto numbers. I deleted one earlier at the restaurant."

"Ha! I think I got the same one," said Zac, holding up his phone.

They'd crashed on the big leather chairs surrounding the fireplace in the mountain house. Eyrún had switched on the gas, and the warmth from the blue-orange flames drove back the coolness. The maquis-tinged air wafted through the open patio doors, bringing with it a cacophony of crickets from the gorge.

Siggy sat up and grabbed her phone from the table. She looked at it and said to Zac, "Let me see your phone." He handed it to her. "Shit. I've seen this before. It's no coincidence."

Zac sat up, pulling his feet off the table. Siggy motioned for Eyrún's phone and laid them side-by-side. She tapped the info button for each message and discovered the one on all three devices had arrived from the same number. "Pegasus!" she spat. "The Syrian government used this on us in the refugee camps."

"Hang on, it could be a clever spammer," Zac said.

"I don't like it," said Siggy, crossing her arms.

"What's Pegasus?" added Eyrún.

Siggy looked at Zac with a you-tell-her expression.

"It's spyware developed by an Israeli cyber-arms company. Hackers use it to gain zero-touch access to devices," he said.

Eyrún's eyebrows shot up.

He added, "It means you don't have to do anything. Just getting a text from Pegasus infects a device without requiring user action."

"How do we know for sure?" asked Eyrún.

"Does Darwin still have the spare laptop?"

Eyrún nodded. Zac asked her to get it, explaining he could use it to determine if their phones had loaded Pegasus.

While Eyrún got the laptop from the downstairs office, he and Siggy refilled their water glasses in the kitchen. When Eyrún returned, Zac turned on the laptop, plugged his phone into its USB port, and kicked off an encrypted backup. While that ran, he asked Siggy if the Syrians had done anything with the hacking.

Her expression darkened. "We don't know. It was chaos. We knew ISIS had infiltrated the camp, but could not distinguish the scared, helpless men looking for their families from the terrorists. Only after several prominent people had been killed did one of our technicians suspect our phones had been hacked. She found Pegasus and traced it from our phones to one of the murdered leaders."

"You never told me." Eyrún put an arm around her sister's shoulder.

"It was horrible. I should—" Siggy's hands went to her face as she broke down in tears.

Zac knew immediately. He'd seen this with one of his team in Afghanistan who'd befriended an informant. He caressed her shoulder and said, "They tracked him through your phone."

Siggy nodded.

He slipped his arm below Eyrún's, and they held Siggy until her sobs quieted. The gentle hiss from the fire and the crickets were the only sounds. Siggy took a ragged breath, huffed a sigh, and sat up.

"You couldn't have known," said Zac.

Eyrún added, "No, Siggy, you couldn't. It wasn't your fault."

"I know," she whispered. "But I hated it. I still hate it. It's why I left." Her voice gained venom.

Eyrún suggested a calming tea and set the kettle on, while Siggy talked about the experience. Zac listened as the encrypted backup finished and downloaded another developer app he needed for the next steps. Eyrún returned with the tea and sat close to Siggy. Zac's fingers danced across the keyboard, text flowing in multiple windows on the laptop screen.

"He's done a lot with our AI," said Eyrún.

Zac entered a script command and hit the return key. Lines of text spun like the numbers on a petrol pump. He turned to the sisters. "Okay, so I got Amnesty International's tool that checks for Pegasus. Whatever it finds will dump into this file." He pointed to an empty window titled *pegasus.stix2*.

Not a minute later, it filled, and Zac parsed the text. "It drops a GPS query, then forwards all messages to a server at this IP address," he said, highlighting a number string. "But then Pegasus raids the phone's contacts app and sends a copy of itself to everyone."

"Wait. What?" said Eyrún. "I got one earlier at the restaurant before I messaged Darwin."

"Whoever this is, they now know where he is," said Zac.

"Oh, my God!" Eyrún's hand went to her mouth.

57

Serabit el-Khadim, Sinai

Darwin left the monastery at dawn, bound for Serabit el-Khadim. His investigation yesterday had pointed to the ancient Egyptians' extensive turquoise mining operations. The initial modern work had been done by Sir Flinders Petrie, a legendary force in Egyptology whom some called the father of archaeology. Darwin liked to think of himself in the same pioneering spirit as Petrie, but he also thrived on what he called Howard Carter moments—those once-in-a-lifetime chances to find what no one had seen for millennia.

As the minibus sped north along the paved road, Darwin drifted into lucid dreams, mainly of his discoveries. He pictured Eyrún, whom he met in Iceland when they discovered a massive lava tube. She'd become his partner in the later discoveries in Alexandria and a Templar's hoard in France. They'd founded the Agrippa Center for Archaeology to foster the importance of their shared past and train archaeologists from countries with little means or interest. While he and Eyrún each had a rich life apart from each other, he hated being unable to communicate with her.

Another vision of Eyrún appeared at the flybridge controls of her powerboat, Hypatia, driving full-throttle. Dark glasses shaded her eyes, and a colorful cover-up protected her Nordic complexion from the blazing sun. The thirty-six-knot wind whipped her ponytail and billowed the coverup like a cape, making Eyrún appear every bit the superwoman he envisioned. She turned and smiled broadly as the boat hit a wake, tossing them into the air.

His head banged on the minibus window, jerking him awake. They'd left the pavement and now were bucking their way up a dirt track. He gripped the handhold for the next twenty minutes until they rolled to a stop in an arid landscape that looked much the same as Saint Catherine's rough terrain. Ancient seas had eroded the peaks and plateaus, leaving horizontal ridges of harder rock and bands of colored bands soil. Scant plant life appeared like stubble on a lightly bearded man.

Darwin fell in with the others behind the guide as they hiked up to the mining camp's remains. The sun seared any bare skin, but the air was temperate. Once at the sprawling mining site, he surveyed its jumble of carved blocks. Overall, the site had been so trodden upon it was hard to make sense of its original layout. Dozens of stele stood amidst the rubble, some twice his height. Many had been repaired, and he quickly determined that most had been re-erected in modern times as the site had evolved into a tourist destination.

Paris

Ramy downed a third espresso, this one from a pop-up vendor on the river walk along the Seine's right bank. He was five minutes late but needed the pick-me-up from his late night with the Toronto woman. She'd pouted when he got up for the meeting, but smiled and rolled up in the sheets when he said he'd be back in an hour.

Kim stood in the same spot he'd met her the other day and was taking photos with her phone. She wore a dress in a nod to the heat wave already bearing down at this early hour. He dropped the cup in a bin next to the cart, rolled his shoulders, and strode onto the bridge. Fatigue and injury, even if self-inflicted from too much drinking, were not excuses in the special forces. You made the team because, short of death, you performed.

The planked surface of Pont des Arts bustled with tourists snapping photos as a barge passed beneath. Summer was his least favorite season in Paris—it was too hot and overrun with foreigners. But he appreciated the women's summer fashions. Kim turned toward him and smiled.

Ramy drank in her more relaxed appearance—a pleated skirt with a dark floral pattern and a sleeveless cross-front bodice. Black platform sandals brought her to his height. Her broad shoulders and well-toned arms telegraphed the time spent in the gym.

She dropped the phone in her bag and greeted him brusquely. "You're late. Don't make a habit of it."

Any excuse would show weakness, so he glossed over it. "What did you find out?"

"The files we traced from his wife's phone tell us they know about the tokamak. And they went to an American nuclear research facility in addition to CERN."

"The Americans must be bidding." He smiled inwardly. *She doesn't know about their visit to the American base in Germany or their $50,000 offer.*

"Possibly," she said. "We need to know what Darwin knows. We leave for Cairo at two. I sent you the flight info. And do yourself a favor: send the Canadian woman home." She smiled pleasantly, but Ramy thought he detected malice.

Or maybe jealousy? His eyes wandered down to her taut midsection. She turned and strode toward the left bank. He retreated and, while walking to his flat, imagined Kim in place of the dark-haired woman waiting in his bed.

Mike finished packing his bag. He'd had it with Ramy's scheming and decided to part company. He wanted no part in North Korean espionage. That road only led to the life he wished to escape.

The door burst open.

Police in riot gear swarmed in, shouting at him. Assault rifles pointed at him from three sides. He couldn't understand a word, but the gun barrels spoke clearly, and he prostrated on the floor.

After the intruders had subdued him, Mike asked, "What's going on?"

"Shut up," a voice came from above the knee in his back.

Rapid conversation flowed between the cops as they packed up Mike's things. Moments later, a young cop walked into the flat and read Mike what sounded like rights.

"What do you want?" Mike asked repeatedly, but after a few minutes, he decided silence was his best option. They bundled him down the stairs and into a waiting van.

At the police station, Mike repeated, *"Je veux un avocat!"* until he was blue in the face, but his request for a lawyer fell on deaf ears. Finally, the same young cop from the flat told Mike he was being held on terrorist charges.

"Why?"

No one answered him. Once, he risked asking for Ramy, only to be informed that the police also sought him. The hellish morning ended with the young cop telling Mike that an English-speaking public defender would come.

"When?"

"Soon."

They shut him in a cell, where after pacing for a while, he lay on the bench to wait.

Damn Ramy! I should've known.

Ramy chased the Toronto woman from the flat, saying he had another meeting that afternoon. He checked his phone—still no reply from Mike. While returning from the meeting with Kim, he'd messaged Mike that they needed to go to Sinai.

He went next door to Mike's flat and rang the bell, hearing it echo inside. He rang again. "Mike? You in there?" Still nothing.

Ramy checked his watch. Ten past noon. There was no time to find Mike and make the flight to Cairo. *He'll get the message and catch up with us later*. It was not the first time they'd improvised on a mission. He returned to his flat and finished packing his case.

An hour later, he checked in at the Egypt Air counter using his Algerian passport and found that Kim had arranged for a diplomatic escort to whisk him through security. At the gate, she frowned at his arrival as the first boarding group was called. *Clearly, "on time" for her meant early.* Ramy lived in the moment, and arriving early to wait meant time wasted.

As the flight was pushed back, Ramy checked his phone once more. No Mike.

"Looking for someone?" Kim asked.

"My colleague, Mike. The one who started all this. He should be going with us."

"Mike's American."

"He's a mercenary. He doesn't give a shit about the Americans. They screwed him over."

"He's a liability."

Ramy shifted in his seat, eyes burning into hers.

"Not to worry. He's come to no harm, he'll just be out of pocket a few days."

Meaning, what? Ramy sat back, gripping the armrest like he wanted to rip it from the plane. *Something's not right. Out of pocket? That's not like Mike.* He tried calming himself, taking deep breaths behind closed eyelids, when he felt Kim's cool, soft hand atop his. Her slender fingers slid between his, gently caressing.

"He'll be fine," she said. "Split the money with him after we find the diamonds. My superiors didn't want to take the risk with any Americans."

Ramy lifted his hand as Kim removed hers. He flexed his fingers, the blood flow returning. *Maybe this is for the better. Mike had been balking at the North Koreans, anyway.* He turned and smiled at Kim, whose mouth turned up into dimples. *With Mike not here, I've got more chances with her.*

58

Serabit el-Khadim

Darwin fought off disappointment at finding no useful clues. The mine had thrived during the Egyptian Old Kingdom, but 4,000 years later, most movable pieces had been hauled off to museums. He unfolded a copy of a nineteenth-century map of the site made by a Prussian expedition and its artist's depiction of how it must have looked. These gave him a better idea of Hathor's once bustling temple layout.

But nothing aided his interpretation of the twin stele with Hathor and Horus. He looked around again, remembering Theophilus had said a Bedouin found the stele in the seventeenth century. *This place was long dead by then. It's got to be closer to the monastery. And the paint on the stele would have long burned away in this unprotected ruin.*

While he'd not expected a revelation here, he knew ideas came to him when he kept in motion—a change of perspective and point of view. Studying and thinking only got him so far. *No,* he looked to the south, *the stele didn't come from here.* Serabit el-Khadim was under a hundred kilometers from Saint Catherine's Monastery as the crow flies. But he let that thought go, as the direct route would be challenging.

Even if someone found the stele here, why would they take it to the monastery? The Red Sea trading routes are closer.

He finished lunch and set aside the stele search to pursue his other reason for coming here—to see a rock cut with ancient graffiti.

Darwin had studied Canaanite while pursuing his advanced degrees and longed to see the earliest example of the modern alphabet. Ten minutes later, he found the spot where prisoners of war, forced to work the mines, had scratched a proto-Sinaitic script in the rocks. The enslaved people had reworked Egyptian hieroglyphs into symbols representing the Semitic language they spoke.

He sat before the stone, trying to imagine the people who had done this. After toiling on the massive temple all day, they had retreated here instead of sitting with the others. *How long did they work on this?* He knew it couldn't have been a lone genius because these scratches had lived on to become the root of Phoenician and Greek alphabets. *No. They didn't just scribble a hundred characters like Twitter and hope it went viral.* They had to socialize it.

People had been speaking forever and had drawn pictures—like cave paintings—to represent stories. Egyptians refined their version of the concept with hieroglyphs. But humans spoke in syllables and pictograms numbered in the thousands. The breakthrough came when clever writers used existing pictograms to represent sounds, not objects. A bee drawing next to a chair could be sounded as *bee-ch*.

Darwin sat in wonder at the proto-script these enslaved people had created. The ancient B symbol replaced the bee picture, and characters for C H combined to make the sound, chair. He smiled at this root of the western alphabet scratched into rock over 140 generations ago.

He leaned back against the smooth rock and sighed, knowing most people didn't share his excitement. The sheer density of human history meant most teaching had to gloss over most topics to cover the curricula.

The early morning start and rich lunch combined with the warm afternoon soon tugged at his eyelids, and he drifted off to sleep.

Cairo

An hour after landing in Cairo, Ramy navigated out of the airport and onto the eight-lane Suez Road. The oppressive daytime heat had lifted somewhat as they'd transferred from the terminal's conditioned air into the garage, where he'd settled behind the wheel of a Toyota Land Cruiser—the twenty-first century's camel.

"He's in Serabit el-Khadim,' said Kim.

"What's there?" asked Ramy as Kim entered the GPS coordinates into the car's navigation system.

"My people say it's an old Egyptian mine. Hurry up."

Ramy accelerated through the light eastbound traffic. The nav showed four hours and twenty minutes to Serabit el-Khadim. "We'll need petrol and a food stop," he said, scrolling ahead on the map. "There," he pointed. "We'll stop in Watanya before the road tunnels under the Suez Canal."

He glanced at Kim, tapping away in Korean on her mobile. She'd spoken little since landing, which was okay with him. While he'd bagged some sleep on the four-hour flight, the previous night's fun had begun to drag on him.

They passed an exit for Madinaty. A Starbucks coffee sign next to a Total Energy petrol stop showed the West's creeping influence. He'd been here three years ago to visit a former commander who'd also left Algeria. The man had lived in a five-bedroom house on a golf course that looked like a wealthy suburb in the American southwest. Manicured lawns and lush vegetation had surrounded the homes that wrapped around a similarly verdant course. Fountains spouting from a large lake that ran alongside the fairway behind his house had betrayed little of the desert wasteland a mere hundred meters beyond. In contrast, the ancient Egyptian canals stayed closer to the Nile River, and modern technologies allowed for much farther movement of fresh water.

Minutes later, the developments that had sprouted around New Cairo City receded into the distance. They'd reach the next bit of civilization in thirty kilometers. Ramy set the cruise control and made a mental list of what to buy. While roads had penetrated the ancient trade routes in the decades following the modern conflicts, oases were still few and far between.

59

Paris

Mike woke at a noise outside the prison cell door. His left shoulder had gone numb at being draped over his eyes to block out the stark ceiling light. He turned on his side, and swinging his feet to the floor, pushed upright. A glance at his bare wrist told him they'd even taken away his ability to know the time.

The door opened, and the jailers escorted him to an interview room where a young woman rose to greet him. "*Bonjour,* Monsieur Carson. I am Annette Leclerc. Have you been treated well?"

Mike shook her offered hand. "Bonjour Mad—" He looked for a ring, but she beat him to it.

"It's *mademoiselle,* but please call me Annette." She motioned for him to sit and requested the jailer leave them. When the door closed, she asked, "What have you been told?"

"Very little—a vague description of terror charges."

"The police said they received a tip about a terrorist operation in the building you were staying in. Do you know anything about that?"

"No."

"Were you staying there legally?"

Mike explained the situation where Ramy was watching the building and had offered him a flat.

"Hmmm." Annette made a note and said, "Your friend Ramy had no such arrangement with the building's owner."

Mike squeezed his fists and stared down at the table. *Christ! I should've known.* Ramy had been the one who set up similar fronts for their criminal work in Afghanistan. *What other lies did he tell?*

"The investigating officers will interview you in a few minutes. You may be familiar with the process, but under French law, you do not have the same individual rights as you do in America. This will go best if you cooperate. The police can hold you here for forty-eight hours without charging you and the prosecutor decides if there is enough evidence to convict you. Do you understand?" she asked.

"Yes."

"Okay, in the few minutes before the investigating officer gets here, please tell me why you're in Paris. They'll ask you the same question, but I need to know ahead of time so I can best help you."

He gave her a compressed version, but left out Ramy's break-in of the Corsica house.

During the interrogation, the investigator, a middle-aged woman in a gray suit who reeked of cigarette smoke, went through preliminary questions, then asked him what he was doing in Paris.

Mike laid out his story as suggested by Annette, beginning with his rehabilitation, studying law, and struggle to gain employment in America as an ex-con. Then he covered his grandmother's death, explaining how her papers pointed to a potential inheritance and how he had filed lawsuits against the Lacroixes. Finally, he described hiring his former colleague, Ramy, as a translator.

"But," said Mike, wrapping up, "I needed help to file lawsuits in France and Ramy introduced me to a lawyer."

The investigator asked him the name. "It's in the court record of the lawsuits," answered Mike.

"I know, but this will save me time," she said.

He gave it. The investigator wrote it down, then asked, "Ramy's payment for assisting was to be a part of any settlement you'd receive. Correct?" When Mike said yes, she continued, "And what role did he play after that?"

Mike sensed a leading question and thought quickly of the last recording where the Lacroixes talked about the break-in and possible video ID of Ramy. *Did Europol recognize him? Probably. An Algerian with a criminal past.*

But the terror charges didn't make sense. *They must have something else.* He was about to respond when the investigator waved her fingers in a "gimme" motion to her associate, who produced Mike's phone.

"If you came here only to file lawsuits, how can you explain the picture the police found on your phone? Our expert described it as, erm," she paused, flipping back a page in her notebook, "a plasma field for a nuclear device."

Mike closed his eyes and sighed heavily. "It's a misunderstanding. I can explain."

"I'm listening. And it's best if you tell us the truth. Your American justice department shared your conviction for smuggling." The investigator folded her hands on the table's edge and leaned in, her breath like a chimney. "I have to say, Mr. Carson, it doesn't look good for you: a felon, pictures of nuclear material, and illegal squatting with an Algerian who's texting a North Korean operative."

Annette interrupted, holding a palm toward Mike. "Don't respond to that." Then she asked the investigator, "May I have a word with my client alone?"

The woman shrugged and left the room. When the door closed, Annette turned to Mike. "What's this about?"

"It was Ramy's idea. He went to Corsica to learn more about the Lacroix family. I had no idea he broke in and planted a microphone."

"And the picture?"

"I looked it up on the Internet. When I heard them talking about a toroidal field, I googled it. The photo's a screen capture."

"What's a toroidal field and what were they talking about?"

Mike explained what Ramy had stumbled into during his visit to

Corsica. She advised him to come clean about everything. He agreed, and she knocked on the door to let the investigator know they were done.

Once she sat down, Mike started his explanation. "I needed first-hand knowledge of the Lacroixes. Ramy was only supposed to gather facts about their current wealth."

"And to plant listening devices in their house," said the investigator.

"Of course not. That's illegal," said Mike, knowing how the game was played—claim the legal and moral high ground.

"But you listened to the recordings?"

"Yes. They talked about diamonds that acted like superconductors. That's when I learned about the toroidal field. But," Mike jabbed a finger at the table, "I told Ramy to stop. I had no interest in diamonds."

"But you knew he went to Algeria?"

"No. Only when he returned."

"What about meeting the North Koreans in Paris?"

"I told him to walk away. I wanted nothing to do with the hermit kingdom—the North Koreans. Look, it's Ramy you should be after, not me. Listen to the recordings. They talked about superconducting and nuclear fusion, not bombs. "

"We are looking for him, Mr. Carson. But before we go, can you tell us why Ramy wanted you to join him in Sinai?"

"What! When did he go there?" Mike looked between Annette and the investigator, who held up Mike's phone so he could read the messages from Ramy.

Mike looked, then said, "I've no idea what Ramy's doing there. Like I said before, I told him I wanted nothing to do with the North Koreans. Listen, I broke the law in Afghanistan and served my time, but I'm no traitor to my country."

At this point, Annette suggested an end to their meeting, saying she would confirm Mike's statements with the lawyer who helped him file her lawsuits as well as the Lacroix's Paris law firm.

"As will we," said the investigator, fingers drumming nervously on the table as if she needed to get to her nicotine fix.

When the police had left, Annette told Mike, "I'll return tomorrow. If there's anything else I should know, here's my card. You are allowed to call your lawyer."

60

Serabit el-Khadim

Just after midnight, Ramy reached the car park at the base of the old mine. Two minivans and another Land Cruiser sat silent, and a quick reconnoiter determined that no one had made a camp nearby. They figured whoever had come in the vehicles must be near the mine and temple.

"Darwin's GPS is still up there," said Kim.

"Let's get some rest," said Ramy. "First light's in four hours." He flattened the rear seats and fashioned a sleeping surface as best he could.

Kim kicked off her boots and lay down on her side, facing the passenger side door. Ramy settled on his back and listened to the night sounds. A jackal howled, joined by another, and the strange human-infant-like squeals echoed in the wadi. As tired as he was, the heat and Kim's soft breathing kept sleep at bay.

Paris

The nightmare closed around Mike again as they put him in a dark community cell that reeked of unwashed men. The other prisoners shifted as he moved into the cell, self-separating like strangers in an elevator until each sat or stood equidistant. None dared more than a furtive glance at the others. One man stood by the door murmuring while rhythmically banging his forehead on its frame.

Mike rested his head against the concrete wall. *God dammit.* He'd spent the last hour envisioning the violence he'd inflict on Ramy when they next met. *But first I have to get out of here.* He went through the investigator's questioning again, trying to determine what they had on him. *What lies did you tell, Ramy?*

Mike had been so focused on replying to the Lacroixes' lawyers that he'd paid scant attention to Ramy's visit to Algeria. His guard had gone up when Ramy mentioned the North Koreans, but he'd heard so much bullshit that he figured it was all talk.

But his message said to meet "us" in Cairo. Who else could "us" mean but the North Koreans? His eyes popped open. *Shit! They're after Darwin. If they kill him, my money's gone. I need him alive. Better still, I need Eyrún to know I helped keep him alive.*

He sprang from the bench. All heads turned at the abrupt movement. The man at the door backed away from Mike's swift approach.

"Guard," said Mike, pounding on the door. "I need to talk to my lawyer."

61

Serabit el-Khadim

A shove to his shoulder followed by, "Let's go," woke Ramy from a hard sleep. Kim was up, boots on, and, from the look of it, had been exploring the area. Ramy stretched and winced at an ache that seemed to run the length of his body. He rolled on his side and tugged up his knees before sitting up. Two minutes later, he relieved himself behind one minivan and returned to their car. Kim had laid out a water bottle next to his pack.

"He's still there. It's three kilometers to the mine," said Kim as she headed up the trail.

Good morning to you too, thought Ramy, drinking long from one bottle before shouldering the pack. He started up after Kim, and a few hundred meters into the steady climb, his body had shaken off sleep. He fell in a few strides behind her and matched her gait. She'd gathered her hair in a ponytail and dressed in a black tank top for the heat, her muscular shoulders glistening in the dawn light.

He considered the mission so far. *This seems too easy. Darwin finds the mine with diamonds. We capture it. Kim pays me.* His gut burned with something other than indigestion from the energy bar he'd eaten a few minutes ago. *Nothing ever goes this smoothly.* He thought of Kim on her phone. *Who's she texting? Where are they?* If he'd learned anything in special forces, it was that plans only worked on paper.

The sun breached the far mountains, its extreme angle blinding them. Ramy donned a ball cap and dark glasses against the visible light, but felt the infrared energy penetrate his skin. In another hundred meters, they traversed carved steps where centuries of weathering and countless feet had worn the rock. Not long after, the trail leveled, and they came upon a vast field of shaped stones. Parts of the walls stood, but overall it appeared like a massive hand had swatted a Lego creation.

Kim made straight for a series of tents, and a dozen people gathered around a camp stove. Most of them were dressed in Western fashion, and half had light-colored hair. Ramy surmised they were Europeans and went to a man crouched over one stove, tending to a pot.

"*Sabah al-kheir*, good morning," said Ramy.

"*Sabah al-noor*, morning of light," the man replied.

Ramy squatted next to him and asked about the group he was hosting. They talked a few minutes before Ramy thanked him, "*Shukran jazeelan*," and rejoined Kim.

"Where is he?" she asked.

"I don't know," said Ramy, "The guide says these people are from Denmark. They arrived yesterday."

Kim studied an app on her phone, then pointed. "Over there." She strode toward the forest of the stele that marked the temple ruin, holding her satellite phone like a divining rod. Then she angled away from the site and darted beneath a large rock.

Ramy followed her and found her probing a hand width gap in a rock. "It's in there. I see it," she said.

Ramy peered in and saw a metallic reflection from Kim's light.

"Looks like an iPhone," he said, scrutinizing at the crack. Ramy tried moving the rocks that trapped the phone, but determined he'd need a substantial pry bar to open the space enough to get a hand in.

"Why would he leave it here?" she asked.

Saint Catherine's Monastery

Darwin looked at his iPad at breakfast, trying to figure out how to dispose of it. Yesterday evening he'd used it to check messages and email, figuring that Pegasus had infected it. All his devices synchronized, so when Eyrún texted him from *I Mazzeri* restaurant, it went to his phone and tablet.

He'd been angry at losing his iPhone at Serabit el-Khadim, but now it seemed prescient. When the tour assistant had roused him to leave the day before, he'd run to the minibus, where the other travelers were grumbling. A half-hour down the road, he patted his empty pocket and discovered his phone was missing. The driver said it was too late to return and he would look for it on the next day's tour.

His iPad had full mobile access and could function as a phone if needed, but Eyrún's email stated that Pegasus had planted a GPS tracker and the North Koreans were looking for him.

I need to hide it. He thought of the Bedouin workers at the monastery, but realized they lived less than ten kilometers away. *That won't give me enough time. I need them thinking I went somewhere else.*

Laughter from across the room drew his attention to a group heading back to Tel Aviv today. On a whim, he approached the Israeli tour guide who'd arrived with him on the luxury bus. He'd suspected she was a member of the Israeli security force from the way she regularly surveyed her surroundings. Less curious. More purposeful.

He walked over and introduced himself and asked if they might talk in private. Once outside, Darwin used his Vatican credentials as the cover, saying he was working to bust a ring of antiquities thieves funneling the money back to North Korea. He needed her help to draw them out into the open.

An hour later, after verifying Darwin's background and running the iPad through a portable scanner she carried on the bus, she'd agreed to take his iPad to Tel Aviv. He loathed losing a second device, but could think of no other diversion.

62

Serabit el-Khadim

Kim and Ramy returned to the man, now cleaning up from breakfast. A faint breeze stirred the tepid air, rippling the colorful tent fabric. He offered them tea and said his partner was leading the Danes on a tour. Ramy offered an energy bar that the man accepted.

Over the next half-hour, the man explained the site and the plethora of mine shafts scattered across its many hectares. They talked about the tour business and that his family had done this for years.

"It's more lucrative than the dirt farming my grandfather used to do. What is the Chinese woman looking for?" the man asked Ramy.

Ramy answered she was investigating the mining potential and translated for Kim, who had been listening while peering into her sat phone. She used the man's question to probe if any of the mines were still active.

"Not that I know of," he said. "There's more money in bringing people up here and much less dangerous work."

Kim swore. "He's at the monastery."

"What?" Ramy turned. "But his phone's here."

"He's got an iPad. At least, that's what my techs told me. He turned it on at the monastery. We need to go. Now," she added when Ramy hesitated.

He ran after her. The trail that had been a mild hike in the dawn air now radiated like a pizza oven. Forty minutes later, his sweat-soaked shirt clung to him as he steered them out of the mountains toward the road to Saint Catherine's.

Ramy kept the Land Cruiser over 140 km/h, sometimes faster, but they'd entered the mountains, and the road hugged the contours.

Kim blurted halfway to Saint Catherine's, "He's moving again."

"Where's he going?" asked Ramy.

"He turned east on the, er, Saint Katherine-Nuweibaa Road," said Kim. "We should make that junction in—"

"Twelve kilometers," said Ramy, pointing at a sign. They rounded a curve, and he stomped on the brakes. "Shit." A tour bus ahead of them lumbered along at 50 km/h, dark exhaust spewing from its tailpipe.

"Pass it!"

"I can't." Ramy waved a hand at the road winding through blind curves.

Kim kept moving her head left and right, trying to see a place to pass. Finally, the road leveled and straightened out, going into the junction. Ramy shot around the bus and, minutes later, just before the turn, he pulled into a petrol station.

"What are you doing?" Kim spat. "We'll lose him."

"We need petrol. That road goes to the Gulf of Aqaba, which gives him two choices," he paused and looked at Kim as he opened the door, "south, which makes no sense, or north, to Israel. Either way, we'll catch him."

Kim grumbled, but used his suggestion to visit the facilities while he fueled up.

In less than five minutes, they were back on the road. The lame tour bus arrived as Ramy exited the mini-store. He'd splashed water on his face and washed the sweat stickiness from his arms. Once settled, he chewed on a nut and date mix he'd bought with the petrol.

"He's thirty kilometers ahead," said Kim.

"No problem." He shoved in another mouthful.

Taba, Israel

Ramy had been right. Darwin's tour bus turned north within the hour, and they caught up with it shortly after passing Nuweibaa. Unfortunately, three luxury buses were driving nose to tail.

Kim shouted into her phone. Ramy made out the word satellite, but nothing else. After a while, she hung up and said, "They have to stop at the Israel border, and everyone gets off. We'll spot him then."

"And if we don't?"

"Then we follow."

Ramy decided it was best not to mention that he was persona non grata in Israel and figured the border police would likely have an unwelcome profile on Kim as well. He settled into the drive and relaxed at the view across the Gulf of Aqaba. Its turquoise water near shore had spurred the development of resorts and diving. He smiled at one such trip in Jordan, a brief respite from a mission in Iraq. He pictured the dive instructor leading the way over a vibrant reef; her fluid kicking had mesmerized him, the surface light in shifting patterns over her body, barely covered by a thong bikini.

He looked over at Kim. Her tank top pushed up her breasts, and he followed the dark shadow of her cleavage down her belly. As if she sensed his stare, she pulled at her top, adjusting its fabric slightly higher. Ramy inserted Kim into his dive instructor fantasy, which passed the time until the traffic backed up at the Taba Border control.

He parked the car at a cafe as the buses entered the border control complex that occupied the last wide spot before the mountains squeezed the road into a chokepoint against the Sea of Aqaba. Passengers stepped out of the luxury coaches and claimed their luggage before joining the customs queue. The Israel-bound passengers would board other buses across the border.

"Split up," said Kim. "You go forward and work your way back. I'll start here."

"Agreed. Text me every ten minutes. If anyone stops you, tell them we're looking for a thief," said Ramy.

They also agreed to meet in an hour and, if one of them didn't show up, assume they were detained and drive away. Ramy had left the key fob atop the rear passenger tire.

Ramy walked toward the front of the line until he reached a point he knew had to be ahead of any bus they'd been following, then returned. He videoed the people in line, covering his move like he was making a video call. His eye, trained to find faces that did not want to be seen, scanned the group as he strolled. Three minutes later, he met Kim, who had moved from the line and stood by one bus.

"It's the woman with the yellow dress. The signal's coming from her purple case," she said.

"Okay. I'll wait here."

Kim walked toward a door, where a guard directed her back to the line. Once near the woman, Kim kneeled to adjust her boot lace, then scanned the people before returning to Ramy.

"He's not with them," she said.

63

Saint Catherine's Monastery

Just before lunch, Darwin sat in the library, trying to find a connection between the stele and the monastery, or at least this southerly region of Sinai. He figured it would be another hour before the North Koreans discovered he was not on the tour bus.

An idea germinated. *What if the alchemist is more charlatan? Henri wrote about sneaking in to see him use psilocybin powder.* He studied the drawings of the stele he'd made in a small notebook. *What if these are fake? Made long ago, for sure, but not 3,500 years ago.*

A chair scraped on the stone floor across the room, and he looked up at the Theophilus. The absence of life's background noises like cars, air conditioners, and even music accentuated the monastery's quietude. A column of minute insects swirled in a shaft of light that Darwin followed up to a window set high in the wall.

Unlatching himself from the day-to-day world allowed calm to permeate him and made space for nagging, unimportant matters to slough off. He'd experienced the same tranquility at Siwa Oasis in Egypt's far western desert. He began to grasp why some sought solitude. *Hermits and mystics have occupied this place for more than two thousand years.*

He shut his eyes and rewound time. The books and walls disappeared. The number of buildings shrank, and the outer bulwark receded, leaving the barest smattering of vegetation among the granite. But some people made a life here and benefited from the life-giving spring still used by the monastery.

Then, Darwin reversed the exercise—more people came with their animals. Far across the Red Sea, Greeks put their stamp on Egypt as Alexandria thrived as a center of learning. The Roman empire spread and a new religious movement took root, its counterculture undermining Rome's power. Its emperors purged the believers. Martyrs chose death, but many fled.

They came here, bringing the monastic life that had sprouted in the cities along the Nile. He pictured the wadis—full of caves and crude dwellings used by hermits. *There were also many Christian factions in those early days.*

A sense of discovery grew, that finder vibe. He plunged ahead. *What if one splinter group blended the occult, part ancient Egyptian, part Christian? And they used psilocybin in their worship?*

He snorted. *They'd be driven underground as Roman Christianity enforced its canon. Even the Coptics would find them too esoteric. The occultists would have to move far from Alexandria and Cairo, certainly out of Roman influence.*

The empty land in his fantasy dissolved, and the modern-day monastery took its place. He reasoned that, even if a strange Christian offshoot took refuge here, it would have been driven out.

But not entirely. He stared at the stele. *What if Henri stumbled on a practitioner? And what if the diamonds had been incorporated into the ritual?*

He paused. He needed data to back up the idea. But dating the stele would take time and equipment he didn't have. *And there is no way the monks will let me take it.* Darwin scribbled his thoughts in a notebook and listed questions to pursue. The first was about documents on esoteric rituals—a long shot. *But stranger things have happened,* he thought while walking to Theophilus's desk.

"Ah, good timing," said the librarian when Darwin approached. "The Israeli tour guide emailed me a message for you. Here."

Darwin took the scrap of paper:

Two people looked for Darwin at the border. An Arab man and a Korean woman. She stopped next to me in the customs line. Tell Darwin he was right. Be careful.

She attached a photo of each. Darwin studied them, but had seen neither before now.

"What's the email mean?" asked Theophilus.

"It means they're coming here, and I need your help to hide."

Darwin used a library computer to forward photos of the Arab man and Korean woman to Eyrún via his secure email service and added:

```
I'm going to ground before they come back.
I'll contact you again in two days.
```

Then he logged in to his Apple account and remotely wiped his phone and iPad. While the Israeli woman had helped him, he was sure their security service would hoover everything off the device, including data on the diamond's tokamak potential.

"Ready," Darwin told Theophilus, after logging off and rebooting the machine to clear its memory.

He followed him into the kitchen, where the monks and Bedouins had finished their weekly bread baking and were packing up the loaves. The librarian introduced Darwin to the men and requested their cooperation.

64

Paris

Later the next morning, Mike followed a guard to an interview room where his public defender, Annette, waited with another woman who looked a decade older. While Annette dressed fashionably, this new woman exhibited the wealth garnered through years of success. Her Chanel handbag, matching necklace, and earrings shouted accomplishment, and the rock on her finger could anchor a small boat. His curiosity was piqued, but also a deep suspicion. Lawyers like her had tried to trap him during the smuggling trial, protecting their clients farther up the chain.

"Mike, this is Astrid. She represents the Lacroix family," said Annette.

He shook Astrid's hand, but remained silent as they sat down. Annette started to speak, but Astrid placed a hand on hers, and the younger woman paused.

"Mr. Carson, I know you were expecting Eyrún Stephansdottir, but we prefer that the police don't make a connection. As far as they know, I'm here as an advisor to Annette."

Mike nodded. He'd been deceived by forked-tongue lawyers before.

Astrid smiled, then continued. "My firm represents Eyrún's foundation, the Agrippa Center for Archaeology. Emelio Lacroix and Eyrún share a special bond, and she interceded to help him."

Mike crossed his arms and leaned back in the chair.

"I'm going to be transparent with you, Mr. Carson. I was the one who advised Emelio Lacroix to take a harsh stance. Given the time lapse since the affair that you say resulted in your great-grandmother and the recent change to French inheritance law, you'd be hard-pressed to find a judge sympathetic enough to hear it. And, it would certainly be taxing on your resources."

"What's your point?" He'd told Annette last night he knew Darwin was in danger and expected to trade the details to get the charges dropped. Having a partner in a high-priced Paris law firm flaunt its prowess pissed him off.

"Emelio sympathizes with your case. He regrets denying your grandmother's request," she paused, but Mike remained stoic. Astrid waited a beat longer before continuing, "And, of course, Eyrún wants to learn about her husband. She thinks you've been set up."

Mike's face screwed up.

"You heard me correctly. Eyrún wanted to tell you herself, but the police will only allow direct relatives or counsel to meet with prisoners."

He leaned forward, sliding his elbows on the table. "Get me out of here, and I'll tell you what I know."

"That's our intention, Mike, but it's tricky. The Paris police remain on high alert from the 2015 attacks. We've filed a motion with the judge, but it could take forty-eight hours to clear you."

Mike's head dropped. He stared at his clasped hands, thumbs rubbing together.

"I know it's not what you want to hear," said Annette.

He locked eyes with her. "I've done nothing wrong. I've told them about Ramy and his dealings."

Astrid laid two photos before Mike.

"That's Ramy and the North Korean woman. Where were these taken?" he asked.

"At the Egyptian border crossing with Israel," said Astrid, repeating what Eyrún had communicated via email.

"They're after Darwin," said Mike. "They've hacked his phone and are following him to—"

Astrid held up a hand, silencing him, and slid a folded sheet of paper across the table. He read it:

Do not react to this note. Read it and hand it back.
Eyrún told us about the diamonds. We are working on getting you out of here. Today. But you must help track down Ramy. In exchange, the Lacroix estate agrees to an inheritance, for you only, of $1,000,000.
Do not communicate any of this with the police.
Nod if you agree.

Mike nodded and refolded the paper. Astrid slid it back into her folio.

"We'll let you know as soon as we hear from the judge," said Annette.

After the women left, the guards escorted Mike back to the communal holding tank. He suppressed a smile as they reached the cell door. He liked the sound of *today*.

Ajaccio

As Astrid met with Mike in Paris, Eyrún received a call from Richard Ndembele in Vatican City.

"His Holiness will talk to the French president in an hour," he said.

"Thank you, Richard. You're a godsend."

Richard laughed. "My superiors don't always think so. Listen, you need to keep to the story of antiquities theft. I suggested the British Museum break-in was linked to this situation and that the North

Korean thieves were trying to plunder antiquities and sell them on the black market."

"Got it, Richard. The break-in is—"

"Don't tell me. I'm sure this is one of Darwin's shortcuts."

"Whatever gave you that idea?" asked Eyrún, feigning innocence. Richard's laughter rumbled over their connection, and when finished, Eyrún said, "Thank you again. And please thank His Holiness for me."

"I shall," he said, and they hung up.

Eyrún sent an encrypted email to Astrid:

`This morning. Be ready.`

Paris

Mike fought back the butterflies in his stomach as the day dragged on, and a shadow fell across the skylight in the cell. He'd heard so many broken promises over the years, and lawyers consistently underestimated the constipation in the justice system.

A short while later, the main cell door opened, and two guards stepped inside. The investigating detective, dressed in the same gray suit, stood at the door. "Mike Carson. Follow me."

One guard cuffed him before leaving the cell, but once outside the relocked door, the investigator said, "Take them off." The guard did so and left.

"You're released. All charges are dismissed. Follow me," said the investigator, turning down the hall. After Mike had been given back his belongings, she led him outside, where she grasped his elbow before he walked away. "Tell me, who do you know?"

Mike shrugged, remembering Astrid's note.

The investigator lit a cigarette and blew out a long smoke trail. "My bosses got a call from the president of the republic. I don't know who you are, but I recommend you leave Paris."

At that moment, a black Mercedes Benz sedan pulled up. A bulky man in a suit emerged from the passenger side and opened the rear door. "Monsieur Carson. Please come with us."

The investigator ground the cigarette into the pavement and beat a path back inside.

Holy shit, thought Mike as he slid across the tan leather, and the door closed. The car rocketed away from the curb. "Where are we going?" he asked.

"To the airport," said the driver.

65

Saint Catherine, Egypt

Darwin woke the following day to voices and hissing from a gas stove. He rolled over and rubbed a sore spot on his lower back from sleeping on the ground. Light penetrated the tent from the open flap, and someone started a nearby car.

"*Sabah alkhayr*, good morning," said Darwin to the man squatting by the teapot.

He returned the greeting, and they engaged in a light conversation. Darwin's speech came more quickly after an evening spent in the Bedouin camp a few kilometers outside Saint Catherine's. He spoke fluent Arabic, but it had been three years since he'd lived in Siwa Oasis, and the dialect here was subtly distinct.

The previous day, Darwin had borrowed a *thoab* from a Bedouin who had been laundering clothes in the monastery while others were baking bread with the monks. He then joined the group in their Toyota pickup. The traditional long-sleeved robe, combined with his skin tone, deeply bronzed from many days on Eyrún's yacht, helped him meld into the group.

While excavating a tomb in the Siwa Oasis, he'd befriended the local Bedouins, so much so that he and Eyrún were married in a traditional Siwan ceremony. Last night, he'd related this to the men here and, to his surprise, learned that one man was a cousin of a family Darwin and Eyrún knew in the Siwa Oasis.

This bit of serendipity that turned Darwin from stranger to friend made it easier for him to ask, "Have you heard of any rituals using mystical drugs? Maybe in a cave?"

They were quiet for a time, and Darwin thought he'd offended them when one man said, "My great-grandfather spoke of a cave."

Darwin's heart leaped, and it was all he could do to remain still while the man looked at the others sitting around the small fire as if seeking their approval to keep going. When no one spoke, he continued, "I don't know where it is." Darwin slumped. "But you can ask him yourself. I can take you to him tomorrow."

He'd slept well and dreamed about the spectacular paintings in the Siwa Oasis tomb built for Alexander the Great but never used. It had been a joyous year with Eyrún, living a simple life.

He adjusted the cotton trousers beneath his thoab and joined his host. He accepted some of the bread he'd carried from the monastery yesterday, and a short while later, the pickup returned. Outside, he stepped into sandals and wrapped the scarf over his head and neck. An hour later, after driving deep into a narrow wadi, they reached another camp. The sun had just risen above the steep canyon wall and brought alive the reds and ochres in the tent's fabrics.

The great-grandson led Darwin into the tent where a shrunken figure sat, a blanket draped across his shoulders. Two older women nodded in greeting, then left the tent as Darwin entered.

"Grandfather, this is the man I told you about."

"*As-salamu alaikum,*" said Darwin.

The old man's gray eyes studied Darwin before he replied, "*Wa-alaikum as-salam.*"

Darwin continued in Arabic, thanking the man for his family's hospitality and protection.

"We have been friends with the monks for more than a thousand years. We look out for each other. The abbot says you are trustworthy."

"Thank you," said Darwin.

The old man continued, "Your Arabic is good, but your accent is terrible."

Darwin sat rigid, unsure what to say, when the old man cackled, slapping his knee and smiling so broadly that all the lines in his face turned up. Darwin then laughed, realizing he'd been had.

The old man waved for tea, and one woman brought a battered silver pot on a tray and poured the tea into glass cups. When she departed, he asked, "Now, what is it you came all this way to ask?"

Darwin began with an explanation of his forebear Henri's study of alchemy during the time of Napoleon, before introducing the stele and its unusual depictions of mushrooms. Then he asked, "Have you ever heard of legends of ancient ceremonies that used ..." he paused and asked the younger man the Arabic word for psychoactive.

"*Muathir nafsiana,*" said the man.

Darwin turned back to the old man, whose expression had darkened. Darwin quickly added, "I'm not interested in the drugs. I seek an object that may be in a cave where psychoactive mushrooms grow."

"Show me the stele."

Darwin opened his notebook and handed over two photos he'd printed in the library.

The old man fixed a pince-nez on his nose. After a long minute, he handed back the photos. "My great-grandfather talked about a cave with a great evil. I never believed it until now."

Darwin leaned forward, waiting for the old man to continue, and when he did not, he reached under his robe and removed a protective box. He took out a diamond and, holding it between his fingers, said, "we think the stele refers to these diamonds, and the mushrooms are found in the same cave. Perhaps a cult blending ancient traditions with newer Christian practices. I don't know, but we have learned these diamonds have useful modern properties. Let me show you."

He cupped the diamond so the old man could see it in the darkness, then asked the younger man, "Take this outside and hold it in the sunlight a minute, then bring it back." He did so while Darwin poured more tea into the older man's cup, then filled his own.

"Show him," Darwin instructed the younger man to show his

great-grandfather the yellow-green glow from the diamond when he returned.

The old man glanced, then waved a hand. "Take it away." As Darwin placed it back in the box, he asked, "How did you get this?"

"Henri, my great-grandfather, stole them from an alchemist in Cairo. Could this diamond have come from the cave you mentioned?"

"My grandfathers said a cult practiced a strange religion and its practitioners came from Cairo to extract their heretical material from a cave. Some of my tribe became followers and had dark visions. Those who stayed in the cave too long died a wasting death. The monks at the monastery helped drive them away. In time, the Cairo people stopped coming as the Prophet, *alayhi as-salām*, directed our people."

"Was the wasting death caused by radiation poisoning?"

"I do not know. It was generations before my time."

Darwin waited and, when it was apparent the old man had finished, he asked, "Do you know the location of this cave?"

The old man nodded.

"Will you show me?" He paused, then added, "People who will use the diamonds to make a weapon are coming."

"No. I cannot let you disturb the evil in that place."

Darwin tried to reason with him, but the old man stood his ground. "We've kept the secret for generations. No one in the tribe will give it up."

When it was clear he would learn no more, Darwin thanked the man, and they said their goodbyes.

66

Roissy, France

Mike sat up as the car exited the highway. He'd dozed earlier when he got no more details from the men in the front. Signs for Orly airport directed traffic to its various terminals. The big sedan turned on a side road marked Private Flights.

A minute later, the driver flashed his badge at a security gate, and they were whisked through to a private jet. Its pilot walked from the adjacent building and met them at the aircraft.

"*Bon voyage,* Monsieur Carson," said the big man, handing over Mike's case from the boot.

"Where am I going?"

The man shrugged.

Mike asked the same question of the pilot as he boarded.

"Corsica," the pilot replied, directing Mike toward the seat.

Once airborne, Mike used the tiny toilet to wash up from his two days in the prison cell and change into fresh clothes. He then fell hard asleep until the wheels bumped the runway ninety minutes later.

Ajaccio

As the NetJet carrying Mike taxied toward them, its fuselage gleaming in the afternoon sun, Eyrún surveyed their readiness one more time. Each had a pack and was dressed in rugged clothing that also allowed them freedom of movement. She knew from experience that going into caves was a messy business.

After she'd offered Mike a settlement in exchange for information, they'd debated the strategy of taking him to Sinai. The Pegasus hack and hearing the North Koreans were involved had spooked her. Darwin was out of communication, and she followed the logic of keeping her enemies close.

"I don't like it," Zac had said upon first hearing the plan. "We don't know this guy. And yes, you're right, I've got a chip on my shoulder about soldiers who broke the law in Afghanistan."

"But he's done his time," said Eyrún.

"And here he is in Europe, suing you and breaking into your house."

"That wasn't him."

"Splitting hairs. It was another convict," said Zac.

Siggy interceded. "What other options do we have? Darwin's gone to ground and has only a vague idea who's after him."

"Fine," Zac acquiesced, "we bring Mike. How do we control him?"

"Emelio and I settled on a million after doing the maths on the company sale and accounting for inflation."

Zac whistled.

"This is about Darwin," said Eyrún, voice catching in her throat. "His life's worth more to me than—" She looked away.

Siggy glared at Zac while wrapping an arm around her sister.

"Oh no, Eyrún. I'm sorry," he said. "I didn't mean to put a value on Darwin's life."

After a moment, she looked up and said, "I know you didn't mean it that way."

An hour later, the French president okayed an order to release Mike, and they hurried a plan together. A half hour ago, they'd gathered at the airport's private terminal to wait.

As the jet rolled to a stop, Zac swung his pack onto his shoulder. Eyrún glanced at it. She'd tested its weight when taking it from the car earlier and knew he carried more than clothes. She hoped they wouldn't need deadly force.

"Zac, let me handle this," she said, stepping in front of him as the jet's door opened. She didn't wait for an answer as she turned and mounted the steps. She knew they had about twenty minutes on the ground while the jet took on fuel, and she wanted to meet Mike alone, and get a firsthand feel for the man Zac had labeled a criminal and con artist. Her face and neck grew hot as she envisioned a similar confrontation with a woman, Tessa Santarossa, who'd deceived Darwin to get at a document in the Vatican's secret archives. Tessa later tried to kill them both, only to bring a horrific death upon herself.

Eyrún paused just inside the door, studying Mike's profile. His disheveled, sandy hair covered his eyes as he leaned over, rearranging his pack's contents, and his wrinkled clothing looked consistent with someone who'd spent the night in a jail cell. He didn't appear dangerous. Astrid had said Mike seemed to be a reluctant criminal, swept up in circumstances not of his own design. But she'd also said he was bright and had learned deceit and manipulation brought results faster than earning an honest living.

Eyrún's brow furrowed. She'd seen his kind of manipulator before. A year ago, blackmailers had sullied the ACA's reputation by using it to launder looted antiquities. She and Darwin were generous with their money and talent and had no patience for people who sought to deceive and steal. *And endanger my husband.* Her teeth ground as Mike looked up.

She swallowed back the emotion and smiled. "Mike, I'm Eyrún Stephansdottir." They shook hands.

"I never intended this—"

"So you say." She studied his face. "What, exactly, did you intend?"

"To get my great-grandmother's rightful inheritance," he said and, when Eyrún didn't reply, added, "the other lawsuit about the *Demeter* was a red herring to get the Lacroixes to settle."

"And the break-in at Emelio's house? What was that for? To steal, in case the lawsuits didn't pan out?" Eyrún checked herself by taking a deep breath. This encounter was surfacing more anger than she'd intended.

"I hired Ramy to help research. I don't speak French. He took it upon himself to come here and see firsthand what was left of the estate. He was to look and ask around. That's it."

"But you didn't stop him once you learned about the diamonds."

"Because I thought he was nuts. Yes, I heard you talk about superconducting and all that, but I got consumed by your lawyer's countermotions. And frankly, I let Ramy chase it to keep him out of the lawsuits. Look," Mike turned his palms up in mock surrender, "like I said earlier, it's not what I intended and I warned you as soon as I found out what Ramy was doing."

Eyrún paused a few beats, then spoke slowly. "I pulled in huge favors to get you out of jail. But," she leaned toward him, "it won't take much to put you back in if you don't cooperate."

Mike sighed. "I didn't lie. Ramy acted on his own."

"Good. That's what I was hoping. I'm also hoping the settlement we offered buys your loyalty to get my husband out of the danger you put him in."

"I'll do whatever I can," he said and glanced at her pack. "Are we going someplace?"

"Sinai. You know what Ramy looks like, and I'm guessing you've seen the North Korean woman."

"Not up close," said Mike.

"Probably doesn't matter. I can't imagine many Korean women are visiting the monastery. Stay here," she said, moving back toward the door. "We take off in five minutes."

Mike looked out the window as the petrol truck filled the wing tanks. The Middle East was the last place he wanted to go, but the payout would be worth it. He envisioned what he'd do with it when a tall, well-muscled man stepped onto the jet, His head bent to fit in the cabin, and his chest and arms stretched the fabric of his polo shirt.

"Who are you?" Mike stood to meet the newcomer.

"Zac Johnson. West Point class of oh-seven. Captain seventy-fifth Ranger Regiment, Iraq and Afghanistan." He dropped his pack on a seat and extended a hand.

Mike shook it, wincing as the larger man squeezed; his green eyes burned with a warrior's intensity. Mike's job in the military had been policing and defending the perimeter. This man's role eliminated trouble before it got close—a hunter.

The hand gripping Mike's suddenly yanked him close, and Zac growled. "Eyrún didn't tell you the other part of the deal: when her husband comes home alive, so do you."

Zac thrust Mike back, grabbed his pack, and took up one of the rear seats.

67

An hour before sunset, Darwin rode back to the monastery with a driver who was picking up the members of the tribe who worked there. Darwin followed the man through the main gate into the kitchen, where the driver stopped to pick up freshly baked bread. Darwin peeled away toward the library.

He crossed a courtyard, still wearing the thoab and a *kufiya* wrapped around his head and neck, and passed the dark green living relative of the venerated burning bush. A group of tourists took his photo. He angled his face downward and smiled, thinking of the stories they'd tell. He cut through a narrow passage and soon entered the library.

Theophilus looked up from behind his monitor and laughed. "Gone native? It suits you."

"I lived in Siwa Oasis for two years," said Darwin and explained he needed to check his email for the translation. Theophilus returned to work as Darwin used another computer to access his encrypted email.

He jumped straight to one from Eyrún:

```
On the way from Ajaccio with Zac, Siggy, and
Mike. I'll explain when I get there. Satel-
```

lite photos show a probable location. Do not reply. I'll find your room at the monastery.

He looked at the time stamp on the email: 12:17. The current computer time showed 16:43. They'd probably landed, but he figured the driving time from Cairo meant they wouldn't arrive until late in the evening. He skipped three other emails, all responses to research inquiries, and went straight to the purple lady's reply.

Thank you for the photo of the reassembled stele. Someday you'll have to tell me how you persuaded the British Museum to part with Hathor's lower half.

Not likely. Darwin still wondered about his fallout from that incident, but pushed it aside.

First, the script. It's demotic, as you suspected, but from a later period. We used two luminescence methods to corroborate the date as 2nd century CE. You've found a piece that fuses old kingdom gods with esoteric rituals from the Ptolemaic period.

That's definitely interesting. This put the stele much more recent than the ancient mining operations and potentially linked it to unknown occultists who'd isolated themselves from the mainstream traditions in Cairo and Alexandria. *Could this be connected to the alchemist Henri met?* He made a mental note to review Henri's journal, then continued reading.

The translation reads like a hodgepodge of demotic spells and incantations taken from the Greek magical papyri. The first lines appear to be directions, possibly pointing to your mushrooms and diamonds idea.

The last line, "eater of souls," must refer to the snake on the stele. I guess this is Apep, a deity who embodies chaos and opposes Ma'at, the goddess who brought order at the moment of creation. But it could have other meanings.

The complete translation follows below. Let me know what you find.

Regards,
Angela

Darwin knew of the Greek magical papyri—it was not a single work but a collection of Greek, Coptic, and demotic spells, hymns, and rituals. Early Christians seeking to consolidate power burned these texts, but practitioners hid enough to give scholars a solid understanding of old-world magic.

He'd read some of the works during a course on early Christian development and remembered that most were difficult to grasp. Reading Angela's translation, he hoped the stele would be more direct.

"Look for Ra in the coming day and enter the third chamber. Where the light transforms Hathor's jewels, take the offering from Horus to open mystical visions and union with the universal spirit.

"Drink from the well of life, but beware the eater of souls who will lead you on a false journey into the great furnace. The mistress of heat and its glow shall consume your soul."

It was not, and he read it three more times, trying to make sense of it. Although the text was vague, he guessed that the third chamber referred to a place inside the highlighted mountain on the stele's map side.

He printed two copies of the email and thanked the librarian before crossing the grounds to the garden gate. After glancing around, he walked to the guest building and entered his room, where he penned a note to Eyrún:

Hi Love, wish I could see you in person, but I don't know who may be following me. This printout is the translated stele script. It's unclear, but I think it refers to the mountain on the map. Maybe your sat photos can narrow it down. I'll make contact tomorrow.

He left the note atop a color print of the stele and left. He found the monk in charge of the rooms and told him that his wife, Eyrún, would stay in his room tonight and he would be away on an overnight retreat. That garnered a raised eyebrow from the monk, but he nodded at the request and went about his business.

Darwin reentered the monastery gate and exited its front entrance, where the Bedouin guides were leaving for the day. He hopped in the pickup's bed, and it pulled away.

68

Saint Catherine International Airport

The western slopes of the red granite peaks glowed in the setting sun as they descended into St. Catherine International Airport. Eyrún didn't want to waste the extra time dealing with airports and driving, and opted for the chartered flight. Commercial flights into Saint Catherine's had been sporadic in Egypt's unstable political climate.

They had bags ready beside their seats. While Richard had arranged diplomatic coverage for them, the pilot had initially balked at landing when the Egyptian authorities had questioned the flight plan. He changed his mind when offered a hefty bonus.

The wheels chirped on a smooth touchdown, and reverse thrust engaged, but when the jet slowed to taxi speed, the pilot opened the cockpit door. "Police. I see cars and lights at the terminal. I didn't agree to this."

Zac jumped up and looked out the cockpit window. "They're waiting. Let us out here and go."

"Are you crazy?" The pilot looked at him.

"Piece of cake. I usually jump from these things at altitude."

The pilot stopped the plane and lowered the stairs just long enough for Zac, Eyrún, Siggy, and Mike to reach the runway before closing the door and spooling up the engines. The police cars began moving toward them fast as the four ran off the cement, and the jet screamed away. Seconds later, the pilot rotated the craft airborne and arced west toward Jordanian airspace.

Zac remained placid as the sure-to-be-angry Egyptian authorities raced toward them.

"I'll deal with them," said Siggy. "Eyrún, give me that email printout."

She took it as the police jumped out of their cars and pointed guns at them. One man approached them, and Siggy launched into them in rapid Arabic. "What is this? We are a diplomatic mission from Vatican City returning a treasured relic to Saint Catherine's Monastery."

She waved the paper at him. "This is an email from His Excellency, the president of the Arab Republic of Egypt. Is this the greeting he intended for representatives from the pope in Rome? Maybe I need to phone our sponsor in Cairo." She took out her phone and began tapping on it.

"Wait," said the man, telling the others to lower their weapons.

Minutes later, they were in the police van heading towards the monastery. "Well, that solved our transportation problem," Zac said to Siggy.

"I put up with too much shit from incompetent police in the refugee camps. It doesn't always work, but sometimes throwing around authority does," she said.

As the sun set, the police dropped them off at the monastery gate, where they quickly beat a path inside before anyone questioned them about what was really on that piece of paper.

Ramy answered a knock on his guestroom door. A Bedouin he'd paid to watch for Darwin pointed toward the front gate and said, "He left with the Jebalya five minutes ago."

"I paid you to follow him."

"I know where he went. I have more news," said the Bedouin.

"Tell me," said Ramy.

"It is worth more."

Ramy yanked the man by his robe and kicked the door closed. He slammed him against the wall. "Tell me, and I'll decide if it's worth anything," he hissed, pressing his forearm against the man's neck.

The Bedouin's eyes bulged in fear and he gagged out. "There was another arrival."

Probably bullshit, thought Ramy, recoiling at the man's rancid breath. He lightened the pressure. "Speak."

The man rubbed his throat, then said, "The police arrived. They escorted two men and two women."

"Describe them."

"One man was tall, strong looking. The other man was smaller, with blonde hair. The women looked like sisters. Both have dark hair and the same face."

Ramy released the man. "Where are they now?"

"In the dining room."

Ramy gave the man a handful of baksheesh and pushed him out the door. "Follow the first man, as I asked."

He waited a long minute, then walked toward the dining room and scanned the diners through its front window. His eyes stopped at a table with two dark-haired women of northern European descent and remarkably similar profiles. One resembled the woman he'd fought in Ajaccio. *Where are the men?*

While they finished their meal, he waited in the shadows and followed the women back to a guest room. One carried a tray with two plates. He stepped behind an olive tree as they reached their room.

The door had not opened far, but Ramy caught a clear view of the blonde-haired guy inside—Mike! *What the hell's he doing here?*

69

Saint Catherine's Monastery

After their dinner, Eyrún and Siggy brought food to Zac and Mike. The plan called for keeping Mike out of view. Over the last few days, the three had choreographed their communication about traveling to Egypt using disposable phones. They'd given their hacked phones to colleagues in Ajaccio to carry around, mimicking their everyday routines, and hoped this diversion would allow them to catch up with Darwin and find the cave.

The men ate while Siggy related what they'd heard over dinner. "Most people are departing at 2:00 a.m. to climb Jebel Musa. People at another table who'd climbed it today talked about the amazing sunrise experience and that they headed back down after a religious service and breakfast."

"Good," said Zac between bites. "I figure if we hit the trail by eight, we'll summit about ten when most pilgrims are gone."

Eyrún wandered around the room, gathering Darwin's scattered clothing. She folded two shirts while listening to the conversation about the mountain and stacked them in his opened case. Then she sat on the twin bed where Darwin had slept, smoothing the sheets.

As if sensing her worry, Zac said, "I'm sure he's fine, Eyrún."

"I know," she said and picked up his note and the printed map.

Zac laid the high-resolution photos next to the print to compare the locations. Eons of water had carved deep wadis, leaving a triangular mountain as viewed from above. In addition, the ancient receding waters had ringed it with dozens of terraces. While the satellite photo was taken at a larger scale, the terrain's features between the map and image matched.

Eyrún ran a finger along the map. "The ridges align with the meteorite impact location, and this highlighted mountain appears to be in the right spot."

"And over here," said Zac, pointing to the photo's upper right. "The trail comes in from where Siggy spotted people hiking. From the car park, it's about ten kilometers to the town of Saint Catherine."

"Could people still be mining?" asked Siggy.

"Possibly," he said, "but I doubt it's commercially viable, especially any hand-dug operation."

She followed up with, "What are the tiny outlines all over this plateau section?"

Eyrún took that question. "Abandoned hermit dwellings, as best I can tell. They're all over this area."

"And that's why it'll be hard to find what we're looking for," said Zac, patting his pack. "Hopefully, the sensors on the drone will distinguish the most traveled paths."

Zac turned to Mike, who sat apart from them. "Seen them yet? They've got to be here." They'd brought Mike along to recognize Ramy, but so far excluded him from their planning.

"No," said Mike, "I've only been from the entrance to here and saw no Korean women. Ramy will be hard to spot with all the Bedouins circulating."

"Keep your eyes peeled," said Zac.

An hour later, Zac and Mike went to their shared room, while Siggy stayed with Eyrún. Mike knew Ramy had to be around as they'd had a day's head start. As he lay on the bed, hands under his head, Zac said he was going to the toilet and to stay put. The guest rooms had shared facilities a few doors farther along the building. Mike snorted. *Right, asshole. Like, I'm not in the middle of nowhere.*

He watched the ceiling fan's blades slowly revolve as he considered his situation—between people who'd offered to pay him off and an unknown number of North Koreans. And while he'd not been included in the conversations, he'd seen the map and photos. Zac's plan had seemed more guesswork than a well-thought out strategy. *How the hell are they going to find a specific cave in the warren of holes?*

The door burst open and Ramy rushed in along with two men. "Mike, buddy. Good to see you're safe."

"What the fuck do you want?" said Mike, sitting up.

The two North Korean men seized his arms and shuffled him outside to meet Kim. Her face under the pool of light by the door showed no emotion, but as Mike looked down at a handgun aimed at his belly, she said, "Your cooperation would be appreciated, but we can also do it differently."

Mike swore under his breath. "I'll cooperate."

"Let's go," said Ramy, directing them toward the low wall surrounding the monastery's outer buildings.

Eyrún was reviewing Darwin's notes again when Zac charged into the room, arguing, "The bastard betrayed us. I knew it!"

Siggy, right behind him, countered, "That's not how it appeared to me."

"It did to me. He must've seen Ramy earlier and waited for the right moment."

"Stop it, you two," said Eyrún. "What happened?"

Siggy began as Zac stormed back and forth. "I was coming out of the toilet when I saw Ramy and a woman standing with Mike, and two other men on the lookout."

Eyrún turned to Zac, who gave his version. "I saw Mike talking to Ramy and the woman. There was no coercion."

"But why would they need four people to pick him up if he volunteered?" Siggy asked.

Eyrún cut into the argument. "Zac, did Mike take anything?"

"No. I had my pack with me."

"Where did they go?" asked Eyrún.

"Out the garden's front gate and into a Land Cruiser; Mike was between the two guys," said Zac.

"A million dollars is a lot to walk away from," said Eyrún.

"So what?" Zac argued. "The North Koreans could be paying more."

Eyrún held up a hand. "Whatever Mike's reason for leaving, he knows our plan. Question is, do we change it?"

She and Zac debated while Siggy tapped furiously on the sat phone. A minute later, she blurted out, "It's her! I knew it!"

"Who?" asked Eyrún.

"Kim Un-jong. It's been seven years, but I got a good look at her face as she passed near the toilet."

"Wait," said Zac, eyes wide. "How do you know a North Korean spy?"

"The Brazil Olympics."

"Her?" Eyrún crossed her arms.

"Yes. Her!" Siggy's eyes smoldered. She threw the phone at a bed pillow. "I never thought I'd see that bitch again. Let alone here."

Zac glanced between the sisters, trying to grasp the significance when Eyrún filled him in. "Kim Un-jong eliminated Siggy from the medal round in a surprise win. The Iceland Olympic committee protested, but we could never prove the Chinese and North Korean judges had cheated."

"Damn," said Zac.

A long silence passed, and Eyrún saw Siggy's old wound suck her in. She'd worked hard after winning the silver medal at the World Championships the year before the Olympics. Siggy understood getting beat by a better opponent. It happened to all competitors. *But losing to a cheater?* The highest level of global sport was supposed to be immune to deceit.

Eyrún's blood boiled. She'd been wrestling with why they were trying to find the diamonds. They could leave them hidden. But now the reason was crystal clear.

The North Koreans didn't just isolate themselves. That would be okay. Any culture deserved privacy if it wanted it. But she'd dealt with North Korea in the antiquities trade. They stole to support a failed economy. And the money went to its supreme leader's family—to create nuclear weapons.

"Maybe we should change the plan," said Zac.

"No!" Eyrún spat.

Siggy and Zac stared at her.

"Sorry. I mean, let's stick with the plan." She explained her reasoning. "It's too late. This confirms the North Koreans know about the diamonds. We know they'll want them for weapons development."

"But Mike doesn't know the location, so they'll have to follow us," said Zac.

"Or follow Darwin," said Siggy.

"Which means they'll have to split up. Let's use it to our advantage," said Zac.

"Okay. Let's work it out when Darwin contacts us in the morning," said Eyrún.

"Agreed," said Zac.

Siggy nodded.

Zac gathered pillows and sheets from his room and arranged a makeshift bed on the floor of the sisters' room. It wasn't optimal for comfort, but they wanted no more kidnappings during the night.

70

Bedouin Camp

Mike sat in the tent where Ramy had left him. They'd driven in silence from the monastery earlier and arrived in a desert camp. Across from him, three Bedouin men murmured in Arabic while making tea on a small stove. Mike understood some Arabic from his military time in Iraq, but could not make out their dialect.

Ramy reentered the tent and made what sounded like a crude comment about Kim. The men laughed, then stood and left the tent. Moments later, Kim walked in. One of the male North Koreans stayed by the open flap while Ramy and Kim joined Mike on the carpet.

"We require your help, Mr. Carson," said Kim. Mike remained silent, and she continued. "It's not a request, Mike. Clearly, the Lacroixes have a great deal of influence as the French do not let terror suspects off lightly. But I need to know where they are going tomorrow."

That Kim knew of the charges spoke volumes, as he'd been told they'd left Paris before his arrest. "The charges had no basis and were dismissed," he said.

She smiled. "I like your resilience, Mike. You manipulated your way out of jail and got yourself brought here. But do you really think you'll get whatever they promised you?"

He had been wondering the same thing. He had heard nothing to back up their promise except the handwritten note from the lawyer—which she'd taken back. Eyrún had seemed sincere, but in his experience, executives who ran multi-million euro operations focused on their objectives, justified by fungible means.

Mike studied Kim's face, her eyes deep in shadow, and decided to test what he was really up against. "Why should I help you?"

Her pale lips spread in a thin smile. "Because if you don't, you will go with the Bedouins on their trek north in the morning. They dislike the Christians in the monastery. To them, it's an abomination in their holy land. They've agreed to leave you in an abandoned hermit's cave —where you and your God can have a long discussion while you wait for the end." She nodded to Ramy and left.

"Mike, buddy, don't piss her off," Ramy said. "Look, I didn't know about the terror setup. I would've never agreed to it. She told me after we left Paris."

Mike looked at him impassively. The guy was out of control, seduced by Kim, or hoping to be. He'd seen how she'd put a hand on Ramy's thigh when she stood.

Mike chastised himself again. *I should have hired someone besides Ramy. Found a student who wanted to earn cash with an easy research project.* Mike had even thought about cutting things off when Ramy had gone to Corsica. But he'd hesitated, and then Ramy had gone to Algeria and got the North Koreans involved. Like before, minor mistakes had led to a nightmare scenario—*just like Iraq.*

Ramy continued, "C'mon, Mike. Whatever they're paying you, it can't be more than twenty thousand a diamond. If this guy Darwin is right, there are hundreds of them. That's millions."

Dammit. Mike considered his options, which had boiled down to a one-way trip into the desert or betraying the people who had got him out of jail. But he thought about the trip here and how Eyrún had treated him. The family ploy had worked to get himself out of jail, but in reality, Eyrún had used him just like the North Koreans were now.

She threw money at me in the same way she was shutting down my lawsuits. And that ranger guy's a hothead.

It had come down to picking sides. *The story of my life.* He sighed, knowing the only side that benefited him was his own. *Best to be neutral. Play this out. See how it goes.*

He decided the best method of staying alive was cooperation. When it all came to a head, he could explain the kidnapping to Eyrún.

"Do you really think Eyrún will pay out?" Ramy asked, as if he knew what Mike had been thinking.

"Doubt it, but what about Kim? Do you trust her?"

"Hell no. But I gave you some of the cash she offered, and one of her agents gave me a peek at a huge wad he's carrying. Once we find the diamonds, we take the money and disappear."

"Fine. I didn't ask them to get me out of jail. They offered to pay because they don't know what you look like," said Mike.

"Cool. You won't regret it. What's their plan?"

"They're climbing Jebel Musa tomorrow and think they can find the cave location from its summit. It's something to do with an ancient meteorite."

"What about the other guy, Darwin?"

"I haven't seen him, but they talked about an ancient map he'd found. And no, they didn't show it to me."

"Perfect. I'll tell her." Ramy left the tent.

Mike stared out through the open flap. The orange firelight flickered on a group of people sitting outside. Once again, Mike found himself alone. Just once in his life, he'd like to feel that someone besides himself looked after his best interests.

71

Saint Catherine's Monastery

The following day at dawn, Darwin traveled back with the Bedouins who worked at the monastery. When he climbed from the pickup, a hand gripped his shoulder. "Someone is following you," said the man whose family Darwin had stayed with. He handed Darwin his pack, adding, "He is lingering by the big tour bus to our left. Look casually and go directly through the tunnel."

"Who is he?"

"He is from a rival tribe. One who opposes the monastery. I don't know what he wants, but be cautious, my friend."

Darwin thanked him and moved toward the monastery. About halfway to the gate, he gazed toward tourists gathering at the bus. Three-robed men were helping to load cases, but one kept looking in his direction. He continued into the dark tunnel through the massive wall and glanced back. The man had followed, but had to pause for a group of women exiting.

Darwin darted into the basilica where the monks were in morning prayers. He quietly moved near a shrine where he could watch the door; minutes later, the service ended. As the monks filed out in silence, he moved from the shrine and tapped Theophilus's shoulder. The man raised his eyebrows at the intrusion.

"I need your help," said Darwin.

Theophilus led him to a door near the chapel of the burning bush and asked, as they turned to the monk's quarters, "Who's following you?"

"Dunno. My Bedouin host said a guy from a rival clan who doesn't like the monastery."

"We've had our share of those across the centuries. Does this have anything to do with the North Koreans?"

"It might," said Darwin, but decided to keep it brief.

Theophilus found a spare robe in the laundry, then suggested both raise their hoods as they walked to breakfast.

"I haven't changed outfits so often since a stage play in university," Darwin said.

"Don't make a habit of it," quipped the librarian, giving Darwin a wry smile.

Once inside the hall, Darwin thanked him again, deciding he liked Theophilus, despite his peevish temperament. He continued through the gate into the garden and toward the small church across from the guest building. No one was in the courtyard, but he caught a whiff of cigarette smoke from the graveyard behind the church.

He moved along the church wall and saw a man taking a long drag as he stood among the tombstones. When he turned to flick the butt, the sun highlighted his face. Darwin couldn't be sure from this distance, but the man looked Asian. Eyrún said the North Koreans were heading to Saint Catherine's, and this lone man, when everyone else had gone, certainly was suspicious.

The man exhaled a long stream, and Darwin beat a path to the guest wing, where he keyed his room's door.

"Who is it?" asked Eyrún as the door opened a crack.

"It's me, Love." Darwin lifted the sides of the hood to reveal his face. "Someone's—"

A brawny arm yanked him inside before he could finish.

"Zac!" said Darwin.

"Shhh," admonished Siggy. She stood on a chair, peering out a window high in the wall. "He just came around the church. I'm pretty sure he's one of the two I saw with Kim last night."

They filled Darwin in on seeing Mike go with Ramy and the North Koreans. Zac emphasized the betrayal. Siggy added her recognition of Kim Un-jong and disagreed with Zac's statement.

Darwin let the arguments play out, and when they'd paused, asked, "What did you make of my note?"

"Well, you seem to have outdone your normal level of arcane with this one," said Zac. "Beware the eater of souls?"

"I think it's a warning."

"No shit." Zac held up the print of the stele. "But seriously, what's with the snake?"

"It's Apep, a deity who brings chaos and is sometimes called an eater of souls." They looked at him with questioning faces, so he continued. "Let's say Hathor's jewels on the stele are the diamonds, and Horus is offering her magical mushrooms. Psilocybins cause an experience of oneness with the divine or, in this case, the universal spirit. For the ancient Egyptians, that's Ma'at."

"Game designers would eat this up," said Zac.

Siggy asked, "So, this snake god, Apep, is Ma'at's opposite?"

"Not exactly. You see, there's another Egyptian god who—"

Eyrún placed a hand on Darwin's forearm. "Not now, Love. We need to get going."

"Right. Sorry," said Darwin, "Problem is the first line. Look for Ra in the coming day. Easy, that's east. But enter the third chamber? The third chamber from where?"

The three smiled in unison.

"You know where?" he asked.

Eyrún spread the satellite photos on the nearest bed while Zac and Siggy explained how a triangular mountain between the wadis aligned with their meteorite strike theory. "And now you've handed us confirmation," said Siggy.

"Well, almost," Zac added. "These hermit caves align east to west, but there are caves at multiple levels on the mountain. And the third chamber? Is that a cave or a chamber inside a cave?"

"So we explore them all," said Darwin.

"No time," said Eyrún. "With Kim and Ramy—"

"And Mike," said Zac.

"And Mike and the two other men following us, we don't have time to poke around every cave. We think this triangle mountain is behind Jebel Musa. We're going up there and using a drone to look closely at the most traveled paths," said Eyrún.

"Do you have a second sat phone?" asked Darwin.

"Yes."

"Good. I have a better idea and a plan to deal with the guy outside."

Darwin walked along the path in front of the guest rooms before looping back to the chapel. He'd slipped out of the room during a distraction caused by Eyrún, Siggy, and Zac. The women had walked to the toilet, talking loudly and laughing. Moments later, Zac headed toward them, asking about breakfast. As the North Korean agent watched them, Darwin approached and coughed to get the agent's attention.

When the man turned, Darwin asked, "Excuse me. Do you speak English?"

"Yes."

"Can I have a cigarette? I saw you smoking earlier. The brothers forbid it. I'm new here, and quitting is killing me," said Darwin.

The man fished out a pack from his jacket and handed it to Darwin, who intentionally dropped it and fumbled to pick it up. "Sorry. Nervous," he said while getting a cigarette in his mouth.

The agent sparked a lighter. Darwin leaned into the flame. Suddenly, the man's hand flew away. Zac had run up from behind and grabbed him in a chokehold. The lighter clattered to the ground as the guy's hands went to his neck. A moment later, he went limp.

"He's out," said Zac, holding the man upright.

"This way," said Darwin, turning to the chapel.

They moved past two benches and behind a small altar to an iron gate. Its latch squealed as Darwin opened it, and Zac carried the man inside. There was little room in the tight space, an ossuary where the monks' bones lay piled almost to the ceiling. The number of monks over nearly two millennia far outnumbered the capacity for individual graves, so their bones were dug up after a few years and placed in the ossuary. The cemetery outside contained only abbots who'd achieved distinction.

Zac gagged the man as Darwin tied his wrists together outside the bars. Two minutes later, they emerged. From the look of the dust-covered pews, Darwin surmised the chapel got infrequent use. "How long will it hold him?" he asked.

"Long enough. And this will help," said Zac, pocketing the agent's sat phone. "As far as the others are concerned, he followed us up the mountain."

Five minutes after Zac and Siggy left for Jebel Musa through the monastery's main gate, Darwin and Eyrún exited the garden gate away from the main monastery. Darwin had called his Bedouin friend from the Jebaliya tribe, who picked them up. As they passed the immense front monastery wall, Eyrún shook Darwin's shoulder and pointed to a group of people who had just arrived. "That's Mike in the blue ballcap."

Darwin swiveled but caught only a fleeting glance of a guy wearing a dark blue hat, its visor angled away from him. Fortunately, no one in the group looked in their direction.

"Do you think they know about their agent?" asked Eyrún.

"Doesn't look like it from their casual stance. By now, Zac and Siggy should be at least two or three kilometers up the trail. And it should be awhile before they find the agent in the chapel." He turned to the driver. "How long will it take to get there?"

"Not long. Half an hour."

"Doesn't give us much time to find the cave," said Eyrún.

"No, but Mike doesn't know where we're going."

72

Bedouin Camp

Mike rode in an SUV with Ramy, Kim, and one agent. He'd learned the other agent had gone back to the monastery long before sunrise to follow Eyrún, her sister, and Zac up on the mountain.

A satellite phone rang. The agent answered it, listened a few moments, then said, in English, "They've not gone yet. The Bedouin reported seeing Darwin enter the monastery, but lost him inside. They have not seen him enter the garden area."

Kim turned to Mike, who, anticipating her question, said, "They mentioned going up after the tourists."

"What about Darwin?"

"All I know is his note said he would make contact in the morning."

"What about their phones?" Kim asked the agent.

"The GPS shows they're in Cairo."

"How did they find out about Pegasus?" she asked rhetorically. Then added, "It must be the American spy." Mike had told her about Zac's military record. She barked an order in Korean to the agent, who spoke into the sat phone, before pocketing it.

They journeyed in silence until reaching the monastery. The sun was fully up, and tourists had gathered to wait for the daily tours. A Bedouin man approached them as they exited the SUV.

Ramy spoke to him in rapid Arabic, then turned to Kim. "He saw Darwin but thinks he went inside the church and couldn't follow him. Like you heard earlier, he has not seen him since. Your man in there," Ramy nodded toward the guest rooms, "is watching the garden-side gate."

The Bedouin added in English, "I found the guide I told you about."

Ramy handed him baksheesh and went with him toward a younger man standing next to a newer model SUV. Kim told Mike to stay put and followed Ramy.

Minutes passed as Ramy negotiated. At one point, the young man's arms waved in frustration, but he relaxed and shook Ramy's hand. Mike guessed they'd reached a deal when Kim returned as Ramy got in the young man's SUV.

"Where are they now?" Kim asked the agent.

"On the trail," he said, pointing to a dot on the sat phone's display.

As the SUV rolled up, Mike asked, "What about Darwin?"

"This man will take us to a cave that he says has the diamonds. The Bedouin will watch for Darwin."

Mike got in the SUV's rear seat between the agent and Ramy, and as they drove away, Kim addressed him from the front passenger seat. "You made the right decision to cooperate with us."

73

Triangle Mountain

About forty minutes later, the SUV bucked to a stop in the uneven riverbed. Darwin removed the monk's habit and left it rolled up on the passenger seat.

Their driver said, "I'll pick you up here before dark," and then drove off in a cloud of dust.

Eyrún and Darwin surveyed their surroundings as the pickup truck's squeaking springs receded. A minute later, silence enveloped them in the flat-bottomed wadi, and they began walking in the dry riverbed toward the triangle mountain. The wadi's sides rose steeply to orange-pink granite peaks, and while not hot, the still air and the sandy soil soon caused them to sweat.

Darwin shaded his eyes and looked up towards Jebel Musa, whose summit Zac and Siggy had started climbing over ninety minutes ago. The plan was for them to connect via satellite phone from the summit. Zac and Eyrún would use their geologist skills to interpret the sites in real time.

Not quite a half-hour later, the wadi curved left, then forked around what they figured was the triangle mountain. It plateaued at about two-thirds the height of the surrounding mountains. When they reached its base, Eyrún stopped to take some soil samples. They scrambled ten meters up the slope and sat in the shade cast by a boulder.

"Get me samples from a few spots," she said, while taking a field microscope from her pack.

Darwin did and drank some water while she hunched over the hand-held device.

She looked at a sample from higher up the slope and said, "Got them. Micro-spherulites. Fortunately, these are big enough to see. Here." She handed the device to him, and he peered at a brightly lit smattering of particles.

It took a moment for his brain to pick out the round objects in the field. "How do we know they're not anthropogenic? This mountain's full of hermit dwellings."

"We can't rule it out without other tests, but I doubt these resulted from human activity. The spheres have a glassy appearance. Gently roll the microscope about."

"I see it." He looked longer before handing it back to her. "Is that enough to confirm your meteorite theory for the diamonds?"

"Not completely, but it's a data point that aligns with the stele."

They climbed down and traversed the stream bed until, at a midpoint of the triangle, then crossed the riverbed to get a full view of the peak.

Dozens of small openings dotted the mountain. A line of caves began about halfway up, where a more expansive terrace had been cut by ancient water flow.

"Nice view for a hermit. Long walk to find food, though," said Eyrún.

Darwin consulted the translation in his notebook. "We're looking for 'eyes in a face.' Maybe Zac's AI analysis of the foot traffic can help narrow it down."

"Already on it," said Eyrún, looking at a photo. She turned the picture, orienting it to the mountain. "The two most traveled trails go up there," she pointed to the left, "and there, in the middle. It zigzags."

"I see it. Starts right behind the rock where we sat." His eyes followed it until it disappeared behind a ridge. "Must be along that level."

"But nothing looks like a face," she said.

"No, but there are three groups of two caves. That narrows it down. Maybe we can see something when closer."

They crossed the riverbed and climbed the trail. Once past the boulder they'd sat on earlier, they found imprints from modern shoes on the trail. Nine switchbacks later, they reached a terrace about five meters wide in front of the six caves that dropped off a cliff into the wadi. Rocks had been arranged in crude yards that separated the caves from each other.

"That's odd. What do you make of it?" asked Eyrún.

Darwin went into the closest cave but found it shallow, less than three meters deep. He turned and bumped into Eyrún, who'd entered after him. The next cave was the same size. They walked back outside and looked at the six openings.

"Which cave is it?" asked Eyrún.

Darwin saw a small red object two caves over. "That one," he said, crossing over the lined-up rocks. He picked up a piece of energy bar wrapper and studied it briefly before declaring, "It's been here about a week based on its fading. Whoever ate it sat here and tucked it under this rock."

Eyrún raised her brows.

"Really," he added. "I wrote a paper on it for an undergrad field archaeology course."

They entered and found a larger round space. "Looks like a communal area," said Eyrún.

"Exactly," said Darwin. "Now it makes sense. Some hermetic traditions in Egypt and Sinai were communal. They used this cave for gatherings, like mealtime. The rest of their days were spent in the smaller caves in prayer and contemplation. The rocks are a simple reminder of separation."

"It's been used recently," said Eyrún, pointing to a niche in the wall that held a modern camp stove, teapot, and cups. "And there are more here." She moved to the cave's rear.

Darwin crossed over as she squeezed through a vertical slot in the wall. "There's writing," he said to her through the gap. "It matches the demotic on the stele. I'd say we're in the right spot."

"What's it say?"

"Death to those who trespass."

"Now, there's a welcome mat."

Jebel Musa

Zac and Siggy summited Jebel Musa mid-morning. The trail had been moderate, then angled sharply upward the last half-kilometer. The desolate, dusty summit reminded Zac of photos from the Mars rovers. Nothing grew in the red granite, enhanced by the sun in the clear alpine air. The sunrise climbers were gathered in knots around the Greek chapel and what appeared to be hermit shacks on the broad, undulating summit.

Siggy rested on a large rock while studying her watch. "One thirty-seven," she said, referring to her pulse. "It's coming down. That last section was brutal."

"Yep. Did you count the steps?" asked Zac.

"I lost count. Focused on beating your butt to the top."

Zac smiled. They'd hit the trail just after tying up the North Korean agent. Siggy had started at a run, and Zac had fallen in but let her set the pace. He'd had the reserves to pass her in the last section, but the trail had narrowed, making it dangerous to pass. He'd also figured today would be long.

He stared out across the ridges that dropped in height before giving way to flat land near the Red Sea—fifty kilometers distant. He'd studied the geological forces exerted on the Sinai peninsula as the African and Asian land masses crushed it. The tectonic forces upended its striated layers, like two hands squeezing a cake. Some sections had tipped vertically, and eons of weathering had reduced sharp peaks to humps. He thought one looked like the stern of a sinking ship, momentarily suspended before its final plunge.

"They went in a cave ten minutes ago," said Siggy, looking at a message on the sat phone. "It's that triangle-shaped hill down there." She pointed into the wadi.

Zac looked, then said, "Let's get set up. If those caves they're exploring don't work out, the additional data might help narrow down the most active trails."

74

Cave in Triangle Mountain

Darwin pushed his right leg through the opening as he followed Eyrún. Away from the natural light, the cave grew danker, and animal urine permeated the air on the other side of the gap. His light revealed an empty creature's den, most likely that had run deeper into the cave.

They both put on headlamps that Eyrún had brought, and she traversed a winding passage. Darwin followed close behind. The smooth, dry walls appeared carved by water. The passage turned hard right, then bent left after five meters. He pushed through a snug gap that opened into a tiny bedroom-sized chamber.

"You feel that?" asked Eyrún.

"Yeah." Darwin noticed the increase in humidity that she was referring to. The moldy smell had dramatically increased in this chamber, and the temperature had risen. Just inside the wider space, his foot slid on a rock, and he grasped the wall for support. His hand came away wet, and his headlamp revealed a slimy moisture trail.

"Look at this," said Eyrún, running her light over the walls. Thousands of soft, hooded mushrooms had sprouted. But something else as well. In gaps between the mushrooms, bits of light reflected. She pried some of the minerals off the wall and examined it with a jeweler's loupe. "Diamonds. Although, these are tiny."

She dug out a handheld Geiger counter from her pack. Darwin's eyes widened in concern as he held out his muddy hand. "It's safe. One point three micro-sieverts," she announced after scanning the wall. She checked his hand and got a similar reading.

"Good." Darwin wiped the mud on his pant leg, then moved toward a wine barrel-sized opening about knee height. Darwin looked into the dark hole and experienced dread, as if something evil was lurking inside, just waiting to pounce. He couldn't see anything and pushed back a memory that had plagued him since childhood of a scene in a horror film of a corpse with its eyes sewn shut. He shivered. *Stop it. There's nothing in there.*

But he still felt a presence watching him from the darkness. He borrowed the Geiger counter from Eyrún and took a reading from the hole. "It's the same," he said and shook off the creepy vibe, telling himself it was just the radiation freaking him out. He crawled into the hole and saw nothing but inky blackness at its other end. The odd feeling returned and sweat beaded on his brow.

He took a deep breath and moved ahead, but the sensation intensified further. It pressed down on him like a weight, making breathing difficult. The suffocating darkness seemed to close in, gripping him with an urge to turn back.

"Are you okay in there?" asked Eyrún.

He jumped, hitting the ceiling. His headlamp went out, plunging him into blackness. *Putain!* He lost his sense of direction. Blood whooshed in his ears. He forced himself back in control of the erupting panic. *Stop! Breathe!*

Eyrún's light shone from behind, giving him a focal point. "What's going on?"

"I'm fine. Just looking at something, and my light went out." Darwin moved onto his left side, using a knee to push his body back to get an arm to his head. His neck ached, having to twist as his fingers fumbled at the headlamp. He found the switch.

His hand registered pain, and a small amount of blood oozed from the scraped skin. The injury refocused him. He'd been underground many times and never felt this way—there was something about this place that made his skin crawl.

Another body length forward, and his headlamp revealed an open space. He emerged in a chamber about four meters across, with a pool of water filling about half the space. The walls were alabaster smooth in some places and pocketed in others; the cavities were irregular and pocked. *It's like standing inside a sponge.*

Eyrún joined him, and after a moment, Darwin said, "This place is weird. I've never felt like this in a cave. Are you—"

"Oh, my God. Exactly," she said. "It's a little like what I experienced in the tunnel under the mountain house."

"Could it be the mushrooms?"

"We didn't eat any, but maybe the spores are in the soil? We breathed in the dust."

"So, I'm not losing my mind. Maybe it's psilocybin we kicked up."

Eyrún shrugged. "Here. Put this on." She handed him an N95 mask from her pack. They used them when caving in dusty sections and to protect pristine environments from human bacteria.

Darwin pinched his mask to the bridge of his nose as he explored the pool. The water was clear but darkened toward its center as it grew deeper. A smooth white rock lay mostly submerged on the pool's far side. *Odd,* he thought, *the color's all wrong. Looks like someone brought it from the outside.*

"*Merde!* It's a skull," he said, kneeling and placing a hand on the pool's edge for a closer look. "It's human." He sat back and examined the site as Eyrún joined him. "There's nothing else here. No signs of a burial." He removed the headlamp and shone the light closer to the skull—its ocular cavities were just below the water's surface. And another hole that shouldn't be there was just above the left eye.

"Is that a bullet hole?" asked Eyrún.

"Yes. Coursework in forensic archaeology taught me how to recognize injuries from weapons. The instructor also introduced modern injuries as a way to gauge the age of a skeleton quickly. This is a modern murder, not the ancient mystery we're trying to solve. Someone shot this person and left them here to rot."

"Where's the rest of the body?"

"Good question." Darwin shone the light around the small chamber, looking for clues to help identify the victim or the killer. There was nothing: no clothing, belongings, or signs of a struggle.

"Maybe the other bones sank in there." Eyrún held her light over the water, but its deep center swallowed the beam.

Mike looked into the wadi below as they neared the caves. That its dry bed had once carried water seemed impossible. He couldn't imagine hermits living here. *It makes no sense unless they thought clinging to life on the fringes brought them closer to the spirit world.*

"Watch your step," said the guide as the trail leveled out. They'd come to a row of caves framed by large rocks. Thirty meters farther, he stopped them again and pointed to a cave at the far end of the row.

Before entering, Kim asked the agent a question. The man consulted his sat phone and answered, pointing at Jebel Musa behind them. Mike looked, but couldn't see its summit from this angle. Kim then waved the agent into the cave first, followed by the guide, Mike, and Ramy. She brought up the rear.

Mike took in the round chamber that looked recently used, judging by the ash content in a fire pit in the cave's center. A carved shelf ringed the walls and served as seating for a gathering. He figured for ten, but as many as fifteen might squeeze onto the rock bench. Egyptian paintings covered the walls in vivid hues that seemed too modern to him.

"Where is it?" asked Kim.

"It is here," answered the guide. "Please sit down. I will begin the ceremony." The guide turned to a small camp stove set in a niche with a teapot, cups, and jars.

"No. Where is the cave?" asked Kim.

"This *is* the cave. I don't understand," said the guide, who pointed to Ramy and continued. "He said you sought the mystical experience to speak with the Universal One."

Ramy spoke to him in Arabic. Mike roughly followed that Ramy had asked about a deeper cave, one that contained a mystical compound. The guide still didn't understand. Ramy held out a diamond from his pocket.

The guide drew back as if shown a deadly poison.

"You know where these are," said Ramy. "Take us there."

"No." The guide waved his hands.

Kim aimed her pistol at the guide's head. "Take me there, now."

75

Darwin found no more clues to explain the skull on the pool's edge, and they retreated into the chamber filled with mushrooms, where Eyrún studied the walls more closely.

"These diamonds are much smaller than the ones in Henri's lab," she said. "There's slime and other organic growth. Sometime in the past, the mushroom spores got in here."

"Perhaps the hermits grew them for food," said Darwin.

"These all can't be psilocybin, then."

"I doubt it. This is out of my realm. There must be a dozen different varieties. Look, over here." Darwin moved to a mound of palm-sized mushrooms the color of tan shoe leather. "I swear these are shiitake. I've seen them in the market."

Eyrún said she'd take his word for it and moved her hand-held light over the walls. "There's no color change in the diamonds and no radiation either."

Darwin probed the mound with his shoe. "I thought so. Someone's cultivating these. They're growing on wood. There's no way this could have lasted since the hermits. Maybe some surviving cult uses this place?" He looked around. "Eyrún?" She'd disappeared.

"In here," her voice echoed from around a corner.

Darwin followed the sound to a small, dry chamber where mushrooms lay drying on wooden racks. From left to right, the mushrooms were spread in batches; the ones on the right were the most dehydrated. A bench carved into one wall contained a large mortar and pestle and a clay jar. Darwin carefully studied it. A brown-gray powder filled it halfway.

"This gets weirder and weirder," said Eyrún. "This must be your cult."

"If this is magic mushroom power—and I'm not ingesting any to find out—then this would be a way to 'open mystical visions' referred to by the stele."

"Is that pool the 'well of life'?"

"Dunno," he said. "But if it is, then I'm wondering about 'the mistress of heat' that the 'eater of souls' would lead us to."

They debated whether the false journey in the incantation was metaphorical for the magic mushroom trip but left the discussion hanging, as their knowledge of Egyptian esoteric was limited. They surmised that knowing the gods and being steeped in the traditions of the soul's journey into the afterlife would influence the psilocybin's effect.

"We need to update Zac and Siggy," said Eyrún. "Maybe they've found a different cave."

Darwin agreed, and they began working their way outside when, at a tricky bend, Eyrún's light fell on paint. "What's this?" She approached a hand-width picture of a snake. "It looks like the one on your stele."

Darwin moved around her to examine the serpent. Its ochre head and body undulated like a sine wave, and a red forked tongue flicked out its mouth. "Wait, there's a crevasse here." He wedged sideways, stepping over rockfall piled on the floor. He slipped and grasped the wall, pulling a chunk from it. Small pieces from the ceiling rained down.

"It doesn't look safe," said Eyrún, shining her light over Darwin's head.

"It looks intact enough, and it widens right here," he said, wiggling his extended right hand. "I'm just going to look."

He shimmied his way to the wider spot and peered around a corner. A dark passage loomed ahead. His nose itched fiercely under the mask, and he brought his left forearm up to rub it through the white material. A moment later, the irritation passed, and he stretched to shine his headlamp into the passage. Unfortunately, the wide beam splashed too much light onto the walls, and he couldn't see into the opening a couple of body lengths ahead.

"Hand me your torch," he asked Eyrún.

She got next to him in the awkward space, stretched a hand under his chin, and placed the light in his right hand that had reached back. Darwin flicked on the beam and aimed it down the gap. "Still too much reflection. Can you turn off my headlamp?"

He felt her search probe the back of his head until she found the switch. The walls suddenly darkened, and he focused the beam from the handheld. "It's another chamber, and there are reflections, like sparkles," he said. "I'm going closer."

Darwin sidestepped toward the sparkles in the chamber, but Eyrún grabbed his arm. "Turn the light off."

"Why?" But she held fast to his sleeve, and he followed her instruction. It took half a minute, but as the light wash faded, his vision picked up objects glowing in the gap ahead. "It's green spots, like cats' eyes."

"Don't move. Here. Give me back the light and take a reading with the Geiger counter."

Darwin bent his arm back toward Eyrún. She swapped the light with the counter, and Darwin slipped his hand back into the gap. He pressed its button, and three seconds later, it beeped.

"What's it say?"

He strained to read the numbers on the dim display. "Looks like five twelve."

"Five point one two?"

"No. Five hundred and twelve."

"Oh, God. Darwin, get out of there now."

"*Putain!*" He sucked in his gut and pushed back into the corridor under the snake painting, almost knocking Eyrún to the ground.

Darwin stared at his right hand like he'd dunked it in poison. His face went pale, and the room closed in.

Eyrún grasped his arm to steady him. Then grabbed the dosimeter in her other hand. She took multiple readings where they currently stood and another reading in the gap beyond the snake. "There's nothing over four millisieverts," she said.

"What about in there?" he asked in a shrill voice. "Five hundred?"

"I don't know," she said.

"Cancer?"

"Only your hand and forearm were exposed. The rock protected your body."

"But I stuck my head in there to look. What do we do?" he asked behind wide eyes.

She put her hands on his cheeks. "Darwin. Look at me."

He focused on her and relaxed.

"I know, Love. It's scary. I was frightened when I first discovered the radioactivity in the lab, but I looked it up. A reading in the hundreds means an elevated risk, but it's not extreme. The danger's time based. You were only exposed for seconds. You'll be okay." When he did not respond right away, she added. "Darwin?"

"Okay," he said.

She hugged him and whispered, "There's nothing we can do now except get out of here."

After a long moment, she turned to exit the cave, but froze at a noise outside the chamber. "Someone's coming," she said, switching off her headlamp. She crouched down as Darwin did the same.

76

Jebel Musa

Zac and Siggy hiked a little downslope to deploy the drone. The thirty-plus tourists milling around the summit would ask questions, and he was in no mood to answer. He unpacked it and powered up its instruments. Its high-end camera could read a coin at a hundred meters, and the microphone could distinguish speech from farther out. The pricey carbon fiber and titanium construction meant bigger, longer-running batteries, but unfortunately, little could be done about the noise from its quad-propellers. At fifty meters, it buzzed like angry bees.

He guided it over the wadi. The updrafts from the warming rock bounced the small craft until he'd flown it out over the riverbed. Then he throttled back and let the drone drift toward the triangular mountain.

"I see people going into one of the caves," said Siggy, peering into powerful binoculars braced on a tripod.

"Is it them?"

"No. I don't think so. Eyrún's sat signal is still offline. There's four, but I can't tell much else about them."

"I can get you closer with the video feed. Put on the VR headset," said Zac.

Siggy fitted virtual reality goggles on her face. Zac had modified them to view the drone's video feed. "Okay," she said. "I see them. It's better than the binoculars, but still too far away."

"Working it." Zac flew the drone as fast as he could without the risk of flipping it in the volatile air currents.

"They're getting bigger," she said, "but it's bouncing pretty bad. Wait. What's that? It got noisy."

"I turned on the drone's microphone."

"Oh, okay." She adjusted the sound on the headset's earphones. "They went inside the far left cave. No. Wait, one came back out. I think he sees the drone. He's got a hand over his eyes, looking right at me."

"It's as close as I can go. The signal's getting weak."

Cave at Triangle Mountain

The guide's eyes went wide, but a moment later, he steeled himself against Kim's threat. "No. There is a great evil."

Mike stepped sideways, away from the guide. Kim's eyes were cold, her jaw set. Mike had seen the look in the Iraqi drug trade. The young man had seconds to decide.

Ramy broke the tension. "You can't kill him. He's the only one who knows."

"You're right," said Kim. "He needs to see an example." With that, she swung the gun at Ramy and pulled the trigger.

The shot roared in the tight space, dropping Ramy like a stone.

Kim brought the gun back to the guide's face. Mike's ears rang, but he heard her say to the guide, "Take me to the diamonds, or you're next."

Jebel Musa

Siggy screamed.

"What?" Zac turned to see her hands over the earpieces.

"A gunshot. Somebody got shot." She yanked off the headset to look at the cave below with her own eyes. "Oh, God, Zac. What if it was Eyrún or Darwin?"

Zac lost the drone's signal and could just make out its black shape over the riverbed. It was programmed to auto-land, and he could see it dropping. "Shit!" He set down the now useless controller and crouched next to Siggy. "Let me hear it."

He put on the headset, then replayed the last sixty seconds, wincing at the sound. "Definitely a gunshot."

In the video, the man outside the cave had turned toward the drone's sound but spun toward the cave at the gunshot. Then the recording shut off as the drone went into safety mode.

"What if they were in there, Zac?" Siggy's face turned ashen, eyes flooding with tears.

"Which cave did Darwin and Eyrún go in? I see six."

"I don't know, but—"

"We need to get down there," said Zac, already in motion, stuffing the gear in his pack. Then, he briefly shut his eyes to picture the mountain's backside from when he'd studied its satellite images. His eyes popped open. "This way." He started down to his right. "There's a chimney that goes from here to the riverbed."

The first meters fell away at a modest rate, then dropped into a tight gap. Zac braced his hands against the granite walls that formed a V in the near vertical shaft as he worked his way over rocks lodged between them. He looked back once when Siggy hollered, but she'd only slipped and landed on her butt.

"I'm fine," she yelled. "Keep going!"

In thirty meters, the gap opened onto a wide, scree-covered slope. His foot shot forward on the loose rock, arms swirling for balance as he brought his other leg around and stopped. His heart slammed in his rib cage, realizing he'd just stopped himself from going ass over tea kettle down the impossibly steep slope.

A crunch and slide sounded behind him. Rocks sprayed his backside as Siggy whooshed by.

"You gotta ski it, Zac." She hopped from one foot to another atop the sliding scree, shifting her weight like a snow skier as she half-surfed the rock wave.

Zac jumped up and mimicked her motions. He'd skied enough times to get the hang of it quickly. But the sliding mess beneath his feet seemed to have a mind of its own, as he nearly pitched over when he snagged his toe on a rock below the surface.

They descended over 500 meters in under two minutes, soon finding themselves in a widening slope of softer material. Here they had to run, but their boots sank into the softer soil. When they reached the riverbed, sweat poured down Zac's face. A glance at his watch told him they'd been on the summit just under twenty minutes ago. The adrenaline rush momentarily distracted him from the situation, but he controlled it. *Stay vigilant,* he reminded himself. *We haven't engaged the enemy yet.*

77

Cave

Darwin steadied his breathing as muffled voices argued in the passage coming from the cave's mouth. A faint light wavered in the gap before him. Eyrún, still beside him, picked up a fist-sized rock and whispered, "Stay here. I'm going to the opposite side."

She moved a short distance, then crouched down, leaving Darwin alone. With few places to hide, his mind raced through workable options. Each of the chambers was a dead end, and one was radioactive. He considered potential weapons as he squeezed a small handheld light. *Throw it in their face? That's stupid. It hardly weighs anything. Wait. Throw it away from them.*

The instant the idea struck, he stood and wedged back into the crevasse by the snake. He forced himself not to think about the radiation as he reached the sharp bend. He flicked on the light and tossed it toward the diamonds. It hit the far wall and clattered to the floor. Its beam glowed brightly on the rock.

"Yes," he mouthed silently, figuring the light would draw whoever looked into the passage. He squeezed himself back out and pressed against the wall beneath the snake painting. In the tunnel, a man's voice, in Arabic, asked, "Where are the diamonds?"

"In a deeper chamber farther in," said another male voice.

It was followed by a woman's voice he couldn't comprehend. He guessed it was Kim.

Merde! He looked in Eyrún's direction. He couldn't see her, but her rock and his bare hands were no match for three. *Maybe more,* he thought. They needed something to buy time. He crossed over to Eyrún in the dim light cast by his smart-watch.

"Follow me," he whispered and led the way back to the mushroom drying chamber, where he grabbed the jar of ground magic mushroom powder. He explained his plan to smash it against a wall beside Kim and the others. "They'll be overcome like you were in the tunnel under our house."

"But where do we go?" she whispered.

"Back in the pool chamber to wait, then go around them when they're overcome."

Eyrún's face screwed up.

"I put a light in the crevasse with the diamonds. That should draw their attention as well."

"Not exactly brilliant," she said.

"Nothing else came to mind. You got any ideas?"

She hesitated a long moment, then said, "No."

"Okay. Let's do it."

He stood a moment while Eyrún went to the pool chamber, then got in position to throw the jar.

He pressed against the right side wall and adjusted his mask, figuring the last thing he wanted was hallucinations in the cramped space. The proximity of voices heralded their approach. Seconds later, lights flashed on the walls.

Closer. Closer. He repeated until the first figure came into view. He jumped into the gap and heaved the jar at the wall nearest two of the figures. The pot smashed, cascading a brownish cloud onto the intruders.

Yells erupted.

Darwin turned, took a few steps, then reached for the opposite wall. The lights behind him receded as he groped along the wall until it opened into the mushroom chamber. A few more steps brought him to the tunnel toward the pool chamber. He plunged in on his belly. A short way in, he paused to listen. Nothing. He shimmied its length toward the pool.

Once inside, he flicked on his headlamp. He looked around. "Eyrún? Where are you?"

A light flashed from beneath a low gap. "In here," she called out.

Darwin noticed some large rocks had been moved down to the gap. Eyrún's face appeared on the other side.

"I moved the rocks and found this. I think it's a way out. Hurry, get in."

He worked his way under, grunting as he wriggled his hips through to a space no bigger than a compact car. Calcification from ancient water dripping ran down the walls, and the beginnings of stalactites poked from the low ceiling. Three tunnels entered the chamber, all from upward directions.

"Did it work?" she asked.

"Hard to tell. I saw a cloud of powder in their lights."

"Let's get going. The opening behind me ascends. Hopefully, it's a way out," she said, turning and crawling in.

Darwin looked at the gap behind him. A sick feeling seized him as he realized it wouldn't take much to block it. He adjusted his headlamp and followed Eyrún's boots as they disappeared into one tunnel.

78

Outside the Cave

Standing in the riverbed, Zac wanted water, at least to wash out his dusty throat, but Siggy raced on. He continued, adrenaline driving him onto the triangle mountain trail. The uphill run seemed to take forever, but they soon reached the level with the caves, flying across the open spaces the hermits had created. She ran toward the farthest cave, leaping over the rock borders.

Zac caught her just before its entrance. "Siggy. Wait," he said, grabbing her arm.

She spun, face flushed red, and tried shrugging him off, but he'd pulled past her, gun in hand. He stopped at the opening, motioning her to hold still. He dropped low and slipped into the cave, scanning the walls, looking for adversaries.

"Darwin!" Siggy screamed, running past him.

A body lay face-down, heels toward them, just beyond the shadow cast by the cave's mouth.

Zac went cold. He stumbled toward her.

But the scene was off—the boots were bigger than Darwin's. Zac rolled the body over. "It's Ramy," he gasped. "Shot through the heart."

"What about Eyrún and Darwin?" Siggy panted.

He spun slowly, trying to figure out what had happened.

Siggy ran outside.

"Shit!" He sprinted after her, catching her as she approached the next cave in line.

"Stop. Let me do this."

"She's my sister!" she yelled, flailing at him.

"Doesn't matter. These people are killers. I'm trained. You're not. End of debate."

Zac studied the footprints and reconnoitered each cave until he found a recent cigarette butt in front of the cave four over from where Ramy'd been shot.

"Stay here," he whispered. She shook her head, so he added, "Then stay directly behind me."

He listened at the cave mouth. They looked at each other with scrunched eyebrows. Someone was singing.

79

Cave

Mike brushed the powder off his shirt. He'd been nearest to the figure who'd thrown the jar. It had shattered on the wall, sending a dust cloud across the chamber. Mike and the guide took the brunt of the powder. The agent behind him looked at the potsherds on the floor and laughed at the feeble attack. But the dust smelled odd to Mike, and a second later, the guide yelled, "Get out."

Kim and the agent were out first, and Mike was last after he'd helped the guide who'd stumbled. He doubled over, coughing in front of the cave, and the guide, struggling through his coughs, explained his reason for the warning. All Mike got was "poison."

The guide coughed again and drank some water.

Kim then turned to Mike. "What did you see? Was it them?"

"Who else would it be?" he said, then asked. "What's the poison?"

Kim asked the agent, who spoke fluent Arabic, and translated for Mike. "No poison. Magic mushrooms."

Great. What next? Mike thought of the amount he'd inhaled, but he didn't know if it was dangerous or would just make him high. He drank more water and snorted some of it off his wet fingers to relieve his nose's dry, dirty feeling.

Kim turned back to the agent and asked another question, who relayed it to their guide. Mike understood the words for "exit" and "behind."

"No," said the guide, coughing again.

"We go back when the dust settles. Half an hour," said Kim.

Mike sat down as the agent explored the other four caves. He stared into the riverbed far below and, over the next quarter hour later, swore the sun got brighter.

He glanced at the guide, who seemed fascinated, moving his hands in and out of the shadow cast by his body. When the agent returned, Mike was intrigued by the vibrant green laces in his boots, enjoying how they snaked over each other.

Kim ordered them both inside the cave and to lie on the floor. "Stay here," she said, but Mike had no intention of moving. She was much less engaging than the patterns playing on the cave ceiling.

She and the agent returned to the cave as he got lost in the shifting colors. A short while later, the guide began singing. At first, it annoyed him, but soon Mike's visions moved with the song, and he drifted with it.

80

Siggy began tossing fist-sized rocks on Zac's signal from where she stood by the left side mouth of the cave. They planned on drawing out whoever was singing. One by one, the rocks clacked against others in the open space, interrupting the desert silence. Zac slipped inside from the right on the third rock toss when no one came out.

Nothing moved, but the singing continued—an up-tempo Arab pop song. Zac's eyes adjusted to the dim light from outside, and he moved to the voice.

It paused when he got there. "Keep singing. I like it," he said to the guide leaning against the wall. Then, he turned to the other figure, lying on its back, a finger tracing something in the air. "Mike?"

"Oh hey, Zac. When did you get here? I thought you climbed that mountain."

"I did. What the hell's going on?" Zac dropped to one knee and surveyed the chamber, not daring to turn a light on.

Siggy walked up to them. "These guys look smacked."

Zac studied Mike. His clothing was covered in dust, more heavily on his right shoulder, as if dirt had fallen on him. But it smelled moldy. He rubbed his finger on a heavily coated spot, sniffed it, tasted it—

mushroom—and laughed. "They are. Somebody dumped ground mushrooms on them, odds on the magic kind."

"Then Darwin was right about the cult practice," she said.

"Mike?" Zac got his attention again.

"Yes," he said, sounding like someone hypnotized, physically present, but mentally in another space.

"Where did the mushrooms come from?"

"A flying jar."

"Who threw it?"

"The darkness."

Zac figured this would get nowhere. While Mike seemed lucid, his answers would probably make no more sense than they had. Zac had tried magic mushrooms once and remembered the synaesthesia that blended the senses and led to a feeling of connection. In such a state, nothing Mike told them would tactically be helpful.

He turned to Siggy. "We're going in blind. We don't know the layout or if Darwin and Eyrún are in there."

"But somebody threw that jar."

"Agreed. Let's say it was Darwin or Eyrún. They probably figured on doing exactly what happened to these two, but," he risked shining a light on the rear wall, "there's no powder in this chamber." He turned to Mike. "How did you and your friend get here?"

"Kim brought us."

"Where is she now?" Siggy pressed.

"Looking for diamonds." Mike pointed toward the cave's rear. "But they're out here. Don't you see them?" Mike's hand waved across the ceiling.

Zac explored the far wall and found the opening. He got Siggy, then said, "Same as before. Stay directly behind me. Do not turn on your light. It's a good target for a shooter. And no talking."

81

Darwin backed out of the tunnel they'd entered fifteen minutes ago and sat in the broader spot beyond the gap to the pool chamber. Eyrún had hit a second dead end. His neck cramped, and he rested atop an outstretched arm.

"How's your head?" asked Eyrún, sliding in behind.

"Sore, I'm just resting." He rubbed a lump above his forehead where he'd whacked it earlier. Typically, they wore helmets underground. Fortunately, Eyrún had brought headlamps. Darwin's neck muscles relaxed, and he was about to enter the remaining possible exit when a light flashed under the pool chamber gap.

He froze, putting a hand up to warn Eyrún. They switched off their lights. Darwin's pulse thumped in his ears as he strained to hear. A muffled voice came through the gap, but sounded too far away to be the person with the light.

Something touched his leg. He jerked, banging the other side of his head. Stars swirled as he rubbed the spot and his cheeks puffed out, holding back a curse. Eyrún's fingers tugged at his pant leg, then pointed to a head-sized rock on the floor.

Glad to realize it was his wife's hand and not a snake, he scrunched down and lifted the rock. Not a great weapon, but it would stop whoever came through the opening below. Sweat ran down his forehead and into his eye. He moved to rub it on his raised sleeve but remembered the magic mushroom powder had half covered him and the people he'd thrown it at. He had no idea what would happen if it got in his eye, so he pinched the lid closed while he kept his other focused on the hole. The irritation soon subsided.

The light outside remained still as the voices argued in Korean. He picked up a scent of after-shave carried on an air current. He leaned farther toward the tunnel they were trying next. The air movement from the gap cooled his sweaty face—which meant it exited at its other end. Once the voices with the light moved away, he sat back and whispered what he'd discovered to Eyrún.

"I'll follow," she said.

Darwin angled his way up. The tunnel then leveled, and his headlamp picked up a gap several body lengths ahead. Eyrún came up behind him, and he turned to tell her.

Suddenly, she screamed and lunged, grabbing both his legs. His body stretched in her grasp as the sound of tumbling rocks reverberated.

"Eyrún!" The air thickened with dust, obscuring his view. "Eyrún? Eyrún!" He coughed as dust seeped under the mask.

All he felt was her dead weight on his legs.

82

Outside the Cave

Zac stayed low, offering as little a target as possible. He'd been in plenty of caves, but was usually better kitted out than today. His least memorable missions in Afghanistan involved routing out insurgents. In those caves, he had night vision goggles, flash bombs, and laser-sighted weapons.

Today, his most useful weapons were stealth and guile. He breathed deeply and slowly, keeping himself centered. Every few steps, he shut his eyes and turned his head, listening for the smallest of movements, but the cave was silent as a tomb.

A rock rolled behind him. He stepped backward and pressed Siggy into the wall.

"Sorry," she whispered in his ear.

He put a finger to her lips and shook his head. She nodded. Then he held the sat phone out into the tunnel, using its glass surface as a mirror. Nothing.

They continued. In a few steps, the cave opened into a widened chamber. Potsherds lay scattered on the floor, and a dank smell hung in the air. A powder had splattered the wall. He risked turning up the light and moved toward the far wall, covered in mushrooms. A slime trail flowed onto the floor beneath them. Nearby, a different type of mushroom grew on a woodpile, fed by the wetness. *Somebody uses this place.*

His light scanned the wall, stopping in a circular hole. He stood at an angle, not giving a clear shot to anyone on the other side. He drifted to a wide opening on his left, where Siggy had entered another chamber. She pointed out mushrooms on a drying rack and a workbench with the mortar and pestle.

Zac crossed to it and tasted the powder in the mortar. Same stuff as on Mike's clothes. He began developing a picture of Darwin's and Eyrún's movements: finding this room, deducing the ground mushrooms as psilocybin, and using it to disable their opponents. *Clever.* His eyes scoured the room with the drying rack and the bigger chamber. *But where are you now?*

He stopped on the large hole and motioned Siggy to move closer. "Have you ever used a gun?" he whispered.

"Some target shooting."

"Then this will be easy. I'm going in there. Shoot whoever comes out, except me, of course."

"What will you use?"

He palmed a sharp knife. She nodded and took up a position to the side as Zac bellied into the hole.

Zac moved through the dark opening. All the breathing exercises in the world could not hold back his apprehension. Fortunately, the faint light from Siggy highlighted most of the small chamber, including a flat dark spot. *Water,* he guessed. He could see no one. *Weird, unless someone's clinging to the ceiling like Spiderman.* He took a quick breath, then dove into the chamber, rolling to his feet beside the pool. He looked about. *Where are they?*

He noted the porous walls, eaten away by water that formed the pool. The other caverns were harder rock. He examined the skull in the pool and determined it was not a mystery involving today, so he left it alone. There was only one other viable exit, besides the hole he'd come from. He probed its opening, but it had filled with rocks.

What the hell's going on in this place? It's like they turned into spirits. A premonition seized him: *Siggy. The other chamber*. He ducked back into the hole and, as he neared the other side whispered, "Siggy."

Nothing. *Shit*. He tried louder. "Siggy, it's me." A light came closer to the hole. He held the knife, ready to strike at anything entering the hole. "Siggy?"

Suddenly, her face appeared from outside. He jumped, whacking his head. Seconds later, he crawled out. "Didn't you hear me?"

"Not at first, but you also said not to talk."

"But I—" he started and let it drop.

Siggy wanted to see the pool chamber, so he stood watch. Three minutes later, she came back. "You're right, it's strange. What's a skull doing in there? And where's the rest of it?"

He shrugged. "I'm more interested in where Kim and her thug are."

"And that jar didn't throw itself," she added. "It's got to be Darwin or Eyrún."

"Stay alert. I feel like we've missed something." He checked his gun again.

83

Escape Tunnel

Darwin couldn't see. The dust had whited out everything. But at least he felt Eyrún atop his lower legs.

"Eyrún," he called.

He tried dragging himself forward, but couldn't beneath her slack body. Something had knocked her out. He looked ahead. The dust had moved. Not much. *But a partial airflow still exists.*

"Eyrún," he called again and kicked his legs gently, like a swimmer, to rouse her.

Still nothing.

He went very still and focused all his attention on his legs, trying to feel Eyrún's breathing. He could not, but he sensed a faint but rapid pulse. *Is it hers or mine?* He put a finger to his neck artery, but still couldn't tell if they matched.

Oh, God. Don't let us end here. He'd never imagined they'd end up in a situation like this. He tried to swallow against a hard lump in his throat. *There's got to be a way.*

But no ideas came. Defeated, he laid his head on one arm as a dark wave of emotion pummeled him.

84

Cave

Zac felt more confident as they backtracked toward the cave's entrance. At least he knew the way out. But the situation made no sense. *Did they leave while we climbed down the mountain? Did Darwin and Eyrún come in here? Why didn't they contact us?*

He was not superstitious, but he sensed they were being watched. *There!* A sound like a tumbling rock came from ahead. He moved cautiously around a bend. His light fell upon a snake painting. What's that? He edged closer to study it. An arm's length away, he traced its body with a finger.

Siggy slipped behind him and whispered, "It looks like the snake in Darwin's stele."

"It does."

She tapped his shoulder. "There's a light."

Zac looked to his right into a perfectly hidden crevasse. A steady light showed a tight turn about two meters away. Another light moved about on the wall. *Someone's in there?*

He eased into the gap but stopped, guessing he'd have a tough time getting his large frame through. *But Darwin and Eyrún could fit. And Siggy.*

"Do think you can squeeze in there?" he whispered.

She nodded and backed up so they could swap places. But before they did, rocks tumbled from the direction of the mushroom chamber.

Zac's light caught a figure coming toward them from the mushroom chamber. "It's Kim!" He shoved Siggy to the floor. A beam hit him in the face as he jumped back into the crevasse.

A gunshot exploded the rock on his right.

He reached around the gap, returning fire. "Siggy, stay down," he yelled as another bullet shattered the wall, splintering bits into his arm and face. He moved to shoot again, but a hail of bullets hit the ceiling, raining down rocks.

He released a volley at Kim while pushing himself from the crevasse.

Kim ran, shoving Siggy aside.

Zac tripped as the ceiling came down.

Siggy reached back to pull him from the pile.

"Get Kim," he yelled. "I can get out."

Siggy spun, giving chase.

85

Outside the Cave

Siggy tripped Kim as she left the cave's mouth. She rolled in the pebble-strewn dirt but lost her grip on the gun. Still on her feet, Siggy got to it first, but Kim gripped her ankle, sending her sprawling. Siggy tossed it into the ravine as she tumbled and rolled to her right. Both women sprang to their feet, shading their eyes against the harsh midday sun.

Lines of rocks on either side of the forecourt separated this cave from the others. And though it was an easy hop to the spaces on either side, the far edge plunged fifty meters into the wadi.

"Just like the Rio games," said Kim.

Siggy said nothing, matching her nemesis's movements. She flashed on that day in Rio: a block of Icelandic flags waved in the stands, the arena hot from a struggling air conditioner. Siggy was favored to reach the medal round.

Kim reached down as if to adjust her boot, but slung a handful of pebbles at her.

Siggy lunged left, reading the move. She came up behind Kim, seized her waist, and, blocking her foot, hauled her down. But she'd misjudged the space. Air burst from her lungs as she landed on a large rock.

Kim broke free and threw a sideways kick. Siggy barely dodged it from her position on the edge of the abyss. When the move left Kim off balance, Siggy landed an open-handed punch to Kim's face.

Kim absorbed it, shook it off, and came back with a roundhouse kick. Siggy blocked it, countering with a snap kick to Kim's stomach, doubling her over.

Siggy moved to finish, but Kim had baited her and rolled, sweeping out Siggy's legs. Both scrambled in the dirt, faced each other, and cautiously stood.

Kim ran to escape, but a tall figure blocked the trail. Zac stood, covered head to toe in chalky dust, arms crossed like a mummy but holding a gun instead of an *ankh*. He moved at Kim.

"Back off, Zac. She's mine," Siggy yelled, her hair a tangled mess, blood streaming down her left temple.

Kim turned back to face her. "You know I'll beat you again. He might kill me, but not before I kill you."

"Where's my sister?"

"You saw."

The women circled each other again, probing for weaknesses. Siggy winced, her left leg moving stiffly.

"Saw what?"

"The hole near the pool. It's blocked. She screamed when I caved it in."

Siggy went slack, picturing the pool chamber with the small opening.

"Aw, I took your medal in Rio, and now I took your sister," said Kim, launching a cage fight move.

The flying kick hit Siggy's chest. She flew backward, smacking her head on the rock near the cave mouth, and crashed to the ground with an audible crunch.

"No rules here," said Kim.

Siggy pushed up on a knee. The judo rematch now a street brawl.

"Your sister's dead. Now I'll finish you." Kim swept a kick at

Siggy's head. She pulled back, but the blow caught her chin, pitching her sideways.

Zac raised his gun as Kim moved in for the kill.

In a flash, Siggy snatched Kim's hair, yanked down, and drove her head up into Kim's chin.

Bones crunched.

"Bitch." Kim howled, grasping her face, then looked at her bloody hands.

Siggy tried to stand, her left hand bracing the ground. Kim lunged to stomp on it, but Siggy pulled away and grabbed Kim's foot, yanking it sideways. Kim hit the ground hard. Siggy straddled her, punching her face. Kim shielded herself, but found a rock with one hand and slammed it into Siggy's ribs.

Siggy screamed, and Kim twisted, breaking free. Both women rolled and staggered upright. Kim kicked Siggy in the left knee. Siggy spun, screaming, and limped heavily toward the wadi. Kim rushed to send her over the edge.

Siggy flashed back to the move that should have won the match in Rio, but the referee from China had called a foul. The crowd had roared in protest as Kim got the win.

Not this time! Siggy fell backward, absorbing the energy from the incoming fist and driving her foot into Kim's gut. She rolled, using Kim's momentum to launch them over the edge.

Zac lurched. "No!"

But as Siggy flung Kim, she twisted mid-air like a cat, hands grasping the ledge and breaking her momentum.

Zac dove, dropping the gun. Siggy's body smacked the rocks, and the impact yanked one hand free.

Zac seized her hand on the ledge. The toes of his boots scored the earth as her weight dragged him toward the abyss. "Grab my hand, Siggy! Grab my hand!"

Siggy's other hand flailed as she twisted in space, finally using her momentum to slap her free hand onto Zac's wrist. She clenched it for dear life as she got her boots against the cliff face.

"I got you. Easy now," said Zac as Siggy worked her way back up the rock, climbing over him like a rope. Once up, she collapsed, panting.

Zac got onto his hands and knees and looked into the wadi. Kim's body lay on the lowest slope of the mountain. Her neck and one leg were twisted at inhuman angles. He winced and turned to Siggy, who'd crawled next to him.

"Helluva fight. She was good," he said.

"Not as good as me," she spat, then jumped to her feet and ran to the cave, screaming, "Eyrún!"

86

Cave

Zac followed. Siggy continued screaming her sister's name as she disappeared into the darkness. He caught her in the pool chamber, where she'd dropped on her belly and was shining her light in the rock-filled opening.

"Eyrún! Darwin!" she shouted into the gap. She grabbed smaller rocks from the hole, hurling them backward. Most splashed into the pool. Zac helped as best he could in the tight space.

Every few throws, she stopped and listened, then yelled their names again. Within minutes, they'd moved all the rocks that could be moved. Siggy crawled into the gap.

"No, Siggy." Zac grasped her waistband. "It's too dangerous."

She kicked him. "My sister's in there."

"It's blocked. Let me look."

She shifted aside, and he wedged next to her. They'd cleared a small space, but Zac found larger rocks had lodged above.

"She's in there, Zac. I know it."

"Maybe. Maybe not."

He sat up and studied the chamber. Boot prints in the dust meant people had been in there. *What did Mike say? Kim is with the diamonds.* But they'd found nothing at this end of the cave except for the pool and the mushroom chamber. *Where are the diamonds? What did we miss?* He pictured the place where Kim had shot at them.

"C'mon," he said. He shot through the hole out of the pool chamber and helped Siggy to her feet. They checked the mushroom chamber once more for any other exits and, finding none, went to the crevasse with the snake.

Knee-deep rock had spilled from the gap, and the ceiling above the snake looked freshly exposed. Zac leaned in but could no longer see the light he'd seen earlier.

"Darwin? Eyrún?" he yelled.

The pile slid. More rock rained down. And another section of the gap collapsed as they retreated. Zac ran his beam over the ceiling. "I don't like it. It's way too unstable."

"Kim said she trapped them. They must be in there." Siggy tried to push past him, but he blocked the way.

"It's too dangerous, Siggy. We need help."

"Help? From who?"

"Egyptian special forces. Let's get to the sat phone. They owe me a favor."

87

Escape Tunnel

After what felt like an eternity to Darwin, Eyrún groaned.

He called out, "Eyrún, Love. Are you okay?"

"I—" she broke into a coughing fit.

Her convulsions shook Darwin, but he had never been happier to feel her body against his.

"How long was I out?" she asked.

Darwin checked his watch. "Seven minutes. Can you move?"

"My legs are trapped. I can feel a breeze, though."

"Yeah. It's moving away from us. The tunnel's clearing, and I see a gap ahead."

"If you move ahead, I'll use your legs to pull mine free."

He agreed, and they waited until Eyrún felt fully conscious. They began tentatively.

"I moved a little," she said and pulled on his legs three more times. "We need a strong pull together."

He stretched and hooked his fingers in a crack. "Ready?"

"Go," she yelled.

He pulled, sliding a forearm's length. Eyrún grunted, yanking hard.

Darwin's fingers and hip sockets felt ready to dislocate, but she moved.

"I'm free—ow."

"What?"

"Something cut my ankle."

"Bad?"

"I don't know. Ah," she sucked through her teeth. "Hurts like hell."

"What can I do?"

"Just keep going to that gap you said you see."

Darwin dragged himself along, pushing off elbows and knees. Two meters farther, the ceiling rose gradually, then opened into a space the size of a small closet. He twisted around and helped Eyrún crawl in beside him. As she sat up, his headlamp caught blood smeared in the tunnel she'd just crawled from.

"Ow!" She pulled her knees up. Her left pant leg had ripped from mid-calf to the hem. "Oh, God. That's not good." A rock had torn the skin on her leg about a hand's width up from the ankle bone.

"Here, drink some before I wash the cut," said Darwin, pulling a water bottle from his pack. "I need to see how deep it is."

She drank and handed it back. He gulped twice before drizzling water on the cut. The dirt ran down her ankle, and blood oozed faster. "Is it deep?" she asked.

He spread the wound. She gasped; blood flooded the gap. He squeezed it closed. "I can't tell how deep, but it definitely needs sutures." He looked at the bloody trail in the cave again, trying to estimate how much she had lost. "How do you feel?"

"Fine, except for the throbbing pain."

He dug around in his pack for extra socks and a bandanna. He folded the socks over the wound, tied it with the bandanna, and pressed on it for a full minute to quell the bleeding. "Let me know if your toes feel numb, and I'll loosen it."

"Okay. Where do you think this comes out?" she asked.

"A sign back there read: Omar's Oasis, one kilometer. I heard it's got a Michelin star."

"Smart-ass." She whacked his arm.

When she was ready, she led the way. Following her through the low passage, Darwin sensed a definite upward incline. In less than two minutes, Eyrún stood up. "Found it."

"What?" He could only see her ankles.

"The way out."

Darwin crawled toward her feet, then stood up in a well-sized vertical chamber. Daylight and blue sky blossomed from a crack high in the rock.

"Merde!"

"My thoughts exactly. What would you say? Twenty, thirty meters up."

"Thirty."

88

Outside the Cave

Siggy moved like a zombie following Zac. The guide had run off, and Mike was in a deep slumber. Zac grabbed his pack as they moved outside, and while he phoned contacts to get help, Siggy sat staring into space, her legs dangling over the ravine.

In less than five minutes, Zac had made all the calls he could think of. The last one ended with a promise they'd call back within the hour. With nothing else to do, he joined Siggy on the ledge.

"I don't want to be alone like this," she said, her voice hollow. "Eyrún was there for me after our father died. She's why I came to Corsica after my breakup. She always knows what to do."

Zac put an arm around her shoulder, and she leaned on him. The mountain glowed in the afternoon sun, and the shadows from the scant vegetation stretched toward it like arms prostrated in prayer.

89

Escape Tunnel

"Ouch! Careful up there," yelled Darwin after being hit a third time.

Eyrún had started up first after they'd estimated the deep cleft in the rock could be climbed by using hand and foot holds on opposing walls. Her ankle bandage had bled through, but they had no more material to wrap it. When she had reached twice Darwin's height, he'd started up but retreated as rocks tumbled down.

He fashioned a helmet by placing his pack atop his head and tying the shoulder straps under his chin. It was awkward but effective. Unfortunately, the rocks still pelted the rest of his unprotected body.

"I need to rest," she called down.

"Not too long. I'm not in a good spot." He wedged his left foot against the wall but only got a toehold for his right. His thighs and calves burned. He risked looking up, then measured the distance down. *Halfway, maybe.*

"Okay. I'm starting up again," she warned. Dirt rained down.

We're gonna make it. We're gonna make it. He repeated the mantra he'd started earlier and focused on making solid holds. He shoved back another vision of Eyrún slipping. *We're gonna make it.* He pushed up with his right leg, leaned into it, and moved his left leg up. Push. Repeat.

Eyrún yelled down. "Do you think Zac and Siggy are still on the mountain?"

"Doubt it. They probably hiked down when we didn't respond."

Eyrún reached the top and poked her head out of the tight hole. She squinted at the brightness of the surrounding plateau. Jebel Musa loomed to her left; its western slope blazed in the afternoon sun. Then she dropped down and pushed her arms overhead until her shoulders were out.

She wriggled up on her elbows and, when she was high enough, used her hands to press up until she got her waist out. Then, sitting on the edge, she lifted out one leg, then the other, and rolled away from the crack. The soil burned after being trapped in the shaded cave, but she welcomed the sensation. She looked around a moment before rolling back to help Darwin.

"You're almost here," she said.

"What's out there?" he grunted.

"An oasis, just like you said. The server's bringing iced tea."

He neared the opening. Another push and the pack jammed in the crack. "What's that?" His hand shot up and grasped the edge.

Eyrún laughed. "It's your fat head. Hold still."

"Hurry. My leg's cramping."

She leaned in and loosened the pack straps under his neck, lifted off the pack, and tossed it aside. After she helped him out, they both lay spent on the flat rock.

Moments later, metallic chimes erupted from the pack.

"What the hell's that?" he asked.

"The sat phone." Eyrún sat up. "Siggy must have sent a lot of messages." She got the device from Darwin's pack and read them.

Siggy: Twenty minutes to summit

Siggy: On summit. Can't see you

Siggy: Gunshot. Where are you? We're coming down the back side of mtn

"Gunshot. Oh, my God," said Eyrún.

"What gunshot?"

Eyrún called Siggy as Darwin got to his feet and looked at Jebel Musa's backside. *How the hell did they get down that?*

90

Outside the Cave

Siggy kicked her legs anxiously over the ravine. Zac looked at his watch again. The hour was almost up.

The sat phone between them rang. They simultaneously looked at the caller ID. Zac's heart felt like it hit pause.

Siggy seized it. "Eyrún?" She hopped to her feet. "Oh, my God. Oh, my God. It's you. Where are you? Are you safe?"

Zac tried to keep pace as Siggy circled the forecourt before halting and looking up. "I see you. I see you." She waved at Eyrún thirty meters up the mountain, then thrust the phone in Zac's hand as she ran up the trail.

Eyrún handed her phone to Darwin and hobbled in the direction where Siggy would arrive.

Zac stared upwards at his friend. "How'd you get up there?"

"It's a long story," said Darwin.

91

South Coast, Corsica

Eight days later, Eyrún stroked the skin on her ankle where Siggy had pulled out the stitches earlier in the day. The jagged pink scar itched, and the warm salt water of the Mediterranean Sea soothed the irritation. She'd driven her powerboat Hypatia to her favorite secluded cove south of Ajaccio. Her other leg swung free in the azure blue water, where she watched Zac and Darwin forage oysters for lunch.

They'd returned to Ajaccio five days ago, but she'd delayed their boat trip until she could go in the water. While waiting, she and Darwin made good on their million-dollar promise to Mike and sent him back to America. Part of Mike's inheritance acceptance included a clause that he did not talk about anything that had happened in Egypt. Zac added in a private conversation with Mike that he would know who to blame if any news of the radioactive diamonds got out.

Astrid's firm created a new Lacroix trust in order to distance future heirs from liabilities, such as Mike's forebears. The mountain house and mansion on Rue des Oranges were deeded into the new trust with Darwin, his sister Marie, their parents, and Emelio as trustees.

Zac's contact in Egyptian special forces never called back, and they had a tricky time explaining Kim's and Ramy's deaths to the local police. At first, Zac, Siggy, Eyrún, and Darwin debated not saying anything. But Eyrún pointed out that the driver who'd dropped them off and picked them up at the triangle mountain could place them all at the scene. Eventually, it went down as antiquities looting gone wrong.

Theophilus corroborated Darwin's story that he was looking for a second-century cult as part of repatriating an Egyptian artifact from the British Museum. Siggy and Zac confirmed using a drone atop Jebel Musa to reveal ancient trails when they'd heard gunshots. Siggy accounted for her beaten-up look by saying she'd fallen while descending the mountain's back slope.

Before the driver arrived, Zac had recovered the downed drone and buried Kim's gun in the riverbed. He'd also collected the brass from Kim's bullets that had brought down the cave ceiling. Darwin explained finding the symbols at the back of the main cave and the snake symbol, but said they halted deeper exploration when the ceiling proved unstable. He speculated about the mushrooms, saying it could be a modern connection to the ancient cult.

When a monk found cut zip-ties in the ossuary chapel, the police hypothesized the person had been involved in the killings. The guide who brought Ramy and Kim to the cave had disappeared.

The extra time at the monastery allowed Eyrún to stay off her leg during the initial healing period. Fortunately, the monks had a well-stocked clinic that Siggy used to clean and suture Eyrún's ankle, as well as tend to her own wounds.

Darwin and Theophilus researched the stele and the possibility of a cult, but the grotto had been too trampled in modern times to piece together more than conjecture. The skull remained a mystery they left behind when departing Sinai three days ago.

Eyrún turned at a splash. Siggy popped up, spear in one hand and two sea breams on a stringer in the other. She tossed the catch on the swim deck, and Eyrún took the spear. Minutes later, the men surfaced with a full net of oysters.

While Siggy and Zac shucked the oysters, Eyrún opened a bottle of her favorite wine. Darwin fired up the grill outside the galley, gutted the fish, and scored their flesh. Then he placed lemon slices inside each cut and laid them over the fire. The wine from the native Vermentino grape paired perfectly with the oysters, and they ate while standing around the grill.

"I could get used to this," said Siggy, wiping her chin.

"I'm with you. How about we go native?" Zac suggested while pointing ashore. "See that break in the maquis? Let's set up a tent and forage for our meals. Eat oysters every day."

"Oh, be serious," said Siggy.

"I am."

After lunch, Darwin and Eyrún remained aboard and lounged in the shade. Zac and Siggy had swum ashore to explore. Darwin gently massaged Eyrún's leg above the cut.

"Careful. It's still tender," she said.

He eased up. "Better?"

"Yes. Thanks. It helps. The muscles are tight." A few moments later, she said, "I've been thinking about what the *mazzeri* said about cancer."

"Still?"

"Not about us. About Henri's daughter, Stéphanie. He gave her the music box, and she probably played with it constantly. At her young age, the radiation probably had a worse effect."

"Probably."

"Sad. He couldn't have known, though."

"No." Darwin's thumbs moved in long strokes over Eyrún's smooth skin. The last months had revealed a side of his family he'd never known: suffering and loss. Emelio was the last living link to the tragedies. Darwin felt a touch of melancholy at losing his innocent childhood memories of pirate adventures and treasure. The reality was a family history of theft and war.

"What's up, Love?"

"Huh?"

"I know that look. You're brooding about something."

Darwin sat up and wiped his oily hands on a towel. "Just the things Emelio never talked about; Henri, Pasquale's death, the wars."

"Men of his generation don't talk about feelings," she said. "He shared some of it with me during our time in the ICU, and said he's made peace with the tragedy."

Darwin sighed heavily.

"He also said that he's proud of you. Not only for your accomplishments but for how you brought the family back together."

"Really?"

"Yes. Let it go, Love. Be more like your friend Zac. He's seen horrible things, but he chooses to live in the moment. Let the past remain where it is. You can't change it."

"You're right. As always," he said. The mention of Zac caused him to look toward the empty shore. "Where'd they go?"

"Exploring," said Eyrún with a knowing smile.

"Hmm. Living in the moment." He slid closer. "Maybe we should try it."

She ran her fingers through his hair. "Maybe," she said, pulling him toward her.

EPILOGUE

Bocagno, Corsica

In late autumn, Darwin got an email from Mike Carson. They'd had a long conversation about the Lacroix family before his departure in late summer, but he'd not heard from Mike since. Darwin had never thought they'd develop a friendship, but Mike was family, however distant.

Darwin made his second triple cappuccino of the morning and sat by the fireplace to read Mike's email.

After two months of soul-searching, I realized I should use the break you and Eyrún gave me to help others who need one, especially those with the least means. I moved to California's inland empire to get far away from my roots in Maryland and help those who need it most.

I established a law practice specifically to help families ravaged by addiction and get on the right side of the law and health. I use the generous inheritance to fund the operation. I've found a purpose bigger than myself. But I'm not writing to tell you about my life.

While looking through a box of files when we moved to a new facility, I found my notes on Henri Lacroix. One thing has always perplexed me: the Demeter spoliation case records show the US court requested a copy of Henri's will. (Remember, I mentioned Henri's seizure of the Mercure, an American vessel carrying gold.) But no will was ever received.
The French court refused to settle with the Americans because it got no gold from Henri. But think about it. Our forebear was a privateer. He would have known many places to hide a vast treasure.
Let me know if you find anything.

Regards,
Mike

Darwin drained the cup and set it aside, then laid down his iPad and stared into the flames flickering around the porcelain logs. He'd pondered the same thing about Henri, but had let it lapse. They'd explored the tunnel more thoroughly when they'd swept the crypt and lab for radiation. They needed to know how much of the diamonds' radioactivity had penetrated their home. Fortunately, it was scant, in line with the background radiation in the granite.

Stéphanie's tomb got a higher reading. Eyrún reassembled the radioactive music box and replaced it in the girl's hands before resealing her tomb. They'd also determined clearing the lower tunnel would require a significant operation that included moving the rock through the mountain house to dispose of it. Neither he nor Eyrún wanted the disruption, so they left the project for some other time.

Darwin had explored the canyon, looking for an exit, but two centuries of growth and weathering had obscured the evidence, and he'd abandoned searching.

Still, his finder sense tickled. He'd grown up listening to stories around the dining table. Emelio would point at Pasquale's portrait to emphasize his points. Later on, Darwin's father scoffed at the tales when about them. *But Emelio had been right about the lava tubes. What else did Pasquale know?*

Henri had lived well into his eighties. The family was embarrassed by Henri's dementia, but his grandson, Pasquale, had lapped up Henri's tales of hidden pirate treasure and passed them down. *Could there be more to this? Why was Henri entombed in a secret tunnel under the mountain house?*

He finally called Emelio.

"Darwin, my boy. How are you today?"

"Fine, Grand-père. And you?"

They discussed the weather and local news a while before Darwin steered the conversation toward his inquiry. "Do you know why Henri might have been buried under my house and not in the family plot?"

"No, but that reminds me of something I thought of while you were in Egypt. The family kept all the legal documents. I moved them years ago to a safe deposit box in our bank. I meant to go look them up, but …"

Darwin listened as Emelio rambled. *He's getting worse.* When Emelio coughed, Darwin asked, "What if we went to the bank today?"

Ajaccio

Three hours later, Darwin and Emelio sat in a private vault at the Bank of Ajaccio with documents from two large drawers stacked on the table. Darwin mentally noted moving these to a document archive at the ACA, where he'd thought of creating a maritime section. While the bank was secure, he didn't like the limited access.

They'd found Henri's will in roughly chronological order, stuffed in a folder with other documents. *Another reason for a proper archive,* thought Darwin as he placed the will on the table between them and began reviewing it.

Dated 23 July 1837, twenty years before Henri's death, it was dry reading until the last lines:

> *Upon my death, I wish to be interred with my daughter, Stéphanie, the light and joy of my life, taken too soon.*

Henri specified burial preparations, including which suit he would wear and instructions to seal his laboratory. The last orders were peculiar:

> *Place my chronometer between my hands and set the security apparatus at the door. Only when these plans are complete will my estate pass to my surviving heirs.*

"That's it?" asked Emelio.

"There's another page attached," said Darwin, flipping it over and scanning it. It was a carpenter's invoice for an armoire built into the wall of the mountain house safe room. "This explains why the tunnel remained hidden, but nothing about a treasure. Why a chronometer?"

"We live in a world of GPS, but in Henri's day, the location was a function of latitude and longitude. And the latter was the most difficult, as you needed a precise time measurement. Not any time, but your difference from Greenwich Mean Time," said Emelio. He wrapped up by adding, "Global empires in the age of sail were dominated by knowing the exact locations of ports and the fastest shipping lanes."

Darwin smiled at Emelio's encyclopedic recollection, but was still perplexed. "Why be buried with it?"

"His favorite, maybe? And it would certainly be obsolete by his death."

"How so?"

"The technology advanced fast. There were competitions to build the most accurate devices, chronometers, meaning time and distance. Winners collected millions in today's money," said Emelio.

Darwin snapped photos of the will and returned the files to the safe deposit boxes. Then the two went to lunch at their favorite quayside bistro. Darwin had been itching to go back up the mountain and look in the crypt, but Eyrún had a full schedule at the ACA, and they had a dinner that night with a visiting dignitary. Throughout the day, he kept telling himself that whatever secret lay with Henri would not change overnight.

Mountain House, Bocagno

The next day after breakfast, Darwin and Eyrún went downstairs to the safe room. They put on puffer jackets against the chill in the tunnel and opened the massive oak door. Fortunately, Darwin had lubricated the hinges during earlier explorations of the lab.

They reached the crypt and entered. The musty odor of long-dead bodies hung in the air. Stéphanie's tombstone had been cleaned and set back in place. And Eyrún had laid new white linen on the chapel altar. The space no longer felt creepy, but Darwin's neck tingled at the prospect of opening Henri's tomb. Both he and Eyrún wore goggles and organic vapor masks in case Henri had employed some other trap.

But the tombstone came away with relative ease when Darwin used a small pry bar to open it. Wisps of white hair hung from Henri's skull. Decomposition was complete, but Darwin was thankful the mask filtered out any lingering smell. A black suit over a disintegrating white shirt covered the skeleton, and a dark wooden cube lay on its upper abdomen between finger bones.

Darwin's face was right against the skull as he reached inside. The surprisingly heavy box lifted free of the bones, and he carefully pulled it from the tomb. He set it upon the altar, and Eyrún moved beside him as he tilted the lid. A white-faced clock set in a brass mechanism had stopped at 3:07 and eleven seconds. He raised the box and tilted it. The gimbal kept the clock face level just as it had functioned aboard a ship.

Back upstairs, Darwin made himself a coffee while Eyrún played with the chronometer, her tea bag steeping. Darwin had wound the clock and set its time using his digital watch to Coordinated Universal Time, the successor to Greenwich Mean Time.

Eyrún turned the box, testing the clock's leveling ability. "Still works great. Wait? What's that noise?" She held it up as she rotated the box. Something made a clicking noise, as if sliding. "There's nothing on the bottom." She shook the box gently. It rattled. "It's in the lid. Behind this brass circle."

Darwin tapped the brass disk affixed to the lid above the clock. "It's hollow," he said, and rummaged through a kitchen drawer to find a screwdriver.

Eyrún held the box as he removed four screws. He lifted the brass disk to reveal a smaller one stamped with numbers.

41° 52' 43.5792" N
8° 35' 39.8364" E

"It's a location," said Eyrún.

Darwin tapped the numbers into the map app on his phone. "It can't be."

Darwin phoned the marina as Eyrún rocketed her Porsche Macan down the mountain. In less than a half hour, they'd backed Hypatia out of her slip and were motoring out of Ajaccio harbor.

Darwin opened the chronometer on the galley counter next to Eyrún. "I'm still figuring out how to read this," he confessed.

"Doesn't matter," she said. "I put the coordinates into Hypatia's nav system."

She throttled up, and the sleek powerboat took less than fifteen minutes to reach their destination: the big Sanguinaire Island. She dropped anchor, and they went ashore in the Zodiac.

The island was desolate as they walked up to its lighthouse. "You're sure it's not that cave you found years ago?" asked Eyrún.

"No, it's too small, and it would be ridiculously difficult to move a large amount of gold underwater," he said, referring to a well-known grotto where he'd found Spanish gold coins.

They approached the towering lighthouse. It had been automated, and its metal door had been fitted with a modern lock.

"What are we looking for?" Eyrún asked, disappearing around one corner of the square base the white and black tower stood on.

"Dunno." Darwin rounded the corner, nearly bumping into her, squatting by the cornerstone.

"X marks the spot," she said.

LAID BY HENRI LACROIX
4 NOVEMBER 1807

AUTHOR'S NOTE

Thank you for reading Sinai Deceit. I hope you enjoyed it and would love to hear from you at dave@davebartell.com, and please write a review, as we authors thrive on recommendations.

If you find anything amiss in the book, please email me directly, and I'll fix it. While I worked with a translator, developmental editor, copy editor, and proofreader, to err is human.

For those who have read *Tuscan Hoax,* Sinai Deceit had to answer the looming question from its epilogue: why did Eyrún scream?

For the last two books, I'd been mulling over Darwin's past and thinking of shaking him up. My family history includes a sea captain who had two families. I heard tales of wealth in the 19th century squandered in subsequent generations. As in many families, my relatives have fading memories of the stories passed down. When I probed them, the recollections quickly reached dead ends. So I brought my fantasy of lost wealth to Darwin's family.

In Roman Ice, I mentioned a Lacroix forebear who was a childhood friend of Napoleon Bonaparte. At that time, in the late 1700s, the Enlightenment had reached its apex. Revolutions had led to government by a constitution (France, United States), but the fledgling United States still grappled with European powers in the Quasi-War.

In 1799, Napoleon, on the cusp of becoming the emperor, led a massive cultural and scientific exploration of Egypt. He organized 151 Commission of the Sciences and Arts members into a scientific corps that produced the Description de l'Egypte, spurring a global fascination with Egyptology.

But science was not yet science as we know it today.

Alchemy conjures impressions of wizards, witches, magic, and the philosopher's stone, turning lead into gold. But its roots are simpler: human search for meaning and how things work. Alchemy deals in the mystical and esoteric. And its origins shimmer from beyond the veil of history.

But alchemy also used precise measurement, disciplined documentation, and knowledge-sharing. One alchemist's formula to transmute metal could be tested by another alchemist. This method of theory, investigation, and interrogation forms the basis of modern science.

What more fertile environment could a writer wish for?

What better shock could Eyrún (a scientist) and Darwin (a seeker of ancient answers) find in the tunnel under their house?

A Templar knight, voices from beyond the grave, and fantastical visions.

After writing the wild scene, I stepped back to bring the story down to earth as we experience it, you know, gravity and taxes. I needed plausible explanations.

A mind-altering substance could cause Eyrún's visions. Mold? Maybe. Mushrooms? Definitely. Medical research in the last decade has shown these "class A drugs" have profound neurological value in healing depression, among other conditions. And mushrooms fit with alchemical and Egyptian esotericism (see papers below), but the story needed more than magic mushrooms.

It needed something scary and deadly.

A recent discovery catalyzed the story: Davemaoite. The compound found inside a diamond had been theorized, but only in the crucible of the Earth's mantle—over 600 miles/1,000 kilometers down. But a diamond's carbon matrix exerts enough internal pressure to contain a fractional quantity of Davemaoite.

Interesting? Yes, but not enough to warrant a global chase.

What if I added a radioactive element with the Davemaoite?

Viola! A diamond with superconductor capacity would have extraordinary commercial value but, in the wrong hands, could trigger a nuclear explosion. Modern science wrapped in an ancient Egyptian enigma made for a story worthy of Darwin's curiosity.

Everything in Sinai Deceit is accurate except for adding thorium and uranium to the diamonds and extrapolating weaponization. Especially the wondrous and beautiful Saint Catherine's monastery and its "world's oldest library" add to the story setting.

Thank you for reading Sinai Deceit. I hope you enjoyed Darwin's latest adventure. If you did, please write a review on Amazon or Facebook and tell a friend about the Darwin Lacroix adventure series.

Have any questions, concerns, or comments? I'd love to hear from you at dave@davebartell.com.

Resources used and recommended for further study:

Netflix

How to change your mind

Fantastic Fungi

Internet

Advanced Light Source: Lawrence Berkeley National Laboratory

Psilocybin Treatment for Major Depression Effective for Up to a Year for Most Patients, Johns Hopkins Medicine

The Sinai Insurgency, Part 3: The Tribal Aspect

Wikipedia

France: Napoleon, Sidney Smith, Quasi-War

Prize courts and Letters of marque

Alchemy: Zosimos of Panopolis (early source of alchemy), Magnum opus, Mary the Jewess, Hermes Trismegistus, Prima materia,

Commission des Sciences et des Arts (Commission of the Sciences and Arts) and the works they produced, Description de l'Egypte

Sinai: Sinai peninsula, Serabit el-Khadim,

Egyptian gods: Apep, Hathor, Horus, Ma'at, Set

Superconductivity

Books

The Greatest Invention: A History of the World in Nine Mysterious Scripts, Silvia Ferrara

The Monastery of Saint Catherine in Sinai: History and Guide, Jill Kamil

Christianity in the Land of the Pharaohs: The Coptic Orthodox Church, Jill Kamil

The Sinai: A Physical Geography, Ned H. Greenwood

Saint Catherine's Monastery Sinai, Egypt: A Photographic Essay, Helen C. Evans & Bruce White

Ancient Egyptian Magic, Eleanor Harris

The Greek Magical Papyri in Translation: Including the Demotic Spells, Hans Dieter Betz

The Egyptian Book of the Dead: The Book of Going Forth by Day (The Complete Papyrus of Ani), Dr. Ogden Goelet, Jr.; Dr. Raymond O. Faulkner; Carol A. R. Andrews; J. Daniel Gunther; James Wasserman

Articles

Alchemy and Science

A brief history of medical diagnosis and the birth of the clinical laboratory: Ancient times through the 19th century, Darlene Berger

Chemistry in the 19th Century

Ancestry

Getting genetic ancestry right for science and society, Anna C. Lewis et al. Science, 15 April 2022, Vol. 376, Issue 6590

Diamonds and Superconductors

Discovery of davemaoite, CaSiO3-perovskite as a mineral from the lower mantle. Science 12 November 2021, Vol. 374, Issue 6569

Natural-Color Green Diamonds: A Beautiful Conundrum, Christopher M. Breeding, Sally Eaton-Magaña, & James E. Shigley. Gems & Gemology, Spring 2018

Optical absorption and luminescence in diamond, John Walker. Prog. Phys. Vol. 42, 1979.

Superconductors gain momentum: Spin-density modulations point to inhomogeneous superconductivity in perovskite, Eva Pavarini. Science 22 April 2022, Vol. 376. Issue 6591

A shortage of tritium fuel may leave fusion energy with an empty tank, Daniel Clery. Science 24 June 2022, Vol. 376, Issue 6600

Soviet-era tech could change the geothermal industry: Gyrotons can

superheat plasma, maybe vaporize 20km of rock, too, Brandon Vigliatolo, Science 28 June 2022

History

Why France really helped America's Founding Fathers fight the Revolutionary War, Willard Sterne Randall (Hint: the snuff trade)

Jill Kamil (1930-2022): A life in Egypt

"Magic mushrooms"

The therapeutic potential of psychedelics: The development of psychedelics as medicines faces several challenges, Emmanuelle A. D. Schindler and Deepak Cyril D'Souza. Science 9 December 2022, Vol. 378 Issue 6624

Hidden Influences: Beliefs about the vital roles played by spirits and gods have long been underappreciated, argues an anthropologist, Jonathan Spencer. Science 6 May 2022, Vol. 376 Issue 6593

The entheomycological origin of Egyptian crowns and the esoteric underpinning of Egyptian religion, Stephen R. Berlant. Journal of Ethnopharmacology 30 September 2005

On the Origin of the Genus Psilocybe and Its Potential Ritual Use in Ancient Africa and Europe, Tom Froese, Gastón Guzmán, and Laura Guzmán-Dávalos. Economic Botany 10 May 2016

Are altered states of consciousness detrimental, neutral or helpful for the origin of symbolic cognition? Tom Froese, Alexander Woodward, and Takashi Ikegami

Does the Nervous System Have an Intrinsic Archaic Language? H. Ümit Sayin. NeuroQuantology, September 2014, Volume 12, Issue 3

The Consumption of Psychoactive Plants During Religious Rituals: The Roots of Common Symbols and Figures in Religions and Myths. H. Ümit Sayin. NeuroQuantology, June 2014, Volume 12, Issue 2

Rock Art or Rorschach: Is there More to Entoptics than Meets the Eye? David Luke. Time and Mind: The Journal of Archaeology, Consciousness and Culture, March 2010, Vol. 3, Issue 1

ACKNOWLEDGMENTS

As this is the fifth full-length Darwin Lacroix adventure (Corsican Gold is a Novella), character development becomes a more critical piece of the series. We all naturally age and grow wiser, and our relationships mature. The same holds for characters. Thanks to Annie Tucker, my development editor, who helps deepen my character's emotional interplay.

Thanks to Pauline Toop & Neil Hall on my ARC (Advance Reader Copy) team who went the extra distance to help ferret out those niggling errors that get through the professional editors.

Pauline brought the nuances of UK inheritance law and suggested that I delve deeper into French inheritance law. The sections with Mike and the French lawyers is now more authentic.

Neil noticed my ability to count diamonds and who had how many needed improving. The number of diamonds Ramy stole (one) is now correctly told in the story

Every book deserves a great cover, and thanks to Patrick Knowles Design, Sinai Deceit has one. This is our fifth collaboration, as he did the covers on Hypatia's Diary, Templar's Bank, and Corsican Gold.

And, thank you to Diane Bartell, my wife, best fan, and most important person in my life. She will soon ask, "Got anything new for me to read."

Again, THANKS, and I invite you to learn about the next Darwin Lacroix Adventure by joining my mailing list at davebartell.com.

Onward to book six!

ABOUT THE AUTHOR

Imagine the wonder of being the first person to open King Tut's tomb. Dave Bartell loves reviving lost history, and his novels breathe "thriller" into archaeology.

As a kid, he frequently tinkered in his parent's garage. His insatiable curiosity to understand how things work led him to study biochemistry and, later, fueled a career in high technology. His what-if mindset and life experiences combine to make his fiction plausible and feel realistic.

Dave lives in Los Gatos, California; a small town tucked into the edge of Silicon Valley. He enjoys hiking in the hills behind his home, where beauty is still analog.

He hopes you enjoy his stories and invites you to share your thoughts at dave@davebartell.com. And visit davebartell.com to get a sneak peek of upcoming projects.

BB bookbub.com/authors/dave-bartell

facebook.com/DaveBartellWriter

goodreads.com/davebartell

instagram.com/davebartell

twitter.com/davebartell

Made in the USA
Coppell, TX
19 April 2023